SUDDENLY THE night was split by an ungodly scream of sheer, animal terror. Then just as quickly all went still, and the lawman could feel a vagrant breeze cooling the sweat on his forehead. Wondering if Bajeca had met his match, Stoudenmire scrambled up the hill, trying to make as little noise as possible. Within moments he topped the rise and plowed down the other side, cocking both hammers on the shotgun as he skidded through the dusty soil. Moving cautiously now, he eased through another stand of juniper and tangled underbrush, gliding silently from tree to tree. Abruptly he broke out into a small clearing and froze dead in his tracks.

Beside a crackling little fire sat Bajeca, calmly wiping his knife clean on Kale's shirt. Glancing up, he grinned like a playful wolf and lifted Kale's severed head from the ground.

"A gift for *el patrón*. One *gringo pistolero* who will kill no more."

NOVELS BY MATT BRAUN

El Paso

MATT BRAUN

St. Martin's Paperbacks

This is a work of fiction. All of the characters, organizations, and events portrayed in this novel are either products of the author's imagination or are used fictitiously.

EL PASO

Copyright © 1972 by Matt Braun.

For information address St. Martin's Press, 175 Fifth Avenue, New York, NY 10010.

ISBN: 978-0-312-97074-1

Printed in the United States of America

Previously published in 1973
Signet edition / March 1989
St. Martin's Paperbacks edition / July 1999

St. Martin's Paperbacks are published by St. Martin's Press, 175 Fifth Avenue, New York, NY 10010.

10 9 8 7 6 5 4 3 2

For
Barry Winston
who stuck through all the wars
and
Elizabeth and Paul Shumski
whose support was ever valued

AUTHOR'S NOTE

El Paso is essentially the story of one man, Dallas Stoudenmire. Lawman, gunfighter, mankiller, he was all these and
more. Yet unlike the cotton-candy heroes of Western folklore, Stoudenmire was imperfect, flawed; a man who lived
by his own code in a land where it was often difficult to
separate evil from good.

Born to German parents who had immigrated to the Lone
Star State, Stoudenmire was named after George Mifflin
Dallas, a Texan who served briefly as vice-president of the
United States. After four bloody years fighting for the Confederacy, Stoudenmire returned home a trained killer; cold,
impersonal, something of a loner. Over the next decade he
became a lawman of formidable persuasion, killing an unre-
corded number of badmen with the precision and stoic disinterest that was to remain his trademark. Along the way, he
served variously as a Texas Ranger, deputy sheriff, and city
marshal, evincing little concern for titles so long as he had a
star pinned on his chest.

When the call came to tame El Paso, Stoudenmire was
ready. Everything past, from the killing ground of the Civil
War through the deadly years as a Ranger, had been but a

preliminary to this main event. Like some intricate jigsaw puzzle of destiny, the toughest bordertown on the frontier and the lone-wolf lawman were brought together in a clash that reshaped western legend.

Although the events depicted in *El Paso* are based on documented records, certain liberties have been taken with time, place, and various names. The fact remains, however, that what is written here was essentially what occurred along the banks of the Rio Grande during that desperate summer of 1881.

Dallas Stoudenmire left his mark on El Paso, as well as on the era of the gunfighter. Yet, in passing, it must be noted that he bore small resemblance to the mythical lawmen of folklore. He was simply a man doing the job for which he had been trained, perhaps colder and more deadly than most, but fairly typical of his breed. Resourceful, honest to a fault, brave beyond the measure of other men; a mankiller who coincidentally happened to wear a star.

Matthew Braun

CHAPTER ONE

—◆—

1

Lieutenant John Tays found himself at a slight tactical disadvantage. He was leading a force of eighteen Texas Rangers, and his orders were to safeguard the journey of three American businessmen. But at the moment, he was standing eyeball to eyeball with close to a thousand Mexican insurgents, and whoever blinked first would very likely wind up cold meat. Somewhat like a man who has a bear by the tail, Lieutenant Tays had developed a sudden liking for far away places.

That morning, as false dawn had given way to first light, the besieged Americans saw that all hope of escape was gone. Under cover of darkness the villagers of San Elizario had encircled with hastily dug rifle pits the adobe hut in which the Americans were trapped, and the sun's brilliant streamers glinted off a solid ring of blued steel. Rangers and civilians alike gazed at the fortifications in dull apathy. After seven days of intermittent fighting, any hope that the army would lift the siege had long since faded. Time had run out, and to a man they knew full well that the Mexicans would exact a grim price for the misery inflicted on them in the last few months.

Waiting for the final attack, Charles Howard could only reflect on the vicious bitch called fate. Earlier that year he had formed a combine with various El Paso businessmen for the sole purpose of cornering the Rio Grande salt trade. East of town, across a hundred miles of barren desert, lay a small chain of salt lakes. Though only recently arrived in Texas, Howard was a man of considerable ambition; an opportunist not above an unsavory deal if enough money were involved. And he was quick to grasp that whoever held a monopoly on the salt lakes could name his own price for that precious commodity.

Though Howard bore a remarkable resemblance to a well-fed hog, he was an affable, persuasive talker. Political skulduggery was a game he understood well, and within a short time, his combine had been allowed to file a claim on the distant lakes. While such grants were normally restricted on public service lands, the burgeoning salt cartel had in effect been given a license to steal. With legal possession of the lakes, they could collect a fee on every *fanega* of salt hauled away, and there were none to prevent them from raising the price to whatever the traffic would bear.

But Howard and his cronies had miscalculated the temper of the people. Throughout the memory of many generations, natives from both sides of the Rio Grande had driven their oxcarts to the dry lakes, braving a fortnight in the waterless desert so that their families might have salt. Moreover, they also bartered salt in the interior regions of Chihuahua, and the gummy cakes they gouged from the earth represented the primary money crop of every village along the border. The El Paso combine posed a threat not only to the natives' own humble needs, but more significantly to the meager livelihood they had been able to glean from the salt trade itself. Reaction was swift and violent.

Under the leadership of Don Luis Cardis, the insurgents had captured Charles Howard at San Elizario, the village closest to the salt lakes. There they forced him to relinquish all claim to the disputed lands, presumably squelching his salt racket in the bud. Then, in exchange for his life, they extracted his promise never to return and sent him packing down the road. Though Howard was built along the lines of a whale, he was hardly a jovial fat man accustomed to turning the other cheek. Ten days later, he caught Don Luis alone in El Paso and gave him an overdose of buckshot, leaving the Mexicans leaderless, if not wholly defanged.

Public officials immediately set the telegraph wires humming, urging the governor to request assistance from troops stationed at nearby Ft. Bliss. Of the fifteen thousand souls along the upper Rio Grande, roughly a thousand were *norteamericanos*. Should a race war erupt, they would be doomed by the sheer weight of numbers. More distressing still, El Paso was isolated by an arid waste of some five hundred miles from the nearest American settlement. With visions of the entire community being wiped out overnight, local politicians demanded forceful action from the government in Austin.

Characteristically, the governor disdained the use of federal troops and sent instead a company of Texas Rangers, commanded by Lieutenant John Tays. Never wanting for a glib argument, Howard somehow convinced Lieutenant Tays that the Mexicans were in open revolt. *After all, fewer than five decades had passed since Texans defeated Santa Anna at San Jacinto. Only a fool would doubt that the greasers remained loyal to Mexico!* Accompanied by the Rangers, Howard and his cohorts had returned to San Elizario, determined to recover what was theirs by right of connivance and political clout.

But natives along both sides of the border were also marching on the sleepy village. Chico Barela had emerged as their new leader, and his call to arms drew upwards of a thousand fighting men even as Howard prepared to reclaim the salt lakes. No sooner had the businessmen arrived in San Elizario than they found themselves confronted by an ugly mob. The cry went up for blood, retribution for the murder of Don Luis Cardis, and the Rangers were barely able to hold them off. Retreating to an adobe hut on the south side of the plaza, the hated *gringos* quickly found themselves under siege by the frenzied Mexicans.

The next week proved a hellish nightmare for the Americans. They ate horse meat, rationed their water, and waited anxiously for federal troops that never came. Instead of attacking directly, the Mexicans pinned them down with sniper fire night and day, certain they couldn't hold out longer than the dwindling water supply in their canteens. Then, as the seventh morning dawned, the natives waited in their newly dug rifle pits, ready for an all-out charge should the *gringos* prove unreasonable.

Shortly after sunrise Chico Barela called for a parley under a white flag. Lieutenant Tays stepped from the adobe, and the Mexican leader's conditions were heard clearly by everyone in the hut. The Rangers would be allowed to depart in peace, but Howard and his partners, John McBride and John Atkinson, would remain as hostages in the village. The *gringos* had one hour to consider the offer, and if they refused, then their company would be killed to the last man. With that, the Mexican flashed an arrogant grin and strode back to the rifle pits.

Turning, Tays moved through the door of the hut, only to be greeted by a deadly silence. None of the Rangers could bring themselves to look at the three businessmen. While they were sworn to uphold the law, they had families to think about, not to mention their own skins. *And besides, hadn't the greaser promised that the three men would simply be held as hostages? Like as not, they'd be released just as soon as things calmed down. Probably no more'n a day or two at the most.*

Charles Howard was many things, but above all else he was a man who believed in hedging his bet. Even if the Rangers agreed to fight, which seemed highly unlikely, he would surely be killed. That was a foregone conclusion. No, the wiser move was to surrender. Although he wouldn't trust a greaser's word any further than he could spit, it made sense to get the Rangers clear and hope they could return in time with a cavalry troop. Briskly confident, he outlined the plan to Lieutenant Tays and saw the strain wash out of the Rangers' faces. McBride and Atkinson weren't too happy with his decision, but then they didn't have a hell of a lot of a choice. Come to think of it, none of them did.

Thirty minutes later Tays and his Rangers pounded out of the village, spurring their horses for El Paso. Behind they left Howard and his partners the featured attraction amidst a howling mob. Some years would pass before even the strongest of them could erase the scene from his memory.

Chico Barela was no less pragmatic than Charles Howard. He remained a leader only so long as he served the will of his people, and right now, his ragtag army was calling for blood. *Gringo* blood! With the Rangers hardly out of sight, the hostages' arms were bound behind them, and they were marched across the plaza to an adobe wall beside the ancient mission. While McBride and Atkinson seemed numb with shock, Charles Howard allowed his captors nothing more than a tight smile. He had gambled and lost. And where he was headed, he had best enjoy the fresh air while he could.

Without benefit of prayer or even a blindfold, the prisoners were shoved against the wall as a firing squad was hurriedly formed. Lacking a sword, Barela borrowed a *machete* and raised it overhead. When it fell, the roar of gunfire thundered across the plaza, instantly followed by the maddened shout of the onlookers. Atkinson and McBride dropped lifelessly in the dust, but Howard had been gut-shot, and he staggered forward, knees buckling.

"¡Más arriba, cabrones!" he moaned through clenched teeth. "Higher, you stinking goats!"

"¡Acábenlos!" roared the delighted mob. "Finish him!"

Chico Barela marched solemnly to the wounded man. Deliberating a moment, he gauged the blow, then swung the *machete*. Charles Howard's head toppled to the ground, ending his brief moment as salt baron of the Rio Grande. Spurting bright fountains of blood, his body simply collapsed, and the crowd went mad with a spasm of sheer joy.

"¡Hecho!" cried Chico Barela. "It is done! Don Cardis is avenged. The salt lakes belong again to the people!"

2

Shortly after suppertime, the men began drifting into the
compound. Spread along the banks of the Rio Grande just
west of town, Hart's Mill was an imposing structure. The
river had been channeled and damned so that it flowed
through a high stone arch erected on one side of the mill-
house. Locally, it was said that the sluggish river was a mile
wide and a foot deep; too thin to plow and too thick to drink.
But as it tumbled from the towering arch, sufficient force was
generated to turn a huge creaking waterwheel. Seth Hart had
copied it directly from those he remembered as a boy in New
England, and along the upper Rio Grande, his was the only
gristmill. Somewhat like its owner, the mill seemed formidable, unrelenting as it ground inexorably on; one of a kind
in a land where industry and determination often fell victim
to the drowsy pace of the natives.

Near the mill stood Seth Hart's home. Overlooking the
river, it was built of foot-thick adobe and surrounded by tall
shade trees. And it was here that various El Paso businessmen who shared Hart's political persuasion met once a week
for a bruising, heads-up poker game. The house rules were
table stakes, check and raise, and a good stiff jolt of rotgut
for those left sucking hind tit. As in his business and political endeavors, Seth Hart played poker to win.

After being greeted by their host, the men took their usual
seats and settled down for a long, spirited night. They were
old friends, each having come to El Paso when it was still a
stopover to somewhere else, and there were few secrets
among them. They loved whiskey and cards, shared a long
standing dream to make El Paso the hub of power in west
Texas, and considered themselves ethical businessmen as
well as adept politicians. They saw no contradiction in this
latter belief, for they readily agreed that a man of substance
must play many roles. While there were no saints among
them, neither were there any scoundrels, and on this bedrock,
their friendship had taken root and grown.

With drinks served and small talk out of the way, the men sat back to await the first deal. But Seth Hart absently riffled the cards, as if pursuing some elusive thought that resisted words. His thatch of white hair spilled over his head like an unkept mane, and the soft, cider glow of the lamp gave his face the flat sheen of weathered rawhide. Were these men his sons, or had this been a land of clans, he would have ruled as patriarch, the venerable elder to whom all others looked for guidance. Although neither condition existed, Hart was still a man of considerable influence, and his four friends seldom made a move without seeking the miller's counsel. Curiosity whetted, they waited in deepening silence as he sifted the chaff from what it was he had to say.

Hart cleared his throat and spat a wad of phlegm at a cuspidor beside the chair. When he spoke his voice was gravelly, as if he had spent too many years swallowing the dust from his own gristmill. "Boys, before we get side-tracked on poker, I'd like to get your ideas on this hornet's nest Charlie Howard stirred up. We're looking down a long, hard road, and if somebody doesn't calm the Mexicans pretty quick it's liable to be a bloody one." He paused, mulling the thought further. "One thing's for certain. Just as sure as we're sitting here, Ed Banning and his bunch aren't going to do a damn thing except keep right on lining their pockets."

"Maybe the greasers'll ventilate Banning the same way they did ol' Charlie." Doc Cummings, owner of the local mercantile emporium, chuckled softly at his own wit. "After all, Charlie was a spoon-fed piker compared to the Banning boys."

Horace Adair reared back in his chair. Noted for his hair-trigger temper, the Irishman was general manager of a mine north of town. "Jesus Christ, Doc! You made your point and missed it, all in the same breath. Granted Ed Banning would skin a flea for its hide and tallow, but he only steals from poor folks indirectly. Political corruption and cattle rustling rarely matter one way or the other to *peones*. Come to think of it, they might even admire him."

Curiously, Horace Adair was closer to the truth than he realized. There were many in El Paso who openly admired

the Banning brothers, and their ranks weren't limited to saloonkeepers, madams, and cardsharps. Ed and Sam Banning
had hit town in the spring of '79, shortly after word leaked
out that three railroads were laying track toward the border.
At the time, El Paso was little more than a crossroads. The
trail from Santa Fe to Mexico City ran directly through the
center of town, while the stage route connecting San Antonio with the Pacific Coast meandered off in the opposite
direction. And El Paso's chief claim to fame lay in the fact
that the Butterworth stage stopped there twice a day.

But with the arrival of Southern Pacific's first train only last
month, the little border town had undergone some startling
changes. Trains were daily disgorging a horde of mercenar-
ies who smelled loose money on the freshening wind. For
those with a strong stomach, there were fortunes to be made,
and whores, tinhorn gamblers, thimbleriggers, and gunslicks
had descended on El Paso like swarming locusts. Hardly to
anyone's surprise, the Banning brothers were running strong
at the head of the pack, welcoming outlaw and harlot alike
with open arms. With liberal doses of bribery, intimidation,
and outright murder, they had taken over city hall and virtually dominated the city council. Although it saddened early
settlers like Seth Hart and his friends, there was no denying
that in only two short years Ed Banning had become the
power to be reckoned with in El Paso.

"Horace, as usual, your logic is devastating." Doc Cummings cast a mischievous smile around the table, amused by
the Irishman's pugnacious manner. "But I'll tell you one
thing. Ed Banning's day is coming. He's got his finger in
everything else, and he'll probably get around to trying to
steal the salt lakes just like Charlie Howard did. Maybe if
we wait long enough, the greasers'll settle his hash for us."

Before Adair could frame a reply, Seth Hart broke in
sharply. "Doc, you and Horace are both missing the point.
Howard trying to grab the salt lakes only aggravated a sore
that's been festering for years. And mark my words, the
Bannings' rustling operation across the river will one day
force the *patrones* to lead their people against us. So far

they've sat back and watched, but if their ranches keep getting raided, they'll organize those *peones*, and God help us then."

The men silently glanced at one another, weighing Hart's words. Nate Hobart, proprietor of the Alhambra Hotel, sucked nervously at his drink and tried to think of something profound to add. But his natural reticence won out, and he merely waited for the shaggy-haired miller to resume.

When the stillness thickened without anyone venturing a solution, Hart tossed out another firecracker. "Boys, what I've been leading up to is simply stated. El Paso is just facing too goddamned many problems all at one time. Ed Banning is stealing the town blind, and when you get right down to cases, his political shenanigans are one of the big causes of our Mexican problems. Appears to me that, if we solve one, we'll have gone a long way toward solving the other. What I'm suggesting is that we put Banning to the skids and send him packing."

"Well, we could always have George Campbell run him out of town," Cummings observed dryly. The comment was greeted with grunts and snorts by the other men, for it was common knowledge that City Marshal Campbell was one of Banning's political flunkeys.

"Shit fire," Adair remarked acidly. "George Campbell couldn't catch his ass if he was tied hand and foot in a tow sack."

"By God, what we need is a *town tamer!*" John Simmons, owner of the livery stable and feed store, suddenly came alive. His eyes glittered with comprehension, as if the answer had been revealed to him alone. "Someone like Wild Bill Hickok, or Bear River Tom Smith. A real head-cracker!"

"There's only one problem with that, Johnny. They're both dead." Horace Adair's sardonic comment brought chuckles from the other men, and a withering look from Simmons.

Doc Cummings abruptly came up on the edge of his chair. "Maybe so. But by Jesus Christ, I know one that's not dead! He's a deputy sheriff up in Colorado County, and, gents, he's the meanest sonovabitch that ever got up and walked on his hind legs. Name's Dallas Stoudenmire, and lemme tell you, he eats knotheads like Ed Banning for breakfast."

"Is that a fact?" Adair inquired innocently, glancing about the table. "And how is it you know so much about a Dutchy gunslinger?"

"Horace, he just happens to be German. Or at least his folks were. And for your information, he's gonna marry my sister later this month."

"Doc, we're not playing for chalkies, you know." Seth Hart gave him a searching look. "This is serious business. You sure you want to get your brother-in-law hooked up in a deal like this?"

"Hell, Seth, I can't see how it'd hurt to ask," Cummings replied. "He's full grown, and I reckon he knows how to say no. Besides, he's been a lawman of one kind or another since the end of the war, and even if he don't want the job, he could sure as hell give us some powerful advice. Offhand, I'd say it's as good a place to start as any."

Hart pondered this for a moment, then nodded. "All right, send him a wire. But don't let the cat out of the bag. Just say you'd like to see him on a matter of some importance."

"And what will we accomplish, even if he's as tough as Doc says?" Adair's bulldog jowls set in an obstinate scowl. "You don't seriously think the city council will fire Campbell and hire a new marshal?"

Hart smiled patiently. "Horace, let's take 'em as we come to 'em. Don't forget that Doc and me both have a vote on that same council. And if we want to play dirty pool, we might just figure a way to ram it through."

The miller ran callused hands through his white mane, then picked up the deck of cards. The discussion had ended. "Boys, let's get down to some serious poker playin'. The name of the game is stud. Ante five dollars and take your licks like real white men."

3

Dallas Stoudenmire wasn't what folks would call a handsome man, but he looked like he had been built to last. Rangy and lean, he was hewed somewhat on the order of an oak door, standing six feet four and weighing in at a gristled two hundred twenty. Few men knew his full strength, and those who had tested it rarely came back for seconds. His very presence was enough to halt most troublemakers in their tracks, and his fearsome impact wasn't lessened by the craggy features, the jut of a heavy brow, and a shock of hair like burnished wheat. His face looked as though it had been hurriedly chiseled from a hunk of granite, and above the hollow cheeks his eyes touched lightly on all about him. As if it concealed some shallowly buried danger, his gaze seemed pale and depthless in its constant movement, like mountain water beneath freshly frozen ice. All in all, he was a solitary sort, a man best left to himself. And most people took him just as they found him. At a distance, in short doses.

When Stoudenmire stepped from the train at the Southern Pacific depot, he felt the stares of those crowding the platform. While he was used to it, the gaping looks never ceased to nettle him, like farmers gawking at some oddity in a tent show. He knew he was different from most men, colder, quicker to strike, drained of remorse once it was done. But it didn't bother him; he accepted it for what it was, wasting little thought on the compassion and gentleness that preachers rated so highly. Time lays scars on a man, bloody welts tracing a path from where he stands back to where he started. In the overall scheme of things, there were some men who needed killing, and it stood to reason that there had to be a few who were hardened to wield the instrument of destruction. Why he had been tapped for the job, or how it had come about, seemed unimportant, lost in the haze of long-ago, faraway things. Somehow it had started, leading him step by step from a wild young hellion to a man with a star on his chest. He was good at it, perhaps the best. And for now, being best at what he did was all that mattered.

Ignoring the stares, Stoudenmire turned his broad back, on the train station and strode off down Main Street. Though he knew little of El Paso, he had heard that it was nestled in the Tularosa Basin and was thus unprepared for the pervasive sense of being encircled by mountains. The *Conquistadores* had named it El Paso del Norte, for it formed a natural pass to the north over the mountains that now joined Texas, New Mexico, and Mexico. The bare, craggy slopes of the Franklin Mountains dropped off from a high rim to the north, and the town itself lay in the shadow of Comanche Peak. To the east lay the arid plains he had crossed by train, broken only by the flat desert mesas, jutting unevenly from the parched earth. Beyond the tablelands, he could see the Hueco Mountains, with the sheer cliffs of El Capitán thrusting skyward as if to escape the desolation and heat.

Turning, he studied the land to the southwest, across the river. In the distance, he saw the Sierra Madre range, forming a backdrop for El Paso's twin sister on the opposite border, Paso del Norte. Even though the towns appeared similar in every respect, he had heard on the train that Paso del Norte was strictly for Mexicans, a place where a *gringo* wandered at his own risk. The thought brought his mind back to the reason for being here, and he crossed the plaza in search of Doc Cummings. The cryptic telegram in his coat pocket said little, and perhaps that was what made him curious enough to travel six hundred miles. Most times the things men left unsaid were what counted in a pinch, and knowing Doc, he had no doubt there was considerable yet to tell.

Later that night, Stoudenmire and Cummings met with Seth Hart and his poker cronies. Although the five businessmen were the only ones who knew the purpose behind the lawman's visit, Stoudenmire's presence in El Paso was hardly a secret. Earlier in the evening, Cummings had taken him on a tour of the town's gamier dives, and there was considerable talk in the red-light district about the solemn-faced jasper with the frosty eyes. But the brief walk through the southside had served its purpose. Within an hour's time the lawman had counted close to thirty saloons, an equal number of dancehalls, and a rash of whorehouses unlike anything he had ever seen. Moreover, he had observed two saloon brawls, a knifing, and a somewhat amateurish gunfight, all within the space of two blocks. Yet not once had he seen a man wearing a badge. Any lingering doubt in Stoudenmire's mind had fast been dispelled. El Paso was in desperate need of a responsible peace officer.

Once introductions were out of the way and the men seated in Hart's study, the miller briefed Stoudenmire on the extent of the problem they faced. Without need of exaggeration, he detailed events leading to the salt war, the general hostility that existed between whites and Mexicans, and the stranglehold the Bannings had secured on the political apparatus of the town. While he spoke, Seth Hart had been sizing Stoudenmire up, and he liked what he saw. But there was more to a man than what met the eye, and that's what they had to find out before the evening was finished.

"Frankly, Mr. Stoudenmire," Hart concluded, "if I were in your boots, I wouldn't touch this job with a ten-foot pole. Course, you're a lawman, and I'm not, so I suppose you know what you're gettin' into." Then he paused, letting the silence mount as he appraised the other man. "Well, no sense beatin' around the bush. What about it? Do you think you're man enough to cut the mustard?"

Stoudenmire's eyes narrowed at the outright challenge, and the room went still as the men waited to see how he would answer. "Mr. Hart, it sort of looks to me like you've got the saddle on backwards. I didn't come here begging a job. You sent for me, near as I recollect. Whether or not I can pull your bacon out of the fire is something you'll have to decide for yourself. My record as a peace officer isn't hard to track down, and if I'm any judge, you've already put out feelers in the right direction."

Doc Cummings couldn't restrain himself from butting in. "Dallas, don't be so infernal high and mighty. He's only tryin' to get your opinion of our predicament. Christ, I've already told them how you fought for the Confederacy and served as a Ranger before you took the deputy job. They know you can clean up El Paso. They're just tryin' to get you to say it."

The lawman just nodded, smiling tightly. "Well, I'll tell

you, Doc. I'm not right sure I want the job. Leastways not until we come to an understanding about a few things."

"If you want my two cents worth," Horace Adair snorted, "I'm not convinced he can handle it. Running the Bannings out of town is gonna be like tryin' to pour hot butter in a wild-cat's ear. All this bullshit about him being a gunslinger might impress the folks back home, but goddamnit, this is the border. If he starts playing the big, tough *hombre* on the southside, those boys are just liable to whittle him down to size."

Stoudenmire's flinty gaze swung around, and he looked at Adair as if he were something hairy that had just crawled out of the gravy. "Mister, I never had much use for little men with loud mouths. Now if you pop off once more, I'll be forced to forget you're Doc's friend. Savvy?"

"Hold it!" Hart's gruff command came just as the Irish-man's jowls swelled with rage. "Horace, sometimes I'd swear you don't have sense enough to carry guts to a bear. Granted Mr. Stoudenmire might be young in years, but it seems you aren't able to see beyond that. There are other ways of mea-suring time, you know. Offhand, I'd say that anyone who has killed six men upholding the law doesn't need a wet nurse, even on the border." The startled looks from his friends brought a benign smile to the miller's face. "Why the sur-prise? You boys know I don't bet without peeking at the hole card. Like Mr. Stoudenmire surmised, I've already gone to the trouble of having him checked out."

Horace Adair glued a sheepish smile on his face and got busy sipping his whiskey. The big sonovabitch was for real after all! Silently, he wondered what went on inside a man's head who killed so easily, and for pay at that. The cold-eyed bastard probably pissed ice water and slept on nails.

"Well goddamn," Cummings crowed. "Are we gonna sit around on our thumbs or do we offer the man a job? How about it, Dallas? Want to try cutting El Paso down to size?"

"Trying won't get it. Not by half," Hart interjected. "He'll have to bet the limit and back every play to the hilt. Otherwise, he'll be cold meat inside of a week. But before we go too far with that, I'd like to hear more about those conditions Mr. Stoudenmire wants us to meet."

The lawman glanced around the room, studying each man in turn before responding. "Gentlemen, with the exception of Doc, I don't know any more about you than I do Adam's goat. You say you want your town cleaned up, and until you prove different, I'll take you at your word. But if I'm going to kick over a shithouse, it'll have to be done my way. That means no interference, no deals, and no special treatment for friends. Whoever gets in the way gets hurt. If you can't swallow that, then let's just shake hands, and I'll see about catching the next train out."

The men stared at Stoudenmire as if hypnotized, certain he meant every word he said. Whoever got in his way wouldn't just get hurt. They would get killed. And in his own way, the lawman was warning them that it could happen. Still, they didn't have a hell of a lot of choice. It was either suffer along under the Bannings or take a chance on a killer who just happened to wear a star. The one bled you dry with political corruption, and the other might just chase the whole damn town up a tree. But you paid your money and you took your chances. The odds came out the same no matter how the nut was cracked.

"Boys, it looks like we've got ourselves a new marshal." Seth Hart's tone left no doubt that the decision had been made. "Now we'd better get down to figuring strategy. I've got an idea the city council is gonna wet down their legs when we spring Dallas on them."

Stoudenmire leaned back in his chair and lit a cigar. As the men began talking, he sipped at his drink for the first time. Good whiskey. Damned good, in fact. And he had to admit that he was impressed with the company, too. Still, he'd seen sure-fire winners turn to busted flushes more than once. Better to bank on himself and forget about handouts. Storekeepers were generally soft in the guts anyway. Besides, when the shooting started, a man did well to forget he had friends.

4

El Paso's city hall fronted Oregon Street on the west side of the plaza. Once a month, Mayor Isaac Porter convened the city council in an upstairs meeting hall. There they met to consider the bagful of problems generated by the town's mushrooming growth.

Since the mayor, as well as two of the councilmen, Simeon Ogleby and Pud Brown, danced to whatever tune the Banning brothers happened to favor, the monthly meetings were generally cut-and-dried affairs. Occasionally, the irascible Doc Cummings would liven up what he called "The puppet show," but more often than not, the meetings made for a dull, frequently wasted, evening. The sole ambition of Mayor Porter and his two henchmen centered on milking the town dry with corrupt schemes, and even Seth Hart in his tenacious, probing way had been unable to get the goods on them to date.

The June council meeting promised to be little different from those in the past. After reviewing progress on current projects, which included a public waterworks contract awarded to Pud Brown's brother, the mayor opened the floor to new business. Hart and Cummings sat back to watch the show. While the council's shenanigans sometimes curdled their stomachs, there was a perverse fascination about the rogues' devious methods; as if a primer in civic malfeasance was being acted out right before their very eyes. Still, tonight might prove more interesting than anyone suspected, for Seth Hart planned to drop a bomb right in the mayor's lap. Just as soon as the four-flushers finished ramming through their latest swindle.

Isaac Porter was a beefy little man, whose spongy face was deeply pocked from a childhood bout with smallpox. Careful grooming did little to improve his chunky figure, and he had the disconcerting habit of peering at a man like some wise, inquisitive bird. The role of charlatan suited him perfectly, and as he faced the council, none doubted that he had few peers in the art of slick manipulation.

"Gentlemen, before the night's over I have every intention of breaking the faro bank at the Monte Carlo, so what do you say we get down to brass tacks? The floor's open, first come, first served."

Simeon Ogleby's hand shot skyward, and the mayor recognized him with a benevolent nod. "Mr. Mayor, I'd like to propose that the council entertain a motion to build a bridge over the Rio Grande. It's a public disgrace for a town of this size not to have a fine, substantial bridge joinin' us with our neighbors across the river. Besides that, now that the railroad has reached us, we should provide some civilized way of importing and exporting goods with Mexico. Trade is the backbone of commerce, and if this town's gonna grow, we've got to start thinkin' *progress*."

Hart and Cummings exchanged glances, never ceasing to be amazed by the sheer audacity of these rascals. Though he knew it was futile, Doc couldn't resist a bit of heckling. "Simeon, what the hell are you gonna do with a bridge? You could wade that goddamn mudhole without gettin' your toes wet."

"Commerce, Doc. Commerce. The backbone of trade." Ogleby floundered, trying to remember if he had his terms in the right order. "And vice versa, of course."

Isaac Porter gave him a devastating look and jumped into the breach. "Gentlemen, I personally find great merit in this proposal. Why, just think of it! El Paso would be the only town on the border with a bridge connecting it to Mexico. The possibilities for international trade are enormous. I might even say, unlimited. As a matter of fact, the idea has such merit that I suggest we broaden the discussion to consideration of selecting a contractor to build this fine bridge."

"Hell, why not give it to Pud's brother?" Doc cackled. "He knows all about working in water."

Pud Brown shot a nervous glance at the mayor and smiled apologetically, like he expected someone to kick him in the ass. Porter studiously ignored Doc's wisecrack and went right on with the meeting. To no one's surprise, a building outfit resting in Ed Banning's hip pocket was selected, and an allocation of twenty-five thousand dollars earmarked for construction. The motion was quickly brought to vote and passed three to two. Hart and Cummings voting *nay* had somewhat the same effect as spitting into the wind.

As the mayor and his two cronies were congratulating themselves on their slippery footwork, Seth Hart decided it was time to rock the boat. But it would have to be done skillfully, in a roundabout manner. For if the Bannings ever tumbled to his real purpose, then no amount of pressure, deftly applied or otherwise, could force them to oust George Campbell.

"Mr. Mayor, I would like to bring a matter of some importance to the council's attention. Just now you made the point that our town is growing by leaps and bounds. And I agree wholeheartedly. Our first bank has just opened, we've got two newspapers, and before the summer's out, another railroad will reach us. All in all, I'd say we're about to become the biggest thing that ever hit West Texas. But if we're ever going to equal the likes of Austin or San Antonio, we've got to bring about some changes. To use your term, Isaac, we've got to get down to the brass tacks of civilizing a town that thinks it's still a frontier outpost."

Hart had their attention, though it was obvious they were waiting for the ax to fall. Looking around the table, he let the suspense build for only a moment, then pushed on. "We're faced with two problems that aren't about to solve themselves. First, there's the Mexicans. The army proved they're unwilling to take a hand in civilian matters when they let Charlie Howard get sliced to ribbons. And Austin isn't gonna keep sending a detachment of Rangers everytime we yell wolf. Which means we must solve it ourselves. As long as there's a threat of violence, El Paso won't be anything more than a jerkwater whistle-stop.

"Now the second problem is just as bad, from a standpoint of the town growing and attracting more business enterprises. Any night of the week you wanna go down to the southside, you can see at least one gunfight and probably stumble across two or three cadavers without even trying. And every last one of you knows it's true. Brawls, shootings, knife fights. The kind of violence people expect from a cowtown, but certainly not a progressive community. And to my way of thinking, gentlemen, the blame falls on our shoulders, not on the townspeople. Calling a spade a spade, I'm talking about the man we appointed to protect the citizens of El Paso. George Campbell is worthless as tits on a boar hog. He not only isn't man enough for the job, he doesn't even try. I can guarantee you he's sacked up in some whorehouse swilling whiskey at this very moment. And with my own eyes, I've seen him make a beeline in the opposite direction whenever trouble starts."

Mayor Porter chuckled softly, then broke in before Hart could catch his breath. "Now, Seth, it's not all that bad. George isn't the best peace officer, I grant you. But he's certainly not the worst. Good Lord, this town's still got growing pains, and you can't expect any man to civilize it overnight."

"Well, by God, somebody better," Cummings snorted. "Otherwise, we're gonna have greasers crawlin' over us like flies on a manure pile. That is, if the rowdies don't kill everybody in town first."

The mayor and his cohorts suddenly began squirming in their chairs. Huddled together at the end of the table, they peered blankly at Hart and Cummings, like a trio of owls caught in a chicken coop. Apparently, the businessmen were in dead earnest, and the Banning underlings had no desire to create a row over such an insignificant post as city marshal. Their crooked little empire was running under full sail, and anyone who made waves would have to answer to Ed Banning personally.

Porter blinked first, unwilling to start a fight without Banning's approval. Then in his oily, politician's voice, he began probing for a weak spot. "Now Doc, don't get yourself in a swivet. We're all reasonable men here. And I'm sure Seth will agree that we can come up with some way to get George Campbell back on the straight and narrow. Think about it calmly for a moment and then tell me where you think the marshal has gone astray."

Cummings regarded him with a brash, amused insolence.

"Isaac, you're slick. Real slick. Remind me of a tomcat I heard about once. Seems like he got the hots for a little skunk pussy and started humpin' a female polecat. Well, sir, after a couple of whacks, he had to call it quits. Hadn't had all he wanted, you understand, just all he could stomach. What I'm gettin' around to saying, Isaac, is that unless you put a damper on the southside and the greasers, the voters of this town might start figuring they've had all of you they can stand."

"Doc's right, Mayor." Seth Hart grabbed the lead before Porter could gather his wits. "The marshal was appointed because you supported him, and everyone knows it, and as any fool can see, George Campbell wilted when the going got rough. He's your responsibility, Isaac, and if you don't do something about it, the decent people of El Paso are going to start having second thoughts about their mayor."

Porter glared at him across the table, trying desperately to muster some reasonable argument. But Hart's words had the ring of truth, and everyone in the room knew it. Ogleby and Brown simply held their breath, like something rancid had been smeared on their upper lips. Yet the silence deepened, and their faces went taut as they waited on the mayor to offer a snappy rebuttal.

Watching them, Doc Cummings couldn't resist the temptation. "Blessed are those who have nothing to say and cannot be persuaded to say it."

The sarcasm brought Porter out of his funk. He shot Cummings a stinging glance, then looked back at Hart. "Exactly what is it you're suggesting, Seth?"

"Not much, really. Just that Campbell be replaced with a man who can make El Paso a safe place to live."

"And I suppose you've got his replacement all picked out?"

"You might say that. We've been talking to a fellow named Stoudenmire. Got a fine record as a peace officer in East Texas. We think he's got the backbone the job calls for."

"And if I refuse to consider a change?"

"Why, Isaac, I suppose I'd be forced to call in the newspapers and tell 'em the mayor got skittish when we started talking about cleaning up El Paso. You know, elections are only a year or so away, and lots of people are just achin' to stir up a reform movement."

Porter mulled it over for a moment, desperately aware of the need to talk with Ed Banning. "Tell you what. We'll take it under advisement and come to a decision at next month's meeting."

"Sorry, Mayor, but that won't cut it." Hart's eyes hardened, and his jaw set in a stubborn cast. "I'll agree to twenty-four hours, which means we meet again tomorrow night. Otherwise I sic the newshounds on you."

Isaac Porter merely nodded, his face flushed with indignation and worry. Rising, he stalked from the room, trailed closely by Brown and Ogleby. Breaking the bank at the Monte Carlo was now the furthest thought from his mind. It had been a rough night, and right at the moment, he needed a good, stiff drink.

Observing their hasty departure, Cummings heard the warm, moist chuckle of a fat man laughing and turned to find Seth Hart thoroughly amused by the new order of things.

"Doc, just offhand, I'd say we've got 'em on the run. Goddamn me if they didn't look like three little shoats that just come out of the cuttin' pen."

The two men shook hands heartily and strode from the meeting hall with new zest to their step. Things were looking up, and if the Bannings weren't careful, they might just wind up snookered in their own game.

5

Some two hours after the council meeting, Isaac Porter wandered into the Coliseum Saloon. His step was slightly unsteady, and his eyes had taken on a glassy sheen, but otherwise, there was no outward sign that he was carrying a load. Since leaving city hall, he had belted down the better part of a quart, and at the moment he was feeling no pain. Still, he was in command of himself, and his confidence had risen sharply as he moved from saloon to saloon along San Antonio Street. Tipping his hat to the bartender, greeting his

constituents with an expansive smile, the mayor eased
through the boisterous crowd and headed for the Coliseum's
back room.

Like most watering holes in town, the Coliseum had a long
mahogany bar with a smattering of nude paintings and French
mirrors hung on the walls. But the similarity ended there, for
the Coliseum was owned by the Banning brothers, and it was
hardly an accident that their establishment was the showplace
of El Paso. On one side of the large hall, there was a row of
gaming tables, offering faro, chuck-a-luck, roulette, and other
pleasant devices for separating the sucker from his poke. Toward the rear of the room, angled across one entire corner,
was a small stage where dancing girls, Irish tenors, and
stuttering comedians took turns competing with the roar of
the crowd. Taken at a glance, it was quite a place, and for
most men, owning the Coliseum would have represented the
end of the rainbow. But Ed Banning had never considered
himself molded from common clay; what was enough for the
average pilgrim was merely a sampler for El Paso's political
kingpin.

After threading his way through the packed house, Mayor
Porter halted before a door at the rear, adjusted his coat, and
knocked lightly. From inside came a muffled command,
barely audible over the hubbub from the saloon. Sucking up
his paunch, Porter twisted the doorknob and entered Ed
Banning's office.

The first thing he saw was Sam Banning. The younger of
the Banning brothers had a way of drawing attention, even
in a crowd. For a big man, he was uncommonly handsome,
and the fact that his nose had been broken on occasion somehow lent character to his broad, rough-hewn features. But
after fashioning his face, the gods in their perverse way had
played a cruel joke on Sam. His wide, heavily muscled shoulders gave way to long dangling arms, and his hands looked
as if they could crush coconuts if the need arose. Still, the
crowning touch was that Sam had grown to manhood almost
as thick through the head as he was through the shoulders.

All in all, the young Mr. Banning seemed only one step removed from walking on his knuckles.

Porter nodded to Sam, then turned to his brother who was seated behind a massive, ornately carved desk. "Ed, how's tricks? Looked like you're making money hand over fist out there." The mayor jerked his head back toward the door, and his hat tilted askew, cocked rakishly over one eyebrow.

Ed Banning regarded the dumpy politician with a speculative gaze. Isaac Porter had achieved minor fame as a boozer in earlier days, and Banning had a sneaking hunch he was on the firewater again. "Mayor, what brings you down to this neck of the woods? Thought you had a council meeting tonight."

"Oh, we did, we did," Porter assured him. "Passed that bridge deal one, two, three, and awarded the contract to our sterling partner in illusion, Ab Roberts."

El Paso's political boss just nodded, observing him closely, certain now that Porter's euphoric mood was about nine parts alcohol. Banning's frowning eyes slanted upward, two cold, ashen sockets in a long, bony face. Unlike Sam, he was a spare man, with a chalky, pallid look, almost as if he had been sickly as a child. Somewhat withdrawn by nature, he was an astringent sort, who usually spoke through clenched teeth, as if his jaws had been broken and wired shut. But the most disturbing thing about him was his eyes, menacing yet somehow lifeless, tinted a strange, dispassionate shade of gray, curiously suggestive of a cold winter cloud in a dead sky.

With the exception of his brother, Ed Banning had little use for other men; cynical of their motives, sharply aware of the imperfections that flawed their character. Remote, purposely holding himself aloof from the crowd, he played on other men's frailties and, with reasoned audacity, brought them to their knees in the crunch. Now, irritated by Porter's weakness for the bottle, he decided to whittle his political front-man down a notch or two.

"Isaac, you're soused. And the only thing lower in my book than a drunk is a reformed drunk. Now, suppose you pull up your pants and tell me what happened at the council meeting to set you off."

The mayor's bonhomie wilted under the biting sarcasm, and his motley features dissolved beneath a mask of outright alarm. "Ed, it wasn't my fault, honest to Christ it wasn't. That bastard Seth Hart has got it in his head that we need a new marshal. And he's threatened to blow the lid off unless we appoint some John Law he's scrounged up. I swear to you, Ed, I didn't have a thing to do with it. Absolutely nothing."

"All right, Isaac, keep your dauber up. There's a difference between having your tit in a wringer and losing all the marbles. Now just start at the beginning and tell me exactly what happened."

"Goddamn, Ed, you ain't gonna get nothin' out of him that makes sense." Sam's eyes flashed like coals of black ice as he gestured comtemptuously toward Porter. His normal disposition was something akin to a boar grizzly with its paw in a rusty bear trap, and right now he regarded the stubby little politician with a hungry glare. "Lemme take old swizzle-guts out and dump him in a horse trough. That'll bring him up talkin' a blue streak."

"Sam, try not to be so rash. Isaac's not that bad off. Are you, Isaac?" Ed Banning paused and Porter nodded dumbly, darting a nervous glance in Sam's direction. "See, what did I tell you, Sam? Isaac's got it all sorted out, and he's going to pony up just like he had balls. Now you go right ahead, Mayor, we're all ears."

Fumbling the words, Porter tried to flush the whiskey fumes from his spinning brain. Haltingly at first, he started to relate the gist of what had happened at the council meeting. Warming to his subject, the old warrior then launched into a vitriolic, damning tirade against Seth Hart and Doc Cummings. Gaining confidence as his grasp for the trenchant phrase returned, the mayor swept into the home stretch with a dire warning that all was lost unless the two businessmen were somehow thwarted in their underhanded conspiracy.

When he finished, standing spent and slightly breathless, the brothers simply stared at him with disgust. Ed Banning finally shook his head with a patronizing smile. "Isaac, if anybody ever takes the trouble to kick all the bullshit out of you, they could bury you in a matchbox."

Sam's hoarse grunt cut him off. "Forget him, Ed. We got to worry about them smart-aleck sonsabitches uptown. I say get 'em in a dark alley and split their heads with a bungstarter. Teach 'em they can't get away with muckin' up the water. Let everybody in this whole goddamn fleabag know who's callin' the shots in El Paso."

"You know, Sam, sometimes I think our old man's oats must've been thinned out when he get around to you. Killin' Hart and Cummings wouldn't do anything but get the reformers out on the street pounding their drums." When the younger Banning gave him a baleful frown, Ed chuckled lightly. "Now don't get all bent out of shape. Lemme have a minute to think this out."

Unlike his brother, who operated solely on raw instinct, Ed Banning was coldly phlegmatic when crossed; a calculating, passionless instrument even with his back to the wall. Leaning back in the chair, his eyes clouded over and fixed on the ceiling, as if the answer lay hidden in the broad crossbeam. Slowly, piece by piece, he took the puzzle apart and put it back together again, examining each possibility with precise care before discarding it. Then, as he stood back and looked at the situation as a whole, the jumbled parts abruptly fell into place, no longer obscured or muddied but suddenly clear and shiny bright.

With the solution now in hand, his eyes focused again, and he found Sam watching him intently. "Brother, it occurs to me that dogs don't lie down just one way. And I think this is one of those times when we're gonna let Mr. Seth Hart go away figurin' he's bluffed us out."

When Sam's forehead wrinkled in protest, Ed held up his hand. "Let me finish. We're gonna let them have this hayseed as marshal. Stoudenmire, is that his name? Well they can have him, and welcome to him. It's no sweat off our balls. So long as we control the courts and city hall it doesn't make a good goddamn who wears that tin star. Without the mayor

or the judges to back him up, Stoudenmire is gonna be floun-
derin' around like a hamstrung calf. And the dandy part of it
is that we have absolutely nothing to lose, whichever way
the dice fall. If he does get the greasers calmed down and
clamps a lid on the southside, then we'll take credit for ap-
pointing the man who cleaned up El Paso. Lookin' at it the
other way, if he falls on his ass or gets himself killed, then
we'll dump the blame right back on Hart's doorstep. Like I
said, there's no way for us to lose. It's like playing with a
stacked deck."

"By God, Ed, you've done it again!" Isaac Porter grinned
broadly, nodding his head with a great show of awe. "I'll just
walk into that meeting tomorrow night and tell Hart to bring
on his horses."

"You do that, Mayor. Only make damn sure Hart and
Cummings believe that their threats worked. Otherwise, they
might shy off and start kicking over more rocks."

Later, after Porter had wandered back into the saloon, the
Bannings broke out a bottle of their own. Downing a shot,
Sam smacked his lips, like a dog sniffing horse apples. Then
he started, as if the whiskey had jarred his dim wits, and
peered quizzically at his brother.

"Say, Ed, I just thought of somethin'. What the hell kind
of excuse are we gonna give George Campbell?"

"Don't worry about it, I'll think of something. Course, we
could send him on a raid across the river. Maybe somebody'd
put a hole through him and let a little of that rotgut leak out."
Lazing back in the chair, he sipped the whiskey, savoring its
pleasant bite as his eyes drifted off. "Sam, if you're ever
gonna amount to anything in this game, you've got to get one
thing through your head. Men are the cheapest commodity
on God's green earth. You buy 'em like pig's knuckles. By
the pound or by the keg. And even then, you've got to figure
you've been robbed. No matter what you paid."

Sam Banning's thick brow wrinkled, and he dimly wondered what the hell his brother was talking about. Then he
decided it wasn't worth the effort, and went back to the more
inviting certainty of the bottle.

CHAPTER TWO

1

"Doc! Doc!" Kate Stoudenmire rushed forward and threw herself into the storekeeper's arms. She hadn't seen her brother in almost a year, and she sorely missed the eldest of the Cummings brood.

"Lordy, Kate girl, just look at you." After a mighty hug Doc held her at arm's length, mumbling appreciatively as he made a slow appraisal. "Yessir, gal, you are purely somethin'. Can't rightly call you my baby sister anymore. All growed up and married. Say, speakin' of husbands, where's Dallas?"

Glancing around, they saw Stoudenmire threading his way through the crowd gathered about the train station. Behind him came two Mexican youngsters who had all they could do to handle Kate's assortment of luggage. Trailing at his heels was the biggest dog Doc Cummings had ever laid eyes on.

As the two men shook hands, Doc saw the dog give him a long, speculative stare. He was easily the most ferocious-looking beast Doc could recall having stumbled across, including a couple of brief encounters with grizzlies. Built

along the lines of a mastiff, he had a deep bull-chest, an enormous furrowed head, and a jawful of teeth that looked like
he'd traded them off a shark. And like his master's, the dog's
eyes were cold, somehow menacing, constantly shifting as he
noted the movement of all about him with a wary scowl. In
the background, Doc overheard the little Mexicans talking
about *el lobo hambre*. The hungry wolf! Somehow it fitted
the dog perfectly, and he idly wondered what the hell Stoudenmire fed the brute.

"Dallas, it's good to see you," Cummings said, tearing his
thoughts away from the dog. "How's it feel to be an old married man? And what have you done to Kate? Man, she looks
like someone just handed her the keys to the goody factory."

Stoudenmire's face cracked in a rare grin. Kate was his
one weakness, the only soft spot in some thirty years of steel-
ing himself to toe the mark in an uncompromising land.
"Doc, near as I can see, I haven't done a thing for Kate. She's
just a natural looker, that's all. Trouble is, you've been sittin'
out here remembering your baby sister, and all the time she
was studying to be a real eyeful."

Kate was a stunner, no question about it, and a man needed
only one look to work up a fit of envy toward the lawman.
Standing about even with Stoudenmire's shoulder, she was
what people back home called dainty. But unlike many delicate women, she hadn't been shorted when the sweetmeats
were handed out. Her oval face was framed by hair black as
obsidian, and her eyes shot sparks of fiery green, like some
ancient feline goddess. She had a devastatingly winsome
smile and a bewitching manner that was both seductive and
impish in the same breath. Yet Kate somehow created the illusion of being one of those fragile, gentle things that would
vanish in a wisp of smoke unless handled gingerly. And beneath these more obvious features was a sense of refinement
and gentility that left even rawboned Texans gulping for
pretty words and mushy phrases.

Although one man's eye for beauty might easily leave another man doubting his judgment, there were few who
wouldn't agree that Dallas Stoudenmire had snared a rare

prize indeed when he got himself spliced to this toothsome young piece.

Cummings slapped Stoudenmire on the shoulder and crowed with laughter. "Maybe I remember her in pigtails, like you say. But I bet I wouldn't be wide of the mark thinkin' you got more than you bargained for too." Rolling his eyes, he chortled and nudged the lawman in the ribs, glancing slyly at Kate. "You're lookin' sort of peaked, son. Not lettin' Katie girl work you overtime, are you?"

"Honestly! Men are so crude." Kate blushed up to her hairline, eyes flashing with mock indignation. "You two act like you're in a stable discussing some high-stepping brood mare. Well you'd better take care, mark my words. I know enough about the both of you that, if I ever started talking, this whole town would roll over on its back."

"God save us, she'd do it too!" Grabbing his sister around the waist, Cummings struck off toward a horse and buggy hitched near the end of the depot. "C'mon, Dallas. Let's take your bride on a tour of the town before she ups and spills the beans." Over his shoulder he darted a quick glance at the dog. "That grizzly bear of yours can ride in the caboose. What's his name, anyway?"

"Tige. And you'd better take care what you call him." The dog's ears perked up at the sound of his name, and Stoudenmire knuckled his wrinkled brow. "He's sort of proud of being a dog, and he don't take kindly to most folks."

"Man or beast?" Cummings called back in jest.

"Both." The lawman chuckled softly, and Tige licked his hand, sensing in some distant way that his master had had the last word.

Shortly, luggage and dog had been loaded on the buggy, and they headed uptown. Chattering like a magpie, Doc Cummings enlightened them on the points of interest, allowing small room for questions. San Jacinto Plaza, renamed for the battleground where Texas had won its independence. The Notice Tree, an ancient shadetree on which proclamations and death warrants had been tacked in times past. The State National Bank, first of its breed on the upper Rio

Grande. And its partner in commerce, the Parker House
Hotel, even then rising from the dust in a whirlwind of mor-
tice and wood.

Pausing at the native market, the storekeeper explained
that the countryside abounded with Mexican *granjeros,* small
farmers who spent their lives coaxing raisins, grapes, and
various fruits from the hostile soil. Centuries ago, hard on
the heels of the *Conquistadores*, Franciscan monks had
planted vineyards across the basin, and Paso wine, along with
a fiery *aguardiente*, were now relished throughout the Southwest and Mexico. While the natives were far from prosper-
ous, they seldom experienced the famines of old, and with
the coming of the railroad, their produce could be marketed
on an even vaster scale.

Kate was all eyes as the buggy trundled through El Paso.
Her life had been spent in the backwoods village of Columbus,
and she had always dreamed of living in a city. While a bit
disappointed, with the monotonous adobe buildings, she
was enthralled with the bright costumes and gentle gaiety of
the people. There were few Mexicans in East Texas, and by
contrast, the border town seemed very colorful and exciting,
almost quaint. Maybe it wasn't Austin or San Antonio, but it
wasn't the sticks either. Besides, she was seeing it all for the
first time with the man who had rescued her from a shabby
life in the backwaters of nowhere.

Dallas Stoudenmire was her savior, sometimes gruff, often
inscrutable, but a man of intense passion and hidden
warmth. He had snatched her from the jaws of marrying some
farmer with one cow and a boil on his rump. Had that happened, she would have ended up like her mother, old and
worn before her time, having another baby every-time someone shook a pair of overalls at her. Now she was somebody,
the wife of a man selected for an important civic post, a
celebrity after a fashion. And while he had never suspected,
she would have gladly kissed her husband's feet on their wedding day.

Thinking about it, she made a tiny gurgling sound deep
in her throat, half wonder, half pure joy. With the excitement

of the moment, it was a heady mixture, and her head spun with the sheer exhilaration of just being alive. Then the moment of reverie passed, and Doc's voice once again intruded on that highly personal little world of her private thoughts.

"Yessir, we're a community that's going places. Agriculture, ranching, mines up north in the mountains. And the railroad just puts frosting on the cake. Everything a town needs to thrive and grow, make something of itself. Wouldn't be surprised but what El Paso becomes a real force in this state's economy before we're through."

"Doc, I think the word you're hunting for is boomtown," Stoudenmire noted soberly. "But from what I've seen so far the biggest business in El Paso is vice. Least-ways most of the *dinero* spent in this town finds its way back to the south-side in one fashion or another. Course, I could be all wet. I'm sort of Johnny-come-lately around here, so I reckon I'll have to wait till I see the full show."

"No, you're right as rain, Dallas. Hit it dead center, as a matter of fact." The storekeeper's face twisted with disgust, and he spat over the side of the buggy. "Sometimes I get wrapped up in what this town *could be*, and I lose sight of what we've got to overcome to get there. Ed Banning and his gang are the nerviest bunch of cutthroats along the border, and they've got to be sent packin' before El Paso will ever amount to anything. That's why we hired you. And being plain-spoken about it, most of the townspeople don't care whether you run 'em out or kill 'em. Just so they're gotten rid of."

"We'll see, Doc," the lawman said. "I don't believe in callin' my hand till all of the cards have showed."

"Perfectly understandable. Anyway, you're the marshal as of tomorrow morning, and you can run it however you see fit." Doc's face suddenly brightened, and he leaned across to swat Stoudenmire on the knee. "Damnation, I clean forgot. Seth Hart pulled a few strings back East while you were gone. Might say he called some political debts. Anyway, he got a pipeline into James Garfield and had you appointed a deputy US marshal. What with wearin' two stars, I'd say you oughta be able to cover just about any play the Bannings make. Course, you might do best to keep that under your hat. Seth figures it's an ace in the hole you shouldn't play till your back's against the wall."

Stoudenmire just nodded, reserving comment one way or the other. "Likely it'll come in handy, but tell Hart I don't want any more favors. I took this job with the understandin' I wouldn't be beholden to anyone. I meant just that, Doc."

"Pull in your horns, boy. Nobody's tryin' to get you obligated. Seth just wants what's best for the town, and he figured you could use all the muscle we could muster."

"Doc, I've got no more use for a politician than a hog does a sidesaddle. Just keep your cronies clear of me and let me do my job. If gettin' the Bannings' ashes hauled is what they're really after, I reckon they won't have long to wait."

Doc Cummings hunched forward and gave the horses a good swat with the reins. Damned if his brother-in-law wasn't as contrary as an old mule about certain things. Stubborn as a Dutchman, people always said, and by God, these Germans sure fitted the ticket.

Seated between them, Kate had remained silent throughout the discussion. Dallas had told her little of what lay behind his appointment, and for the first time she became aware of the task he had undertaken. Deputy sheriff of a settled county was one thing, but marshal of an untamed border town was more than she had bargained for. As they drew up before the house Doc had rented for them, Kate decided that something would have to be done about finding her husband a safer line of work.

2

The dim light of a quarter-moon cast a faint glow over Paso del Norte. Along the main street, soft music drifted from a scattering of *cantinas*, and in a large building to the west, the lively tunes of a *fandango* floated across the plaza. Horses lined the hitchrails, standing hip-shot in the warm, sleepy night, yet the street was nearly deserted. The festivities had only just begun, and those not attending the dance had settled in for a night at their favorite saloon.

But the sleepy tranquillity of the village was abruptly shattered by coarse laughter and drunken shouts that were unmistakably American. The doors of a *cantina* burst open and four men stumbled into the street, steadying each other as they lurched to a halt. They reeked of *tequila*, and as they wobbled about, their eyes searched the night for some devilment worthy of their rowdy mood.

"For Chrissakes, boys," roared one with a thatch of red hair, "I still say we oughta slip on down to that *fandango* and find us some little chili peppers."

"That's the ticket!" another agreed drunkenly. "I'm a man that needs to get his log sapped, and them Mex gals purely know how to jitterate your juices. Whooeee! They is somethin', ain't they, Red?"

Before Red could answer the oldest member of the crew cut him off. "Listen you goddamn nitwits, you go down to that dance and you're gonna end up shootin' marbles with your balls. Them greaser bastards don't like whites messin' with their women."

With a wild screech a runty, bowlegged little man reeled away from them, violently flapping his arms to keep from falling. "Yellow sonsabitches! Yer nothin' but a bunch of gutless shitkickers. Gonna let them greasers run it over you? Bullshit! There ain't a man alive that can make me back up."

With that, he stumbled backwards and sat heavily in the dusty street. The other men regarded him solemnly for a moment, dimly attempting to sift out the gist of his angry tirade.

"Goddammit, boys, he's right," Red growled. "Them greaser pricks ain't gonna brace us. Long as we stick together and keep our guns handy, they'd let us hump their mammy right in the middle of that dancehall."

The horny one perked up at that, and the older man merely mumbled sourly to himself. The decision made, they ambled forward and clumsily lifted their sidekick from the dirt. Just then, an obscure figure materialized from the darkness and silently glided past them, hugging the shadows near the adobe buildings.

Glancing up, Red batted his eyes and squinted hard, not sure he was seeing right. "Boys, if these old peepers ain't playin' tricks on me, that there is a livin', breathin' chili pepper."

The men's heads swung around, and for a moment they stared drunkenly into the shadows. Then their eyes came uncrossed, and without a word, they moved toward the dim figure. Fanning out, they formed a half-circle, bringing their ghostly quarry to bay against a wall.

"¿Quien es?" a small, quivering voice implored. "What is it you want, señores? I was only on my way to the baile. I meant no harm."

Trapped between them stood a young girl, hardly more than a child. Her eyes went wide with terror, glistening in the soft moonlight as she cowered against the building. She pressed herself flatter against the cool adobe, paralyzed with fear, whimpering as the men advanced on her. Then they leapt forward like a pack of wolves on a bleating calf, dragging her to the earth in a silent rush. Beneath her simple cotton dress they could feel the ripe young breasts, the warm thighs, the gentle swell of her girlish hips. Suddenly their tongues went thick, and the brassy taste of lust flooded their mouths. Red clamped his hand over her face, and they wordlessly lifted her. Gripped with shock, the girl stiffened under their hands like some frozen little bird with a broken wing. Moving swiftly, they ducked through the alley and faded into the darkness.

Less than a quarter-hour later the men reappeared from the alleyway, brushing dirt from their clothes. The edge had been blunted on their drunken mood, and their words came in terse, surly grunts.

"Shit, boys, I've had better poontang'n that screwin' a knothole. Come to think of it, Mother Thumb and her four daughters has got that gal beat."

"Goddamn right! That little bitch just laid there like a

board. I'll bet she didn't wiggle her ass once the whole time I was humpin'."

"Quit pissin' and moanin', will ya? It was free, and that's likely the first time you ain't paid for it since you quit jerkin' your pud."

"Listen, you little turdknocker, I've had about enough of your lip for one night. Keep it up and you're gonna get . . ."

The four men came to a halt as they emerged onto the street, falling silent as they blundered into the path of several horsemen. Riding past were seven *vaqueros* mounted on their best cow ponies, clearly dressed for the *fandango.* The Mexicans eyed the men haughtily, their gaze wavering between curiosity and outright contempt. Then, just as they drew even with the Americans, the girl stepped from the darkness at the *gringos'* backs. Blood streamed down her legs, staining her torn skirt the color of burnt ochre; the bodice of her dress had been ripped apart, revealing the delicate bud of her childish breasts. Her eyes seemed wide as saucers in the pale light, and beneath them lay the dull gaze of one who has just walked barefoot through the coals of hell.

The *vaqueros* reined their horses viciously, wheeling toward the Americans. Startled, the four men turned to see what had attracted the Mexicans and found themselves face to face with their own handiwork. The specter advancing toward them froze the Americans in their tracks, like the sightless dead come to exact some nameless vengeance. Suddenly the feisty little man with the bowlegs snarled and spun about, clawing at his six-gun as he turned. But before he could clear leather, the *vaqueros* cut loose with a ragged volley, and pockets of dust spurted from his shirtfront. As he slammed backwards, his legs folded beneath him, and he dropped to the earth with a dusty thud. His partners briefly considered making a run for the darkness, then discarded the thought. They had no more chance than a flea on a wet hog; any sudden movement would leave them as dead as the sawed-off runt lying at their feet. Slowly they raised their hands, halfway expecting to get it in the back even as they did so.

Within the hour, the villagers of Paso del Norte had gathered before the local *calabozo*. Inside the jail, Pedro Vazquez, their *alcalde*, was attempting to piece together the story. As mayor, it was his responsiblity to determine the charges and hold these men for the *rurales*. Quite by chance, his nephew, Ramón Vazquez, was the leader of the *vaqueros* who had captured the Americans.

Listening to Ramón recount what had happened, the *alcalde* sensed that the temper of the crowd was better suited to a quick hanging. But these were his people, and they would never go against his wishes. Quite clearly, the *norteamericanos* were guilty, and they would be executed without doubt. But all according to law. So long as he was *jefe* of Paso del Norte, there would be none of the senseless violence that went on across the river.

As his nephew finished speaking, Pedro Vazquez heard a sullen muttering erupt from the crowd and turned to see people easing away from the door. Then a man and a woman appeared in the doorway, shielding the girl between them. With great dignity, they moved across the room and stopped before the *alcalde*, looking neither right nor left. The girl simply stared at the floor, unable to look at anyone.

"Mi niña, I would spare you this if it were within my power." Pedro Vazquez lifted her chin and kissed her gently on the cheek. "But we must know who did this terrible thing. So you must be brave and force yourself to look upon these men. If they are the ones, then it is your duty to make this known. Have no fear. Just look and tell what you see."

The girl slowly turned her head and stared for a heartbeat at the three men, now securely locked in cells at the end of the room. Huge tears welled up in her eyes, rolling down over her cheeks, and she nodded. Just once, almost shyly. Then her gaze went dull, and a merciful darkness swept over her eyes.

When the girl had been led away by her parents, the *alcalde* turned back to the prisoners, speaking in broken English. "You have been identified as the men who did this horrible thing. Were it up to me, I would hand you over to the people. Instead, you will be tried by law and executed before a firing squad."

"Listen, you tub of guts," Red shouted, "we didn't do nothin' to that bitch that ain't been done before. She's a whore. You understand, a *puta?* Just come right out and offered it to us."

Ramón Vazquez advanced on the cell, his face twisted with rage. "*Gringo bastardo.* Only filth like you would do that to a young girl. She was an *inocente*, a virgin!"

Red swallowed hard, but he didn't back off. "You're not spookin' us, greaser. We're Americans and we know our rights. Besides, we work for Ed Banning, the big *hombre* across the river. If you do anything to us, he'll burn this goddamn pigsty down around your ears."

"*Tien cuidado, bárbaro!*" The *alcalde*'s warning sounded with all the finality of a death knell. "Take care, barbarian! Do not offend your God. You will have need of him where you are going."

"*Sí*, my uncle advises you well," Ramón Vazquez added. "Look to your God for *absolución*. You will find none from Señor Banning. Scorpions like him eat their young when the road grows hard."

The prisoners' faces took on a wooden look. They understood, even halfway believed it. But they didn't like what they heard. The horny one slammed up against the bars and shook his fist in Ramón's face. "You greaser sonovabitch! Your day's comin'. You just wait. We'll get out of here, and when we do, I'm gonna cut your nuts off and feed 'em to the pigs."

The *alcalde* turned and walked to the door, pausing before the jailer. "*Alguacil*, if these *gringo* dogs so much as rattle the bars on their cages, you are to shoot them without hesitation."

Pedro Vazquez stepped into the night, followed closely by Ramón and his *vaqúeros*. The jailer closed and barred the door, then pulled an ancient Colt from its holster. Cocking it, he eased himself onto a stool and regarded the Americans like a fat snake.

Right about then, Red got to wishing he had a stump between his legs. Damned if it wouldn't make life a hell of a
lot simpler.

3

Stoudenmire crossed the plaza with Tige hard on his heels.
The morning sun was barely two hours old, but already the
broad square was a beehive of activity. Everyone in El Paso
got an early start, for as midday approached, the heat became
oppressive, downright unbearable for some. While greenhorns were known to laugh at the town's casual pace, they
quickly learned that the afternoon siesta was a touch of ge-
nius born of sheer necessity. Those who didn't heed the message like as not ended up with sunstroke.

Walking north across the plaza, Stoudenmire reflected on
the unsettling bit of news Doc Cummings had passed along
only moments before. When he had stopped in at Doc's store,
the tale of last night's trouble in Paso del Norte was already
making the rounds. Bad news travels fast, and the young girl's
rape along with the killing that followed had spread alarm
among the townspeople. Something like this could trigger a
shooting war with the greasers, and most everyone agreed
that El Paso was sitting on a powder keg with a short fuse.
The new marshal was of a similar opinion, for it was well
known that the Mexicans thought highly of their women. And
deflowering a virgin was damn near the last straw for anybody! Whichever side of the river they happened to call home.
Thinking about it, Stoudenmire decided he hadn't come to
town any too soon.

But at the moment, he had a more immediate problem.
Namely George Campbell and his deputy, Bill Johnson.
Against his better judgment, Stoudenmire had agreed to keep
them on as deputies. Somehow he was skeptical of any man
who meekly accepted demotion from marshal to deputy, and
it occurred to him that George Campbell would likely try to
undermine his efforts at policing the town. Seth Hart had
termed it good politics, but it had left a bad taste in Stouden-

mire's mouth from the very start. Still he had agreed, and like it or not, he would have to go through the motions.

Entering the office, he found Campbell seated behind the desk and Johnson stretched out on a rickety bunk. One glance was all he needed to catalog this pair. Throughout the war and almost ten years as a peace officer, he had dealt with their breed more often than he cared to remember. Shiftless, slovenly men without roots; warped in mind and filthy by choice; willing to cut their own mother's throat for a decent meal or a shot of cheap whiskey.

The men returned his look with casual indifference, neither stirring from their indolent pose. Plainly they had every intention of giving him a hard way to go, right from the start. Their attitude made it clear that taming El Paso was his ball of wax, and they were merely paid observers. They figured to lay up on their backsides and wait for him to get his nose bloodied. Chuckling to himself, Stoudenmire recalled he'd played this same game before, and he had picked up a few dodges that even these sharpies hadn't seen.

"Off your ass and on your feet, gents. The reins just changed hands, and we're gonna operate a little different around here from now on. In case you hadn't heard, my name's Stoudenmire, and that's my desk you're sittin' behind."

This last remark was aimed at Campbell, who blinked like a horny toad that had just stepped on a rattler's tail. He was a thin, stringy sort of fellow, who looked as if he had been stretched out to dry and left in the sun too long. As he unfolded from the chair and came to his feet, his beady eyes glinted with outright hatred. "Sure thing, Dallas. You just set right down and take over the ship. And if it gets a mite leaky, why Bill and me'll be real proud to give you a hand bailin'. Won't we, Billy boy?"

Johnson mumbled something under his breath and heaved himself off the bunk with considerable effort. From the look of his eyes, he might bleed to death at any moment, and anyone who doubted he was a confirmed rummy just couldn't read sign. Twenty years of beans and sowbelly and green rotgut were starting to show at his beltline, and from all appearances, he couldn't have fought his way out of a rotten gunnysack.

Stoudenmire merely glanced at him, then leveled a flinty gaze on the former marshal. "Campbell, let's get something straight from the outset. When you speak to me, it's Mister Stoudenmire, or Marshal. I'm sorta particular that way, and you'd do well not to make me tell you twice."

"Well, yessir. Marshal, sir. You play the fiddle and we'll do the dancin'. And Billy, let's not forget to salute when *Mister Stoudenmire* starts barkin' orders."

"Gents, I've got a feeling that ridin' double with you two is gonna be more than I could stomach." His pale eyes settled briefly on the rummy, then shifted back to Campbell. "There's two things I never had much use for. Tin-horns with a flannel-mouth, and a swizzelguts that can't wean himself off the juice."

Campbell's face blanched, and his Adam's apple bobbed like a fishcork. "Lemme tell you somethin', *Marshal*. We been around a long time before this town ever heard of you, and we're gonna be around a long time after you're gone. There's more'n one way to skin a cat, you know. And I got an idea somebody's gonna nail your hide to the wall before you even get started real good."

"Is that a threat, sonny?" Stoudenmire deliberately goaded the man, enjoying himself immensely now that it was out in the open. "Or are you just makin' promises you can't keep?"

"Mister, you're walkin' on eggshells, and you don't even know it. If I was you, I'd take to avoidin' dark alleys and lonely places."

"Campbell, you just tied a can to your own tail." Stoudenmire's glare raked the other man. "You and Johnson pick up your gear and clear out. You can collect your wages at city hall."

Campbell took a step forward, his fists clenched. "Listen, you overgrown sack of shit, you can't fire me. I don't take orders from anybody. . . ."

A pistol suddenly appeared in Stoudenmire's hand, and he laid it upside Campbell's jaw like a sledgehammer. Fiery sparks erupted inside the skinny man's brain, and the whole left side of his head went numb. Without a sound he crumpled to the floor as if his backbone had been snatched clean.

Across the room, Johnson's hand edged slowly toward his gun, almost as though he wanted someone to stop him before he worked up the guts to make a try for it. Snarling, Tige padded forward with hackles raised, baring his fangs. Johnson froze, eyes bright with fear, as if he had been turned to stone. One wrong move and he knew the ferocious-looking bastard would start at his boot tops and eat him alive.

Once he saw that Tige had Johnson cornered, Stoudenmire hefted Campbell, lugged him to the door, and tossed him into the street. Returning, he grabbed Johnson by the collar, waltzed him across the floor and planted his boot straight up the rummy's tailbone. Johnson shot through the door as though propelled from a cannon and came to a shaky halt beside his fallen partner.

Massaging the seat of his pants, he tried to suck up the nerve to stand and fight. "Marshal, you're a real stem-winder. But you ain't as big as you think. Things are gonna get plenty sticky around here, and it might just be I'll take a hand in it personal."

Leaning against the doorjamb, Stoudenmire smiled sardonically. "Johnson, find yourself another trough to swill at. You mess around with me and you'll get hurt."

Unable to stand up under the lawman's cold stare, Johnson turned and helped Campbell to his feet. Bleeding freely from a wide gash in his head, Campbell moaned something that didn't make much sense and slumped against his cohort. Supporting him, Johnson started off at a slow walk across the plaza. Every few steps, he turned to peek back over his shoulder, like a jowly old rooster twisting his neck to hunt for lice.

Stepping back inside, Stoudenmire took a seat behind the desk and waited for the explosion. Twenty minutes later it came. Mayor Isaac Porter stormed through the door in a faunching rage. Before the lawman could open his mouth,

Porter launched into a frothing tirade that would have turned a faith healer green as pickle juice.

"By all that's holy, Mr. Stoudenmire, you are a very temperamental sort of man. You can't just go around whipping the bejesus out of your own deputies and dumping them into the street. Something like that creates a bad example for the rest of the town. Sets law and order back on its ear. Gives it a black eye, if you see what I mean. This is a civilized town, Mr. Stoudenmire, and we can't have the law fighting among themselves. It just won't do. By glory, it won't do at all!"

Porter's overbearing manner left the marshal thoroughly unimpressed. "Mayor, you might as well save your breath. What's done is done, and that's the end of it."

"Not by a damnsight it's not, Marshal. When you appeared before the city council to discuss this job, we took you to be a reasonable man. It was agreed that Campbell and Johnson would be retained as your deputies, and I'm just afraid we'll have to hold you to it." Porter's voice had risen sharply as he spoke, but he suddenly lost wind as he noticed Tige eyeing him with a strange look. "And if you don't mind, please call your dog off. I don't care for the way he's staring at me."

Stoudenmire rubbed behind the dog's ears, smiling faintly. "You can relax, Mayor. Politicians are a little rancid for his tastes. But that's neither here nor there. I've given your stooges the gate, and that's how it stands. If you or the city council try to interfere, then you can start hunting for a new marshal. Now, I haven't got all day to stand around listening to you preach, so fish or cut bait."

Porter was on the verge of blowing his cork when he thought better of it. Banning had ordered him to let the German have his head. And by God, that's just what he'd do. *He'd let the arrogant sonovabitch hang himself!* "All right, Marshal. Don't do anything rash. There's no need to get riled up over such an insignificant matter. We hired you, and we'll back you to the hilt. Even if we don't fully agree. But I feel duty bound to warn you that this isn't a town that can be policed by one man alone."

Stoudenmire grinned cockily. "Don't get yourself in a

lather over that, Mr. Mayor. Just happens there's a fellow on his way here that I've already signed on as deputy. Name's Jim Gillette. He's not much to look at, but he's tougher'n most. Found that out when we rode together in the Rangers."

Mayor Isaac Porter just nodded and plastered an assy smile across his face. Someone had just been feinted into position and given a first class screwing. And he had the very distinct feeling that it was Mother Porter's youngest son. The slow one.

4

Ramón Vazquez had awakened earlier than usual that morning. There was a taste of ashes in his mouth, and it occurred to him that what lay suppurating in a man's mind often surfaced in his gorge. Dressing slowly, his thoughts returned again to last night, and he silently offered a prayer that it had been his bullet that killed the *gringo cerdo.* Since squeezing the trigger that once, he had cursed himself a thousand times for not continuing to fire until all the filthy beasts were dead. *Muerte!* That is what they each deserved, quickly and simply, without the mercy one shows even a dumb animal.

But then, a man could not easily escape the lessons of his youth. And a Vazquez would never lower himself to act in the manner of the barbarians across the river. Especially one who had risen to the position of *caporal* over the largest ranch in the district. After all, Don Miguel Salazar expected him to set the example! *El patrón* would hardly bestow his blessings on a foreman who taught *vaqueros* to shoot men down in cold blood.

Somehow the thought filled him with disgust. Mercy and aristocratic conduct were for the *hidalgos,* the ruling class. Perhaps compassion was a luxury the common people, the *peones,* could no longer afford. The time for civilized behavior was when one faced an honorable enemy, not when the *gringo* jackals were snapping at the heels of the poor and the defenseless. While he had been revolted by the brutal executions of the *norteamericano* businessmen at San Elizario, it came to Ramón that there was much to be said for dealing harshly with such scavengers. *¡Madre de Dios!* What he wouldn't give to be an Apache for a short time. There was a form of moral conduct the *gringo bárbaros* could understand. And never forget!

Leaving the bedroom, Ramón walked toward the center of the house. Though this was the *casa* of his uncle, he thought of it as his own, for he had grown to manhood within these walls. And it was good to have spent such a night in the place of his youth. Somehow he seemed stronger for having slept in his old bed again. Moments later, he entered the dining room to find Pedro Vazquez already seated at the head of the table.

"Buenos días, mi tio," he greeted the older man. *"¿Como está usted?"*

"Bueno, Ramón." The *alcalde* paused just long enough to note the hollow cast to his nephew's eyes. *"¿Y tu?"*

Ramón merely shrugged, sliding listlessly into a chair. After pouring a cup of hot chocolate, he idly stirred it with a spoon, clearly absorbed with his own worrisome thoughts.

"A quien madruga, Dios le ayuda," Pedro Vazquez observed. "God favors those who rise with the dawn. Are the circles beneath your eyes from early prayer, *mi hijo?"*

Ramón shook his head, then gestured heavenward. "Does He also favor those who cannot sleep for want of destroying their enemies?"

"My son, God overlooks much, but he would be displeased to see your hatred so quickly aroused." The older man examined the dregs in his cup thoughtfully, as if seeking some further enlightenment. "Ramón, no rational man could deny that the situation worsens between the *yanquis* and our people. I, too, spent a restless night considering this very thing. But if those to whom the people look for guidance were to sanction violence, then the Rio Grande would run red with blood. *¡La jugo de muerte!* The juice of death."

"¡Bueno!" Ramón's dark gaze crackled with sudden ferocity. "So long as it is *gringo* blood, then I would gladly cut

the first throat. We have lived too long under the oppression of this filth. It must end. *¡Pronto!*"

The *alcalde* flinched, his face gone tight with shock. "And is spilling blood the only way it can be ended? Are we not reasonable men who can employ persuasion with our enemies? Have we learned nothing from the suffering of our *antepasados* under the Spaniards?"

"You talk in riddles, *mi tio.* The yoke of oppression was lifted from our people only after Juarez led them to war. It would seem that the way of our ancestors contradicts your cry for reason."

"So you would have our people take up the sword and march on El Paso. Slaughter the *norteamericanos* as if they were hogs in a charnel house. Is this what you are telling me, Ramón?"

The younger man flushed and looked away, shamed by his uncle's heated rebuff. "You twist my words, *padrino.* I meant only that we should defend ourselves and have no mercy on these jackals when they swim the river to violate our lands and our women. How could anyone who values his manhood do less? Can you look inside yourself and state with certainty that the *gringos* would ever be swayed by reason? Even if they were, what would be gained besides a moment in time? We have seen them break faith again and again with the *indios* of the north. Are we *ingeui niños* to believe that they will treat Mexicans with greater honor than they have shown the red men?"

The *alcalde* nodded, more in understanding than agreement, as though weighing the younger man's words before he spoke. "Since your mother and father died and you came to live with me, I have tried to raise you as a son. *¡Mi hijo!* And now I will repeat a blasphemy to you that a man would dare whisper to none but his own flesh. I have lived long and seen much of the evil men practice among themselves, most of it so terrible it is best forgotten. As *jefe* of this village, I have learned that brotherhood is merely a word employed by priests, for if God smiles on a man, then he must afterward hold himself beware of his neighbors.

"But wisdom such as this often makes a man *cinico*, and we are confronted by problems, Ramón, that will never yield before cynicism alone. Certainly we can open our eyes to the *gringos'* treachery, but to fight them is to do battle with the wind. There is no end to it. A man must ultimately tire, and when he does, he will be blown away, as chaff from wheat. Somehow we must seek out men of reason among the *yanquis* and deal with them not so much from trust as from necessity. Until then, we must not provoke our people to foolhardy acts. Among the old ones it is well known that even the bravest *toro* can thrash himself to death in a spider web."

Ramón heeded the wisdom of his uncle's counsel, but it did nothing to lessen his hatred of *gringos*. Nor did it have much effect on his fear that even then the *norte-americanos* were planning reprisals against their village. Although it was true that the cloud of rage no longer blinded his thinking, he still saw the situation for what it was.

Last night's tragedy was but a quirt to the hostility that existed between the two races. Perhaps the last in a dreary chronicle of injustice and duplicity that would soon drive his people beyond the point of reason. Regardless of his uncle's belief that decades of humiliation could be resolved with pretty words and unstinting faith.

Long before his time, it had started with the Treaty of Guadelupe Hidalgo. That infamous document, which had allowed a river to split a city in half, leaving thousands of their people to suffer under the rule of arrogant *tejanos*. While it had never touched him personally, he had seen with his own eyes the degradation of those who lived north of the Rio Grande. It was not a sight easily forgotten.

Yet that was only the beginning. Wherever a man turned, he seemed to find *gringos* blocking his path, scheming and clawing to satisfy their monstrous greed. There was the constant rustling of cattle from Mexican *ranchos*, an indignity that *patrones* and *vaqueros* alike had suffered for much too long. The *yanqui* mining interests were burrowing like moles throughout Chihuahua, sapping the strength and the spirit of *peones* enslaved in those dungeon pits. Even the salt war had

been the *norteamericanos'* fault, for it was they who sought
to rob the poor by withholding the very substance of life
itself.

Now they had committed the unforgivable indecency.
Despoiled a young girl of her virtue. And he had no doubt that
those across the river were at that very moment planning to
rescue the three barbarians held prisoner in Paso del Norte.

The *alcalde* had waited patiently while his nephew sorted
out his thoughts. When Ramón finally looked around, he
smiled and clasped the younger man's arm. "It occurs to me
that you are a good man, *mi hijo.* Never had I heard you speak
out against the *gringos* with such anger until the ordeal of this
young girl. Compassion for the weak is a commendable thing,
particularly in a man. But never should it be allowed to cloud
your judgment. The people look up to you, and in time, you
could become their *jefe.* Yet I would caution you that there
is more to being a leader than making impassioned speeches
and provoking men to spill blood. A fool often regrets his
words, but a wise man seldom regrets his silence. You would
do well to think on this in days to come."

Ramón stared at the old man for a long time, wondering
if wisdom and reason could, after all, bring about justice for
their people. Troubled beyond measure, he had allowed himself to be persuaded that nothing should be done to incite
violence. And for the moment, he would respect his uncle's
wishes. But persuaded or not, he fully intended that the *cabrones* in jail would never again cross the Rio Grande. Except
as dead men.

5

Jim Gillette arrived on the afternoon train. While he was
glad to get his feet on solid earth once more, he didn't waste
any time gawking at the sights. Like the man, his gear was
honed to essentials, and he came straightaway to the office.
When he stepped through the door, he carried a warbag, a
mule-eared sawed-off shotgun, and a Colt .44 cinched high
on his hip.

Stoudenmire came around the desk, and the two men shook hands. Though they hadn't seen each other in over a year, they had kept in touch, and there was little need for small talk. They liked each other, respected one another's skills as a peace officer, and felt confident enough in their friendship that there was no need to prime it with meaningless words.

With greetings out of the way, they had gotten down to business. Gillette hitched a chair over beside the desk, and Stoudenmire proceeded to brief him on what they faced. In a detached, unemotional voice, he related each incident in the long chain of bloodlettings leading to the present tensions between Mexicans and Yankees. Then he covered the Banning Brothers in similar detail, stressing their political stranglehold on the town and their dominance of the vice district. Much as an afterthought, he next outlined the support they could expect from Seth Hart and the council of businessmen, noting wryly that it was something on the order of a fresh water spring in an alkali desert: just when you needed it most, it would more than likely go bone dry.

Gillette toyed with his mustache and asked few questions, occasionally snorting like an old plow horse when a particularly juicy item was ticked off. In one form or another, he had seen this pathetic little drama repeated almost endlessly across the frontier. After twenty years, he had become a jaded warrior in a land where every dusty, ramshackle crossroads had both an arena and its own version of the Christians and the lions. Only the names and faces changed. And sometimes the death list.

Observing his calm, unruffled manner, Stoudenmire was again reminded that the former Ranger wasn't much to look at, coming or going. Gillette was whipcord lean, gaunt as a skinned lizard, and his washboard ribs gave the impression he hadn't had a decent meal since he quit the farm. Beneath a mop of shaggy hair, his narrow face was set in a woebegone, saturnine mold, as though he toted the troubles of the world on his bony shoulders. While he wasn't a jolly man, occasionally he would grin like a horse eating briars, and at

the oddest times. Like at a funeral or when he was headed
into a gunfight. His watery eyes were uncommonly tranquil,
like a pool of maize pudding, and to all outward appearances
he seemed mild as a sucking dove. But a man's looks could
be curiously deceptive. Stoudenmire had seen this long drink
of water in action. When push came to shove, he was fast as
a snake, and what he could do with that old Colt .44 made
greased lightning look like molasses at twenty below.

The rest of the afternoon had been spent in war council,
with the two men discussing how best to approach the double-
barreled dilemma confronting El Paso. Stoudenmire's
disposition improved markedly just knowing Gillette was
on hand to back his play. Having the gloomy-faced deputy
around was much like pulling on an old pair of boots, comfortable and somehow reassuring. Along toward sundown,
they had mapped out their opening strategy, leaving plenty
of room for fancy footwork in the clinches. Once they started
booting asses, there was small likelihood of predicting which
way the worm would turn, and neither man tried to fool himself on that score. Looking ahead, they were agreed that,
after a certain point, they would just have to play the cards
as dealt.

Stoudenmire invited Gillette home for supper and posi-
tively glowed under the old lawdog's praise of Kate and her
cooking. Afterward, they strolled downtown and began a
systematic tour of the southside dives. Much to the marshal's
amusement, Gillette's doleful features took on a spark of live-
liness as they inspected row after row of whorehouses, saloons, and gambling dives. Never had he seen so much vice
crammed into so little space, and he noted that, heathen for
heathen, the sporting crowd of El Paso more than likely
topped Dodge City in its heyday. Then the pensive look returned to his face, and the deputy observed that it was a
shame to put the skids under such a testament to man's moral
blight. After all, it was the nature of the beast to wallow in
fornication and sin, and who were they to upset the Good
Lord's grand design. Stoudenmire just chuckled, never quite
sure whether the old fox was pulling his leg or actually

making some profound comment on the shaky state of men's affairs.

Later in the evening, they swung back toward the plaza and decided to have a look at the Coliseum Saloon. So far, they hadn't seen anything they couldn't handle, and the only unknown factor remaining was the Banning brothers themselves.

"Just might as well let 'em know we're in town," Stoudenmire remarked. "Sooner we put a bad taste in their mouth, the quicker we'll get 'em to come out in the open."

"Dallas, you're a natural wonder. Back 'em into a corner, twist their tail, and make 'em howl! Yessir, there's more'n one way to make a dog shit peach seeds. Present company excepted, of course."

Gillette glanced down at Tige, who was trotting along at Stoudenmire's side. The dog returned the stare with a kindly light in his eyes, and even gave his tail a patronizing wag. The new deputy was one of the few men Tige tolerated as an equal, and Gillette considered it an honor that he had been accepted into the dog's select circle of friends.

Together, the three of them marched through the swinging doors of the Coliseum and halted to give the place the once-over. Other than the fact that the room was jammed to the rafters, there wasn't anything noteworthy going on, and after a few moments they took up positions at the end of the bar. But even in the mad swirl of roughly dressed men and spangled saloon girls, their arrival hadn't gone unnoticed. As they bellied up to the bar, an undercurrent swept through the crowd, and within moments everyone in the room knew that the town's new marshal had paid an unofficial visit on El Paso's political kingpin.

Before Stoudenmire and Gillette appeared out of the night, conversation at the bar had centered around the three men being held in Paso del Norte. Sam Banning had been right in the thick of the discussion, occasionally prodding the crowd on with a bitter comment about the uppity greasers. Talk had slackened momentarily with the arrival of the lawmen, but hard whiskey makes for loose tongues, and before long the angry shouts began anew.

"Boys, you can say whatever you damn well please," barked a chunky man built along the lines of a beer keg. "But I'm here to tell you that there ain't a man-jack among us that's safe once them Mexicans get the idea they can jail a white man."

"Goddamn right!" growled a beefy miner with hands like ore crushers. "We oughta go over there and wipe out the whole fuckin' village. Just like the Indians." He slammed his fist on the bar, and bottles rattled its entire length. "Nits and lice, by Christ!"

Sam Banning's bullish roar drowned out the crowd's response. "Now wait a minute, boys. You're going off half-cocked. There's no need to start a war. The way to teach them greasers a lesson is to show 'em we won't stand still for white men being arrested. Ride over there a couple of hundred strong and just flat-ass free them three men. Show them *cholo* bastards who's boss around here, and by God I'm layin' money our troubles are ended."

"Sam, you're all wet," the big miner shot back. "There's only one thing them sonsabitches understand, and its name is Judge Colt. What we gotta do is make a lead mine out of a few of them greasers. That'll take the kinks out of their tails once and for all."

While the men were arguing, Ed Banning had eased through the crowd and now stood beside his brother. Word had reached the backroom that Stoudenmire was on the premises, and the boss decided to have a look for himself. What he saw left him thoroughly unimpressed, and it occurred to him that the crowd would enjoy a little sport at the marshal's expense. *Might as well put the big bastard in his place right from the start!*

"Marshal Stoudenmire, we'd like to hear your opinion about all this." The crowd went silent, sensing that Banning was out to gig the new lawdog. "We know you haven't had time to get your feet on the ground just yet, but we'd be interested in hearing how you'd go about freeing those poor boys."

Everyone at the bar turned to look at Stoudenmire. Although they had heard of him, few had seen him before tonight, and they were openly curious as to where the new marshal stood. Stories were already circulating that the city council had been blackjacked into hiring the German, but as yet no one had figured out to what purpose.

Stoudenmire's flinty gaze rested on Banning for a moment, then swung around the crowd. "Gents, if you want some good advice, you'll stay on this side of the river. Mexicans are about as fair as anyone else unless they're curried the wrong way. If those three fellows really did gang up on a young girl, then I reckon they deserve whatever they get."

A murmur of resentment swept through the crowd, ending with hoarse muttering from those nearest the lawman. Then the one built like a beer keg spoke out. "Shit, I always heard that rapin' a Mexican gal was no more a crime than humpin' a nanny goat."

The men laughed good naturedly, turning back to the marshal for his reaction. But the miner with the fearsome hands wouldn't let it drop. "You know, I've heard of nigger-lovers. But I'm a sonovabitch if I ever heard of a greaser-lover. Marshal, you're wearin' a badge on the wrong side of the river. Why, over there, I'll bet your shit wouldn't even stink."

In one stride, Stoudenmire was on him, pistol barrel flashing in the dull glint of the overhead lamps. The Colt landed with a mushy thud, and the miner's eyes rolled back in his head like glazed stones, flat and unseeing. With a great sigh, he simply collapsed and sank to the floor.

Stoudenmire spun on the crowd, his eyes cold as chilled glass, every fiber of his body prickly and tensed. This was the part he enjoyed, the moment that made all the drudgery and routine bearable. Meeting the bullyboys and hard-cases head-on, cracking their skulls with the old buffalo trick, or forcing their hand until they did something even more foolish. Like going for their guns.

"Anybody else got something on his mind?"

The crowd remained curiously still, stunned by the speed with which Stoudenmire had floored the ruffian. They were also distinctly aware that Gillette was covering the marshal's back, which meant that whoever got brave would be caught in a cross fire. To make matters worse, Tige had materialized beside his master, showing a row of teeth like a shark. Between the guns and being chewed on by a snarling brute, the men just held their breath and waited it out.

Then the blood pounding against his temples eased off and Stoudenmire relaxed. "Gents, in case someone forgot to mention it, the Bannings are playing you for fools. The men being held over in El Paso del Norte are on their payroll. They were just setting you up to do the dirty work for them. If I were you, I'd think it over before I risked my neck to pull someone else's fat out of the fire."

Casually reholstering his gun, Stoudenmire turned his gaze on Ed Banning and waited. But the political boss wasn't about to face another man at his own game, especially with the deck stacked against the house. Smiling tightly, he just nodded. This was only the opening gambit, and until the odds suited him better, he wasn't going to be pushed into anything hasty.

After a moment Stoudenmire turned and walked leisurely from the saloon, trailed by Gillette and Tige. As the batwing doors swung shut, the crowd let out a huge sigh, and everyone started talking at once.

El Paso had a new marshal, and he gave every indication of being man enough to handle the job. But anyone who had seen the look of evil stamped on Ed Banning's face would have laid odds that Dallas Stoudenmire was a walking dead-man.

CHAPTER THREE

───◆───

1

Sam Banning kept a loose rein on the high stepping bays, letting them pick their own way over the rutted, twisting trail that led eastward from El Paso. Beside him, Ed sat lost in contemplation, stewing on the way Stoudenmire had jackassed him the night before. The political boss was a man easily affronted, and he wasn't about to overlook outright contempt from anybody. Especially a two-bit lawman set on making a name for himself. Stoudenmire had called the tune last night, but there were ways of bringing the big German to earth.

Their buggy raised a rooster-tail of dust as they traversed the desolate country east and north of the Rio Grande. It was an arid, hostile land, filled with sand, rattlesnakes, and thorny chaparral. Yet it wasn't a barren land, not if a man knew where to look. There were vast, hidden stretches of buffalo and grama grasses, generally sharing the soil with yuccas that sprouted stalks of brilliant, white blossoms. Scattered waterholes seldom went dry even in late summer, and spring rains usually brought the countryside alive with Tahoka daisies, buttercups, and fiery paintbrush. Stands of lacy mesquite and barbed cat's-claw fought for the earth's moisture, but somehow the sparse grasslands survived, mocking the fallow plains that dominated the cardinal points of the compass. And curiously enough, that remote, seemingly ravaged land provided a bountiful life for great herds of longhorn cows.

But while the arid flatlands offered bounty of sort for the mossyhorns, they held forth even greater lure for the Banning brothers and their night riders. Within such desolate country was to be found the isolation and secrecy so highly prized by those who prey on other men's possessions. Especially the four-footed variety.

Shortly after arriving in El Paso two years earlier, Ed Banning had undertaken a search for ranchlands far removed from the settlements along the Rio Grande. After crisscrossing the countryside for nearly a month, he finally found exactly what he had in mind: a rundown spread so far back in the wastelands that a man needed a map to find it. The next step had been to hire a crew and flush out the half-wild longhorns inhabiting the brush and thorn patches dotting the land. Once he had a going concern, Banning began greasing the right palms, and before long his outfit was awarded the beef contract at Fort Bliss. With a legitimate front firmly established, he then branched out, regularly ordering his crew into Chihuahua and Sonora to raid the wealthy Mexican *ranchos*. The rustled cattle were herded back to the ranch, given a brief introduction to a running iron, then either sold to the army or trailed to Fort Worth. With the coming of the railroad, the operation was simplified even further, and the gratifying part was that hardly anyone cared how or under what circumstances the cattle came to be north of the Rio Grande.

The ranch itself was little more than a wilderness outpost, consisting of two adobe buildings, a cookshack, and a log corral west of the compound. Northeast of the ranch, the terrain lifted gradually to a chain of stunted mesas, and in the distance hung the towering peak of Cerro Alto. Beneath the sheer cliffs of this great mountain, the adobe structures looked small and insignificant, dwarfed by the immensity of rock and sky that dominated the landscape for twenty miles in every direction. All things considered, it made for a fore-boding, uninviting scene. The kind that people normally went out of their way to avoid.

When the Bannings pulled up before the main house, Tom Kale stepped through the doorway and ambled toward the buggy. Kale had worked for Banning from the beginning, ramrodding the ranch, organizing and leading forays into Mexico; in general, contributing greatly to the devious schemes of his boss. He was a leathery man, tightlipped and unsmiling, as if the merciless sun had long ago melted both the suet and the humor from his lean frame. Weathered by a lifetime in the saddle, his features looked as though whittled from some dark, resisting wood, and his nose jutted from be-tween sharp cheekbones like a jagged outcropping of rock. There was no sign of warmth in his long, dour face, just as flaked stone seems all the more cold for its lack of expression.

Those who best knew Tom Kale seldom let their guard down whenever he was near. For like the land itself, the Banning foreman was a brutal, often murderously savage man who derived some queer satisfaction in watching both man and beast suffer at his hand.

After alighting from the buggy, Ed Banning led the way toward the house without uttering so much as a word. Kale knew a thundercloud building when he saw it, and rightly suspected that a storm was about to break. Once inside, out of sight of the bunkhouse, Banning turned on him like a sore-tailed bear in fly season.

"Kale, you've got my ass between a rock and a hard spot, and something has to change or else you're gonna be look-ing for a new meal ticket. I've told you till I was blue in the face that our men aren't to be allowed in Paso del Norte. Yet you just go your own way and let 'em do as they damn please."

Kale opened his mouth to speak but Banning cut him off with a dismissive gesture. "Now don't give me any of that horseshit about having to play nursemaid. You're paid to ram-rod this outfit, and that includes seeing to it that they follow orders. Well, by Christ, crossing the line and raping a Mexican girl right in the middle of the village isn't my idea of sticking to business."

In a cold, metallic voice, Banning related the gist of what had happened in Paso del Norte the night before last. Sparing no detail, he then recounted Stoudenmire's visit to the Coliseum and the duel of wits that had subsequently ensued. When he came to the part about the marshal's outright challenge, Banning's face blanched. As he remembered how he had been ridiculed before the townspeople, his voice went shaky with rage, and for a moment, Kale thought he was going to come unglued. But Banning quickly got hold of himself and resumed in the flat, menacing tone he normally employed.

"I blame you for this whole goddamned mess, Kale. If you'd been minding the store none of it would've happened. And just in case you've got any doubts, *you're* the one that's gonna get it straightened out. We've got too much at stake to let things get out of hand now."

Tom Kale got busy rolling a cigarette and made a stab at changing the subject. "Boss, I've never let you down yet, even if them knuckleheads did sneak across the river. But the thing that's got me bumfoolzled is this new marshal. What the hell's he doin' in El Paso anyway? Some of the boys say they heard of him when he was a Ranger, and the way they tell it, he's just about as good with a gun as he makes out. You reckon we've done bit off more than we can chew?"

"That big crock of shit?" Sam blurted angrily. "Listen, when Ed gives the word, I'm gonna tie a knot in his tail so hard he'll never sit down. Near as I can tell, the only thing he's good at is makin' fools out of other people."

Ed glanced sourly at his brother. "You don't need to keep harping on it. But you're right about one thing. We've got to act fast to save face in town. Stoudenmire has rigged it so that everyone is waitin' to see if we're gonna let those boys go up against the wall. If we leave 'em to a greaser firing squad, we're gonna be the laughingstock of West Texas."

Kale peered at him owlishly through a haze of smoke. "You mean you want us to raid that Mex jail?"

"Kale, if you had dynamite for brains, you couldn't blow yourself off a jonny pot." Banning shook his head sadly, as if reprimanding a backward child. "Now pay attention, just like you had good sense. Tonight I want you to raid one of the big *ranchos* south of Paso del Norte. Make it worthwhile in terms of cattle, but the important thing is to shoot up the *hacienda* and the Mex crew. That'll scare the bejesus out of every greaser in the district, and tomorrow night they'll all be home with their doors barred."

"Then we raid the jail!" Kale laughed, slapping his thigh.

"No, you goddamn nitwit! You're not to go anywhere near that jail. I wouldn't trust your boys to piss on a dead dog. What I'm gonna do is send a buggy over there about an hour after suppertime. Three of my girls will be decked out like housewives, and they'll say those boys are their husbands. Only they're gonna have guns under their dresses, and when they leave, those boys won't be so helpless anymore. Later, they can make a break and swim the river. If nobody shits and steps in it, I figure we can get 'em free and make an ass out of Stoudenmire all in one stroke."

"Boss, that's slick," Kale snorted, shaking his head with admiration. "We'll have them boys back over here before anybody even tumbles to 'em being gone."

Banning's eyes leveled down on the foreman, fixing him with a malevolent glare. "And once you get 'em back here, I want you to march them over to the bunkhouse and shoot 'em right in the doorway. It's time you and the rest of these bastards learned that when I give an order I expect it to be followed. Savvy?"

Tom Kale wasn't easily frightened, yet he swallowed nervously under Banning's harsh scrutiny. Killing was his stock in trade, and adding three more to the list was all in a day's work. But the death sentence he had just heard pronounced indirectly included him. Should he foul Banning's nest again, his life wouldn't be worth a plug nickel. Kale's mouth suddenly turned dry as a gourd, and his guts went stone cold. Working for this ruthless scutter was like being harnessed shoulder to shoulder with Lucifer himself, and he had the very distinct feeling that he was running dead last in a two-horse race.

2

Doc Cummings could smell the aromas while he was still a good stone's throw from the house. No doubt about it, Kate had acquired their mother's knack for southern cooking, the kind that stuck to a man's ribs and left him wishing he could have eaten more. He could tell from the smell alone, and it set his mouth to watering. Reflecting back over the carefree days of their childhood, Doc was suddenly warmed inside by the thought of having Kate so near. She had always been his favorite of the Cummings' brood, and he was immensely pleased that he had been able to finagle a way for her to live in El Paso. Suddenly it occurred to Doc that things were really looking up.

As a widower, he had become used to the heartburn served up in the local greasy spoon, but with Kate in town, it stood to reason he'd get a decent meal occasionally anyway. Perhaps being invited to supper tonight was only the beginning. Maybe if he played his cards right, it would become a regular thing. Whistling a catchy little tune, he entered the Stoudenmire home, beaming like a chessy cat as Kate came to greet him.

When she led him into the living room, Doc's mouth popped open in astonishment. "Great jumpin' jehossafat! Katie what have you done to this place? Why it looks like a palace. A goldang palace!"

Kate flushed, and her eyes took on a little girl sparkle. Considering that she'd had little to work with, she was justly proud of the transformation. That first evening in El Paso she had stood looking at the austere interior of this adobe monstrosity, wondering how in the world she could ever make it appear anything more than a mud hut. But in only three days she had wrought a minor miracle, decorating it with all the frills and foofaraw so dear to a woman's heart.

Each window was now festooned with gay curtains, done

in bright, cheery colors that distracted the eye from the stark
adobe walls. The spartan furniture did little to liven the room,
but somewhere, Kate had found an ornate Persian rug, that
covered nearly the entire floor. Like a peacock amongst a
flock of brown hens, the rug somehow lent beauty to the dull
ugliness of the room itself. Pictures of solemn ancestors and
pastoral landscapes had been hung judiciously along the
walls, and everywhere there was evidence of Kate's remarkable cleverness with crochet and needlepoint. From the native market she had bought great batches of wild flowers and
small boxed plants, which even now were beginning to sprout
tiny blossoms. But the *pièce de résistance* had been reserved
for the mantel over the fireplace. There in somber dignity
hung a strangely lifelike portrait of Kate and Dallas on their
wedding day. Framed in gilded wood with a delicate carved
design, the portrait dominated the room, evoking a degree of
elegance that was curiously foreign to the wattled adobe.

While the Stoudenmire home was located on Magoffin
Avenue in the better district of El Paso, there were few houses
that could match its comfortable atmosphere and simple
grace. Kate had ample reason to be proud, and as she luxuri-
ated in Doc's praise, it somehow seemed right that her brother
was the first outsider to observe the results of her handiwork.

The meal she served was no less impressive than the house
itself, particularly to a widower who had grown accustomed
to the chili pepper and raw spices of local cafes. Spread across
the table in lavish array was fried chicken, mashed potatoes,
cream gravy, blackeyed peas, snap beans, cornbread, and a
huge pitcher of buttermilk. For a crowning touch, she served
a steamy peach cobbler with great gobs of fresh whipped
cream.

Doc Cummings unbuckled his belt and set to with the
gusto of a starved mongrel trailing a gut wagon. Between
mouthfuls he raved incessantly about the food, the house, his
sister's beauty, and his own great fortune in them having chosen El Paso as their home. Watching him, Stoudenmire was
reminded of a gluttonous bear fresh from a winter's hiberna-

tion. And it came to him that with little or no prompting Doc could easily become a steady boarder.

After a particularly effusive compliment on the house, Doc helped himself to another load of potatoes and gravy. "Dallas, you oughta be mighty proud of this gal. It's not every woman that could turn an outsize *jacal* hut into a dazzler like you've got here."

Stoudenmire pretended to consider it a moment, watching Kate out of the corner of his eye. "I expect you're right, Doc. Course, this place might be too fancy for some folks' tastes. Not everybody can get used to being just another ornament in his own house."

"Oh, what gratitude!" Kate's eyes flashed with feminine outrage. "Dallas Stoudenmire, sometimes you drive me to distraction. After I work my fingers to the bone, you have the unmitigated gall to say it's too frilly. Honestly!"

She knew he liked the house from the little things he had said, but it exasperated her no end that he was so close-mouthed with compliments. Still, she should be getting used to it by now. This great bear of a man she had married was no talker, to put it mildly. What he left unsaid about home, job, and his own thoughts would fill volumes. She sometimes had the feeling it was like extracting teeth to get him loosened up for even a pleasant little chat.

Stoudenmire grinned slyly at her obvious indignation. "Doc, I hate to carry tales on your sister, but she's laying it on a little thick. The fact of the matter is, she enjoyed sprucin' this place up so much that I couldn't get her to quit till it was plumb finished. Put me in mind of a speckled pup with a fresh bowl of cream."

"Yeah, her mama was like that." Doc paused with a drumstick in midair, and a mellow look came into his eyes. "Turn her loose cleanin' a house or whippin' up a big meal, and she acted like the Good Lord had just passed out a dipperful of heaven on earth."

"You two should just hear yourselves," Kate exclaimed. "Honest to gracious! It's like you were talking about a doll that just happens to speak passable English. Doc, if mama were alive she'd jerk your britches down and paddle your rump with that drumstick. I swear she would."

The two men couldn't help but laugh, and after a moment, Kate gave in, smiling good-naturedly. But Doc wasn't about to risk spoiling his chances as a steady guest, and he very shrewdly changed the subject.

"Dallas, there's talk around town that Banning is planning something that'll bring both sides of the river up short. Nothin' you can hang your hat on, but the word is out that he means to show everyone just who's runnin' El Paso. You heard anything?"

"Not much. People are still a little leary about where I stand in this deal." Stoudenmire stirred his coffee thoughtfully for a moment. "There's one thing you can bank on, though. Banning will have to act soon. He can't afford for folks to get the idea he's going soft. Which is what'll happen if he lets the Mexicans get away with killin' his men. Just offhand, I'd judge he's giving it some serious thought."

Doc came up for a breather after his second helping of peach cobbler. "Well it's for damn certain he's been too quiet. Especially after you faced him down in the Coliseum the other night. To my way of thinkin', that's a sure sign something big is brewing. But when and where it'll happen is up for grabs. Most of his boys develop lockjaw when anything really salty is hatching."

Stoudenmire's mouth lifted in a tight, sardonic smile. "Just between you and me, we're real lucky he opened his mouth in front of that crowd. I'd been wonderin' how we could stop a mob from crossing the river, and he set it up easy as pie by tryin' to show off. The way things worked out it's a matter of *his* honor at stake. Unless the wind changes, none of the townspeople are gonna get involved, no matter what he does. Now if we can just keep it that way, then maybe folks'll think twice about taking pot shots at one another across the river."

"Oh, I've got no doubt it headed off an open war between us and the greasers. But I'm not so sure I agree with your bracin' Banning the first crack out of the box. Seems to me you might've led up to it slowly. This way he knows you're after his hide even before you've started."

"Doc, there's no easy way to rid yourself of lice. Banning has to be crowded so hard he'll get mad enough to act, and sooner or later he's gonna make the *big* mistake. Think back to when you were a kid, and you'll remember that, once the hounds start snapping at a coon's heels, he doesn't have time to make plans. He has to move fast and hope he doesn't stub his toe along the way. That's why there's more dumb hounds than there are smart coons."

"Maybe you're right." The dubious look on Doc's face belied his words. "I just hope you haven't stirred up a hornets' nest before you're ready to burn 'em out. Now, for example. What've you got in mind if Banning sics his gang on your tail? You know, it's just possible he's got plans to run you out of town. Did you ever think of that?"

"Doc, if I'd let you, I suspect you'd talk the molars right out of my jawbone." Stoudenmire pulled a huge pocket watch from his vest, noting the time as he pushed his chair back. "But I've got evening rounds to make, and Gillette's gonna be champin' at the bit if I keep him waiting. Now you just have another piece of cobbler and don't get yourself in a lather about me and Banning. When he stumbles, I'll be there to dust him off, and it'll likely be all over before you even hear the shoutin'."

The lawman gave Kate a peck on the cheek, then walked from the dining room with Tige at his heels. After a moment, the front door closed with a gentle thud, and the house went still. Brother and sister sat staring at each other, both troubled by the same doubts yet tempted to leave their thoughts unsaid.

3

Throughout the meal Kate had listened silently to the casual exchange between Dallas and Doc, learning more in a few minutes than her husband had told her in three days. Now she felt herself being swamped by an outpouring of fear and

downright bafflement about the grim, unyielding man she
had married. Suddenly she couldn't hold it in any longer.

"Doc, I'm so worried I don't know what to do. Dallas
treats this whole thing so lightly. He won't even talk to me
about it. Whenever I bring it up, he just pats my head like I
was a child and goes back into his shell. But the way you talk,
he's got half the men in El Paso out gunning for him."

Doc made a good try at grinning and clucked sympathet-
ically. "Katie, don't let your imagination run away with you.
All of that was mostly talk, nothin' else. Listen, you've got
one hellava man there, and he cut his teeth on hardcases like
Ed Banning."

"That's something else that bothers me." Kate's words
came awkwardly, and she found it difficult to look at him.
Somehow her thoughts seemed too terrible to share with anyone, even her brother. "Dallas changes when he starts talking
about the law. Almost as though killing another man was
some kind of game. It's frightening to say, Doc, but he's like
a cat playing with a mouse. Only he's not playing. He's deadly
serious, and it's as if he just can't wait for those men to start
fighting back." She shook her head numbly. "I just can't understand the change in him. When we're here alone, he's so
warm and gentle. Then he puts that badge on, and he becomes
someone else, a stranger almost. And that part of him scares
me, Doc."

Doc Cummings just looked at her, searching desperately
for something to say. But what could a man say to a sister who
had blindly married a gunfighter? She hadn't the slightest notion that her husband was a trained killer, the kind that hunts
men much as a great cat instinctively hunts animals of prey.
How could any woman understand that the man who shared
her bed was a specialist at a very dirty game? Dallas Stoudenmire was a professional mankiller, and anyone with a lick of
sense never doubted it for a moment.

Doc glanced at her out of the corner of his eye. "Sis, what
do you know about Dallas?"

"That's a strange question to ask." Kate gave him a mildly
puzzled look, not quite sure what he meant. "I know that his

folks, came over from Germany and he was born outside Mineral Wells. He's thirty-three, doesn't drink much, and behaves himself around women. I know lots about him, Doc. Enough that I wanted him to be my husband."

"Sure. But those are things girls're just naturally interested in. What I'm drivin' at is, do you know anything about his life before you met him? What he was doing for thirty years before he turned up in Columbus."

"Well, of course, I do," Kate said indignantly. "I'm not some schoolgirl ninny with stars in her eyes. He was city marshal at Nacogdoches, and before that he was a Texas Ranger, and before that he fought for the Confederacy. Just for your information, he'd never been married before, either."

Doc poured himself another cup of coffee, trying to keep his tone casual. "Didn't that strike you as a little odd? Him being that old and never married, I mean."

Kate shook her head, more puzzled than ever. "Why would it strike me as odd? Lots of men wait till they've sown their wild oats before they settle down. They don't all jump the broomstick with the first thing that comes along in skirts."

"Dallas never seemed to me like a man that'd sowed any wild oats." Doc hesitated, mulling it over, and his next words were those of a man thinking out loud. "Unless I miss my guess, there wasn't much to tell on that score."

"That's ridiculous, Doc. Why should he tell me things like that, anyway?" Kate was growing exasperated with her brother's prying manner. "If you're hinting that Dallas isn't . . . oh, damn, you make me so mad sometimes I could just scream. If you're trying to say that Dallas isn't like other men, then you'd better drink your coffee and go on home."

"Katie, I don't mean it like you think, but in a way, that's what I've been drivin' at. He's not like other men." He faltered for a moment, wracking his brain for a way to open her eyes about the man she had married. "Did he ever tell you that his folks were killed by the Comanche when he was just a kid?"

She stared at him blankly, hardly able to credit her own ears. "Indians?"

"You remember when I came home to visit last year?"
Kate bobbed her head, and he went on. "Well I decided to
find out about this fella my little sister was stuck on. So I took
Dallas out and got him drunk. Leastways as drunk as Dallas
can get. Loosened up might be more like it. Just enough so's
he would talk some."

"But, Doc, I don't understand. What have his folks getting
killed got to do with anything?"

"I'm comin' to that. Just give me time. You see the Civil
War was going rough for the South about then, so he ups and
enlists. Course, he lied about his age, but the Confederates
needed men, and since he was bigger than most already full-
growed, they didn't ask any questions. He ended up fightin'
with General Joe Johnston. Matter of fact, he was still at it
when Lee called it quits at Appomattox."

Kate nodded impatiently, somewhat irritated by his roundabout manner. "I know all that. He told me about being in
the army."

"Sure, but I'll bet he didn't tell you what it was like." When
she failed to answer, he smiled dryly. "Thought so."

There was a pause while Doc collected his thoughts,
searching for some way to break it to her gently. "Well now,
keep in mind he was only fifteen when he started in at this
business of war. Maybe you never thought about it, but that's
sort of an early age to get baptized in the ways of killin' men.
Fact is, he wasn't but seventeen when the war ended. Those
two years had a mighty big effect on him, Katie. Had to.
Couldn't have been no other way. There he was, just a kid,
watching men being slaughtered like cattle, seeing 'em
maimed and going mad with fear. Still, them things was only
part of it. More'n likely just a small part. What I'm gettin'
around to sayin' is, they took an overgrown kid and taught
him to kill, showed him how easy it was. Just pull the trigger
and a man falls down. More'n that, though, they taught him
there wasn't nothin' wrong with killin'. Not so long as a man's
in the right. Don't you see, they wiped away that old buga-
boo about 'Thou shalt not kill.' A green kid marched off to
war, but an old man came marchin' back. Something had

been burned clean out of his soul. Call it feelin', or pity, or whatever you want. Killin' came natural to him now, and he didn't have no more conscience about it than if he was swattin' flies."

Kate stared at him in sheer horror, her eyes wide and glistening wetly. When she spoke her voice was tremulous, shrill. "Doc, are you trying to tell me that the man I married isn't human? That he's some kind of mad-dog killer. If you are, I won't listen to another word. That's sick, to talk like that, and you're no friend of Dallas's to say such wicked things."

Doc winced, stung by her fiery accusation. "Kate, I was your brother before I was his friend. Maybe it's not pretty, and like as not I'm being rash tellin' you all this, but if you don't come to understand the man, your life's gonna be pure hell."

"Understand him? Don't try to play God, Doc. I understand him very well. He's a gentle man underneath all that bluster, and I know it in ways that nobody else could know."

"Is that why he keeps that man-eatin' dog with him all the time? 'Cause he's so gentle." The little merchant's face saddened, and he cursed himself for having ever broached the subject of Stoudenmire's character. "Sis, I'm not tryin' to run Dallas down. I like him, even admire him in a way. Guess I always have. But if I didn't understand him, I'd find him mighty hard to like. Maybe you oughta give that some thought where lovin' him's concerned."

"You're the one I don't understand." Kate appeared bemused, uncertain of her feelings just at that moment. "You tell me all these dreadful things, and in the same breath, you try to convince me that it's for my own good. How, Doc? How is knowing all this going to make my life with Dallas any better?"

"Because there's more to being a man's wife than sleepin' with him. More'n likely, you've already found that out." He studied her for a second, watching the hurt and fear kindle in her eyes, yet he was determined now to see it through. "Kate, this man's whole life is tied up in some funny kind of

way with doing what he thinks is right. Upholding the law,
destroying the lawless. Sorta like the great god Jehovah visitin' wrath and damnation on the sinners. After the war, he
drifted around for a while, then joined the Rangers. First he
fought the Indians up north with Jones's company, and con-
siderin' how his folks was killed, I suspect he took few prisoners. Later, he served with McNelly down on the border, and
that wasn't no picnic either. Don't you see what I'm gettin'
at, Sis? Ever since he was a kid, somebody's been trainin' him
to kill and givin' him a license to make it legal. They taught
him that killin' is all right so long as it's the sinner that gets
killed. That's how he was raised up and that's how he believes."

Then Cummings hesitated, groping for some justification
that would absolve the man his sister had married. "Whatever your man is Kate, he's what the people of Texas made
him. What they needed, what the times called for. That's all
I'm tryin' to say."

Kate regarded him vacantly, her face drained of emotion.
"You're saying he kills other men because he has to, because
no one ever showed him another way. You don't condemn
him, but at the same time, you don't approve. He's the lesser
of two evils. A good badman hired to hunt down the common, garden-variety badmen. That's very charitable of you,
Doc. Almost Christian."

"Damn, I wish I'd never opened my big mouth." He rubbed
his face with both hands, like a man that has sore eyes and a
long way yet to go. "Kate, regardless of what you thought I
said, I don't believe there's a bad bone in Dallas Stoudenmire's body. Matter of fact, he's about the most decent man
I ever met. Otherwise, I'd have raised holy hell before I let
you marry him. I'd trust him with my life sooner'n anybody
I know, and you damn sure don't put that kind of faith in a
man that's not straight. That's what I meant a while ago about
him being my friend whatever he is. What he isn't has got
nothin' to do with it."

Kate didn't say anything for a few seconds, almost as if she
had dismissed the subject from her mind. Then she glanced

up with renewed curiosity. "Did Dallas tell you all this the night you got him drunk? Or are you just guessing?"

"Tell you the truth, Seth Hart had him checked out through the governor's office. Most of it came out there. The rest I put together from little things Dallas said. Damn little, I'll admit. He's not the most talkative man I ever met."

"No, he's not that." Kate smiled wanly and sighed. "But deep down he's as good a man as any woman could ask for. And somehow, I'm going to get him out of El Paso and make him forget this horrible life. I don't know how, but I will."

Later, walking back to his room over the store, Doc Cummings had the feeling that he had only made matters worse. He had meant it the right way, for it was plain to see that Kate couldn't go on much longer with the way things were. But then, as parsons were so fond of reminding folks, the road to hell was paved with good intentions. Chalk one up to damn fools and good deeds. Lately they seemed to be a matched pair.

4

They came like ghostly shadows in the night. The moons' golden streamers lighted the compound with a dusky glow, just bright enough for a man to catch his rifle sights when the time was right. Kale placed each man in position, carefully selecting an open field of fire, and by midnight they had the *hacienda* surrounded.

The night riders had split into two parties after Tom Kale personally scouted the layout. The smaller group was to raid the northernmost herd of cattle just as soon as firing broke out in the compound. Leaving nothing to chance, Kale had selected to lead the assault on the *hacienda*. The sole purpose of this raid was to punish the greasers in their own backyard; scare them so badly that they would be posting sentries for a month to come. The cattle herd was strictly a secondary target, and like any guerrilla leader worth his salt, Kale had chosen to direct the main attack himself.

The *hacienda* of Don Miguel Salazar lay some twenty kilometers southwest of Paso del Norte. The aristocratic *hidalgo* had inherited a Spanish land grant from his father and ruled a small kingdom stretching to the headwaters of the Rio Santa Maria, nearly a hundred kilometers further south. Located on a tree-sheltered plain alongside a sleepy brook, the *cuadrilla* consisted of the master's *casa* and various outbuildings, which included bunkhouses, *jacal* huts, stables, and storage sheds. The compound was enclosed on three sides by a low adobe wall with the brook forming the remaining boundary. Don Miguel's large, sprawling home overlooked the stream just south of the main gate and commanded a view of the entire *rancho* headquarters.

Kale had posted half his men on the far side of the brook behind trees and the remainder in a grove of giant *maguey* near the opposite side of the compound. Once the shooting started, the Mexicans would be caught in a deadly cross fire, with virtually no chance of mounting a counterattack. While greatly outnumbered, the Banning night riders had the element of surprise working in their favor, and their tactical advantage promised to make it a costly night for Don Salazar's *vaqueros*.

Shortly after midnight, three of Kale's men slithered into the compound and set fire to a large stable near the west wall. Within moments the building was engulfed in flames, and squeals from the terror-stricken horses could be heard a mile away. *Vaqueros* poured from the buildings in their nightclothes, forgetting guns, boots, and all else in their rush to save *el patrón*'s prized breeding stock. Among the first to reach the blazing stable was Ramón Vazquez, who had served as Don Salazar's *caporal* for close to five years. Shouting commands above the raging inferno, Ramón quickly organized a bucket brigade, then led a handpicked crew through the flames to rescue the panicked horses.

Waiting patiently, like a tawny panther watching a game trail, Kale bided his time as the crowd thickened around the stables. Soon every man on the place was frantically engaged in dousing the fire, and the leaping flames silhouetted their every movement within the confines of the *cuadrilla*. Observing the rushing figures closely, Kale selected the one who seemed to be giving all the orders. Carefully aligning his sights on the man's chest, Kale squeezed the trigger and felt the Winchester buck against his shoulder.

Ramón Vazquez would always think back on the night of the fire as a moment of *buena fortuna* for him personally. Had he been standing still he would have been a dead man, *muy muerto.* But at the split second the rifle cracked, he stooped to retrieve a fallen bucket, and the slug ripped through the fleshy part of his arm. Spun around, he dropped to the earth, knowing even as he fell that his people had been skillfully lured into a trap.

Suddenly the night came alive with the yellowish flash of gunfire, and lead hissed across the compound like a swarm of angry wasps. *Vaqueros* fell right and left, clutching their wounds, and those left unscathed after the first volley ran for cover. Rolling beneath a *carreta,* Ramón peered cautiously around the wooden wheel, trying to ignore the dull throb in his left arm. One glance was enough to confirm his suspicions. Their attackers had them neatly scissored in a cross fire, and unless something was done fast, every man in the *cuadrilla* would be snuffed out like defenseless insects.

"¡Dispersad, hombres!" Ramón shouted over the roar of flames and rifle-fire. "Scatter! Run for the buildings! Get your guns and form along the walls. *¡Pronto, hombres! ¡Pronto!"*

The *vaqueros* came off the ground as if electrified by his hoarse command. Scuttling crablike across the open compound, they dodged and weaved in headlong flight toward the adobe structures. The gunfire increased in tempo as they ran, upending an even half dozen before they reached the sanctuary of the buildings. Moments later, they boiled from their *cabañas* like frenzied ants, clutching rifles and bandoliers as they darted toward the walls. Five more of their number jackknifed into the dust as they ran the gauntlet of lead for the second time, but more than forty *vaqueros* made it safely. Within the beat of a heart, their rifles leveled over the walls, and the night was split with a thunderous fusillade as they returned the raiders' fire with a vengeance.

* * *

Three miles to the northeast another deadly engagement was being played out with equally savage results. Ten raiders had infiltrated the cattle herd, moving stealthily through the pale darkness as they waited for the signal. When the ragged sound of shooting drifted in from the *hacienda*, they opened fire on the night guards, presumably killing every man in the first volley. But among the *vaqueros* was an *anciano* of great resourcefulness and daring. The slug meant for him had pulverized his pommel instead, and he very cunningly tumbled from the saddle, squirming off into the brush with the noiseless wrigglings of a chubby snake. From there, he watched silently as the bushwhackers mounted their horses and set about trailing the restless herd in a northerly direction.

But this ancient one wasn't a man who accepted such insult lightly. In his prime, he had been *macho hombre,* and it went against the grain to cower in the brush like a steer with an empty bag. Removing his rowled spurs, he waited until the herd had been lined out and started north. Just as he suspected, one of the *gringo ladrones* fell back to ride drag on the skittish longhorns. With that, the *anciano* exploded from his hiding place, displaying the agility of one half his age as he collared the raider in a bounding leap. Cartwheeling over the horse, they struck the ground, and he scrambled erect as if shot from coiled springs. Balanced catlike on the balls of his feet, the ancient one's heart thudded with the excitement of an old *guerrero* who has forgotten nothing about the deadly games men play. Jerking a battered cap and ball Remington, he clouted the raider upside the head, grunting with satisfaction as the man settled limply into the dust.

¡Caramba! The old fox had lost none of his juices after all. And he, Hector Lizardi, the *vaquero* they had thought to retire to the goat herd, would personally present *el patrón* with this *gringo abominación. ¡Madre de Dios!* It had been a good night indeed for old men.

While Hector Lizardi was gloating over his prisoner, Tom Kale decided it was time to break off the fighting and make a run for the border. Withdrawing his men in small bunches, he managed to keep the *vaqueros* pinned down until everyone was mounted. Moments later the raiders thundered northward, intent on putting distance between themselves and the Salazar *rancho.* Circling back to assign a rear guard, Kale was astounded to find that he hadn't lost a single man in a firefight that had raged for nearly a half-hour. If the cattle raid had come off anywhere near as well, he'd really have something to crow about to the Bannings!

But if Tom Kale was exultant, Ramón Vazquez was seared clean through by a fury unlike any he had ever known. The Salazar *hacienda* was devastated, a burned-out ruin where only an hour before there had been a magnificent ranch. With no one to halt its advance, the stable fire had spread rapidly to other buildings, and the entire *cuadrilla* now lay in smoky rubble. With the exception of Don Miguel's *casa* and a single bunkhouse, every building in the compound had been leveled to the ground.

Still, buildings could be erected again; their loss was but a thing of the moment. Men were something else entirely, and short of *Jesucristo* himself, there was no one with the knack of pumping life back into the dead. With a quick count, Ramón made it eleven dead and twenty-six wounded, some mortally. There would be much wailing in the *vaqueros'* quarters before another dawn, and the thought of his people being shot down like dogs brought a sickening taste to Ramón's mouth. Someone would pay dearly for this slaughter, eye for eye, just as it has been in the old days when they fought Comanches instead of *gringos.*

After seeing to his men, Ramón sought out Don Miguel, who was wandering through the rubble in a numbed daze. *El patrón* had little to say, staring blankly at the carnage and death about them. Ramón tersely explained what must be done, then left him gazing sorrowfully upon a brood mare that had not survived the fire. Ordering horses brought in from the nearby *remuda*, he called on every *vaquero* who could ride to take the saddle. Less than a quarter-hour after the shooting had ceased, the *caporal* led a force of nineteen men toward the Rio Grande.

With fresh horses under them, the *vaqueros* set a blistering pace, and some ten kilometers from the border, they over-
took the *gringo* column. Kale and his raiders had joined the
tail end of the rustled herd only minutes before and were
hanging back in event the greasers gave pursuit. Upon sight-
ing the Mexicans, Kale ordered the longhorns stampeded toward the river and formed his men to fight a delaying action
until the herd was safely aground on Texas soil.

Over the next hour, a running battle raged across the countryside. The villagers of Paso del Norte heard the gunfire
and promptly bolted their doors. Those engaged in the fighting seemed to be doing a good job of it, which meant that
only the *estúpido* would venture forth to satisfy their curiosity. Wise men minded their own business, behind locked
doors, leaving other men to attend to such affairs as they
saw fit.

But the villagers' relutance by no means extended to
Ramón's *vaqueros*. Repeatedly they charged the *gringos*,
only to have their attack blunted by the accurate fire of the
Texans' rifles. Kale kept his men fanned out in a compact
crescent behind the rushing herd, never once allowing them
to bunch together. After losing several men in futile charges,
the Mexicans splintered off, every man for himself in a
ghostly, moonlit duel. But Kale directed the raiders' fire with
telling deadliness, and as the last of the herd was driven into
the river, the *vaqueros* called it quits.

Drawing to a halt on a rise overlooking the Rio Grande,
Ramón and his men watched helplessly as the raiders swam
the lazy current. On the other side was Texas, and over there
a *vaquero* had one foot in the grave when he stepped from
the water. Better to wait, to make plans, Ramón counseled.
There was always another day, and the *gringos* had departed
owing a debt that would be collected manyfold in time to
come.

Reining his horse about on the opposite bank, Tom Kale
observed the distant Mexicans with a throaty chuckle. By
God, this was a good night's work well done! He had lost only
two men, and as near as he could count, they had put at least

a dozen of those greaser bastards under for keeps. That's the kind of fighting any man could be proud of!

Thinking on it, he decided he might just hit the Bannings up for a raise.

5

The sun had barely topped the horizon when Don Miguel and Ramón came out to survey the damage from last night's raid. While the *hacienda* itself had suffered only minor damage, the outbuildings were nothing but charred ruins, and a sense of loss hung over the compound like a shroud. Upward of two hundred steers had also been lost in the raid, but among Don Miguel's people, there was a greater sorrow that left no room for smoldering homes or scrubby longhorns.

After the abortive chase to the Rio Grande, there were now fourteen dead *vaqueros*, and the mournful cries of their women was enough to make a strong man lose his breakfast. When Ramón saw the bodies laid out, his guts shriveled into a hard knot, strengthening his resolve that retribution must be swift in coming. There were some things upon which no price could be set, except in blood.

Later in the morning, after the dead and the wounded had been attended to, the captured *norteamericano* was brought forward. Hector Lizardi had become an overnight hero among his people, once again *macho hombre*, proudly leading the barbarian around for everyone to see. The prisoner was a large, fleshy man, towering over his shrunken captor, but a deft tug on the rawhide *reata* around his neck quickly brought him to heel.

When the raider was hauled before Ramón, the *caporal*'s rage centered wholly on him, just as a hawk selects a single dove in flight. This lone man was the one visible symbol of the unspeakable filth that had devastated their homes and murdered their *compañeros*. What he had to say would make interesting listening, and the *vaqueros* gathered closer, eagerly awaiting Ramón's choice of persuasion.

The raider was jerked and shoved across the *cuadrilla*

grounds and roughly bound to a tree near the brook. The
questioning began, but the prisoner proved a stubborn witness. First, he professed no understanding of Spanish, then
when Ramón switched to broken English he simply refused
to speak, sulling up like a paunchy old mule. The night rider
had no illusions about what was coming; he had lived on the
border long enough to know that his fate was sealed. It was
only a matter of what device would be used and how long it
would take. Determined to go under like a man, he clamped
his jaws shut and gave every indication of never opening them
again. These greaser pricks could do whatever they wanted,
but he'd show them the kind of grit a real *hombre* had.

Ramón studied the problem for a moment, then stepped
off a few paces and drew his pistol. Aiming with utmost
care, he squeezed off a shot, and the man's right ear disappeared in a frothy, pink spray. The prisoner banged his head
against the tree as he jerked backwards and a steady stream
of blood trickled down his neck. Ramón waited, giving him
an opportunity to speak, but the Texan merely gritted his
teeth and returned the stare defiantly. The *caporal* raised his
pistol again, and when it exploded, the man's left ear disintegrated in a shower of bloody tissue. The raider groaned, yet
so slightly that only those standing nearby heard it, and spat
a wad of phlegm at Ramón's feet.

Ramón glanced at Don Miguel, who was standing off to
one side, and smiled tightly. This *gringo* promised to be a
tough one; but the day was long, and they had plenty of time.
Perhaps he had greater fear of a slow death than a quick
one, and in that, they could accommodate him easily. The
caporal ordered the prisoner's shirt removed, then looked
slowly around the circle of hard, brown faces. For what he had
in mind, there was one above all others who deserved the
honor, and he selected Hector Lizardi.

"*Abuelo*, it comes to me that your knife needs practice.
This vermin is yours to whittle on, old one. But take care you
do not kill him. The *bárbaro* has much to say before we allow him to die."

The old man's eyes went moist with pride. "*Sí jefe*. I will treat him gently, as if he were merely a child whose manners must be corrected."

Walking forward, Hector Lizardi stopped before the prisoner. With great ceremony, he slipped a long, wicked looking stiletto from its scabbard. Testing its edge with his thumb, he squinted up at the raider, flashing a mouthful of scraggly, brown teeth. "*Amigo*, you are about to witness a miracle. With one swift stroke of the blade, I will reveal how it is possible for you to change from man to *manso*, the tame bull. Have you ever seen a man gelded, my friend? It is an ugly thing, and sad. Very sad. No longer will his pole grow stout, and the women find him a source of much amusement."

Suddenly the narrow blade flicked out and down, slashing the man's belt and pants so that they fell over against his hips. A thin ribbon of blood appeared from his bellybutton to his groin, seeping down over the short, curly hairs that showed above the crotch of his trousers. The raider's buttocks slammed up against the tree as his manhood flinched from the knife. Then he sucked up his nerve and closed his eyes, waiting for the final cut.

But men are unlike cattle, as Hector Lizardi well knew. They die quickly from loss of blood or simply from shock when their *pequeñas rocas* are cut from the sack. Better merely to carve on the *gringo* dog and break his spirit little by little. Suiting action to thought, the old man hefted the stiletto like a surgical instrument and began tracing a pattern of precise slits across the man's belly. When that failed to draw any response, he neatly severed each nipple, watching the exquisite agony on the raider's face as the blade razored through his tender flesh. Still the *ladrón* refused to speak.

Losing patience, the ancient one grasped the Texan's lower lip between thumb and forefinger and gauged an arc from corner to corner with the tip of the stiletto. But as the blade pierced the man's fleshy jowls, Ramón halted Hector Lizardi with a sharp command.

"Enough, grandfather! I see now that this *piojo* is more stubborn than we suspected. Either that, or he is more of a man than his fat belly would lead you to believe. Still there

are ways to loosen any man's tongue. Eh, old one? Perhaps
we should let him share a moment with the crawling death."
Turning to his men, Ramón searched their faces. "What do
you say, *caballeros?* Shall we introduce our silent friend to
el culebra?"

The men roared their approval, flashing curious glances
at the prisoner as they nudged one another in the ribs. While
the raider hadn't the faintest idea of what was coming next,
it seemed fairly clear that it would be worse than what he had
already undergone. Bathed in a slime of his own sweat and
gore, he sagged against the ropes, thankful for even this brief
respite. Galvanized by Ramón's brisk orders, the *vaqueros* set
about collecting empty grain sacks and took off in all directions across the parched countryside.

Don Miguel spoke briefly with his *caporal*, nodding occasionally at the prisoner, then walked off toward the *hacienda*
What was about to happen wouldn't be pretty to watch, and
there were some things that even *el patrón* preferred not to
witness. While he saw the necessity, it nonetheless left him
revolted. As he knew full well, Ramón and his *vaqueros* had
not fought the Apaches and Comanches without learning
something about the limits of a man's courage. And the Texan
was about to be tested in a way that Don Miguel considered
harsh even for a *gringo*.

Shortly the prisoner was marched to a small, open-sided
ramada and stripped naked. Four ropes were thrown over the
rafters and secured to his hands and ankles. Then, before he
had time to gather his wits, the man was hoisted aloft in a
spread-eagle position. *Vaqueros* strode forward clutching
sacks and dumped the contents on the earthen floor of the
ramada.

The morning stillness instantly came alive with an ungodly buzzing sound, and a dozen furious rattlesnakes coiled
to strike. Leaping back, the *vaqueros* grabbed long poles
and surrounded the shed, forcing the snakes to remain inside.
Being poked and shoved with the sticks infuriated the rattlers
even more, and their angry warning swelled to a deafening
pitch.

Ramón stepped as close to the shed as he dared and peered up at the helpless raider. "*Gringo*, you can halt this game whenever you feel the urge to speak. From this moment on, whether you live or die is a matter of your own choosing."

Moving back, Ramón barked an order, and the Texan was slowly lowered from the rafters toward the floor. After a moment, the snakes became aware of the new threat and switched their attention from the *vaqueros* to this strange enemy who hovered overhead like a taloned hawk. The raider jerked violently, arching his buttocks high in the air, trying desperately to push himself back up the ropes. But his struggles were in vain, for the lines inexorably lowered him into the viper pit below. As he neared the floor, the snakes poised to strike, and the enraged whir of their rattles came like the call of death itself. Dripping sweat, his eyes bulged out of their sockets, shot through with crazed terror.

Suddenly the man gasped as he spotted one especially large rattler eyeing his dangling manhood. Every fiber in his body strained backwards with inhuman will, for it now became clear that whatever part of him reached the snakes first was exactly what they would strike. Already he could feel the slithering filth gnawing on it, gouging and chomping as they pumped their venom deep within his precious rod. Death came to every man, and once cold, it mattered little how he had gone under. But not like that. *Holy Mother of God, not like that!*

The *vaqueros* watched in frozen awe, wondering if the *yanqui* would hold his tongue until it was too late. Some of his breed were *muy valiente*, brave beyond the measure of other men, and perhaps this fat-gutted barbarian was one. Whatever he was, he would shortly be dog meat unless he opened his mouth soon.

Then, with little more than a yard separating him from the rattlers, the Texan broke. Screaming hysterically, his face etched with mortal fear, he swore to tell all if they would only save him. Ramón ordered him hoisted aloft, but refused to untie him just yet. Drained of the last ounce of courage, the raider hung limply from the ropes, swaying overhead like a gutted steer. Every muscle in his body quivered uncontrollably, his eyes twitched with spastic madness; like a man already dead, his bowels flushed in final release.

The questioning began again. This time Ramon was confident that they would come to an understanding, for they were both reasonable men, and as such, there should be no secrets between them. But should he prove stubborn with certain answers, of course, they would not hesitate to lower him again among those who waited below. *¿Comprendes, amigo? ¡Bueno!*

6

Shortly after noon that day, a carriage crossed the Rio Grande and drove straight to the Paso del Norte jail. There three girls alighted, their faces wan and solemn, dressed demurely as befitted housewives. Their driver escorted them into the *calabozo*, and as they entered the door, the portly jailer came forward to meet them. Four *gringos*, three of them women, was hardly an everyday occurrence in his flea-bitten lockup, and he instinctively grew wary.

"Buenos días, Mariscal," the driver greeted him in passable Spanish. "These *señoras* are the wives of the prisoners now in your custody. They humbly request permission to speak with their men for a few moments. Since it is well known that their husbands are slated for *rapida ejecución* the ladies feel honor-bound to look upon them once more."

The jailer sucked up his stomach and sauntered around for a better look at the ladies. Seldom had he been called marshal, and the title had a heady effect on him in the drowsy heat. Still one could never be too careful where *gringos* were concerned. They were a devious race, given to great cunning and duplicity in their dealings with his people. Yet the man looked harmless enough, and the women certainly presented no threat. After all, he, José Flores, was a man of some experience in such matters, not to mention his remarkable facility for sizing up a person in one glance. Besides, he was a family man himself, and it was only right that *hombres* who had an appointment with the firing squad should be granted one last visit with their loved ones. Such a thing would do much for a man on his way to hell.

"*¡Hecho!*" His eyes warmed, and he smiled benevolently. "Consider it done, *señor*. But the ladies will be allowed only ten minutes, and under the circumstances, I fear they will be afforded no privacy."

"*Gracious, Mariscal.* You are very kind." Looking around at the women, the driver related the gist of the conversation, then turned back to the jailer. "The *señoras* thank you and indicate that ten minutes will be more than enough. After the beastly thing these men have done, the ladies wish only to fulfill their wifely duty, and nothing more."

Tipping his hat to the women, the driver turned and walked out the door. José Flores smiled solicitously and ushered the ladies toward the rear of the jail. This was a sad thing, and he felt very *simpático* about these poor, betrayed women. Still, they were exceptionally pretty in that pale, *gringo* way, and doubtless they would have little trouble finding better husbands once this dirty business was finished. He would light a candle and pray to the Virgin that their bereavement not be too incapacitating.

Red and his two cellmates had watched this little charade with mounting interest. They weren't too sure about the play, but there wasn't a doubt in the world that Banning had hatched this scheme personally. The girls were regulars in the Coliseum Saloon, and they wouldn't be here unless the big boss had a hand in this deal. While the prisoners' grasp of greaser talk was limited, they had caught enough of the conversation to understand that the women were posing as their wives. Considering that each of the girls would hump a drunk Indian if the price was right, the three men had all they could do to keep from laughing. Watching the tubby jailer herd them along like lily-pure doves was more than a man could rightly stand with a straight face.

When the girls stopped before the cell, the three Texans crowded against the bars. José Flores thoughtfully backed off a few paces, not wishing to intrude on their tender, yet

somehow pitiful, moment. Out of the corner of his eye he saw
the men clasp their wives' hands, and the soft murmurings he
took to be words of endearment brought a sorrowful frown to
his face. ¡Madre mio! It was indeed a cruel thing that these
men had brought such disgrace to their women. The sooner
they faced the firing squad the better for everyone concerned!

Suddenly the girls' escort appeared in the doorway and
again stepped inside. Instantly alert, the jailer walked toward
the front of the room, keeping his hand near the ancient Colt
resting on his hip. But the driver seemed peaceful enough,
wishing only to inquire if it would be possible to get a cup of
coffee. José Flores apologized profusely, for the coffee pot
had grown cold since morning. More to the point, he was disgusted with himself at having suspected the man simply because he was a gringo. Chattering like an amiable bear, he
walked the driver back to the door, and they parted with a
warm handshake.

While José Flores was salving his conscience, things in
the back of the jail were moving at a furious pace. In a flash
the girls hiked their skirts, pulled guns from their under-
clothes, and passed them to the prisoners. With the jailer's
attention thoroughly diverted, it was a simple matter for Red
and his partners to stash the guns beneath their mattresses.
When the alguacil returned, he found everything as serene
as a high mass, marred only by an occasional sniffle from
one of the women. Again he was struck by the rightness of
allowing these doomed men one last glimpse of their wives.
Somewhere a man's good deeds were being recorded for that
final day of judgment, and his actions here this afternoon
would not go unnoticed.

When the girls were ready to leave, he escorted them to
the carriage and stood watching as it pulled away. Dabbing
at their eyes with delicate hankies, they waved goodbye, and
José Flores felt a lump the size of a gourd form in his throat.
¡Madre de Dios! Such gentle creatures to be married to those
filthy cabrones back inside.

The day passed uneventfully, and after giving the prisoners their supper, the jailer stepped outside to sit on the front

step. Each evening when darkness fell, a freshening breeze drifted in off the river, and it was good to be rid of the heat for another day. The night seemed alive with fireflies and the chirp of crickets, and for the first time in longer than he could remember, José Flores felt at peace with himself. This was a thankless job, one seldom appreciated by the people, but it had its moments. Gazing up at the sky, he watched the moon play hide and seek with the clouds and reflected once again on the skinny beauty of *yanqui* women. *¡Sí!* Today had been one of those moments.

Back in their cell, Red and his cronies stared up at the same moon through a barred window. Yet their thoughts had little to do with cool breezes and pretty women. They would have much preferred a dark night for a jailbreak, but beggars couldn't be choosers. The greasers could easily take it into their heads to march them before a firing squad at any time, and escape might be tonight or never.

They had spent the afternoon planning just how it would be done, and with the village quieted down, there was no reason to wait longer. On signal, two of the men started scuffling, cursing one another in loud, fluent terms. Jerked from his reverie by the commotion, José Flores hurried into the cell block, ordering them to cease fighting. But the tables suddenly turned, and before he suspected what was happening, the jailer found himself staring down the bores of three Colts.

"All right, you greasy tub o' guts," Red snarled. "We'd just as soon kill you as not, so don't fart around or I'll put a slug right through your gizzard. Now get them keys and be damn quick about it."

The jailer wordlessly crossed the room and took a ring of keys from a wall peg. But as he turned back, his offside was hidden for a moment, and his hand stealthily crept toward the gun on his hip. *¡Jesucristo!* If he let these animals escape, the villagers would more than likely decorate a tree with his plump neck. Three to one were bad odds, even for a *pistolero* like himself, but he had to try.

"Hold it!" Red's sharp growl brought him up short. "Listen you fat prick, you're about a hair away from going under.

Savvy, greaseball? Now heist your hands and trot over here
with them keys."

José Flores did as he was told. Even the most fearless *guerrero* knew there was a fine line between bravery and foolishness, and the big, black holes centered on his bellybutton
seemed very persuasive indeed. Besides, he had seven children, who would take it very unkindly if their father suddenly
left them orphaned. Unlocking the cell door, he stepped aside
to let the Texans out.

Without warning Red whacked him over the head with the
heavy Colt. The jailer's knees buckled, but the *gringo*
thumped him twice more before he hit the floor, striking savagely as one would club a fattened steer. José Flores made
no sound as a widening pool of blood puddled up around his
head. Had Red not feared risking a shot, he would have been
a dead man instead of one with a cracked skull.

Easing through the front door of the jail, the Texans stuck
to the shadows and began a cautious approach to the river.
The streets were deserted, and Paso del Norte seemed quiet
as a graveyard. But they took no chances. Moving silently
from building to building in the tawny moonlight, they passed
through the village without arousing a single dog. Though
this struck Red as curious, he chalked it off to an overdue
change in luck and plowed on toward the border.

Minutes later, they reached the river, and the sight of it
made them bolder. Freedom lay on the other side. A land
where there were no lice, ravenous fleas, or firing squads. The
thought alone made them dizzy with relief. Sliding down the
bank in a shower of dust, they plunged into the water and
went splashing across the Rio Grande like frisky yearlings.

But even as they ran, Ramón Vazquez and fifteen *vaqueros* emerged from the treeline bordering Paso del Norte.
Armed with rifles; they watched impassively as the Texans
neared the opposite shore, awaiting their *caporal*'s order.
When it came, the night was rendered with a hollow roar, and
the three renegades pitched forward on the riverbank, dead
even as they hit American soil. The *vaqueros* continued firing until their rifles were empty, shredding the lifeless bod-

ies with a hail of lead. Only when the hammers clicked on empty chambers did they lower their weapons and fade back into the trees.

The debt had been repaid in part. Not fully by any means, and after the savagery of last night, perhaps never. But now there would be no doubt as to the fate of those who violated Mexican women or ravaged the land of their fathers.

CHAPTER FOUR

1

El Paso was alive with talk of last night's brutal slaying of the three Americans. Frank Hollingsworth, the local butcher, happened to be on his way home and had actually witnessed the slaughter, which was the term already being applied to the killings. The townspeople were in a shaky mood, appalled by the savagery of the incident. Though the dead men were generally considered nothing more than common rapists, border scum really, they were human. When the riddled bodies had been carted up to the funeral parlor, word quickly spread that they were as full of holes as a leaky sieve. Such an end was better suited to animals, for whatever else they had been, the men were Texans. The way things were shaping up, no man was safe outside the sanctuary of his own home. Maybe not even in it.

Although the people were unnerved by the Mexicans' savagery, there was also an undercurrent of ill feeling directed toward the Bannings. They had clearly masterminded the escape attempt, and it had been their ranch hands who had stirred up the Mexicans. Though no one could fault them for trying to save their own men, it now became clear that the life of every *anglo* along the river had been placed in jeopardy. The Mexicans meant to fight if pushed, and stirring up a hornets' nest to save three men was hardly the act of a civic benefactor. What had been whispered in the past was now being bandied about openly. Ed Banning was a conniving bloodsucker, and so long as he ended up with all the marbles, he didn't give a tinker's damn for the fate of the town itself.

Tom Kale rode into town late that morning, eager to report the success of his raid. Touching up the brands on the rustled longhorns was taking longer than planned, and he had finally decided it was best to ride on in and let the Bannings know what was happening. Besides, he was a little concerned that Red and his two partners hadn't shown up at the ranch. Assuming the jailbreak came off without a hitch, he had fully expected them to come loping into the home base sometime last night.

Upon entering the office in the Coliseum he found the Bannings sour-tempered and curiously untalkative. The grim scowl on their faces was clear enough to read, and to an old scout like Kale, the sign said to walk lightly.

"Mornin', boss," Kale's voice was neither chipper nor solemn, just sort of neuter in tone. "How's tricks, Sam?"

"Not worth a shit." The burly man's features twisted in a bilious grimace, like he was having gas pains and couldn't break wind. "In case you hadn't heard, somebody just kicked the crapper door off the hinges."

"Yeah? Well maybe I've got a little news that'll cheer you up some." The ramrod wasn't sure what Sam's cryptic observation meant, but where the Bannings were concerned he had found it best not to prod them with questions. "Night before last we whipped the livin' piss out of them greasers and got away with near two hundred beeves. The boys are finishing up the brandin' right now. Sorta puts a new light on things, don't it?"

Ed Banning came erect in his chair. "Kale, you're a day late and a dollar short. Last night your asshole buddies got themselves pumped full of lead. What Sam's trying to tell you

is that the greasers let 'em get to this side of the river before
they gunned them down. Evidently they got wind of the break
somehow and had a whole goddamn regiment lined up along
the south bank."

"Sorta like a turkey shoot," Sam growled. "Only your boys
didn't have near as good a chance of walkin' away."

"Well I'll be dipped in shit," Kale said, clearly thunderstruck by the news.

"We're all gonna be double-dipped if we don't get things
back on an even keel pretty damn quick." The gang leader's
waspish comments sizzled with anger. "Instead of busting
those three nitwits out of jail and making a fool of Stoudenmire, we've made jackasses out of ourselves twice running. Once more and folks around here are liable to start
thinkin' we've gone soft in the head."

"That's for damn sure." Kale shook his head ruefully, still
slack-jawed with the turn of events. "Us losin' five men in two
days might give the wrong people some big ideas."

"Five men?" Ed Banning snapped. "What the hell are you
talkin' about? I only count three."

"Oh, I lost two in the raid the other night. Taylor and Pickens. Guess I forgot to mention it."

"Just clean slipped your mind, did it? Like you'd lost a
couple of steers out in the brush somewhere. Kale, honest to
Christ, sometimes I think your wits are about as sharp as a
dull butcher knife."

"Boss, I ain't no dummy, but you plumb lost me." The
foreman glanced at Sam for some clue and got only a dour
look in return. "We've lost men on raids before. Plenty of
times. Where's the difference this go-round?"

"You thickheaded ox. If you had sense enough to pour piss
out of a boot, you wouldn't have to ask." Banning's eyes narrowed with scorn, and it was all he could do to hold his rage
in check. "The greasers got hold of one of your men and made
him talk. That oughta be plain enough even for you. Otherwise how would they've known about the jailbreak and had
a whole goddamn army waitin' with Winchesters?"

"Well hell, Mr. Banning, I ain't no mind reader. We shot

it out with the greasers the better part of the night, and I just
sorta figured them boys went under when I wasn't lookin'."

"That's the trouble with you, Kale. You figure too much.
That kind of thing has been known to ruin a man's health."

Banning's surly threat brought the ramrod up short, and
he wisely concluded that it was best not to try defending his
actions further. Sam was just looking for an excuse to beat
the whey out of somebody, and if the elder brother blinked
in his direction, he might easily come out on the short end of
the stick. Not that he was afraid of Sam one way or the other.
It was just that if he had a choice, he'd rather fight a cross-
eyed gorilla.

When Kale held his silence, the gang leader cooled down
somewhat, sinking back into his chair. "If you'd let me know
in time, we could have changed the plan, instead of making
asses out of ourselves. But there's no use cryin' over spilt
milk. What we've got to think about is that the greasers are
holdin' either Taylor or Pickens over there somewhere. And
sure as Christ made green apples, he's talking his head off,
whichever one it is. If the greasers got cute and handed him
over to the Texas Rangers, we'll be hung by our balls on a
short string."

Banning's gaze shifted to the ceiling, and his eyes went
cloudy, somehow out of focus. Sifting the known from the
unknown, and holding it to the light of what urgently needed
doing, he slowly came to the only reasonable solution. "Kale,
whoever they've got, they're probably holding him at the
same hacienda you raided. I want you to make sure he never
sets foot off that place except in a box. If you foul this up,
you'd better keep right on going."

Kale just nodded, needing no explanation. Once more and
he would be playing on borrowed time. That was the message,
and he had every certainty that, if he stumbled again, it
would be a long fall.

Sam's brutish grunt snapped his thoughts back to the present. "Well I'm damned if I see why we ought to bother about
somebody the greasers've got. There's only one man we've
got to thank for this whole mess, and it's that shit heel marshal.

I say get rid of him. Once he's out of the way, them bleedin' hearts uptown won't have anybody to hide behind."

"That's the ticket!" Kale agreed brightly, trying to regain lost ground in his deadly race against ill wind and piss-poor luck. "Hell's bells, I'd be willin' to do the job just to see the bastard's face when he got chopped down."

"You two make a pair," Ed Banning observed testily. "Damned if I ever saw anything to beat it. If Stoudenmire turned up dead, everybody in town would know who did it, and there's a limit even in El Paso. That's all the reformers would need. Give 'em a martyr and they'll start poundin' drums all the way back to the statehouse. Now both of you pay attention, 'cause I'm only gonna say this once. Until I give the word, we'll just lay low and keep our eyes open. One way or another, we'll get Stoudenmire, but nobody makes a move till I say the time is ripe."

When neither man seemed inclined to argue the matter, Banning waved his hand dismissively. "Why don't you two trot out and get yourselves a drink. I've got some things to think out."

Sam bobbed his head dumbly and turned toward the door. Kale followed him out, amused by the fickle tides that momentarily put him to rowing with the boss's brother. Over drinks at the bar, they agreed that Ed was a very deep man, hard to understand. But other than this shallow observation, they were unwilling to speculate further about the man they both served so meekly. Some things were just better left unsaid.

2

Shortly before noon, Stoudenmire was crossing the plaza when he met Mayor Porter headed in the opposite direction. Although the two men were on speaking terms, neither was laboring under any illusions about where the other stood. Stoudenmire served but one mistress, the law, while Porter had cast his lot with corruption and personal gain in the form of the Banning machine. Like two battle-scarred old dogs eyeing the same bone, they feinted this it way and that, sparring verbally whenever they met, each seeking some advantage before the fight was joined. Though the marshal respected Porter's skill as a manipulator of men and things, he found the mayor an insufferable bore, not to mention the fact that he was something of a windbag in the bargain. Porter was simply scared witless of the marshal, for after twenty years on a lawless frontier, he had grown accustomed to a certain tolerance where men's misdeeds were concerned. Clearly Stoudenmire couldn't be classed as a tolerant lawman, and it was a bit unsettling to meet a man who had some Jehovah-like concept of himself as the dispenser of justice.

Stoudenmire nodded to the mayor and started to pass on by. But Porter had other ideas. "Marshal, I wonder if you have a moment? As a matter of fact, if you're not too busy, I'd like to buy you a drink."

"Thanks just the same, Mr. Mayor, but I rarely drink before noon." The sarcasm was thinly veiled, just the way Stoudenmire meant it. "Besides, my wife is expecting me home for dinner."

"Well land's sakes, man, she'll keep it hot for you." Porter's tone seemed almost desperate, and he clutched at the marshal's arm with a feeble, birdlike grasp. "This is important. Official business in a manner of speaking, and I'd think that takes precedent over a paltry noon meal."

Stoudenmire sensed some curious change in the politician. Nothing he could put his finger on, but a noticeable crack in the wall nonetheless. "Since you put it that way, Mayor, I'll take you up on the offer. But no drinks, just talk. Suppose we try your office instead of a saloon."

"No. Not city hall," Porter said a bit too quickly. "Let's go to your office. There'll be less . . . ah . . . interruption that way."

Without a word, the marshal turned and began retracing his steps across the plaza. Whatever was on the portly little man's mind, it would prove a hell of a lot more interesting

than Kate's incessant whining about the risks he took. Come
to think of it, there were times a man could get a gutful without ever touching food.

Trotting along at his side, the mayor would have given considerable for a drink right at that moment. Isaac Porter was
a troubled man, more than he cared to admit. He sensed that
the townspeople were growing more and more disgruntled
with the state of affairs that existed along the border. They
had been brought to the brink of outright warfare with the
Mexicans more times than anyone cared to remember;
there was no longer a soul among them who questioned how
far the Mexicans were willing to go to exact retribution. The
fact that the Texans were vastly outnumbered sobered them
even more, and it was hardly surprising that few men expected to come out of it alive if the bloodletting ever started.

More significantly still, word was spreading that the
Bannings, along with their political and business cronies, were
at the root of the trouble. Though this was only partially true,
Porter could see that any further problems could easily bring
about the downfall of the political machine he had helped to
establish. Should that happen there was every likelihood that
some of his more unsavory deals with the Bannings would
come to light, and he had no wish to end up as an ornament on
a telegraph pole. Which was just where this game might
lead if something wasn't done fast. The Bannings weren't
about to look out for anyone but themselves, even if the whole
town was leveled to the ground; so that left it up to him. But
it would be touch and go if Ed Banning ever got wind of what
he had in mind.

When they reached the office, Stoudenmire sent Gillette
to see about his own dinner, and they had the place to themselves. Porter took a chair across from the desk and gave the
room a quick once over, like he expected a barrel of whiskey
to roll out from under the corner bunk. The marshal just sat
and waited, an old hand at the game of "out of the skillet and
into the fire."

Porter had a distinct aversion to silence, as if a moment
uncluttered by words was an opportunity lost forever, and he

soon broke under the lawman's stony gaze. "Marshal, instead of beating around the bush, I'll come straight to the point. El Paso is faced with a crisis. Perhaps the one that could break the camel's back, in a manner of speaking. The killing of those three scoundrels last night has unsettled the people more than any other single incident I can recall. Even the salt war didn't frighten them like this. It's just too close to home."

"Mayor, before you start stretchin' for a second wind, why don't you get down to the point. It's beginning to look like a long day on an empty belly."

"To be sure, Marshal Stoudenmire. To be sure. But let me first impress on you the need for urgency. The Mexican populace on both sides of the river is only one step away from being up in arms. It would take nothing more than some insignificant mishap to put them at our throats."

"Like raping another little girl?" Stoudenmire remarked stiffly.

Overlooking the sarcasm, Porter pulled out a large handkerchief and mopped his face. "Perhaps. Who knows what governs a Mexican's actions. The thing I'm leading up to is this. I believe the citizens of El Paso to be in greater mortal danger at this moment than ever before. The Mexicans lack only a leader to bring them storming across the river by the thousands. While we could put up a stiff fight with the help of the army, I harbor no illusions about the outcome. And unless we move quickly, that day may arrive sooner than anyone suspects."

"I'll have to hand it to you. You're just a sack full of surprises." Stoudenmire scrutinized the politician's face for a long moment before resuming. "Let's get our cards out on the table. You could talk till you were blue in the face, and I still wouldn't believe you're worried about the townspeople. Now suppose you quit making speeches and tell me what all this is about."

"My boy, there are times in a man's life when he must set aside the lessons of the past and deal with the moment on its own merits. Perhaps your cynicism is well founded, but is it so hard to believe that even a politician can want what's best for his community?"

"Maybe. Maybe not. Most times when a politician gets to worrying about the lowly citizen, it's brought about by some threat of his own political survival. If that's what you're sayin', then I reckon I could swallow it."

"Marshal, I won't deny that a certain concern for my own skin prompted me to arrange this discussion." Porter swabbed his face again with the handkerchief, shrewdly appraising his adversary. "Just between us, I would even admit that those who view me as being corrupt are not without cause of a sort. But even if those things are true, a man can still have a genuine feeling for the people."

Stoudenmire snorted contemptuously and gave the older man a flat, uncompromising stare. "Whatever it is you want, why don't you just spit it out? All this hemming and hawing won't change things between you and me one iota."

"Very well. To be perfectly frank about it, I was hoping you would have a talk with the *alcalde* of Paso del Norte. Word is spreading that you have done your best to head off trouble, and I have a feeling the Mexicans would listen to you. They already know what you've done to calm folks over here, and a request from you to hold their own people in check would carry a lot of weight. More than anyone else in this town, you have a strong chance of preventing further bloodshed."

The mayor paused, meeting Stoudenmire's gaze squarely for the first time. "Whatever your opinion of me, I hope you'll believe that I'm sincere in wanting to halt this violence."

"Sure, I believe you. Your kind always gets squeamish when they see blood." The lawman gave him a look that would have raised frost on a brass cannon. "I'll see the headman across the river, but don't think its got anything to do with you. If it was up to me, I'd feed you and your cronies to the Mexicans like dog meat."

After a moment of strained silence, the mayor rose and walked out the door. There was nothing more to say. Stoudenmire would see the Mexicans well enough, but afterwards, he would be right back dogging the Bannings' tracks. And if some of the Banning underlings happened to get caught in the crunch, it wouldn't bother the marshal in the slightest. Thinking back to those cold eyes, it came over the dumpy little politician that Stoudenmire would probably even enjoy it.

Isaac Porter suddenly needed a drink in the worst way. The furies seemed to be gathering, and he had fought enough battles for one day.

3

Later that afternoon Stoudenmire crossed the Rio Grande and inquired directions to the *alcalde's* home. The somnolent village was like a hundred others he had seen along the border while serving with the Rangers, and it occurred to him that time had little effect on the casual pace of these people. Naked, taffy-skinned children rolled in the dirt right alongside mangy dogs, runty pigs, and a motley assortment of bleating goats. Women in sleazy, faded dresses tended the dirt-floored adobes while their men rested in the shade, ever confident that *mañana* would bring about a sharp reversal in their fortunes. They asked little of life, expected less, and somehow struggled along on the lean times that were part and parcel of border living.

Watching them as he rode along the dusty street, Stoudenmire was reminded again that at heart the Mexicans were warm, peace-loving people. They wished only to bask in the mellow sun, to be left alone. Still, even the most gentle creature on earth would turn and fight when driven to the wall. Thinking about it, he recalled that Mexicans weren't exactly disciplined fighters, but they were mean as a barrelful of snakes when it got right down to cut or be cut.

Dismounting before an unusually large adobe, he walked to the door and knocked. Even before the sound of his knuckles faded, the door swung back, revealing an elderly man who somehow appeared taller than he actually was.

"Buenos días, señor," Pedro Vazquez greeted him. "How may I serve you?"

"Buenos días, Alcalde." The lawman flashed that rare smile, which made it seem all the warmer. "I am Dallas Stoudenmire, marshal of El Paso. Pardon this unannounced intrusion, but I come hoping we might speak of matters mutually important to our people."

"Come in out of the heat, Marshal. I am honored that you would call on me and always welcome an exchange of ideas with our *americano* neighbors."

The *alcalde* led him back to a cool, high-ceilinged study and courteously offered refreshments. While they sipped hot chocolate, Vazquez held the conversation to idle small-talk, obviously trying to put the lawman at ease. After an appropriate round of pleasantries, centering on the weather and the merits of Paso wine, the older man sat back in his chair and folded his hands. With formalities out of the way, the serious business could now begin.

"My friend, I have long wanted to talk with a leader from your side of the river." Chuckling, Pedro Vazquez tapped his chest with a deprecating gesture. "But I am an old man given to excesses in speech. Suppose I first listen to what you have to say, for I am sure your errand is of no small consequence."

"Gracias, Alcalde. Your concern is not misplaced, I assure you." Then, without mincing words, Stoudenmire came straight to the point. "I am here seeking some way to bring about peace between our people. Failing that, I would hope to arrange a truce of some sort so that tempers on both sides of the Rio Grande might have time to cool."

The Mexican's brow furrowed in thought as he studied his guest. "This is no small thing you seek. Your countrymen are not noted for their peaceful ways, and unfortunately my people long ago lost faith in the honorable intentions of any *yanqui.*"

Stoudenmire's mouth tightened at the blunt words, but there was no denying the truth behind them. *"Jefe*, your words are harsh, but not without justification. Like most men, Americans come in all shapes and sizes, some good, some bad. Yet it is a curious thing that the bad ones are always more visible; that they somehow seem to lead the good without a struggle, much like a tame bull with a ring in his nose. Still, if those same people are shown a way, they would much prefer to live in peace. Perhaps I reach too high, but should we be content with anything less than our people living as neighbors once more?"

"We also have our bad ones, the *bandidos* in the hills But strangely they prefer to prey on their own kind." The *alcalde* puzzled on this for a moment, wondering why the bandits never dared cross into Texas. It was a thought that would bear examination. "How would you propose to bring about this truce? It is an ambitious undertaking."

"Ambitious perhaps, but not impossible." The lawman searched Vazquez's face for any sign of guile, then decided to go whole hog. "The men responsible for our troubles are mostly Americans. This I admit freely. Already I have taken steps to calm the good ones among my people. Now, I will reveal for your ears alone, that I have taken the trail of the bad ones and hope to have them in jail soon. They are called Banning, and once I bring them to earth, many of our problems will be resolved."

"Yes, I have heard that name. Are these men responsible for the terrible raid of two nights past?" When Stoudenmire nodded, the Mexican came up on the edge of his chair. "This is a good thing you do, Marshal. *Bichos*, vermin like these men, should be stamped out wherever found."

Vazquez had watched his visitor closely, purposely letting him do the talking. Now he was convinced that this large, soft-spoken *gringo* before him was an honorable man. Within the last week, he had heard tales from his people across the river about Stoudenmire's efforts to avert open hostilities, and there appeared every reason to credit them as true. Suddenly a thing he had once said flashed through his mind. *There are times in a man's life when he must blindly trust other men, even* yanquis. Perhaps this was the place to start.

"Marshal, I wonder if you would care to join me in a humble supper? I wish to send for my nephew so that you might speak with him. What he has to say will prove most interesting, you can be sure."

Stoudenmire readily agreed, not quite sure what the *alcalde* had in mind but willing to gamble a few hours to find out. The supper they shared was far from humble, consisting of choice beef, various native dishes, and an unusually fine wine. After working his way through a second helping of everything, it occurred to the lawman that Mexican politicians must eat as high off the hog as their American counterparts. Still, the old man was chock full of amusing stories, and over brandy and cigars it came to Stoudenmire that he wasn't being entertained so lavishly without some purpose in mind. Whatever the game was, the stakes seemed right, and as long as he had taken a seat, he decided to enjoy himself. Listening to the *alcalde* launch into another whopper, he came to the conclusion that the old Mexican might just be a match for Doc Cummings. The two of them in the same room would probably be more than a man could take in one night.

Toward dusk, Ramón Vazquez arrived on a lathered horse and went into a whispered conference with his uncle. He, too, had heard stories concerning this *gringo* lawman and felt there was no harm in discussion. Walking forward, he shook Stoudenmire's hand with a firm grip.

"Our people across the river say you are *simpático* to the Mexican cause. We find this a very strange trait in a *yanqui*, especially one who serves the will of the *ladrones* who rule El Paso."

Stoudenmire was amused yet a little nettled by this shallow test. "You are a foolish young man to judge people so casually. Were I working for the *gringo* thieves, I wouldn't have missed." Jerking his chin, he indicated the arm that Ramón favored with every movement.

"*¿Quien sabe?*" Ramón shrugged, gigged on his own shaft and unable to wriggle free. "Who knows, perhaps there is such a thing as an honest *yanqui*?"

"Perhaps." Stoudenmire's mouth curled in a tight, dry smile. "But if you meet one, I wish you would point him out to me."

The young *caporal* laughed outright, turning to his uncle.

"This hombre bears watching. It comes to me that the man hasn't been born who could order him against his will."

"In your own way, *mi hijo*, you have come to the right conclusion." The *alcalde* had been sitting back watching the exchange with much zest. "Now that you have taken his measure, I suggest you tell him of the matter we agreed upon."

Ramón glanced back at Stoudenmire, less suspicious now, but still not wholly trusting of any *gringo*. "Even if you betray us, I see no harm that can come of it. We are holding one of the raiders prisoner, and he has been persuaded to talk. Other than the details of the jailbreak last night, he has also revealed that one calling himself Ed Banning is the head of these *piojos*. We are still thinking on ways to make use of the one whose tongue has been loosened."

The lawman paced to the window and stood staring out into the night. Here was a chance to put a rope around Banning's neck, and it had been handed to him on a silver platter. Mexican silver at that. But if he was to pull it off, it would take the help of this young firebrand, and that might require some powerful convincing.

Facing the two Mexicans, he thanked them for their trust and asked that they consider what he had to say without judging it too quickly. Then in a terse, businesslike manner, he outlined his plan.

Ramón must accompany him to the Banning's ranch and identify the stolen cattle. As a US marshal, he would then arrest the Bannings and arrange their extradition to Mexico on charges of rustling and murder. With the testimony of the captive raider, they were certain to be convicted. Once they had had their moment before the firing squad, peace would again come to the border. There were many dangers involved, and the plan could easily fail. But as leaders of their two peoples they were obligated to try.

The *alcalde* thought on it for only a moment, then drew Ramón into another guarded conference. There was much risk to the plan, just as the *yanqui* lawman admitted. But then peace was rarely purchased cheaply. Somewhere in the midst of all this violence and bloodshed, men had to begin trusting one another. If the men to whom the people looked for leadership were unwilling to try then where would it ever begin? They must place themselves in the hands of this quiet *tejano* and pray to the Virgin that their faith had not been misplaced. How could a *jefe* do less and still look his people in the eye?

The old man and his nephew swung around to find Stoudenmire watching them closely. Ramón Vazquez stepped forward and extended his hand. He would appear at the marshal's office in the morning.

4

El Paso was just coming to life when Ramón crossed the river accompanied by two *vaqueros*. Townspeople blinked the sleep from their eyes and gaped in astonishment. Considering the temper of the moment, it was most unusual, if not downright alarming, for armed Mexicans to boldly ford the Rio Grande. Word raced ahead of them along the street, and by the time they reached Stoudenmire's office, a small crowd had gathered on the plaza. Speculation was rife as to their purpose, for it was indeed baffling to see greasers calling on a Texas lawman. That was one for the book, no doubt about it!

Then someone recalled seeing the marshal cross to Paso del Norte just yesterday. Suddenly this strange turn of events took on even more significance. Yet to what purpose? The reason for the Mexicans' presence still eluded them despite a rash of conjecture, and the onlookers were more bewildered than ever.

But if the townspeople were mystified, Ed Banning struggled under no such drawback. One of his men had spotted the brand on the *vaqueros*' horses, the Salazar Bar Lazy S. Hotfooting it over to the saloon, he blurted out that it was the same brand they had doctored on the rustled steers. The ones grazing contentedly on the Banning ranch right at that moment. Only the new brand was still fresh, and any fool would take it for exactly what it was. The Bar Lazy S doctored with a running iron.

Banning was a man who believed in hedging his bet, especially in a game where the stakes included his own neck. After pondering the matter briefly, he sent a rider to warn Kale. Under no circumstances were the Mexicans to reach the ranch alive. Stoudenmire wasn't to be touched, but if the greasers came anywhere near Banning range, they were to be gunned down on the spot. Perhaps they were in town for another reason entirely, stranger things had happened. Still, there was nothing to lose by playing it safe.

When Ramón dismounted before the jail, Stoudenmire stepped outside. "I see you have drawn a crowd, *amigo.* Come inside where we may talk freely."

"*Glacias*, Marshal," the *caporal* replied. "I would be the first to admit that such a pack of *gringos* makes my back itch in a most peculiar way."

The *vaqueros* left their horses ground-reined and followed Stoudenmire through the door. Gillette came forward with a glum smile, and after introductions had been attended to, they got down to the business at hand. Motioning Ramón to a chair, the marshal took his seat behind the desk.

"I am pleased to see that you had no second thoughts about out little venture. Many men would place a greater *precio* on their lives."

"*De nada.*" Ramón waved aside the compliment. "It is nothing, I assure you. There are many things a man can live with, but fear makes a jealous companion."

As he spoke, the Mexican glanced uneasily at Tige. The big dog hadn't moved from Stoudenmire's side, and Ramón found it difficult to ignore his cold stare. "This one could teach us both the meaning of courage, I suspect. With such a dog even the darkness holds no secrets for a man. *¿El lobo bajo, eh?*"

"The little wolf?" Stoudenmire gave Tige a rough pat. "Yes, I suppose he would accept that well enough. Yet he was named for the one *vaqueros* have learned to respect above all others. *El tigre.*"

"*Sí*, and rightly so. Never have I seen a dog whose manner so closely resembles that of the spotted death. But enough of such things. We have more important matters to discuss. How are we to proceed with our own hunt?"

The lawman tilted back in his chair, hands locked behind his head. "The Banning *rancho* lies something over twenty kilometers to the northeast. We will ride there and conduct a quiet search for your cattle. If we can avoid being seen, so much the better. If not, then we may be forced to fight. Either way, we will stay until we find what we seek."

"¡Está bueno!" Ramón flashed a pearly grin. "I like your view of things, *amigo*. We go, we look, and if anyone objects, we fight. *¡Madre de Dios!* You should have been born a *vaquero.*"

"Perhaps it is good I wasn't." Stoudenmire smiled lightly. "One *charro* of your boldness seems to be all Chihuahua can afford at the moment. Now, let us come to the crucial part of what we do. Suppose you draw for me the brand used by Don Salazar. Then we will attempt to determine how these *ladrones* might have altered it."

Ramón took the pencil and paper Stoudenmire indicated and slowly began sketching the Bar Lazy S. Gillette and the two *vaqueros* moved in closer until the five men were huddled around the desk. Once the drawing was completed, they began experimenting with various ways it could be changed. But they had more ideas than pencils, and before long, a lively debate was raging as to exactly what they should look for once on Banning land.

Some twenty minutes later, Stoudenmire and Ramón rode east from El Paso, trailed by the two *vaqueros*. Gillette had argued to be taken along, but the marshal ordered him to remain behind. Someone had to police the town, and it would never do for both of them to be gone at the same time. Tige didn't care much for the arrangement either, and as the four men rode off, it occurred to the long-faced deputy that they had been left to hold a fort that hardly rated defending.

After traveling eastward on the main road for some miles, the horsemen swung north on a narrow, rutted trail. There wasn't much to see in this desolate land, and Stoudenmire used the time to get better acquainted with the young *capo-*

ral. The lawman found him a very likeable sort, maybe a
shade too formal for a Texan's tastes, but the kind of man a
fellow wouldn't mind having at his side when push came to
shove. Like many Mexicans, he was a little short-fused, and
there was no doubt that he was headstrong. Too much so. The
way an unbroken stud has a mind all its own. A pound of daring in the same keg with fiery temper made for an explosive
mix, one that could get everyone around it blown sky high if
sparks ever flew the wrong way. Still he was an engaging cuss
when he wanted to be, without a devious bone in his body,
and it was a damn cinch he didn't fear anything this side of
perdition itself. That kind were few and far between, and a
man was lucky if he crossed trails with two or three in an
entire lifetime. Yet Stoudenmire wasn't the sort who committed himself quickly where people were concerned. Ramón
had the stuff to make a good friend, no two ways about it.
Something on the order of Jim Gillette, only a feisty pepper-
ball instead of plodding foxiness. But there was plenty of
time, and thinking about it, he decided to reserve judgment
until they had been back to back a couple of times.

Something over an hour after taking the winding trail, the
riders approached a small chain of sandhills, bordered by an
outcropping of huge boulders and mesquite trees. While there
were no fences or boundary markers, the men knew they
were nearing Banning land, and they became alert for any
sign of cattle. As the road entered a draw, flanked on either
side by higher ground, Stoudenmire felt his hackles come up.

Something was out of kilter, but he couldn't quite put a
name to it.

Before he could react, both sides of the draw came alive
with a sharp crack of Winchesters. The lawman rammed his
spurs home, but his horse needed little urging. The chestnut
hit a gallop in three strides, and Stoudenmire hunched low
over the saddle. Out of the corner of his eye, he saw two of
the Mexican horses falter and go down, then he was out of
the draw and running clear.

Glancing back, he caught a quick glimpse of Ramón and
another *vaquero* returning the fire from behind their downed

horses. The other Mexican was spraddled beside the road, obviously dead. But even as he turned his horse to assist the trapped men, the hills and rocks erupted with flame, slamming Ramón and the *vaquero* to the earth.

Wheeling the chestnut, he cursed himself for a fool and rode north, circling the sandhills. The blood pounded against his temples, and his teeth gritted so hard his jawbone hurt. *Why them and not me*? Did some ungodly specter ride with him that neither he nor his horse had been hit? By what miracle had he come through that hail of lead without so much as a scratch?

Then it came clear. *They hadn't meant to shoot him!* They were after the three Mexicans, and as sure as Christ was spiked to a cross, that stolen cattle herd would be off Banning range before nightfall. For that matter, the bastards might already be trailing the longhorns toward some more remote spot. But with the thought came a vivid kaleidoscope of the murderous fire he had just ridden through, and he knew that every gun on the Banning payroll must have been hidden in that draw.

Suddenly it dawned on him why he had been allowed to live. The Mexicans would blame him for Ramón's death! When violence flared anew, he would be caught squarely in the middle, and he could almost hear the angry chant of the townspeople when they denounced him as a meddling fool.

The chestnut grunted as he raked savagely with his spurs and cut cross-country toward El Paso. The least he could do was get a wagon and return the dead men to their native land.

Then he'd see about settling the Bannings' hash. After today they were past due. Way past due.

5

Shortly after midnight Stoudenmire walked through the doors of the Coliseum with Tige at his heels. Word of the ambush had swept through town like wildfire, and a hush fell over the crowd as he crossed the room. The head barkeep exchanged nervous glances with a pug-nosed bouncer, but neither of them stirred from their tracks. Something about the look on the marshal's face made a man think twice, and it took more nerve than they had between them to try blocking his path. Without bothering to knock, Stoudenmire entered Banning's office and slammed the door behind him.

Ed and Sam Banning were startled by the lawman's sudden appearance, yet they returned his cold stare evenly. Stoudenmire's features were ashen, somehow wooden looking, as though he had just cut the cards with death itself. His hooded eyes gave off a flat sheen, like stained glass in strong sunlight, and every fiber in his body seemed taut as shrunken rawhide.

Ed Banning had seen the killing urge in men's eyes before, but he wasn't particularly intimidated by Stoudenmire's flinty gaze. He had faced many mankillers in his day, and he was still around to tell the tale. Fear was what got a man laid out on a cold slab, while caution was what separated the quick from the dead. The lawman had plainly come looking for trouble, primed to kill—the way a bear thinned by winter noses fresh scent. The gang leader never doubted for a moment that one miscue on his part would trigger a gunfight. But this deal shaped up as a cold deck, and he hadn't the slightest intention of being provoked into a showdown. Stoudenmire's death at their hands would serve no useful purpose, and Banning had already decided to remain calm in the event he forced the issue.

"Evenin', Marshal. Have a seat and rest your feet." Banning's amiable manner was decidedly strained. "Sam, get Marshal Stoudenmire a drink of the good stuff."

When Sam started out of his chair, Tige gathered himself, growling low in his throat. The burly ruffian eyed the dog, then glanced up at the lawman. "Call your hound off or I'll twist a knot in his tail."

"Sonny, you lip off to me and I'm gonna stunt your growth." Stoudenmire's tone was flat, deadly, clearly inviting him to pick up the dare. "Crawl back in your cage or get stomped. Your choice."

"Back off, Sam!" Banning's sharp command froze the

younger brother in his chair. "Just keep your mouth shut and let me do the talking. Now, Marshal, let's get down to brass tacks. Since you're not here on a sociable visit, suppose you just state your business."

"Banning, your string has run out in El Paso. From here on it's devil take the hindmost." The words whipped across the room like pearls of stinging frost. "If you're still around when your number's called, I'll come looking."

The Bannings simply watched him, neither man moving so much as a hair. Stoudenmire remained motionless just inside the door, yet he somehow seemed calmer, even stoic now that he had kicked the lid off. But his unruffled manner was merely the cool shell that settles over an old hand as he steels himself for a fight. His hand hung loose, poised at his side, awaiting some flicker of movement that would send it streaking toward the Colt on his hip. He was ready to kill, and they both knew it.

"Marshal, that's a real pretty speech, but it won't hold water." Banning was very careful with his hands, but his voice was steady and firm. "You're gonna find yourself choppin' tall cotton if you try to run us out of town. And I don't think you've got what it takes to shoot us down in cold blood."

"Banning, you've been drawing aces so long you forgot what it's like to wind up on the short end." Stoudenmire saw they weren't going to fight, but he wasn't ready to call it quits. "Tonight I posted a wanted circular on the Notice Tree. It's got Tom Kale's name on it, and the charge is murder. I'm tempted to save the state the cost of a trial when I run him down. On the other hand, I might just bring him into court and let him put a noose around your neck. Sorta makes your milk curdle, don't it?"

For a moment Ed Banning was too dumbstruck to reply. The Notice Tree in the center of the plaza hadn't been used since Texas won independence. Only in extreme cases was a man's name tacked to the ancient trunk, for it meant he was wanted dead or alive. And few were ever brought in except across the back of a horse.

"Stoudenmire, it appears to me your luck is runnin' a mite thin. I assume you're talkin' about those Mexicans getting killed north of town this morning. But it's gonna be kinda hard to hang a man without witnesses. Course, you're such a smart fellow you might figure out some way to bring them greasers back to life."

The lawman's mouth twisted in a grim smile. "I already have. Leastways one of them is healthy enough to identify your ramrod as one of the bushwhackers. Besides, I was there myself, and I'm not likely to forget Kale's face. Offhand, I'd say my testimony, along with the Mexican's, would just about make him a cinch bet for the scaffold."

This latter statement was sheer bluff. Stoudenmire hadn't seen anything but smoke and gunflashes that morning, and even that had been from the back of a galloping horse. Still there was no one to dispute his claim, and it might just force Kale to come looking for him.

The marshal glanced over at Sam, then back to the older brother. "Banning, I always believe in giving a man an even break. I'll spot you gents a headstart, and we can settle this whole deal right now. Otherwise, I'll crowd you so hard you'll kiss my ass and bark like a fox before we're through."

Ed Banning was tempted, but only for a moment. While one of them might get the lawman, he was damn near certain that the big bastard's first slug would catch him about brisket high. And he hadn't the slightest intention of becoming the late political boss of El Paso.

"Sorry to disappoint you, Marshal, but we'll sit this hand out. And if you're bankin' on that tin star to see you through, you're gonna find out it's nothin' but a damn fine target. When you walk out that door, you'd better keep right on going."

"Banning you can cut your wolves loose anytime you want. Makes no difference to me. I'll still get you."

Stoudenmire turned and walked from the room. When the door slammed shut, the Banning brothers breathed an immense sigh of relief. They had come close, perhaps closer than they had ever been in their lives. For the last few minutes,

Old Scratch had been leaning over their shoulders, and his
breath had a hot, fetid smell. Like a bouquet of dead snap-
dragons.

Crossing the plaza moments later, Stoudenmire cursed the
Bannings for a pair of gutless fourflushers. While they
wouldn't hesitate to shoot a man in the back, they didn't have
the stomach for a face to face showdown, even with two to
one odds. The thought touched a raw nerve and his mind
drifted back to that afternoon when he had returned to the
draw with a wagon.

Already the vultures had gathered, circling ever nearer as
the sun warmed their supper. The Mexicans called them *bui-*
tres, and the name fitted like a glove. Filthy scavengers who
spent their lives squabbling over rotted carrion in a land that
seemed as dead as the flesh they ate. Watching them glide
overhead, he had thought that it really didn't matter much one
way or the other. When you are dead, a box or a buzzard
amounts to about the same thing. Maybe one is a little slower,
but no less final.

When he pulled up in the draw, the Mexicans lay just as
they had fallen. Walking among them, he again cursed the
dirty bastards who had gunned them down so mercilessly.
But when he rolled Ramón over, his pulse quickened, and
cold beads of sweat popped out on his forehead. Astonishing as it seemed, the young *caporal* still had a spark of life
in him. Not much, but a hell of a lot more than Stoudenmire
ever expected to find in a man carrying at least four slugs.

Plugging up the holes as best he could, the lawman loaded
Ramón in the wagon and raced for El Paso. A doctor worked
over him until late evening, pronouncing it an act of the Almighty that the greaser had survived. Somehow none of the
slugs had struck a vital organ, and while his days as a *vaquero*
were finished, the sawbones gave him a fifty-fifty chance of
pulling through.

Leaving Gillette to guard Ramón, the marshal had then
returned to the jailhouse to think out his next move. With his
blood running cold, the decision wasn't long in coming. *Force*
the Bannings up against the wall. Make them fight or run.

But the Bannings seemed disinclined to jump in either direction. They refused to fight, and they showed no signs of making a run for it. Like the *buitres*, they were going to wait and watch, and whatever they had up their sleeves would more than likely come on a dark street when a man least expected it.

Passing the Notice Tree as he headed back to check on Ramón, the lawman had a feeling that El Paso was about to live up to its reputation as the toughest town along the border.

CHAPTER FIVE

———◆———

1

El Paso hadn't exactly returned to normal, but in the two weeks since the bushwhacking, a guarded calm had settled over the town. Like a man holding a stick of dynamite with a sputtering fuse, the townspeople waited for an explosion that seemed dreadfully slow in coming.

Though an inquest into the killings was to be held, it had been delayed until tempers on both sides of the river cooled down. Ed Banning had pulled strings to force an immediate hearing, but when Stoudenmire threatened to expose it as a political fix, the coroner hastily backed off. The local gadflies chalked this up as another point for the marshal and sat back to await results.

Mayor Porter trotted out one lame excuse after another for the postponement, but the real issue behind this political infighting was hardly a secret. Stoudenmire was determined there would be no inquest until his key witness was able to testify. As the sole survivor among the ambushed Mexicans, Ramón Vazquez had much to tell, and the gambling frater-

nity was laying odds that his testimony would send half the
Banning gang scurrying for their holes.

After a week of guarding the *caporal* around the clock,
Stoudenmire had secretly moved him to Paso del Norte, figuring he was considerably safer among his own people. Ramón's
recovery had been little short of remarkable, considering his
wounds; yet he was mending slowly, and the marshal had to
curb his impatience as best he could. Until an inquest was
held, the wanted circular on Tom Kale was strictly unofficial, and he desperately needed the Mexican's testimony in
open court to nail it down tight.

Then, as the uneasy standoff entered its third week, the
turning point came. Just before leaving the office for his noon
meal, the marshal received word from Pedro Vazquez that
Ramón was much improved and anxious to testify. Stoudenmire immediately paid a call on the coroner, who seemed delighted that the troublesome affair was at last coming to a
head. When Stoudenmire suggested that the fewer the
spectators the better, the nervous little official agreed
wholeheartedly and set the inquest for the middle of the week.
That way people would have to choose between curiosity and
their livelihood, which would hold down the size of the crowd
some at any rate. Whether it was enough to maintain order
remained to be seen.

Arriving home for dinner, Stoudenmire seemed in a zest-
ful mood for the first time in longer than Kate could remember. As she was serving the table, he playfully swatted her
on the rump, something he hadn't done since the day of the
ambush.

"Better watch it, missy." Patting her hips again, he gave
her figure an appraising look. "Feels like you're putting on a
little beef in the wrong places."

Kate shot him an indignant glance and moved around the
table to her seat. "How would you know? The last couple of
weeks I began to think you had lost interest in things like
that."

"Lost interest? Hell, I've just been restin' up." Smearing

butter over a slice of bread, he grinned mischievously. "You pretty near wore me down to a nubbin' there for a while. Course, I'm not complaining, mind you. It's just that I thought I'd married a tabby cat, and it turns out I got myself a lady catamount."

"Oh, that's not fair. You're the one that always starts it." Kate's face turned beet red as she toyed with the food on her plate. "Besides, you said yourself that there's nothing wrong with a woman wanting to please her husband."

Stoudenmire chuckled deep in his throat. "And herself, too. Don't forget, it takes two to ring the bell."

Kate had never seen him so talkative. And playful, like a naughty little boy with some prank in mind. Coming out of a clear blue like this, it left her a bit flustered. "My, but aren't you chattery today. Did the city council give you a raise or something?"

"Better than that." The lawman paused in the midst of spearing another pork chop. "Ramón Vazquez is ready to talk, and we're gonna hold the inquest day after tomorrow. Christmas comes early this year."

She watched his sure hands carve the pork chop, her own food now forgotten. "That means you'll finally get the evidence you've been waiting for."

"Not just evidence, Katie. There's more to it than that. Once Vazquez says his piece, it'll force the Bannings' hand and they'll have to fish or cut bait."

"What you really mean is that they'll have to fight or run. And either way, you'll go after them."

"Sure. What do you think I've been after since we came here? Tom Kale is their foreman, and once he's indicted, it'll smoke the Bannings out in the open. That's what I've really been waiting for. Evidence is all right, I reckon, but the only way to nail the Bannings and make sure they stay nailed is to crowd 'em into a corner."

Stoudenmire's eagerness for this encounter was readily apparent, for he clearly saw it as the most expedient means of putting the Bannings on ice. Seldom was he so enthused about anything, and it was as though the prospect of a good

fight had rekindled his sense of humor. But Kate found it difficult, if not outright impossible, to share his mood. They
had been married less than two months, and she was discovering that the law is a demanding mistress. Stoudenmire
seemed like a man possessed, as if his every waking thought
was devoted to the downfall of the Bannings. That left room
for little else—wives included—and more than ever, she had
begun to question the wisdom of marrying a peace officer.

With some reluctance, she had admitted to herself that she
was jealous of his dedication to the law. This wasn't married
life as she had envisioned it, especially since the gaiety of
their courtship had been replaced with his grim compulsion
to tame El Paso. Still, even that would have been bearable if
she weren't so frightened. This stranger who shared her bed
was plainly more concerned about some piddling inquest
than he was with the shaky state of their marriage. But while
she resented that fiercely, she felt numbed by the thought that
the hearing would place him one step closer to a showdown
with the Bannings. Some inner premonition told her that
he hadn't a prayer of living through the fight that was sure to
follow.

After all, what effect could one man have on a town like
this? He was backed only by Gillette and that ungodly dog,
while the Bannings had a small army at their beck and call.
It wasn't just foolish, it was downright thoughtless! When it
was over, he would be conveniently dead, and she'd be left to
do all the suffering alone. Just thinking about it made her
blood boil, and it came over her that she must have been mad
to marry a selfish little boy who liked dangerous games better than he did a warm bed.

"Dallas, we're going to have this out here and now. You
have no right to go out and get yourself killed. It's just not
fair. Even if you don't care for your own sake, you should be
thinking about me."

Stoudenmire just smiled and shook his head, thoroughly
amused by her petulant little tantrum. The thought of getting
killed had never entered his mind. The likelihood was so far-
fetched that it was almost laughable. "Kate, you're gettin'

goosebumps where it's not called for. Whenever I start something, I generally manage to finish it."

"Dallas Stoudenmire, don't you dare take that tone with me! I won't be treated like a simpering little schoolgirl, not by you or anyone else. And while we're at it, you might as well know that I didn't get married just to become a grass widow before I've even gotten used to sleeping with a man."

"C'mon, Kate. You're acting like a spoiled brat, yet you want me to treat you like a woman. You know a man can't turn his back on a job and walk off. Not and live with himself."

"You would if you loved me! Don't you understand, Dallas? I want a live husband, not a dead hero. If you loved me, you'd take me away from here this very day, before something terrible happens."

Stoudenmire rubbed his forehead with growing exasperation. "That's what I'm trying to tell you. Nothing's gonna happen. Not to me leastways. Why can't you get that through your head?"

Huge tears welled up in Kate's eyes, and she hid her face in her hands. "Oh, Dallas, please take me away from this horrible town. Please. I just don't know how much more I can stand."

Stoudenmire came around the table and took her in his arms, tenderly consoling her. But the more he talked the harder she cried, and it seemed like a losing proposition. Then a curious thing happened. Irritating as her nagging had become, something about Kate's utter defenselessness aroused him, making his breath come short and fast. Switching tactics, he began to kiss the soft hair at the nape of her neck and, after a moment, started fondling her breasts. At first she lay rigid and unyielding in his arms; then she slowly began to respond, and a hungry little moan escaped her lips.

"Oh, God, it's been so long. I thought I'd just shrivel up and die waiting for you to touch me again."

Stoudenmire kissed her gently, rubbing his hands lightly along her thigh. "I know. I'm a damn fool to get so wrapped up in a job. But everything'll be all right now. You'll see.

There's nothin' at the office that can't wait, and we've got all afternoon to ring those bells any way you want."

Lifting her in his arms, he felt Kate nuzzle softly against his shoulder. Women were strange creatures, so easy to neglect and so damned miserable to live with when they weren't being bedded properly. Maybe an afternoon of diddling every now and then was just what she needed. Certainly it would keep her spirits shored up, and that alone would make it worthwhile. Come to think of it, a matinee here and there wouldn't do him any harm either.

But even as he carried her toward the bedroom, he knew it wouldn't change things for him. The job still had to be done.

2

Ed Banning sipped at the whiskey, only vaguely aware that the henna-haired whore had snuggled closer to his lean body. She had been working on him for nearly an hour without noticeable results, and it seemed apparent she would have to go some to earn her keep tonight. Yet the gang boss made no sign that he wanted her to stop, and the girl never once slackened her efforts. She had seen what happened to other whores who couldn't get it up for Banning, and her instinct for survival was too finely honed to take chances like that. But as her fingers teasingly probed his body, she wished mightily that his rod could become as hard as his face. Around the house, the girls had coined a saying for men like this. *Stone face—soft tool*. And with the exception of a wooden Indian, she couldn't think of anyone who had a better claim to the title than this unresponsive turd sharing her bed at the moment.

Boss Banning was a man with a wide assortment of problems, most of which remained obscured behind an aloof, somewhat haughty manner. The outward, more obvious troubles had to do with the threat to his control of the town. He was a lifelong believer in the process of corruption and deeply suspicious of those who advocated the straight and narrow. From his warped perspective, men were greedy,

selfish, lacking in either scruples or anything even remotely
akin to brotherhood. While he hadn't invented the rules, he
was a master of the game and found it well suited to his
ruthless nature. Corruption and fear were the tools of his
trade, employed mercilessly in his drive to dominate those
around him. The strong ruled the weak, just as it should be;
the only part of the earth inherited by the meek was the six
feet that marked their passing. And until Dallas Stoudenmire came to town, the essential weakness of other men had
served him well.

But on this particular night, Banning's thoughts were
focused on a problem that had little to do with politics and
forthright lawmen. While he would be the last to admit it, the
gang leader was a man of flawed character. The obsession
with power that governed his life was merely a manifestation
of some inner compulsion; the need to be accepted as a man of
substance and stature. His origins were of the dirt poor,
beans and sowbelly variety, and within him smoldered the
effects of having been born on the wrong side of the blanket.
Every facet of his life was tainted by the lowly circumstances
of his birth, and from it sprung a bitter resentment of both
the haves and the have-nots. He despised the masses for their
docile fatalism and hated the wealthy few with the passions
of a man reared amidst constant want. The gritty flintstone
of his life had chipped and flaked with each blow, leaving a
man of choleric malice in the aftermath. As if human warmth
had been seared from his being, he was a man devoid of compassion, even for himself. The only emotions he had ever
known were a hard fist and a stiff prick. So it was that his
life had become a mockery of what other men held sacred,
one in which there was neither feeling nor mercy. In Ed Banning's world, force of will alone prevailed, and strength was
rarely tempered with selfless motives.

Yet something had gone awry in his relentless pursuit of
prominence. The most visible symbol of all he coveted was
denied him, and without it he remained but a pale reflection
of the man he had set out to become.

Never in his life had he lain with a decent woman.

Well-bred girls wanted nothing to do with a man whose very existence was a blasphemy in itself, and since boyhood, his overtures had been met with the casual disdain reserved for those beneath contempt. Instead of the mansion and genteel wife he had envisioned, he constantly deluded himself in the belief that saloon girls could actually be seduced. When even that became too bothersome, he simply returned to the whorehouses. Strangely, he felt some kinship with these soiled ladies of the night, for his own origins were only one step above the kingdom of whores. And although he detested himself for wallowing in such filth, it was almost as if he had come home each time he returned.

But it was far from a satisfying experience. Amidst frowzy women and stale whiskey, he attempted to elude the furies of his personal hell, only to find that a man can never really outdistance the stench of his own soul. That fickle bitch called fate had allowed him to play with crooked dice well enough but loaded them in her own sly way so that he turned up craps with every roll.

There, sipping whiskey and watching a whore sweat over his intractable body, was where Tom Kale found him. When the knock sounded at the door, the redhead hastily covered them both with a sheet, as if modesty dictated that only her partner of the moment be allowed to gaze upon the merchandise.

"Come on in," Banning called. "We're not bashful."

The door opened, and Kale stepped into the room, peering owlishly through the cider glow of the table lamp. "Howdy, boss. Didn't mean to catch you with your pants down, but I've got to see you *pronto*."

Banning untangled himself from the girl and gave her what passed for a smile. "Sugartit, why don't you run down and get us another bottle. Give me ten minutes, and then we'll pick up where we left off."

The whore scrambled from the bed and into a robe, then headed for the door. She was happy for the respite, no matter how brief. Maybe with a little rest the cold bastard would get some lead back in his pecker. Otherwise, she was in for one long, asshole of a night.

When the door closed behind her, Banning's words came like a slap in the face. "You pinheaded sonovabitch! I oughta have you skinned alive. You've got a lot of nerve showin' up here after you let one of them greasers get out alive."

"Boss, you're treein' the wrong squirrel." Kale moved toward the bed, trying his best to look innocent. "Honest to Christ, them greasers looked deader'n old horse turds. There wasn't no reason to think otherwise, and we was in a hurry to get on back to start trailin' that herd outa there."

"I've told you before, you're not paid to think. You're paid to . . ." Banning bit off the words with a sharp click of his teeth. "What the hell are you doing in town? I thought I sent word for you to lay low."

"Sure, I know. But I got somethin' I figured you wanted to hear."

"Well isn't that dandy? Stoudenmire's got you posted, and you come lollygaggin' into town like school had just let out. You fuckin' dingbat, what if he caught you up here whispering in my ear? You figure to talk us both out of jail?"

"Boss, if you'll quit rawhidin' me, I'll say my piece and get on back to the ranch." The foreman sucked up what backbone he had left and met Banning's stare head-on. "Hell, I wouldn't have come in if it wasn't important."

The gang leader snorted derisively and polished off his drink. "All right, Kale. I'm listening. But you'd better make it damned good."

"It's better'n that." Kale leaned over the brass frame at the foot of the bed, grinning like a skunk in a cabbage patch. "I just had me a little sashay across the river, and I found out where them greasers are holdin' the boy we lost in that raid. They got him locked in a shed close by the *hacienda*, and they feed him once a day, just like he was some kind o' pet dog. I was sorta thinkin' me and the boys would scoot in there some night and bring him back to the fold. That'd really teach them Mex bastards a lesson."

"Your thinkin' is gonna get you killed yet." Banning jabbed his finger in Kale's face, and the ramrod backed away from the bed. "I don't want the sonovabitch rescued. I want him dead! He broke once and he'll break again, even if we get him out. They're planning to spring him on us at the inquest, just as sure as you're standin' there. And if they do, we're gonna be up shit creek without a paddle. Understand, Kale? We'll be swingin' on the wrong side of a long rope."

Kale shook his head with a bewildered frown. "Boss, you're gonna have to run that one by again. How can they lynch us for rustlin' Mexican cattle?"

Banning sighed heavily, staring at the foreman with disgust. "The law calls it corroboration. They've got that greaser you missed, and they've got one of our own men. If those two get up in court and tell the same story, then the fact that we rustled those steers will tie us to the killings. In case it slipped your mind, in Texas they hang people for murder. Even if it was greasers."

Kale nodded dumbly, thoroughly convinced they were in mortal danger. The gang leader poured a shot of whiskey and knocked it down in one gulp. Only then did he look back at the bemused ramrod.

"I don't care how you do it, but I want you to make sure neither of 'em gets to that inquest on his feet. If you miss this time, don't bother coming back. That's my last warning, and you're a dead man if you don't deliver the bacon this trip out."

Kale didn't even bother to argue the point. Banning held the case ace, and only a fool bet into a sure-fire lock. The ramrod simply nodded and walked from the room.

Banning watched him out the door, then settled back against the pillows. No damn wonder he couldn't get up a boner lately, what with Stoudenmire breathing down his neck and numbskulls like Kale stepping in shit everytime they turned around. Thinking about it reminded him of the redhead, and he began listening for her footstep. Maybe the little bitch had thought up a new trick while she was gone. If she knew what was good for her, she had better come up with something. His pole needed greasing, and this goddamn

waiting around for her to get it hard was enough to set a
man's teeth on edge.

3

The day of the inquest was overcast and unusually muggy,
a bad sign according to those who believed in such things.
Tension among the townspeople was thicker than ever, and
as the final hour approached, a crowd began to gather on
the plaza. Stoudenmire's hopes of holding the hearing without a bunch of hotheads jamming the streets were fast dwindling. The people of El Paso had as much at stake as the
Mexicans, maybe more if violence erupted, and they fully
intended to be in on the showdown.

When it became known that a time for the inquest had finally been set, word circulated through town that an army of
Mexicans planned to attend the hearing. Like most rumors,
nobody knew if this one was true or not, but it was enough
to make grown men lay awake at night. The town began to
bristle with armed men, carrying not just pistols but a regular arsenal of rifles and scatterguns that hadn't seen use since
the last Indian scare. The stage was set for a bloody war, one
the Americans couldn't hope to win, and Stoudenmire suddenly awoke to the fact that he desperately needed help.

Bracing Mayor Porter two nights past, he had demanded
official action of some sort. The army had already shown its
reluctance to interfere in civilian matters; and on the face of
it, that left only the Texas Rangers. Porter had no choice but
to approve the marshal's request and promptly fired off a wire
to Austin appealing for reinforcements. Once again, the aging politico found himself unable to guarantee the safety of
his own town. Perhaps Ed Banning would raise hell about
calling in state police, but under the circumstances, their op-
tions seemed severely limited.

After a flurry of telegraph messages between Porter and
the capital, the governor had finally authorized his request.
But there was considerable resentment in Austin about the
whole affair, and Porter was given to understand that he had

better straighten the mess out once and for all, and be damned quick about it. Otherwise, the governor would declare martial law and dump the entire nest of worms right in the army's lap.

The Ranger company had arrived late last night on the evening train. This time they were commanded by no less a veteran than Capt. Frank McCormak, and it was clear that there would be no repetition of the salt war fiasco. Though McCormak and a goodly number of his men were old friends, Stoudenmire found them strangely distant. Their attitude inferred that he, like everyone else in El Paso, had his own bone to pick. With so many factions in contention, the Rangers simply couldn't afford to take sides, and McCormak made it clear that, unless violence broke out, his company would remain in the background.

When Stoudenmire attempted to brief him on the Bannings and the political struggle underlying the conflict with the Mexicans, Capt. McCormak had cut him off short. The Rangers were interested in safeguarding the citizens of El Paso, and nothing more. The political bickering among the town leaders was none of their concern, and Stoudenmire would just have to skin that cat the best way he could. The marshal had turned on his heel and walked off, thoroughly baffled by McCormak's contemptuous manner. So far as he was concerned, the Rangers would be about as much use as a busted paddle, and he had the very distinct feeling that it was going to be all upstream from here on out.

The hour for the inquest was drawing near, and as the crowd on the plaza continued to swell in number, Stoudenmire found himself growing more apprehensive by the moment. This deal had about it everything necessary for the worst massacre since the Alamo, yet there wasn't a damn thing he could do to head it off. Worrying about Kate, and Ramón, and how to nail the Bannings had been enough for any man, not to mention the subtle pressure from Seth Hart and his crowd. But wondering if the Rangers were going to sit on their thumbs until it was too late had hatched a quandary that left him surly and foul-tempered. If the bastards weren't anything more than official observers then they should have stayed in east Texas, where the battles had already been fought. Still, their presence alone might put the damper on a few hotheads, and right now, he would take all the help he could get. Folks always talked about not looking a gift horse in the mouth, and in this instance it seemed to fit.

Abruptly, his sullen mood was broken when yells went up outside that the Mexicans were coming. Stepping to the door, Stoudenmire watched with some amazement as Ramón drove up in a buggy, surrounded by nearly fifty mounted *vaqueros*. The Mexicans presented quite a formidable appearance with their wide brimmed, floppy hats, bandoliers crossed over their chests, and rifles resting on the pommel of each saddle. They plainly meant business, and if anybody was fool enough to try crossing them, there would be a whole batch of new widows in El Paso tonight.

Walking toward the buggy, Stoudenmire gestured at the *caporal's* escort. *"¿Que pasa, Ramón?"* Such a show of force is indeed surprising. I thought we had agreed to keep this affair peaceful."

Ramón was dressed in the traditional short black jacket with large silver coins for buttons, and his pants had a faint silver pattern woven down each side. Despite a slight pallor to his features, he appeared as fiery as ever, and it seemed hard to believe that he was still recuperating from the murderous wounds of a fortnight past. He looked like a young *caballero* on his way to a fiesta, though on closer examination, there was something older and infinitely sadder about his eyes.

Leaning forward, his voice dropped to a near whisper. *"Hombre*, much has happened this day. None of it good. The *gringo* prisoner was to be brought from Don Miguel's *hacienda* to Paso del Norte early this morning. I regret to say that he and his guards were ambushed by *yanquis pistoleros*. He was killed with the first shot, and it goes without saying that he has been silenced forever concerning who is behind the *conspiración* among your people."

"Dirty bastards." Stoudenmire's eyes narrowed, and he

unconsciously glanced in the direction of the Coliseum Saloon.

"*Sí*. That is the least of what they are." Ramón's mouth was set in a tight, thin line. "Without the *gringo*, I fear our cause is hopeless, but I am still willing to testify. As for these *vaqueros*, I had no choice. Don Salazar refused to allow me across the river without a large escort. You would do well to caution your people, for after this morning, these men would gladly spill *gringo* blood."

The lawman was silent for a time, gazing thoughtfully at the armed horsemen. "*Un momento, amigo.* Let me have a word with the Ranger leader."

Turning, he walked toward the Rangers, who were standing in a small knot beside the jail. Capt. McCormak saw him approaching and stepped forward a few paces.

Stoudenmire gave it to him straight, without any frills. "Frank, those *vaqueros* are spoiling for a fight. We can go into the reasons later, if you're interested. Right now, we've got to keep 'em apart from the local hotheads, or we're gonna have more dead bodies around here than you've seen since Shiloh."

McCormak studied the Mexicans for a moment, then looked back at the lawman. "I reckon we can help you that much. I'll put it down in my report as a preventive measure."

Stoudenmire's mouth twisted in a sardonic grin. "You're a real sport, Frank. The next time you see the governor, be sure and tell him I said to kiss my ass."

Wheeling about, he returned to the buggy and helped Ramón to dismount. The Mexican hobbled a bit from his wounds, but he was game as ever, and Stoudenmire led him toward the coroner's office on the north side of the plaza. McCormak quickly brought the Rangers forward and formed a line separating the *vaqueros* from the townspeople. In a loud, contentious voice, he announced that no one would be allowed inside the hearing room except officials and witnesses. A sullen groan went up from the crowd, but nobody made a move in the direction taken by Stoudenmire and the *caporal*. The Rangers alone would have been enough, but with fifty armed greasers right behind them, it was a little more than anyone cared to tackle on an empty stomach.

Jim Gillette fell in on the other side of Ramón, and as the three men neared the coroner's office, Gus Krempkau, the court interpreter, stepped outside. After being introduced to the witness, Krempkau briefly outlined the inquest procedure, then turned and started back toward the hearing room.

Suddenly a volley of gunfire erupted from the opposite side of the plaza and a storm of lead swept over the four men. Spurts of dust mushroomed off the back of Ramón's jacket, and he staggered on a few steps as if nothing had happened. Then his knees buckled, and he slowly toppled over, dead before he hit the ground. Directly in front of him a few paces, Krempkau clutched his gut, his eyes gone wide and horribly white with shock. The force of the slug had slammed him up against the building, and he very gingerly slid down the wall. But even before he touched the boardwalk, his head lolled over at a crazy angle and he slumped forward in a pool of blood.

With the outbreak of gunfire, the townspeople scattered like fat quail, running for the nearest cover as fast as their legs would pump. Capt. McCormak and his Rangers fanned out in an arc before the *vaqueros*, covering them with cocked Winchesters. While they were outnumbered, the Rangers had the drop on the Mexicans, and for the moment no one seemed inclined to push the matter further.

Stoudenmire and Gillette had instinctively dropped to the ground when Ramón was hit, jerking their sixguns in the same movement. But within a split second, they came up firing, racing across the plaza in a dodging, bobbing run. The bushwhackers had split and run by the time the lawmen reached the opposite corner, presenting them with something of a problem. Then Stoudenmire caught sight of Tom Kale and George Campbell hurrying down a side street and took off at a dead lope. Turning the corner at the end of the block, they saw Kale already mounted and spurring south out of town. Campbell's horse had suddenly gone skittish, rearing and backing away as the former marshal fought to catch a stirrup.

Gillette opened fire on the fleeing Kale, emptying his pistol in a staccato roar. Just then Campbell abandoned his horse and turned to fight, triggering three shots at the lawmen. Stoudenmire's arm came level, and his Colt spouted flame. Deliberately, with precise care, he stitched a pattern of bright red dots across Campbell's shirt front. At each shot, Campbell's body jerked uncontrollably, and he lurched backwards, sinking lower and lower until the last slug pounded him into the dust.

A blue haze of gunsmoke hung in the still air as the lawmen began shucking empties and reloading. Without a word, they came together and turned to stare toward the river. In the distance they saw Tom Kale flogging his horse through the shallow ford, headed southeast into Chihuahua.

4

Stoudenmire and Gillette returned to the plaza only to find themselves confronted with an even graver situation. Townspeople were scurrying about the stores and buildings fronting the square, preparing to defend El Paso. Everyone fully expected the *vaqueros* to begin shooting at any moment, and not a man among them doubted that the Mexicans in Paso del Norte would come running after hearing gunfire. Barricades of trade goods and furniture were being erected on the boardwalk outside a number of stores, and already the plaza seemed encircled by an ominous ring of gun barrels.

The marshal took only a moment to gauge the situation, then turned to his deputy. "Jim, hotfoot it around the plaza and tell those nitwits to get inside and stay there. The man that fires the first shot will answer to me personally. You tell 'em he won't like the way I ask questions, either."

Gillette moved off at a brisk trot, and Stoudenmire headed across the square toward McCormak and his Rangers. But before he had gone ten paces, he heard his name called and turned to find the town leaders bearing down on him like a phalanx of scalded owls. Mayor Porter headed the delegation and close on his heels was the full city council, including Seth Hart and Doc Cummings.

"Marshal Stoudenmire, this madness has gone far enough!" Porter's tone was one of outraged indignation. "You're the one that brought these Mexicans into our town, and I demand that you resolve this dreadful affair immediately. I warn you, sir, we won't stand by and watch our people slaughtered like so many sheep."

Stoudenmire advanced on the jowly politician with a swiftness that rocked him back on his heels. "Porter you're nothing but a conniving old blowhard, and I've had about all of you I'm gonna take. Lip off to me once more, and I'll break your back. That's a promise."

Porter swallowed hard, wilting under the lawman's brutal glare. When Stoudenmire saw that the mayor had run out of juice, he wheeled around and started off. But Seth Hart's gruff rumble again brought him up short.

"Marshal, that won't cut it. We're the elected leaders of this town, and we have a right to know what you're planning. After all, we're not talking about jailing a bunch of rowdy drunks. Man, this whole town could be put to the torch!"

Stoudenmire spun on him, freezing the miller in his tracks with a flinty look. "Mister, you've sorta forgot who's callin' the shots around here. When I took the job, we had the understanding you'd stay off my back. The only conditions were that I run Banning out of town and get the Mexicans cooled off. Maybe it's not as neat and pretty as you'd like it, but that's what I'm doing. Now if you'll just button up your pants and quit dribblin' nonsense, I'll get on about my business."

Doc Cummings stepped forward, grasping the lawman's arm as he turned to leave. "Dallas, don't go off halfcocked like that. These men are only trying to help. They're concerned about the town and trying to figure out what our next move should be. Just slack off and listen to their ideas for a minute. That won't hurt anything."

The marshal shrugged his hand off, scowling at the other

men as if they were worrisome gnats. "Doc, I don't have time to listen to a bunch of politicians blather about if maybe and how come. While they're talking, this whole goddamn deal could blow up in our faces. I know what needs to be done, and as soon as things get quieted down around here, I'll do it. In the meantime, I've got no use for a lot of preachin' from these bullshit artists."

When a crestfallen look came over Cumming's face, Stoudenmire clasped the older man's shoulder. "Listen, Doc, I appreciate what you're trying to do. But if you really want to help, you can go over to the house and keep Kate company. I left Tige with her, and that ought to be enough in case of trouble. But it'd sure take a load off my mind if I knew you were with her."

Cummings just nodded, clearly hurt that he was being elbowed aside like some doddering old man. But Stoudenmire didn't have time to spare his feelings. Out of the corner of his eye, the lawman saw that things were coming to a head between the Mexicans and the Rangers. Without another word, he took off across the plaza at a fast dogtrot.

Though the Rangers still had the upper hand, it was something akin to having a tiger by the tail. Outnumbered as they were, the peace officers wouldn't have a chance if the Mexicans ever went for their guns, and that was exactly what had brought the kettle to boil. As he approached, Stoudenmire heard McCormak arguing with a *vaquero* who appeared to be the spokesman for the Mexicans. When the Marshal came to a halt at the Ranger's elbow, McCormak turned away from the *vaquero* with a troubled frown.

"Dallas, we've got ourselves a real pisscutter. I offered to let these greasers ride out if they'd just lay their guns down, but it's no dice. This bird says they'd as soon die fighting right here as get shot in the back before they reached the river."

Stoudenmire looked from McCormak to the Mexican and back again. "Can't say as I blame him much. In case you hadn't noticed, this town's pretty damn close to being a shootin' gallery."

McCormak glanced around the plaza, and his eyes

squinched up like an old coon. "Maybe so. But we better do somethin' *pronto* or these boys are gonna get tired of pala-verin' and start doing some shootin' of their own."

"Tell you the truth, Frank, I don't know what's holdin' 'em back. If it was me, I'd have shot my way out of here ten min-utes ago." The lawman's gaze again wandered over to the Mexican, who was staring at them with a hostile frown. "Tell you what. Let me have a crack at him. Maybe we talk the same language."

McCormak just shrugged and stepped aside. Stoudenmire turned to face the *vaquero,* gripped by an awareness that what was said in the next few seconds might easily leave El Paso's streets littered with dead. This was the crunch old tim-ers liked to talk about, and it was a damned uneasy spot to be standing in, no matter how big a man's boots were.

"*Está día triste, amigo.* Very sad. We share a great bur-den in the death of your *caporal*, and no one mourns his pass-ing more than I."

"Don't call me friend, *gringo*." The Mexican spat the words with an angry hiss. "You have a peculiar way of re-maining alive while your friends are being killed."

"Perhaps. But your leader believed me to be *simpático* to your cause, and he was not a man easily fooled." Stouden-mire felt his mouth go dry as he prepared to turn the cor-ner. "Still that is neither here nor there in this thing of the guns. The *tejanos soldados* want only to see you safely across the river, and they will guarantee your lives with their own."

"*¡Válgame Dios!* You must think me *loco*." The *vaquero* gestured toward the coroner's office, where the bodies of Ramón Vazquez and Gus Krempkau lay as they had fallen. "There is the truth of what comes to those who trust *grin-gos*. We keep our guns! Let us say no more about it. Anyone who tries to take them from us will pay dearly."

The lawman knew a dead end when he saw it and, on the spur of the moment, decided it was whole hog or none. "Let us compromise then, *señor*. You may keep your guns, but the *tejanos* will accompany you to the river. That way we can watch each other. If you are truly the *teniente* of Ramón Vazquez, then you will see the wisdom in what I propose."

The other *vaqueros* had been listening closely to this exchange, and they now edged forward, awaiting some reaction from their new leader. But before the Mexican could answer, Frank McCormak stepped between the two men.

"Stoudenmire, you just hold your horses. Before I take them greasers anywhere, they're gonna give up those guns. There ain't no two ways about it."

"Whatever you say, Frank. It's your tea party." The lawman moved back a pace and waved McCormak toward the Mexicans. "Just walk right in there and collect their rifles. There's only fifty of 'em, and I seem to remember you always did like long odds."

The debate ended right there. Capt. Frank McCormak decided to temporarily join forces with the *vaqueros* and get them the hell out of El Paso. It had been a trying kind of day, and his only regret was that he couldn't leave with them. Chasing bank robbers and horse thieves back on the Pecos was beginning to look like real soft duty.

While Ramón's body was being loaded in the buggy, Stoudenmire pledged to the *vaqueros* that his killer would not go unpunished. They didn't say much, and he let the matter drop there. But he knew the promise would get talked about across the border, and it might just hold the Mexicans in check until Kale could be caught.

When the *vaqueros* were mounted, Stoudenmire and McCormak led the procession across the plaza. Gillette fell in at the rear and the Rangers rode shotgun on either flank. Once out of the center of town, everyone began breathing easier. The real danger was past, and the Rangers were no less relieved than the Mexicans. Moments later, they reached the river without incident, and the *vaqueros* spurred their horses through the shallow stream. Watching them cross to Paso del Norte, Stoudenmire reflected back over the morning and decided it had been a sorry mess for everyone involved. Especially Ramón Vazquez.

Back on the plaza, the townspeople slowly emerged from the buildings under a sky that was curiously chilling to the bones. They still clutched their guns, like little boys playing at being soldiers, and when they spoke, there was a trace of false bravado to their words. The greasers were gone for the moment, well enough, but few believed the trouble would end there. The murder of the Mexican *caporal* was certain to bring reprisals. Maybe not tomorrow, or the day after, or even the day after that. But it would come.

5

Stoudenmire stepped from the courthouse, crossed South Oregon, and headed back toward his office. He had just sworn out a federal warrant for Tom Kale. The next step was to hunt the backshooter down and capture him. Or kill him. That was up to Kale. So far as the lawman was concerned, it made little difference which way it went. If the bastard resisted, Stoudenmire meant to kill him, with no wasted motion. With or without Kale, he would still get the Bannings. Even if he had to call them out in public where they had no choice but to fight or get laughed out of town. Justice could be served in many ways, and when a man started out killing snakes, he couldn't be too squeamish about his methods.

But as he strode along streets that now seemed hauntingly quiet, it came to the marshal that he was letting his temper get the upper hand. Though Kale deserved no more mercy than a rabid dog, there were factors that overshadowed killing him out of sheer revenge. Alive and kicking, he represented a greater threat to the Bannings. On a witness stand in court, the ramrod could put a rope around Ed Banning's neck without batting an eye. It was entirely possible he even had a few juicy tidbits to relate about the political shenanigans going on in town, which was another can of worms that badly needed opening. And nothing would warm the heart quite so much as watching the Bannings accompany Kale to the gallows. That was for damn sure!

Reflecting on it, Stoudenmire decided there was much to

be said for the majesty of the law. Without it, the world would be a dog-eat-dog slaughterpen, with the little guy coming out on the short end of the stick everytime. Not that it wasn't much the same even with the law, but at least the fainthearts had some chance so long as there were courts and men willing to pin on a star. There was even something wholesome about an old fashioned neck-stretching every now and then. Strange as it sounded, folks went away feeling just a little more civilized after seeing a renegade take the long drop. Just knowing that the covenant of an eye for an eye even existed was somehow reassuring, and when a hired killer like Kale tried walking on air, it made a man think twice about flaunting the rights of others. Naturally, if the men who gave the orders, like the Bannings and Isaac Porter, got strung up in the bargain, it made the law seem all the more invincible. God-like somehow, as if nobody was immune from the rope.

Still, awesome as the formalities of the law might be, there was much to be said for a good, clean bullet just below the brisket. It was neat, saved the state a lot of money and, in the long run, served justice near about as well as a hangman. Folks respected a bullet, too, maybe even more than the rope. And when a fellow started chalking up things like personal satisfaction, there just wasn't anything so deep-down gratifying as putting a slug through some badassed jasper that hadn't gotten the message. Especially a sneaky shitheel like Tom Kale.

Yessir, the law was a good thing. Made people mind their manners and probably converted more heathens into straight-arrow Christians than any Bible-thumper ever thought about. But with snakes like Kale and the Bannings, there was a swifter, more certain law. Which meant that the man wearing the star sort of had to play it by ear. Depending on how the cards fell, some might get hung and some might get shot. Like any sporting proposition, you pays your money and you takes your chances.

Chuckling to himself, Stoudenmire entered the office, noting in the back of his mind that the Rangers had just trooped into a cafe for dinner. The fact that three men had been killed this morning didn't seem to bother their appetites in the slightest. The thought jarred some dim memory of the war, and the lawman remembered how he had always been ravenous as a gaunt wolf after a day on the killing ground. Odd maybe, but nothing startling. Lots of things made men hungry, and if killing happened to whet a man's appetite, that didn't make him some kind of freak. Just different.

Gillette looked up from pouring himself a cup of coffee, his expression just the least bit puzzled. "I sorta figured you'd gone home for dinner. Anything wrong?"

"Nothing that can't be cured I reckon." Stoudenmire eased down in a chair and propped his boots on top the desk. "I'll head home directly. Thought I'd check in with you first."

"Well you needn't have bothered." The deputy took a cautious sip from the steaming mug, then cracked a sly grin. "After you left, I took a little jaunt around town, and it's quiet as a church full of bats. Maybe too much so. But I'll tell you one thing. It's a damn cinch nobody's gonna be visitin' Paso del Norte for a spell."

"If I was you, I wouldn't lay any money on that." Stoudenmire leaned farther back in the chair, locking his hands behind his head. "The way things stand now, I'll be on the other side of the river before nightfall."

"Jesus Christ!" Gillette's startled look was one of sheer bafflement. "What in the raw name of common sense would cause you to do a thing like that?"

"Well, for one thing, I want to have a talk with the *alcalde* over there. See which way he figures his people are gonna jump. For another, I've got it in mind to bring Tom Kale in. Tracking a white man in Mexico won't be hard after what happened here this morning."

Gillette squinted, lifting one eyebrow scornfully. "Dallas, I'm gonna flat-out tell you something. You're out of bounds crossin' the river. Even a US marshal don't have no jurisdiction over the border, and them Rurales are gonna howl like you'd just stuck a hot poker straight up their ass."

The marshall didn't appear too impressed with the argument. "I reckon Ramón's *patrón* will keep the Rurales off my back when he finds out who I'm after."

"In a pig's ass!" Gillette snorted. "Sometimes talkin' to you is like feedin' oats to a dead mule. Even if you run Kale down, the greasers'll likely declare first claim. And to get him back here you're gonna have to fight your way across half of Chihuahua."

"Maybe. Maybe not. But I'm going after him whichever way it works out." Stoudenmire lowered his feet to the floor and began rummaging through the desk drawers. "Ramón got killed because he trusted a *yanqui*, and people over there aren't gonna have any faith in our word until Kale's been measured for a box."

"Pardner, I'm tellin' you for your own good, you'd better chew on this deal for a while. Chances are Mama Stoudenmire's firstborn ain't too popular over there right now. If you keep pushin' your luck, we're liable to have to gather you up with a rake."

The lawman grinned in that cryptic way, like he was thinking of some secret, highly personal joke. "Stranger things have happened. But there's one thing you can't argue. If we're gonna head off a bloodbath along the Rio Grande, then we've got to show that the authorities over here won't condone the killing of Mexicans." Locating a box of shells in a drawer, he paused and began filling the empties in his shell-belt. "Besides, Pedro Vazquez went out on a limb to help me nail the Bannings and lost his nephew in the bargain. I owe the old man, and I mean to pay up."

"Oh, you'll pay all right. Don't fret that." The deputy stared into his coffee mug, as though something profound might be revealed in the dregs. "Trouble is, I've got a feelin' you won't care much for the interest they're gonna ask."

Stoudenmire came around the desk and selected a rifle, then a sawed-off shotgun from the rack on the wall. "Listen, we could sit here jawbonin' till hell freezes over, and it wouldn't change a thing. Unless someone goes after Kale, we might as well shit in one hand and wish in the other. 'Cause

he's not coming back this way. Not as long as he's able to talk
and get the Bannings fitted out for a rope."

Gillette shook his head slowly, searching the marshal's
face for some sign that still eluded him. "Dallas, there's times
you act like some kid that's green an' limber an' full of sap.
Every now and then I get to watchin' you, and it plumb baf-
fles me where the hell you got off to when the good Lord was
handin' out nerves."

"Don't get your bowels in an uproar, Jim. I'll be back before you can say scat. Come to think of it, instead of worrying about me, you oughta light a candle for Mr. Kale."

"Well, you're full growed for a fact, and I reckon your
mammy taught you what teeth was for when she weaned you.
Just make sure you get first bite."

The two men shook hands, and Stoudenmire walked from
the jail. Turning the corner, he headed toward Magoffin Avenue and home, dreading the scene he would face there. After the shootings this morning, the fireworks were sure to go
off the minute he walked in the door. But when Kate found
out he was riding into Chihuahua alone, she would likely
pitch the granddaddy of all screaming fits. Already, he could
hear her pleading with him not to go, snuffling and sobbing,
harping on those lame-brain premonitions of hers.

Women were damned hard to savvy. When they got married, they prayed to the Almighty that they had gotten themselves harnessed to a real man. Then little by little, they tried
to cut his balls off.

CHAPTER SIX

———————

1

Shortly before sundown, Stoudenmire crossed the Rio Grande. The Winchester was snugged down in a scabbard beneath his leg, and the shotgun hung from a rawhide thong over the saddle horn. His chestnut gelding was as frisky as a colt after two weeks on oats and hay, and behind him trailed a packhorse loaded with grub. Like any hunter of dangerous game, the marshal had come prepared.

Running Kale to earth wouldn't be done overnight. The outlaw had a good lead, more than Stoudenmire cared to admit, and had doubtless swung southwest toward the Sierra Madres after circling Paso del Norte. Once in the mountains, he could lose himself for a lifetime, for few there cared if a man was being hunted. Since the time of the Spaniards, the Sierra Madres had been a haven for *bandidos* and *insurrectos* alike; so long as a man tended to his own knitting, there was no safer hideout within a thousand miles in any direction.

Though the lawman had few qualms about the outcome of the hunt, he would have felt even more confident with Tige along. The big dog was like an extra right arm, an infallible sixth sense that never faltered. Without him, it was as if Stoudenmire had left part of himself behind, and it wasn't a good feeling. But where he was headed wasn't a fit place for a dog, or a man either when it came down to cases. Before reaching the mountains, he had to cross vast stretches of desolate wasteland, and just worrying about himself and the horses was going to be chore enough. Besides, Kate needed some sort of protection around the house, and next to a double load of buckshot, Tige had few equals at scaring off uninvited guests.

Right now though, he had other things to worry about. Riding along Paso del Norte's dusty main street, Stoudenmire could feel the villagers' hostility all about him, almost as if their malevolence were alive and breathing deeply of his loathsome scent. Though they refused to look at him directly, he sensed their dark eyes boring holes through his back. It was somewhat the same feeling a stray dog has when he wanders into strange territory, not hunting trouble but pretty damn certain the neighborhood pack is going to give him a good chewing just on general principle. When he reined to a halt before the *alcalde*'s home, the lawman felt a mixture of surprise and relief. That no one had taken a shot at him wasn't just remarkable, it was downright astonishing. As he dismounted, it occurred to Stoudenmire that it might be a sign. A good sign, for a change!

Pedro Vazquez admitted him with the haggard look of a man who has lost that which he treasures most. The *alcalde* was a widower, and after Ramón's parents had died in an epidemic, he had taken the boy to raise. Through the years, they had become like father and son, and Pedro couldn't have been more grief stricken if Ramón had been of his own flesh. But misery was the companion of all men in Mexico, with the exception perhaps of the land-wealthy *hidalgos*. Those who survived learned to bear the pain of life with grace, for within this stoic fatalism lay their only measure of defense against the hardships each must endure. Pedro Vazquez had learned the lesson well over his threescore years, and as he led Stoudenmire inside, his face was a stony mask. Yet beneath this outer serenity, he was a crushed man; it showed in his eyes, vast pools of exquisite sorrow.

Ramón was laid out in the parlor, his face frozen in waxlike tranquillity. The coffin was a simple affair, as unpretentious and as lacking in vanity as the man himself had been. But as Stoudenmire stood over the casket, looking down on the dead man's pallid composure, it struck him that Ramón in death wasn't anything like the fiery young *vaquero* he had grown to admire. Maybe death was the great leveler after all, just like the wise men said. Perhaps when a man went under, he left the bad things behind, all the heartaches and inequities that seemed to dog a fellow's tracks while he was alive and kicking. How else could you account for that petrified smile on Ramón's face? If ever a man crossed over with reason to hate a goodly share of those left behind, it was this young Mexican. And the peaceful calm spread over his features right now was a far cry from the rage he must have felt in those last moments. It was damned strange, more than a man could rightly come to grips with. Like something out of a jumbled-up dream that didn't make much sense but seemed real as hell all the same.

Still, whichever way the dice fell, Ramón was long past caring. The warm climate made it unwise to keep the dead above ground longer than overnight, and by morning he would have a fight of another kind on his hands. Earth to earth and dust to dust, the preachers always said. But the fellow being turned into worm meat might see it a damned sight different. Especially since he was planted six feet deep and couldn't outrun the slimy little bastards.

Villagers filed past the coffin in a steady stream, and a priest was mumbling and waving his hands around like a rainmaker in a dutch oven. Watching them, the lawman wondered who they pitied the most, Ramón or themselves. The young *caporal* would soon be buried and forgotten, but they'd still be trudging along in the same old sea of shit. Before he had time to think that one through, Pedro Vazquez took his arm and guided him toward the study.

After seating Stoudenmire, the *alcalde* went to stand

before the open window. Gazing out into the dusky nightfall, he seemed worn and beaten, a tired old man who had
outlived everything that mattered. His shoulders slumped,
giving him a stooped appearance, as if the burden was simply
too much to carry farther. The lawman regarded him silently,
sharing his remorse to a small degree, yet somehow compli-
mented that the *jefe* would allow him to see beneath the
passive mask. Then the older man's bent figure straightened,
and Stoudenmire realized that it had been only a momentary
lapse. When Pedro Vazquez turned, he was himself again.

"I have often thought that the good die before their time,"
Vazquez said, taking a seat across from the Texan. "After today I am convinced of it."

"In my country we have a saying, *Alcalde*. Only cream
and bastards rise to the top. So it is with death. Sometimes
evil flourishes on the bones of those who least deserve to
go under."

"There is much truth to that. Yet I wonder if it is *mala
suerte* or did God intend it that way? Perhaps the good ones
have merely lost the instinct for survival in this harsh land."

"Perhaps. But that is a question best left to those wiser
than myself." Stoudenmire thumped his head with a deprecating gesture. "I am a practical man, *sin astuto*, and for me
the direct path is the most agreeable. When I see a snake, I
kill it, and in time there will be no snakes where I walk."

Pedro Vazquez gave him an appraising look. "Senor, it
comes to me that there is more than one kind of cunning. I
believe you are attempting to tell me something that resists
words."

The lawman nodded, returning the old man's quizzical
gaze with a solemn frown. "*Jefe*, so long as I remain above
ground. I will blame myself for Ramón's death. Had I been
wiser, he would not be lying in the next room at this moment. But while I live, those who killed him will sleep in fear.
Tonight I begin the search for the one who actually held the
gun."

The *alcalde*'s eyes brightened and he came up on the edge
of his chair. "*¡Madre de Dios!* It is what I had hoped to hear

you say. After this morning, I am convinced that revenge is a good thing. When we heard the *gringo asesino* was riding south, I prayed it would be you who took his trail." Then the old man leaned forward, giving Stoudenmire a fatherly tap on the knee. "But on this other thing, you do yourself an injustice, my friend. Ramón was a man, and he conducted himself as a leader should. What he did was done for our people, and your influence played only a small part. Do not reproach yourself. He died fighting for our cause, and few men go to their grave with such honor."

Before the marshal could answer, a knock sounded at the door, and Don Miguel Salazar stepped into the room. Striding forward he embraced Pedro Vazquez, mumbling condolences in a choked voice. Watching them, Stoudenmire decided it would be a tossup as to which one had loved Ramón the most. Then they separated, and the *alcalde* began talking so fast the lawman could catch only a word here and there. But he heard his name mentioned a couple of times, and when Don Miguel glanced in his direction, it became apparent that their discussion centered on him. After a final exchange, *el patrón* smiled and came forward, offering his hand.

"I have heard much of the *yanqui* whose words are untainted, and I am honored to meet you. Pedro tells me you are going after Ramón's killer, and for this gesture you will be doubly honored among our people."

"*Gracias.* But it is not a gesture, señor. It is a debt owed to a brave man."

"*Sí.* He was that above all else. A man of courage." The *hidalgo's* eyes glistened and he swallowed hurriedly. "But you chose a bad night to ride south, my friend. Chihuahua is no place for an *americano* to be caught alone. Not tonight, perhaps never."

Stoudenmire's expression remained firm. "That is a chance I will have to risk. To delay longer would mean losing the man's trail entirely."

"Yes, I see your point." Don Miguel grew thoughtful for a moment, then suddenly clapped his hands together. "*¡Caramba!* Perhaps there is a way after all. Señor Stoudenmire, tonight you will be a guest at my *hacienda*. Since it is south of here, it is in the direction you travel. Tomorrow I will provide you with the one thing that insures success on any hunt. Regardless of the quarry."

Stoudenmire didn't have the least idea what he was talking about, but there was no reason to refuse. He had to spend the night somewhere, and so long as it was headed south, one spot was as good as another. The two Mexicans chatted a few minutes longer, then *el patrón* indicated it was time they be on their way.

Pedro Vazquez walked them to the door and took the lawman's big paw between his hands. "Ramón will rest easy knowing that you ride in his place. *Vaya con Dios, mi hijo.*"

Only after he had mounted and pulled the chestnut abreast of Don Miguel's stallion did the *alcalde*'s words register on Stoudenmire. Wasn't that something! That old bugger calling him son. He'd been dubbed lots of things for taking a man's trail, but usually it was closer to sonovabitch. Maybe things were looking up after all.

2

Although Jim Gillette hadn't let on to Stoudenmire, he was just a little put out with the lawman's brash scheme. Maybe the marshal's plan to sweet-talk the *alcalde* would work. And maybe it wouldn't. It seemed just as likely that the stubborn German would get himself killed poking around Paso del Norte, and that would really tear things. One thing was sure, the greasers wouldn't be real fond of the man who had gotten Ramón Vazquez killed. Expecially when he was the same one that had gotten those *vaqueros* perforated in an ambush only a couple of weeks back. Where Mexicans were concerned there was a time to be tough and a time to be smart. Some men never lived long enough to learn which was which. But right now, everybody on the other side of that river had a mean hair up his ass, and it would have been a dilly of a time to lay back and play it smart.

Still, there was more at stake here than Stoudenmire's

neck. There was a whole damn town sitting on a short fuse, not to mention a deputy that couldn't hardly work up a good spit. Though he had no qualms about handling roughnecks or diving into a gunfight, this deal was just a bit over his head. The only consolation in the whole sorry mess was that the Rangers were still in town, and if the greasers came storming across the river, he would damn sure dump it square in their laps. But what the hell would he do if they suddenly decided to move on?

While he was ruminating on that unpleasant dilemma, Doc Cummings walked through the door. The storekeeper was just on his way to supper, but he had stopped in on the off chance he could finagle an invitation to one of Kate's meals.

"Evenin', Deputy." He gave the office a quick once over. "Dallas already gone home?"

"Last time I heard, he was headed for points south." Gillette's tone was dry, slightly caustic. "First stop bein' Paso del Norte."

"Paso del Norte!" Cummings parroted incredulously. "What in the name of Christ is he doing over there?"

"Funny. That's the same thing I asked him." The old lawdog grinned like his teeth hurt. "Said he was gonna pour a little honey over their *jefe,* and then he figured to beat the bushes for Tom Kale."

"Well kiss my ass! Doesn't he know a man could get killed that way?"

"Your guess is about as good as mine, I reckon. Dallas is double wolf on guts and savvy, but sometimes I get to wonderin' if he hasn't got more of one than he does the other."

Cummings batted his eyes nervously, thoroughly perplexed by the whole affair. "Damn, I grant you Kale has to be caught, but trailin' him across the border is overdoing it. Dallas oughta know better'n anyone else that he's got no jurisdiction over there."

"He knows, right enough. Just didn't pay it no mind." The deputy spat a black stream of tobacco juice in the general direction of a spittoon. "Thing about Dallas is, he don't like

folks fartin' around in his business. Once they do, he'll chase
'em clean to hell and back. I got an idea Tom Kale is gonna
learn that the hard way."

"Well, everyone wants to see Kale's neck stretched. But
tryin' to take him in Mexico is nothin' but damn foolishness.
Right now those greasers figure any white man is fair game."
The storekeeper dropped into a chair, staring morosely at the
wall. "Besides, it's the Bannings we oughta be worryin'
about. Kale's just hired help."

"I don't know as I'd get all bent out of shape worryin'
about Dallas. Tanglin' with him is sorta like kickin' a porcu-
pine. You generally come away wishin' you hadn't." Gillette
grew silent for a moment, puzzling over something that had
only just now occurred to him. "Course, maybe I was a little
too quick to fault Dallas. Appears to me he figured the Bannings could wait. 'Bout the only thing that's gonna put a
damper on them Mexicans is to get the fellow that actually
done the killin'. Lookin' at it that way, I reckon Kale sorta
comes up with a ring in his nose."

Cummings was becoming testier by the moment. "Well I
don't know as I'd buy that. We're facing a bad situation
here, and Dallas has no business off chasin' around Chihuahua. Brother-in-law or not, he was hired to protect this
community, and his place is in El Paso. All I've got to say is
that his plan better work, or we'll all be out on our ear."

"Mr. Cummings, where I come from, folks used to say
hindsight ain't no better'n hind tit. Dallas did what he thought
was best, and I reckon we'll just have to wait and see how it
pans out. Come to think of it, we haven't got a helluva lot of
choice. Once he gets his mind made up, he's mighty hard to
swing around."

"Damned if that's not the truth. I never met a man so all
fired set in his ways. Now you take this Banning thing, for
instance. We tried to keep him from crowding them so fast.
But no, he had to shove 'em up against the wall. Bang! Bang!
Bang! And now look where it's got us."

The deputy eyed him quizzically, wondering if the man
knew the first thing about bringing law to a border town. And

making it stick. "Just offhand, I'd say that Dallas has got 'em suckin' wind. Every move they've made has turned sour, and if he brings Kale in, their goose is cooked. Course, Dallas would just as soon shoot 'em as send 'em to jail. Can't say as I blame him much."

"Well let me tell you something, deputy. He might not get the chance to do either one." The storekeeper hunched forward, lowering his voice to a conspiratorial whisper. "Seth Hart says he has it on good authority that they're gonna try to kill Dallas just as soon as this Mexican scare eases off. Now, what d'ya think of that?"

Gillette had been a lawman too long to get in a dither over small town rumors. "Seems to me they're going about it bassackwards. Why not just have the city council fire him? Solves the whole problem."

"Not accordin' to Seth Hart, it don't. If they fired him, it'd turn into a political bombshell, and come election time, their boys might just get eased out of city hall. Besides, Dallas is still a US marshal, and gettin' him off the city payroll wouldn't mean a hill of beans."

"Yeah, I can see that. But damned if it don't seem like killin' him would stir up an even bigger political rhubarb. I mean, it ain't like nobody'd have to be told who did it."

Cummings tapped the desk with his finger, grinning like a bloated old cat that had just swallowed the last canary. "There's where you're missin' the boat. People just naturally give a fellow the benefit of the doubt. Even a no-account bastard like Ed Banning. They're too goddamn lazy to get all worked up over something that can't be proved. Especially if there's a chance it might get them shot, too."

The deputy pursed his lips, mulling it over for a moment. "From what you say, it's a matter of who eats who first. That being the case, if I was Dallas, I'd get Banning before he got me. There's all kinds o' ways to egg a feller into a gunfight, you know."

The storekeeper's head jerked around and his eyes widened. "You're talkin' about forcin' a man to fight just so you can use the law to kill. That's a little cold-blooded, isn't it?"

"Why not? You think the sonovabitch is gonna be man-nered about it when he has Dallas backshot in some alley?"

"No, I don't suppose he would. But that doesn't excuse us-ing the law to suit your own ends. I've got a strong hunch the respectable people in this town wouldn't condone that kind of thing. Not for a minute."

"Shit fire and save the grease!" Gillette's rubbery mouth twisted in an amused grin. "Man, you've got a lot to learn about the law. It's not what's written down in books. It's what men like Stoudenmire can enforce at the end of a gun. Any-time you don't believe it, you just try pullin' the props out from under the man holdin' that gun. That's the day you'll quit havin' law. *Muy pronto.*"

"Well, that's neither here nor there, is it?" Cummings was on the verge of losing an argument, and he decided to pull in his horns. "All I know is that Dallas acts too hastily some-times, and one of these days, it's going to be his downfall. Assuming he makes it back from Chihuahua in one piece, tell him I said he'd better watch his step around the Bannings."

"I'll do that very thing." The deputy smiled wryly. "Dallas'll be right proud to know you're lookin' after his wel-fare."

Cummings saw nothing to be gained by arguing further with the contentious old lawdog. Bidding the deputy good night, he walked from the office and headed uptown. Maybe Dallas Stoudenmire didn't know enough to stay at home where he belonged, but that was no reason to let good food go to waste.

Quickening his pace, the storekeeper hurried toward Magoffin Avenue, savoring the smell of Kate's cooking as if he were already seated at the table.

3

Stoudenmire awoke shortly before sunrise and dressed hur-riedly. Through the window, he noted that the dawn sky was metallic, colorless clear to the horizon; to the west he could make out the rugged humps of the Sierra Madres. There was no wind, no sign of rain clouds, nothing to cover a horse's tracks through the parched lands this side of the mountains. A good day for a manhunt.

Moments later, he was striding down the long corridor leading to the center of the house. The lawman had seen many fine homes in his time, but Don Miguel's *casa* was in a class by itself. Though they had arrived late in the night, he could tell that a stranger would do well to have a map if he started roaming these halls alone. The passageways, corridors, and wings would be damned confusing if a man wasn't familiar with the layout. Maybe when things calmed down a little, he would come back with Kate and let the old man give them a guided tour. But right now wasn't the time, not with Kale making dust somewhere ahead.

Stoudenmire's gut rumbled, and his thoughts turned to food. Hopefully he could find the kitchen and get something hot in his belly before riding out. While he would have liked to wait around for a chat with Don Miguel, he just couldn't spare the time. Whatever *el patron* had in mind to help him with the hunt would just have to wait for another day. Every minute lost merely widened a gap that was already pushing twenty-four hours, and that was too big a lead to give any man on the run. Still he was curious about the old *hidalgo's* cryptic offer of last night. *Something that insures success on any hunt.* Damned strange when a man stopped to think about it.

Heading in the general direction of where a kitchen ought to be, he walked through a wide doorway and came to an abrupt halt. Don Miguel was seated at the head of a table big enough for a platoon, calmly working his way through a bowl of fruit. The lawman hadn't figured him to be stirring around at this hour. It was something of a shock to find a *grandee* bright-eyed and bushy-tailed so early in the day.

"What troubles you, my young friend?" The Mexican indicated a chair beside his own. "You appear startled. Is it so remarkable that an *anciano* like myself still rises with first light?"

"De ninguna manera, Patrón." Stoudenmire seated himself as servants began carrying in platters of food. "Not at

all. It is only that I fear your sleep has been disturbed on my account."

"Old men sleep lightly. Particularly when all they hold dear is being destroyed about them. *¡Bastante!* Enough of my troubles. I have ordered the *tejano* breakfast for you, pork and eggs. I hope it meets with your satisfaction."

"Gracias, Don Miguel." The lawman dug in hungrily, bothered not at all that his plate was swimming in grease. "It was kind of you to be concerned with so small a thing."

"No, not kind. *Egoista.*" The *hidalgo* smiled benignly. "But selfishness to a purpose. I want your stomach content and your mind strong for the ride ahead. Even Pedro Vazquez's desire for vengeance pales beside my own."

"That was clear last night, *Patrón.* Only a blind man could have failed to observe your sorrow. I suspect Ramón was as much your son as he was that of the *alcalde's.*"

Don Miguel's eyes clouded over, the bowl of fruit now forgotten. *"Sí. Mi hijo.* He was that and more. When the Comanche killed my wife and children some years ago, I became a man without a soul. Then Ramón came to the *hacienda* as a simple *vaquero.* What a man, even as a boy! He was what I hoped my son would be. And soon that is what he became. *Mi hijo segundo."*

The old man fell silent, staring at his plate as if some vision from the past had been brought to life on its glossy surface. The moments ticked by in utter stillness, and a tiny smile played at the corners of his mouth. Finally, the mist of what once had been faded from his eyes, and he glanced back at the lawman, blinking sheepishly.

"Usted dispense, amigo. Excuse me for looking back to more pleasant times. Today it seems I have nothing to look forward to but the quick death of the one you seek. Now! Tell me how you would go about trapping this *bárbaro.*"

Stoudenmire pushed his plate away and sat back. "I believe he will attempt to reach the Sierra Madres. Chihuahua to the south has many villages, and it seems unlikely he would ride in that direction. The mountains would appear a safer refuge, and if I am right, I will cross his trail somewhere to the southwest. The man must have food, and wherever he stops he will be remembered."

"Your reasoning is sound. It is obvious you have had much experience with *piojos* of this sort." Don Miguel hesitated, searching for a tactful way to phrase his next question. "But what if he reaches the mountains, my friend? The *bandidos* rule the Sierra Madres like kings. Not even the *rurales* dare to travel there. Should this man ever join the *bandoleros*, he would be safe for as long as he cared to remain in Mexico."

"This is true, Don Miguel. Somehow I must overtake him before he crosses the flatlands this side of the mountains. Speaking of that, I fear I must take leave of your hospitality. The one named Kale is many hours ahead of me, and I must find a way to narrow his lead."

"Now you touch on the heart of the matter. This is precisely why I asked you to be my guest. Come, we are expected outside."

The *hidalgo* pushed back his chair and headed for the door at a fast clip. Stoudenmire tagged along in his wake, still thoroughly puzzled by the old man's air of mystery. When they emerged on the front porch of the *casa* a cluster of *vaqueros* waited at the bottom of the steps. As *el patrón* came to a halt, the men doffed their sombreros, darting hidden glances at the *americano*. The marshal returned their looks with growing curiosity, and in that moment, his eye was drawn toward a man at the rear. Looking closer, Stoudenmire suddenly realized that the man wasn't Mexican. He was a *mestizo*. A half-breed Indian.

Don Miguel motioned with his hand, and the breed edged through the crowd, slowly mounting the steps. When he came to a stop before the old man, the Indian bowed his head, not humbly but proudly as a warrior would honor a king. Watching him, Stoudenmire was struck by the sheer force of the man's physical presence. Unlike the plains Indians he had known, this *mestizo* was remarkably tall, with broad shoulders, a deep bull-chest, and bulging, sinewy legs that looked like gnarled saplings. His hair hung loosely over his shoulders, black as the darkest ebony, and his sharp, angular features brought to mind images of a fierce, predatory hawk. Strapped around his waist was a knife distantly related to a machete, and his clothing consisted solely of breechclout and moccasins.

But the thing that men remembered most about this *mestizo* were his eyes. They were black and piercing, in the way fire sears whatever it touches, and among the *vaqueros* it was said that this strange one could see through other men's souls. The lawman wouldn't soon forget those eyes either. When the Indian looked at him, Stoudenmire could think only of Tige. The same inhuman brilliance, somehow bristling with hunger; the eyes of a beast that had been weaned on raw meat and warm blood.

Like Tige, the *mestizo* also served but one master, in this case Don Miguel Salazar. Observing the Indian's manner before *el patrón*, it occurred to Stoudenmire that any one who messed with the old man was the same as dead. It was a handy item to keep in mind. While the Texan had never been bested in a fight, he sensed instinctively that tangling with this half-breed could get a man killed. Stone-cold—and sliced to ribbons in the bargain.

Don Miguel waited until they had finished their inspection of one another before he spoke. "Señor Stoudenmire, this is the man who will guide you in your hunt. His name is Bajeca. If you were familiar with his tribe, you would know he is a Yaqui. A race of *guerreros*, descendents of the Incas. Unfortunately, Porfirio Diaz declared war on them some years ago, and the Yaqui nation is now scattered across all of Mexico. When Bajeca came to us, he was near death. But we nursed him back to health, and he has remained with us ever since."

Turning, *el patrón* smiled benevolently, and a spark of warmth flickered and died in the *mestizo*'s eyes. Glancing back at Stoudenmire, the old man waved his hand toward the distant countryside. "We only see him occasionally. He lives out there among the wild things. No one knows where, or cares to know I would imagine. But when we need him, he somehow comes to us, and never have we needed him more.

Bejeca can track *el tigre* through running water, and if ever a man lived who can find the *gringo pistolero* in that wilderness, you are gazing upon him at this moment."

"Bejeca," Stoudenmire spoke the name with simple dignity, extending his hand. "I am honored to have a *yaqui guerrero* at my side. Together we will bring this pale-eyed *comadreja* to bay."

The *mestizo* pumped his hand once, then dropped it, staring through him as other men would look past a shadow. "Among the people of *el patrón*, it is said that you are *macho hombre*. When a man sets out on the *jornado del muerto* that is a good thing to be."

"The man we pursue will determine if it becomes a journey of death. If he resists, then he must die. But there are reasons for wanting him taken alive."

The Indian shrugged, inscrutable behind a stony expression. "How had you thought to conduct this hunt?"

The lawman gestured toward the Sierra Madres. "Unlike *el zorro*, this man is not cunning. He will run toward the mountains without bothering to cover his tracks. Somewhere to the southwest we will find his sign."

Bajeca studied him for a moment, watching everything and nothing in the same look. "It comes to me that this *cabrón* you seek was wise to run. If he fears you as greatly as you believe, then we will find his tracks at the village of Los Papalotes. That is the fartherest from the Rio Grande a horse could run without resting."

With that, he turned to Don Miguel, bowed his head slightly, then walked down the steps. The old man looked around at Stoudenmire and smiled. "Bajeca is not a tactful man, but he will never fail you. Give him a free rein, and he will lead you to the *gringo* dog."

Out of the corner of his eye, Stoudenmire noted that the *mestizo* was already mounted and had led his own horses forward. Nodding to Don Miguel, he moved down the steps and climbed aboard the chestnut. Without a word, Bajeca wheeled his scruffy mustang and rode south from the compound.

El patrón clearly wanted Kale brought back in a basket.

Stoudenmire had no doubts on that score. And unless he
missed his guess, the breed had been ordered to do the dirty
work. The only thing that had him puzzled was what the old
hidalgo had in mind for a certain *tejano* lawman.

4

The meeting had been called to decide their next move. By
now it was common knowledge that the lawman was off hunting Kale, and if he were captured, then the fat was in the
fire. Ed Banning laid it out in cold, precise terms. Kale could
send them all to jail, probably even get them hung, despite
the fact that every judge in town was on their payroll. Should
the ramrod be returned to El Paso, their chances were slim
indeed, for there was every likelihood they would never live
to stand trial. Lynch mobs couldn't be bribed or scared off,
and once Kale started squealing, the townspeople might just
decide to take matters into their own hands.

Isaac Porter was only about half-stewed, but far enough
along to be amused by this little charade. Ed Banning had
his mind made up before this meeting was ever called, and
to say that they were here to decide a plan of action was like
the Almighty asking Moses what should be inscribed on the
rocks. It was downright laughable, assuming a man could
keep his sense of humor while he was being insulted. They
didn't want his advice today anymore than they had in the
past. They only wanted to make sure his hands were as dirty
as their own. That way they could always toss him to the
wolves if and when a mob came pounding on the door. It was
the oldest trick in the book. Divert the pack's attention with
a juicy bone, and then run like hell.

But on the face of it, there was damn little Isaac Porter
could do to protect himself. Though he bitterly resented the
Bannings' imperious manner, there was no way he could
avoid being used by them. They made the decisions, and it
was up to him to perform the political skullduggery. They
were always in the background, screened by the simple expedient of staying out of sight. Though everyone knew who

pulled the strings, it was the mayor standing stage center who actually danced the jig. And that made him a very vulnerable fellow. People had a way of remembering what they saw rather than what they heard, which meant he was a prime candidate for a lynching bee if things ever came unwound.

Yet if it weren't for the Bannings he would still be scratching out an existence in one grubby scheme or another. They had made him mayor, and like it or not, he was bound to them by a cord that could take a half hitch around his windpipe if he weren't careful. Once a part of their organization, a man did well to toe the mark, even if he didn't care much for their methods. Where the brothers Banning were concerned, loyalty was wisely cultivated. Regardless of how disgusting it might be to play the toady for outright hooligans. Otherwise, a fellow ran the risk of claiming his reward in the hereafter somewhat prematurely.

Whenever he was with them, he felt like a man juggling vials of nitro. Sam was the most dangerous simply because he was the least predictable. He was nothing more than a common thug with a brain the size of a dried prune, someone to be avoided whenever possible. Even Ed had his darker side, though he could be reasoned with if a man had a sound argument. But that made him no less dangerous. Those who crossed him never lived to regret it, no matter how fast they could talk. Generally they just disappeared, buried out in the desert probably, and the message wasn't lost on whoever remained.

Still, a man had to protect himself in the clinches. Even if it meant jabbing Ed in the eye when he wasn't looking. The way things were shaping up, someone was being ticketed for a lengthy stay at Huntsville, maybe even a noose. And it damn sure wasn't going to be Isaac Porter. Listening to Ed rehash their predicament, he decided that a wise man would start hedging his bet. After all, there was no harm done if he put out feelers in the other camp. Not if he played it close to the vest and kept his mouth buttoned when he was drinking.

"Kale is gonna have to be rubbed out." Banning's words came as no surprise to the mayor. This was what the gang

boss had been leading up to for the last ten minutes. "If
Stoudenmire brings him in, we've got no choice. Maybe he
won't talk, but that's a risk we can't afford to take. Better men
than him have cracked when they came face to face with
a hangman's knot."

"Very true, Ed. Very true indeed." Porter nodded sagely,
wondering all the while if Banning's last comment hadn't
also been meant for his benefit. "The expedient thing is to
silence him. Otherwise, our own necks go on the block."

Banning shot him a curious look. "Isaac, you must be
getting smarter in your old age. What happened to all that
holier-than-thou bullshit about never resorting to violence?"

The mayor made a game effort at grinning wickedly. "An
extreme disease requires an extreme cure. Sometimes a man
must forfeit his life so that those about him can carry on the
good fight."

"Jesus Christ," Sam growled. "What kinda crock is that?
We're gonna kill him 'cause he's got a big mouth. Why don't
you just say it straight out?"

"Sam, don't let him get under your skin." Ed cocked an
eye in Porter's direction. "When our friend here starts soa-
kin' up the juice, he just naturally can't resist two-dollar
words. Isn't that right, Mayor?"

"Ed, you do me a grave injustice. Nothing could be farther from the truth. Why, I'm sober as a judge and twice as
circumspect."

"Porky, lemme tell you somethin'. When my brother says
you're drunk, you're drunk." Sam jabbed at the pudgy little
politician like his finger was a battering ram. "And if you're
not careful, I'm gonna give you a fat lip to go along with your
fat head."

"All right, that's enough horsin' around. We've got more
important things to talk about." Ed's crisp tone stopped both
men cold. "That's better. Now whether Stoudenmire brings
Kale in dead or we kill him only solves part of the problem.
The biggest thing hangin' over our heads is the German himself, and as long as he's kickin', we're not safe. Believe it or
not, I've come around to Sam's way of thinkin'. Stoudenmire

has got to go. Until he's laid out, we're up to our necks in a bucket of shit."

"Hotdamn! Now you're talkin' my kind of game." Sam swelled up his chest and crowed loud enough to raise the sun. "I'll break that sorry bastard's head in so many pieces he'll look like a junebug in a meat grinder."

Ed glanced around at Porter, again eyeing him in an odd way. "What about you, Mayor? How's your stick float now?"

Porter appeared shaken, though he tried desperately to hide it. The murder of Ramón Vazquez and Gus Krempkau had aroused the townspeople unlike anything in the past. They knew the gang was responsible, and if an innocent bystander like Krempkau could be gunned down, then nobody was safe. What was even more unsettling, they believed the town to be on the verge of a war with the Mexicans simply because the Bannings were out to protect their own hides. Graft and corruption could be tolerated in reasonable doses, but people drew the line when their lives and property were endangered. Just as sure as he was sitting here, the mayor knew that, if Stoudenmire were killed in the wake of yesterday's murders, it might well be the final straw.

"Ed, I'm not sure but what that wouldn't be a mistake. Killing Kale is one thing. Nobody's going to shed any tears over scum like him. But killing Stoudenmire might just be more than the people will stand for."

"Then I reckon that's something we'll have to worry about when it happens. Stoudenmire is more dangerous to us alive than dead, even if it splits this town right down the middle. I'm gonna tell you something, Porter. I think that bastard is crazy as a loon. He means to shovel dirt in our face even if he goes under doing it. When you're up against somebody that likes killin' that much, you'd better get him before he damn well gets you."

Isaac Porter didn't say anything. From where he sat, there was nothing left to say. Banning had clearly made up his mind, and if he talked till doomsday, it wouldn't change things by a hair. They were going to kill Kale, then Stoudenmire; and afterward, the whole goddamn town would come crashing down around their ears. And when it did, anyone standing close by was going to be sucked under with them. If he wasn't sure before, he was now. The time to make a deal with the opposition was before the worm turned. Which meant that he would have to move fast, before these lunatics had a chance to start taking pot shots at the marshal.

Later, reflecting back over the discussion, Ed Banning came to the conclusion that his political frontman was getting weak-kneed. The signs were all there, and if he was right, it could be serious. Damn serious if the old reprobate started talking to the wrong people. Kale was bad enough, but if Porter ever started blabbing, then the Bannings might as well eat shit and bark at the moon. That's about all that would be left.

After puzzling over it for a while, he ordered Sam to have the mayor watched around the clock. It wouldn't hurt anything, and it might just be the shrewdest move he'd made yet.

5

Stoudenmire and Bajeca pulled into Los Papalotes as the red ball of fire in the sky came directly overhead. They were covered with grit and sweat, and a growing uncertainty. Along the road south they had stopped at a dozen or more native huts, only to be told the same story each time.

The *gringo* they sought had not passed this way. On that the natives were emphatic, for it was a much discussed event when a lone *yanqui* dared to travel so far from the border. Had the man they described ridden past, someone would know, which meant that everyone would have known.

Still the lawman hadn't abandoned hope so easily. This was a much-traveled road, and a man riding fast might have gone unnoticed. On the other hand, perhaps Kale was foxier than he thought. If he had laid up somewhere yesterday and ridden through the night, then there was little likelihood that anyone would have spotted him. Had Stoudenmire been on the run that's what he would have done. And at the moment, he was damn hopeful that Kale had figured it the same way.

Otherwise they could spend a month crisscrossing the countryside before they picked up the trail.

Stoudenmire waited outside while Bajeca entered Los Papalotes' one general store. Maybe if the *mestizo* was alone, he could get more information. Mexicans down this way certainly made no effort to hide their dislike of white men, and it could be that his presence was putting a quietus on the whole deal. Through the open door he could see the storekeeper nodding and flapping his arms around like a windmill whenever he answered a question. The man's eyes were wide as saucers, and even from a distance it was obvious that he was frightened out of his wits by the fierce-looking breed. After a final volley of excited chatter, the storekeeper jerked a soiled rag and began mopping his face. Without so much as a thank-you, the Indian spun on his heel and walked from the store.

Something about his stride alerted Stoudenmire that they had struck paydirt. The *yaqui* swung into the saddle before looking at the lawman, but his eyes smoldered with a peculiar glint.

"The fat *cochino* inside says he was awakened at dawn by a *gringo* not unlike the one we seek. This man purchased food and an *olla* for water, then departed hastily."

"That is good news, Bajeca." Stoudenmire had the feeling his companion wasn't too keen on sharing all he had learned. "And which direction did this man take upon departing?"

The *mestizo* seemed impatient to be off, but he gestured down the road. "This pig of a merchant says he rode south along the road. Yet he made the *consulta* about a trail across the dry lands."

"Then he is headed toward the mountains as we suspected. Is there such a trail?"

"Only in a man's head and his nose. Even a *gringo* can cross the *arido tierra*, but not without much difficulty."

"*¿Quantos los Sierra Madres?*" The lawman pointed toward the distant mountains. "How far across the bad lands?"

Bajeca shrugged, seemingly bored with the incessant questions. "*Quien sabe. Todo día.* Perhaps a day. Perhaps more. Much depends on the man and the horse he rides."

"And what of the horse our friend rides? Did the *mercante* relate the condition of his mount?"

"*Sí.* The fat one says that the *caballo del gringo* had been ridden hard and would most certainly collapse unless treated gently." The *mestizo* cast Stoudenmire a scornful look. "While we talk, the *yanqui* filth moves farther from our reach. *¡Andale!* Let us ride before he eludes us forever."

Bajeca jerked his mustang around and kicked him in the ribs. The lawman was only a few strides behind, and they trotted southward in the noonday sun. Thinking back over what they had learned, Stoudenmire estimated that Kale was probably five hours ahead of them. Six at the outside. More to the point, he was riding a jaded horse, and it was a cinch he couldn't push the animal over the wastelands this side of the mountains. Most likely he figured no one was on his trail at this point and wouldn't risk killing his horse. Maybe he would even hole up somewhere during the heat of the day. If they could somehow cut his sign, there was every likelihood they could close the gap by nightfall. The other side of the coin wasn't pleasant to consider. By morning Kale would be in the mountains, and tracking him there was a foolhardy proposition any way a man sliced it.

Once they were out of sight of the store, Bajeca left the road and began casting in ever widening circles over the broken ground to the west. Kale wouldn't have headed for the mountains until he was sure no one could see him, and this was as good a spot to start as any. Within a quarter-hour the *mestizo* found sign and signaled Stoudenmire. The lawman had only to look at the tracks, and he knew they were on the right trail at last. Yesterday, after Kale had spurred out of El Paso, he had inspected the hoofprints carefully. Two caulks had been built up more than usual on the inside of a back shoe, and it left a distinctive imprint. This track matched it perfectly. The road south had been too heavily traveled to make out one hoofprint from another, but there was no doubt in his mind now. He nodded to Bajeca, and they struck out at a steady lope headed due west.

The earth was sandy in most places, with clumps of

stunted mesquite and yucca scattered over the countryside, all of which made tracking fairly simple. There wasn't a tree worthy of the name for miles around, and in the distance they could see the Sierra Madres range climbing skyward from the desert floor. The terrain grew more hostile as the afternoon wore on, and the sun hammered down with a ferocity that was unlike any heat Stoudenmire had ever known. Bajeca took it all in stride, seemingly oblivious to anything save the tracks stretching westward before them. But the lawman felt as though every ounce of sweat in his body had been drained off, leaving him as dry and parched as a weathered slab of rawhide.

Surprisingly, there was no sign that Kale had any intention of halting to rest his mount. The tracks showed that the horse was nearly spent, dragging his hooves through the clutching grip of the sand. Occasionally the rider had dismounted, walking a ways to give the animal a breather, but it was all too clear that Kale meant to cross this desolate wilderness before the day was out. The two hunters held to a grueling pace, taxing the endurance of their own mounts to the limit. They were gaining, and each time the trail showed signs of freshening their spirits climbed. But they couldn't slacken the pace or allow time for even a brief rest. Kale was still running scared, and if he was to be caught, it might just be now or never.

Through the afternoon they trudged on, following tracks that deviated only to skirt stands of giant saguaro, prickly pear, and Spanish bayonet. Rattlesnakes, tiny desert rodents, and a startling variety of lizards were the only life they saw stirring, and along toward sundown it became apparent that there was small likelihood of overtaking the hunted man. As dusk settled over the vast emptinesss surrounding them, the two men decided to call it quits for the night. There was no sense in going on and running the risk of losing Kale's tracks in the dark. Better to wait for first light and put on a final burst of speed in the hope they could close the gap before he reached the sanctuary of the mountains.

They halted to make camp in the foothills bordering the

Sierra Madres. Here the land was a jagged upheaval of deep
canyons, arroyos, and treacherous barrancas, all the more
reason not to chance traveling at night. Although water was
to be found only during the spring rains, their *ollas* were still
half-full, and they could at least afford the luxury of quench-
ing their thirst. What remained would go for their horses, to
prepare them for the sprint that would come with false dawn.

Stoudenmire had just begun loosening the straps on the
pack horse when he heard Bajeca grunt in that odd way Indians use when they run up on something unexpected. Turning, he saw the *mestizo* staring off toward a distant hill at a
somewhat higher elevation. Though dusk had fallen there was
still a murky half-light in the sky, and he could just make out
a stand of gnarled juniper trees on the hillside. There wasn't
anything strange in that, and for a moment he thought the
breed must be having a bit of fun at his expense. Indians had
a peculiar sense of humor, and they weren't above a practical joke on occasion. Then he took a closer look and saw a
slight movement among the trees. Rubbing his eyes, he peered
into the gloomy twilight, and any doubts fast went by the
boards. A wispy tendril of smoke floated skyward through
the stand of junipers.

Tom Kale had just played out his string!

Clearly he was on the back slope of the hill and had built
a small fire in the belief that there wasn't anything but coy-
otes and gila monsters within miles of his camp. It wouldn't
be easy crossing this nightmarish terrain in the dark, but with
any luck at all they would have him trussed up like a year-
ling steer before the stars came out.

Moving up to stand beside Bajeca, the lawman nodded
toward the hill. "It appears the pale-eyed *diablo* has been
brought to bay."

The *mestizo*'s eyes remained fastened on the smoke. "An
animal being hunted is allowed no mistakes. This one was
cursed by a *bruja* even before he started."

"Perhaps it is so." Stoudenmire paused, watching the
Indian closely. "Bear in mind, he is to be taken alive unless
there is no other way."

Bajeca's stoic features gave no hint of what he was thinking. Without a word he strode to his horse and pulled an ancient Henry repeater from behind the saddle. Stoudenmire thought of saying something else, but gave it up as a waste of breath. Walking to the chestnut, he jerked the scattergun and quickly checked the loads. After a few moments discussion, the two men separated and melted into the darkness. Bajeca would circle in from the south, and the lawman would approach from the north. Once in position, they would sneak up and try to jump the man as he slept.

Working his way through a series of arroyos and rock studded hogbacks, Stoudenmire spent the next hour in a cautious advance. After skinning both knees and a set of knuckles, he was worming his way up the hillside when the dull boom of a pistol shattered the inky stillness. No mistaking it, the shot had come from a Colt and not a Henry repeater. Whatever was happening on the other side of that slope, Kale had gotten in the first lick.

Suddenly the night was split by an ungodly scream of sheer, animal terror. Then just as quickly all went still, and the lawman could feel a vagrant breeze cooling the sweat on his forehead. Wondering if Bajeca had met his match, Stoudenmire scrambled up the hill, trying to make as little noise as possible. Within moments he topped the rise and plowed down the other side, cocking both hammers on the shotgun as he skidded through the dusty soil. Moving cautiously now, he eased through another stand of juniper and tangled underbrush, gliding silently from tree to tree. Abruptly he broke out into a small clearing and froze dead in his tracks.

Beside a crackling little fire sat Bajeca, calmly wiping his knife clean on Kale's shirt. Glancing up, he grinned like a playful wolf and lifted Kale's severed head from the ground.

"A gift for *el patrón*. One *gringo pistolero* who will kill no more."

CHAPTER SEVEN

1

Stoudenmire rode into Paso del Norte just before noon two days later. Since there was no need to push themselves or their horses further, the lawman had set a leisurely pace on the trip back from the mountains. The chase was over, and the bloody sack hanging from Bajeca's saddle horn made it unnecessary to reach El Paso with any haste. Tom Kale's death had turned the clock back almost to where he had started, for without the ramrod's testimony, there wasn't much to be gained by dragging the Bannings into court. The marshal had thought about it plenty in the last couple of days, roundly cursing the way fate sometimes bollixed up a man's best shot. It was a bitter pill to swallow, but there just weren't any witnesses left. First the rustler captured in the raid on Don Miguel's *hacienda*, then Ramón, and now Kale. People who had the goods on the Bannings somehow seemed to wind up stone cold and six feet under. It was a sorry goddamn mess, no two ways about it.

When Stoudenmire and the *mestizo* had ridden into the *rancho* the evening before, Don Miguel insisted he spend the

night. They had much to celebrate, *el patrón* announced, and
he promptly ordered a royal *banquete* in honor of the suc-
cessful hunt. After presenting his gory trophy, Bajeca had
quietly disappeared. Clearly he preferred the solitude of the
wilderness to a Mexican shindig, and Stoudenmire couldn't
fault him there. The lawman wasn't in a particularly festive
mood himself, what with being fresh out of witnesses. But
he had little choice in the matter since everyone on the place
took to addressing him as *compadre*.

Damned if a man could figure these people out. Only a
few days ago, the *alcalde* started calling him son, and now
he had been appointed sidekick to a whole crew of Mex
cowhands. That was heady stuff, and he could see how the
hidalgos had made a good thing for themselves by playing
on the herd instinct of their people.

Kale's head was mounted on a pole in the courtyard
and anyone who could still fog a mirror filed past to have a
look, women and kids included. The *vaqueros* swarmed
around Stoudenmire throughout the entire night, pumping
his hand till it was sore. He was *macho hombre*, the man
who had avenged the murder of their young *caporal*, and
from this night forward, his name would be honored among
the people of Don Miguel. Somehow Stoudenmire took it
all in stride, and even managed to loosen up a bit after a few
shots of tequila. But Kale's swollen eyes staring down on the
festivities played hell with a man's appetite, no matter how
much firewater he downed. The lawman ignored the food
and stuck to drinking, all the while wishing there were some
way to wind that head up and let it speak its piece in a court-
room.

Thinking back on it as he reined to a stop before the
alcalde's house, Stoudenmire seemed to recall having held a
conversation with the head sometime during the night. But it
was all a little muddled, and he couldn't remember exactly
what Kale had said. If anything. That tequila was wicked
stuff, probably the very drink people had in mind when they
started talking about popskull. Anytime it made a stray
head start popping its jaws, there was damn sure more to it

than a fellow might suspect. But what the hell, he was among friends. And near as he could recollect, they had listened to the conversation like a flock of stewed owls anyway.

Pedro Vazquez threw open the door at his knock and embraced him with a great show of affection. The *alcalde* had already heard about the outcome of the manhunt, as had everyone in Paso del Norte. Ramón's killer had been tracked down and executed, which was the kind of justice people understood best; and so far as the old man was concerned, Stoudenmire wasn't far shy from walking on water.

Vazquez ordered a lavish meal in his honor, then made him sit down and relate every detail of the chase. When the lawman came to the part about finding Bajeca with Kale's severed head, the *alcalde*'s eyes glistened brightly, and for a minute Stoudenmire thought he was going to jump up and shout *¡Ole!* But the aging politico merely nodded with vast approval and listened attentively as the Texan concluded with the highlights of Don Salazar's impromptu fiesta. When he finished, Vazquez chuckled happily and slapped his knee.

"¡Madre mio! I would have given much to see that *monfeta*'s head on a pole."* Then he darted a sheepish glance at the lawman. "Do not be offended by our barbaric ways, *amigo*. We Mexicans are a peaceful race, but even the *santos* might become bloodthirsty if their loved ones were being slaughtered like mad dogs."

"My only regret, *jefe*, is that the head belonged to Kale instead of the man named Banning. But that is a problem I will face tomorrow. Tell me now of what happens between our people during my absence."

"Absolutely nothing, my friend." The old man scratched his head as if studying an unusually complicated riddle. "Trade has come to a standstill, but other than that there have been no *incidentes*. Not even one. It surpasses all understanding."

Stoudenmire found it equally bewildering, even unsettling in some curious way. "That is more than I had hoped for. I expected the pursuit of Ramón's killer to calm the more reasonable among our people, but there are many hotheads on both sides of the river. Perhaps the *salvajes* among us tire of fighting after all."

"Perhaps. Yet it is known that a stillness always moves ahead of the storm. Pardon an old man's *cinismo*, but I fear that even a slight rupture would once again set the people at one another's throats."

"*Sí*, there is truth in that. Though the one who must enforce the law sometimes finds himself wishing it were not so."

"You are a young man, and it is only natural that you would wish away the bad. I have lived much too long for such things. Occasionally I can deceive myself into believing that the human race is human after all, but only for a moment. Late at night when I face my God and myself, I must admit that brotherhood is a false dream echoed by false prophets.

"You paint a bleak picture, *anciano*." Stoudenmire tapped the star pinned on his shirt. "Perhaps if men like myself kill enough of the evil ones, there will one day be peace over this land."

The *alcalde* chortled skeptically. "You had best start with the women, my friend. Only when there are none left to bear sons will we eliminate the greed that drives men to kill. The Spaniards took this land from the *indios*. The *juaristas* took it from the *españols*. And now the *gringos* would take it from my people. There is no end. Only change."

"You are no doubt correct, *jefe*. Still there are many who would prefer to live in peace. Otherwise, they would not hire men like me to rid the world of lice. Perhaps the day will yet come when the good ones can set their *diferencias* aside and live in harmony."

"Only a foolish man would cease to pray for such things. To abandon all hope is to renounce *Jesucristo* in the same breath." Pedro Vazquez's deadened eyes belied his words, and it occurred to the lawman that Ramon's death had turned the old man into a devout cynic.

"I am not a religious man, but in my own way I help *Padrenuestro* along." Stoudenmire rose and settled his gunbelt

in place. "Now I must leave you. There are those across the
river who grow anxious for my return."

Vazquez came erect and shook his hand warmly. "What
will you do now, *mi hijo?* All who could have helped you have
been silenced forever."

The lawman grinned. "I will do what it is that I do best,
jefe. Kill a few more of the evil ones."

"Excelente! There is always room in the graveyards for
those who prey on the weak. *Buena fortuna*, my young friend.
Walk lightly and *vaya con Dios*." The *alcalde's* eyes twinkled
and a sardonic smile spread over his brown features. "*Y el
diablo* if need be."

Ten minutes later Stoudenmire nudged the gelding into the
water and forded the Rio Grande. For no particular reason it
passed through his mind that Pedro Vazquez was a man who
had lost his grip on his own soul. The old Mexican no longer
believed in anything, least of all himself. Losing faith in God
was one thing, that happened to lots of men who still somehow managed to toe the mark. But when a man lost faith in
himself, he was treading on a real hellish piece of quicksand.

The marshal's hand lightly brushed over the holstered
Colt, finding curious reassurance in the cold metal. There
were some things a man never lost faith in, no matter how
troublesome times became.

2

People along San Antonio Street stopped to stare as the lawman rode past. Behind him Stoudenmire could hear their
excited chattering, and as he neared the plaza, a small crowd
had formed in his wake. They appeared neither pleased nor
distressed by his return; their attention centered solely on the
fate of Tom Kale. Everyone knew the marshal would come
back, and seeing him in the flesh only piqued their curiosity
all the more. What they really wanted to know were the par-
ticulars of his widely discussed manhunt in Old Mexico.

Presumably Stoudenmire had caught up with Kale; that
much was taken for granted. But the wanted man wasn't

strapped across the marshal's packhorse, and that raised questions of an even more intriguing nature. Had he killed the Banning ramrod and buried him across the border? Or had Kale somehow outwitted him, maybe even outshot him, and reached the interior safely? Both possibilities had an appeal all their own, and the crowd batted them back and forth as if Stoudenmire weren't anywhere within spitting distance.

The lawman wasn't especially interested one way or the other, and he simply ignored them, reining the chestnut catty-cornered across the plaza. He was so tired he felt like he had been run through an ore crusher; over two hundred miles in less than three days was enough to wear any man's tailbone down to the nubbin. Yet physical weariness was only part of the dull ache that rode with him. Tom Kale's death had been a bitter disappointment and returning without a witness against the Bannings only rubbed salt in an already festered sore. Maybe if it had been he who killed Kale, it wouldn't have galled so much. But he felt like he had just been along for the ride, and the scenery damn sure wasn't anything to write home about.

The crowd was still hard on his heels, and their curiosity had been whetted to the point that one man finally worked up the gumption to address Stoudenmire directly. "Marshal, if it ain't too much trouble, we'd be obliged to know what happened over there."

"Mr. Kale won't be coming back." Stoudenmire didn't bother looking at them. Instead, he kicked the chestnut into a trot and left the crowd gawking at his broad back.

But his cryptic answer was clear enough, if somewhat short on details. *Tom Kale had gone under!* How or where wasn't all that important, not at the moment. The thing that mattered was that Stoudenmire had returned, and the wanted man was dog meat. The news swept through El Paso like wildfire, cresting from building to building as if fanned by a hot wind. *Dallas Stoudenmire had pickled the fastest gun in town, and the Bannings were next!*

The marshal didn't give a good goddamn what they thought. By tonight it would be all over town how Kale had actually died, and that would really give them something to talk about. Maybe it would even put the fear of God in some of Banning's cutthroats and set them to making tracks for parts unknown. As for the Bannings themselves, they might just drop around to shake his hand. Kale's death had damn sure gotten them off the hook, and unless he missed his guess, the Coliseum would start serving drinks on the house in about ten minutes. Cursing under his breath, Stoudenmire dismounted in front of the jail and looked up to see Gillette hurrying across the plaza.

The lanky deputy ambled to a halt and eyed him critically. "Well I see you made it back. But damned if you don't look like somebody rolled you over a cliff in a gunnysack."

Stoudenmire tied the horses to a hitch rack and smiled tightly. "Jim, that's pretty much how I feel. Either I'm not used to sittin' a saddle three days straight, or else my rump's gone soft with city living."

"Probably a little bit of both." Gillette craned his long neck around and gave the packhorse a quick once over. "See you didn't bring Kale back after all. Don't tell me now, lemme guess. The Rurales have got him, and they've done thrown away the key."

"Matter of fact, I didn't see a Rurale the whole time I was gone." The lawman grunted as Gillette's wiseass grin evaporated. "C'mon, let's get in out of the heat, and I'll tell you all about a sneaky half-breed I've been keepin' company with."

Once inside, Stoudenmire got himself a cup of coffee, then settled down behind the desk. Skipping minor details, he briefly sketched out what had happened across the river, winding it up with a step by step account of the manhunt's grisly finish. Gillette appeared speechless for a moment, and the lawman chuckled to himself. Anything that could silence this old turkey-gobbler must be hair-raising enough for the best of them.

"Jeeesus Christ!" The deputy looked like a man with a harelip trying to quote scripture. "That's the god-damnedest thing I ever heard tell of. Them bastards sorta play for keeps, don't they?"

"Yeah, I reckon you could say that. They sure as hell snuffed out our last witness against the Bannings, and that's about as permanent as you can get. Looks to me like we're right back where we started."

"Noooo. Not just exactly, that is." Gillette rubbed the back of his neck, and his forehead wrinkled in a frown. "Way I hear it, the Bannings are about half-froze to lift your scalp. So it's just likely you might've smoked 'em out in the open after all."

Stoudenmire's mouth cracked in a tight smile, and the weariness seemed to drain out of his face. "Well now, that's a horse of another color, sure enough. Did you happen to hear when they would make a try, or how they'd go about it?"

"Nope. Just heard that Ed Banning's been kickin' up dust like a pony going off in four directions. Don't take much savvy to figure out how they'll try it, though. Their kind always comes at a man from behind."

"I expect you're right. But it doesn't make much difference one way or the other. Just so long as we can force 'em to show their hand, I won't be too particular. Where'd you run across a juicy tidbit like that, anyway?"

"Well it starts to get a little dicey right about there." Gillette absently twirled the ends of his mustache and cocked one eye. "Doc Cummings got it from Seth Hart who got it from somewheres else. Accordin' to Doc it came straight from the horse's mouth, or pretty damn close thereabouts."

The lawman grimaced and shook his head skeptically. "Hell, I thought you'd got it from one of those unimpeachable sources the newspapers are always carryin' on about. Listening to Doc talk is like pourin' shit through a tin horn. No matter how it comes out, there's not a clear note in the bunch."

"Maybe. But I've been hearin' the same story all over town. The word's around that Banning's not just bowed up anymore. You got him plumb spooked and from where he sits, it's you or them. Folks allow that he don't mean to leave any loose ends this time, either."

"Jim, it sounds to me like someone just made an educated guess and started themselves a fair-sized rumor. Hart and

Cummings can speculate all they want, but that's not gonna get the Bannings off their duff and into the street."

The old lawdog splattered the spittoon with a brown wad and licked his mustache. "When it comes to hardheaded, you could spot a jackass a city block and win going away."

Stoudenmire blew steam off his coffee and mulled it over for a minute. "I'm not sayin' it won't happen. Where there's smoke, there's always fire. Even if it's only a little one. I just don't happen to think the Bannings are rattled enough to start doing their own dirty work. Not yet, at any rate. If they try anything, it'll come from one of those knuckleheads on their payroll."

"Damnation, that's all I've been tryin' to say! Somebody's gonna be layin' to kill you. What the hell difference does it make who it is?"

"None, I suppose. Except that the only way we're gonna get the Bannings is to rawhide 'em into a gunfight." The marshal considered that at some length before he looked back at Gillette. "What about Hart and his crowd? How are they taking all this?"

The deputy's mouth split in a big, horsey grin. "Well, I'll tell you. 'Pears to me they don't know whether to shit or go blind. First they got a case of the hives 'cause you lit out after Kale. Then they started bendin' my ear about Banning plannin' to catch you in a dark alley. Sometimes I get to wonderin' if they've still got to have a light when they get tucked in every night."

Before Stoudenmire could frame an answer, Kate burst through the door and ran around the desk. With a tiny cry of delight she threw herself into his arms and began smearing his face with wet, sticky kisses. Gillette guffawed behind his hand, watching the lawman turn beet red with embarrassment as he tried to fend Kate off.

"Slow down, girl. I've only been gone three days."

Ignoring him completely, she smoothed back his hair and settled more securely into his lap. "Oh, it's so good to have you back. It seems like you've been gone forever, and I promise I'll never be cross again. I was over in Doc's store, and when I heard you were back, I said to myself, the very first thing I'm going to say is that I'm sorry. Well, I'm sorry. So don't you dare act grumpy." Clutching him around the neck, she gave him a big kiss square on the mouth.

Stoudenmire lifted her easily and set her feet on the floor. Rising, he gave Gillette a helpless look. "Jim, how about taking care of my horses. I can see we're not gonna get much work done around here today."

With an arm around Kate's waist, he headed for the door, and she snuggled hungrily against his chest. Just as they disappeared through the door, he turned and called over his shoulder. "Mind the store, deputy. I just decided to take the night off."

3

After checking in with Gillette next morning, Stoudenmire strolled over to the mayor's office. Overnight a scheme had occurred to him that could easily drive another nail into the Bannings' coffin. Whether it worked out or not, he had nothing to lose except a little conversation. Talk was cheap enough, and he might just wind up with a songbird who knew where all the skeletons were buried.

After Kate finally fell asleep in his arms, he had lain awake far into the night sorting through the alternatives that remained. There were many ways to make a gang run for cover. The quickest was to force their boss into a gunfight, but Ed Banning showed a decided reluctance to accept the challenge. Some men preferred to hire others to do their killing for them, and the weasel-faced saloon owner was plainly of that stripe. Whatever it was that would make him stand and fight hadn't come clear as yet, so the lawman set that tactic aside until he could get a better handle on what made Banning tick.

Another method was to whittle away at the lesser gang members, undermining confidence in the boss as his flunkeys were fed to the meat grinder one by one. This was the tack he had followed from the start, yet he had to admit that the score seemed a bit lopsided. Campbell and Kale had gone under to be sure, but at a cost of Ramón, a court official, and two *vaqueros*. Somehow it seemed like a damned poor trade, even though Banning had lost four men in the rhubarb over the young Mexican girl. Besides, taking a bit here and there was the slow way to get results, and he needed something to speed this deal up.

Staring at the ceiling, he had wracked his brain for some foolproof way to clobber the Bannings once and for all. Just when he was about to chuck the whole mess and get some sleep, he remembered the old saw about divide and conquer. Look for the weakest link in the chain and twist till it broke. Once it snapped, Ed Banning would never get it spliced in time to save his own neck. With his grip on the town loosened, both the political machine and the gang itself would come apart at the seams. The more Stoudenmire thought about it the better he liked the idea. And unless he had lost the knack of sizing up men, Mayor Isaac Porter was the weak link.

Stoudenmire found the politician alone in his office, seated behind a desk staring listlessly at a stack of ledgers. His heavy tread brought Porter's head around, and the marshal sensed that this wasn't the same man who had berated him the morning of Ramón's death. Something about his eyes had changed. Nothing a man could put a name to, but it was there just the same. Like a gopher when it's cut off from its hole and no place to run. Suddenly his plan took on a new dimension, for the easiest man to buffalo was the one that had already scared himself.

"Morning, Mr. Mayor," he said, nodding at the ledgers. "How goes the fight?"

Porter darted a nervous glance at the gray-bound records. "Oh, these. Nothing really. The city fiscal year is upon us, and I was just going over the books."

Stoudenmire was well aware that such matters were generally left to accountants, but he let it pass. "Well that's a little out of my bailiwick. Never was much of a hand with figures. If you can spare a minute, I thought I'd fill you in on my trip south."

"No, no. That's quite all right, Marshal." His eyes widened, flashing an unnatural amount of white. "We can dispense with your report. The story's all over town. As a matter of fact, people aren't talking about much else."

"Yeah, something like that would just naturally get people to beatin' their gums." The lawman dropped into a chair and crossed his long legs. "Course, I'd better give you the lowdown anyway. Folks have a way of twistin' things out of shape, and you might've heard the wrong version."

The mayor sighed and slumped back in his chair with an acute look of resignation. "If you insist. But keep it to official matters. I've already heard the gory details."

"You mean about Kale?" Stoudenmire's expression was deceptively bland, but when Porter stiffened at his words, he knew he was on the right track. "Damned if that didn't beat anything I ever saw."

"Please, Marshal." The politician squirmed uneasily and a nervous tic surfaced beneath his left eye. "Just hold it to the facts, if you don't mind."

"Well, Mayor, I reckon the way a wanted man goes under is part of the facts. Come to think of it, not much else matters when it comes down to an official report. Wouldn't you say?"

Porter opened his mouth to reply, but the lawman plowed dead ahead, waving aside his sputtering objections. "You see, it was like this. I was teamed up with this breed, and we had trailed Kale to the foothills this side of the Sierra Madres. That night we separated with the idea of sneakin into his camp and taking him alive. Well wouldn't you know that damned Injun got there before me. I came wormin' through the brush, and there he sat. Holdin' Kale's head up like he was huntin' for fleas. The sonovabitch had whacked it off the way a man would split a fresh melon."

Stoudenmire flicked his hand across his throat in a slicing motion, and beads of sweat popped out on the mayor's forehead. For a moment the lawman thought Porter was going to swoon dead away, but he somehow got a grip on himself and straightened in his seat. "That will do, Marshal.

I'm not a violent man, and I see no need to belabor how Tom Kale died."

"Why hell, Mayor. How he died is only half the story. What happened the next night was the real gutbuster." Stoudenmire hitched his chair around and leaned forward, eyeball to eyeball with the little man. "Them Mexicans got a fiesta going and the guest of honor was none other than old Tom Kale himself. The bastards stuck his head on a pole and spent the whole goddamn night dancin' around it like a bunch of wild Apaches. Course, I'll have to admit that it smelled a little rank by then, and those eyes bulging out of their sockets was enough to gag a dog off a gut wagon. But it was purely something to see. Just think of it! Jammed up on a pole and grinnin' like a jack-o'-lantern."

Porter's face turned green, and the lawman scooted back, certain the mayor was going to puke at any moment. The politician jerked a handkerchief and clapped it over his mouth, breathing heavily. Then he fell back in his chair and closed his eyes, taking short, fast gasps like a man trying to clear his head of a sickening stench. After a brief struggle to hold down his breakfast, his color returned, and he slowly opened his eyes.

Stoudenmire poured him a glass of water from a beaker on the desk, then let him have it right below the gizzard. "Porter, I told you that little story just to give you an idea of what's in store for anybody that stands in my way. I intend to scuttle the Bannings and all their cronies, even if it means fighting dirty in the clinches. And when I said *all* their cronies, I meant you especially, Mister Mayor. Course, I don't need to paint you a picture. You're smart enough to figure who's gonna be left holdin' the bag when the rats start scurrying for safety."

Isaac Porter blanched, and he suddenly felt sick in a different way. Stoudenmire's last statement jibed perfectly with his own estimate of what would happen when the Bannings were finally put to flight. Someone would be left behind as a sacrificial goat, and he had a pretty fair idea of who that *someone* would be. But that didn't shake him nearly as much as the knowledge that the coldblooded bastard seated across from him would be right there waiting. Ready, willing, and able to supply the noose that would stretch his plump neck.

The mayor wanted desperately to talk to someone; to unburden himself and erase the sense of doom that was with him constantly now. Yet there was one unknown in this whole ghastly mess. *Could he trust Stoudenmire?* Or should he go to Seth Hart? Maybe even the governor. It was a critical decision, and a man in his position couldn't afford even one mistake.

Glancing back at the lawman, he spoke with a bravado that seemed curiously out of character. "You're just trying to frighten me. But you'll find I don't fold so easily, Mr. Stoudenmire."

The marshal regarded him with mild disgust. "Porter, I'll make it easy for you. Swap sides now and testify against the Bannings, and you can walk away a free man. Otherwise you'll swing with the rest of 'em. The offer's good for forty-eight hours. No longer."

Stoudenmire rose and walked to the door. Then he turned as though an afterthought had suddenly occurred to him. "Something you oughta keep in mind while you're thinking it over. I can protect you from the Bannings. But the Banning's can't protect you from me."

The door opened and closed, leaving Isaac Porter alone with his fear.

Crossing the plaza, Stoudenmire wondered if he really could deliver on that last statement. He damn sure hadn't had much luck protecting people from the Bannings so far. But, what the hell! There was plenty of time to start worrying about a grubby politician if and when he decided to switch horses. The thing to do now was to take up the slack and see if a little judicious pressure wouldn't pop that weak link right under the Bannings' nose.

4

The Bannings were involved in working out a scheme of their own. Late that afternoon Ed and Sam came together in the

backroom office to discuss how it should be handled. Stoudenmire had to be snuffed out, on that they were agreed. The
sooner the better for everyone concerned, particularly themselves. The marshal's bulldog tenacity showed no signs of
weakening, and by his own word he wouldn't slack off until
they had been plowed under. Even if they were disposed to let
things rock along for a while, the surly bastard seemed determined to force their hand. Each day he lived, he became a
greater threat, that was plain enough for anyone to see. And
only a fool greenhorn let another man pick the time and place
for a fight.

Whatever remnants of the code duello that remained after the war hadn't taken root in El Paso. Here the only recognized code was survival, and whoever struck first was
generally thought to have something besides beeswax between his ears. The logic was really quite simple, profoundly
earthy in its own way. Stoudenmire had poked his nose where
it didn't belong, which was the kind of thing a man could
overlook only so long. The German clearly didn't know when
to let well enough alone, therefore he had to be killed. That
was the only kind of language some people understood, especially hard-nosed lawdogs.

But Ed Banning was of the opinion that it had to be handled discreetly, in a manner that could never be traced back
to them. Although elections were still more than a year away,
they couldn't afford to take any chances. Voters had a long
memory when it could be proved that a town's political boss
was playing dirty pool, which meant that the Banning name
had to be kept out of it at all costs. And right there was where
Sam bowed his neck.

"Dammit, Ed, that's not fair." Sam was just dense enough
to think it should be kept in the family. "I've got a personal
score to settle with that shithead, and you got no right to let
somebody else do the job."

The elder Banning shook his head wearily, as though involved in a senseless argument with a slow child. "Brother,
I'm tellin' you, it's not worth the risk. You can get your jollies
off just as well watchin' somebody else do it."

"Ah, horse apples!" The burly ruffian slunk down in his chair and petulantly slewed his eyes around the room. "That's like sayin' I'd get my load off watchin' some jasper fuck my best girl."

"Now there you go again," Ed snapped. "Making dumb comparisons that you can't back up. You know goddamned well those things have nothing to do with each other. This is business." He sighed heavily, glancing sideways at the younger man. "Besides, you don't even have a best girl."

"Now look who's harpin' the same old tune. One of these days I'm gonna get tired of you raggin' me about girls. You just wait and see. I know a few stories about you that ain't been told. Don't think I don't."

Ed's eyes scrunched up at the corners, and he regarded his brother with a wary gaze. "Is that a fact? Well suppose you just tell me what you know if it's so goddamn earth-shattering."

Sam darted a secretive look at him. "Oh, I know something. Don't you worry about that. Them girls over at Lizzie Pride's do a lot of talkin', and I got big ears."

"No shit? Up beside a jackass I'd never have known. Now suppose you quit playin' ring-around-the-rosie and tell me what the hell you've heard."

Sam's mouth twisted in a juvenile smirk, and he giggled nervously, not unlike a schoolboy telling his first dirty joke. "They say you can't get it up. They're all the time laughin' and carrying on about it when they think nobody's around. That redhead swears up and down you couldn't stick your pecker in a pail of soft lard."

Ed Banning's features went red as ox blood, and he half rose from his chair. "That rotten little bitch! I'll cut her tits off and stuff 'em down her gullet. Then we'll see how much talkin' she does." The rage slowly drained out of his face, leaving it a mottled purple. After a moment he settled back, raking his brother with a furious scowl. "And you better keep your mouth shut, too. If I ever get wind of you talkin' out of turn, I'll crack your balls good. Savvy?"

"Sure, Ed. Whatever you say." Sam clamped his legs shut,

dimly wondering why a sharp pain had suddenly pulsed through his seeds. "I was just funnin.' You know I didn't mean no harm."

Ed drew a deep breath and released it slowly, forcing his mind back to the more immediate problem. "All right, let's drop it and start thinkin' about Stoudenmire. You're not gonna do it, and that's final, so don't give me any lip. The way I've got it figured, we need ourselves a stalking horse."

When Sam gave him a baffled look, the gang leader broke it down into two-bit words. "That's someone who has reason to want the German six feet under. Then everybody'll think he had a personal motive, and we won't be connected to it. He does the killin,' and our hands are clean. Sort of like havin' your cake and eatin' it too."

Sam digested his brother's scheme in an unhurried way, and a brightness slowly kindled in his eyes. "Yeah, that's real smart. Maybe we could even hire us a greaser to do it. Folks around here think greasers are dumb enough to do anything."

"No, we don't have time to go scoutin' up some Mex pig-sticker. We need somebody that's handy, and it's got to be a man with a first class grudge against Stoudenmire. I've been giving it a lot of thought, and I think I know just the man."

"Well hell, there's your answer, slicker'n rat shit. Who is he?"

"Bill Johnson."

"Bill Johnson?" Sam parroted the words with gaping disbelief. "That goddamn alky couldn't hold a gun steady enough to hit a bull in the ass across a fence."

"That's the whole point. We're gonna get him stiffer'n a board. Then we'll start talkin' about Stoudenmire. How he fired Johnson and booted his ass out the door. How he killed George Campbell, the only friend Johnson had in his whole miserable life. Before you know it, we'll have him foamin' at the mouth like a blind dog in a butcher shop. Then we'll open the back door and turn him loose. Everybody in town'll figure he had a shitpot full of reasons to kill the German."

"You know somethin', Ed? You're nothin' but a goddamn wizard." Sam nodded sagely for a moment, then blinked as though some part of the riddle remained unanswered. "Say, I just now thought of somethin'. You never did tell me if it was true."

Ed was still preoccupied with engineering the marshal's sudden demise. "If what was true?"

"What them girls said. That you couldn't get a hard-on no more."

Banning came up out of his chair. "Get your ass out of here! Go find Johnson and tell him I want to see him tonight. And you'd better listen to me close, little brother. Don't you ever again start runnin' your tongue about what those girls said. Not unless you want me to cut it out."

Sam backed slowly across the room, easing through the door without once meeting his brother's smoky glare. When he was gone, it passed through Ed's mind that he looked like a little boy who had just had his wrists slapped. The hell of it was that the dumb brute would always look like that. If he lived to be a hundred, he'd still be a half-grown kid masquerading as a man. And big brother would still be giving him a sugartit to suck instead of letting him fend for himself. Shit!

Later that night Sam returned with Bill Johnson in tow. But as it turned out, they didn't have much of a chore getting Johnson squiffed. The former deputy had installed himself as the reigning town drunk, and he was generally able to cadge enough drinks to stay half-crocked around the clock. When he came through the door, he was already walking on his heels, and within an hour Ed had floated his gizzard with a liberal dose of forty-rod.

Things went pretty much as Banning had predicted. Once they had Johnson cross-eyed, the gang leader started baiting him. *Hadn't Stoudenmire fired him, made a fool out of him in front of the whole town? Hadn't the marshal also killed his best friend, shot him down in cold blood? No real man would take something like that flat on his back. Anybody with any guts would make sure that the sonovabitch was laid out stone-cold dead. The sooner the better!*

Johnson responded to the goad more readily than Banning had expected. Staggering about the room in an alcoholic

rage, he swore he would settle Stoudenmire's hash that very
night. Before he could have any second thoughts, Banning
thrust a shotgun into his hands and shoved him out the back
door. Get him when he makes his night rounds, the gang leader
whispered, down by the old church on Texas Street, Johnson
nodded drunkenly and reeled off into the darkness, mumbling
to himself. Banning watched for a moment to make sure he
was headed in the right direction, then stepped back inside.

Sam was grinning like a short-fanged hyena. "Ed, it's just
like I said. You're a fuckin' wizard."

Banning's eyes swung around, boring holes clean through
him. "Listen close you big ox, 'cause I've only got time to
say this once. Stick on Johnson's trail like a leech. If he gets
it when the fireworks go off, then we've got no problem. But
if he's still kickin' after he gets Stoudenmire, then you kill
him on the spot. Got that? Blast him before he moves out of
his tracks. Make it look like the German got him. The one
thing we sure as shit don't need is another witness. Now
vamoose. And mind what I told you."

Shooting clay pigeons was old hat to Sam, and he took off
like the dinner bell had just caught him out in the north forty.
When the door closed, Ed Banning settled into his chair,
pouring himself a long, tall drink. It had been a grueling
night, but for the first time in weeks he felt like a man holding all the cards.

Then he chuckled. After tonight he'd be the *only* man
holding the cards.

5

Doc Cummings came through the jail door shortly after
eight that evening. His face was furrowed with solemnity
and concern, the way an undertaker looks at an expensive
funeral. The storekeeper had purposely avoided Stoudenmire's house for this discussion since he didn't want to upset
Kate needlessly. Tonight he meant to talk some sense into
his brother-in-law's thick head, and the kind of language he
had in mind wasn't exactly suited to a lady's ears.

The marshal was seated behind the desk paring his fingernails. When Cummings entered, he glanced up, then casually went back to work with the jackknife. "Evenin', Doc. How's tricks?"

Somehow Stoudenmire's unruffled composure grated on the little merchant. It put him in mind of a big cat calmly cleaning its paws as the hunters closed in for the kill. His eyes darted about the office, noting that the lawman was alone. "Where's Gillette, out makin' rounds?"

"No, I gave him the night off." Stoudenmire met the older man's stare, then grinned furtively. "He was overdue, and tonight seemed as good as any."

Cummings couldn't speak for a moment; couldn't bring himself to believe that anyone would be that calculating. Then it came to him that the man his sister had married was just cold-blooded enough to do it.

"Jesus H. Christ. You let him have the night off just to bait somebody into takin' a shot at you. Didn't you?" When Stoudenmire didn't answer, the storekeeper dropped into a chair, now thoroughly exasperated. "Dallas, I'll swear to God, sometimes I get to thinkin' you're on a steady diet of loco weed."

"Doc, you're a born worrier." The lawman chuckled and went right on scraping his thumbnail with the big knife. The abrasive sound sent a chill down Cumming's spine, like chalk screeching across a blackboard. Without looking up, Stoudenmire commented, "The town's peaceful as a church social and I just figured Gillette could use a good night's sleep. Quit your frettin'. Nothin' is gonna happen that I can't handle."

The marshal had a point, and Cummings about halfway believed him. El Paso seemed to have recovered from the shock of the recent killings, or perhaps folks were just learning to take such things in stride. They had damn sure had plenty of practice in the last month or so, enough to last any sane man a couple of lifetimes. But whichever way a fellow looked at it, there was no disputing that the fear of bloodshed had subsided noticeably. Word had gotten around about Stoudenmire's peace talks with Pedro Vazquez, and the townspeople were convinced that they at last had a lawman worth his salt. Still, there was more to it than a bunch of grubby Mexicans. A hell of a lot more where the marshal was concerned.

Cummings made a church with his hands, then flexed his fingers into a steeple. Although Stoudenmire's concentration centered wholly on his fingernails, the storekeeper knew damn well he was watching out of the corner of his eye. Since shouting would obviously accomplish nothing, Cummings decided instead to play it cool and devastate the stubborn German with sheer logic.

"Dallas, I've just come from a meeting with Seth Hart and the rest of the boys. Since you're so all-fired touchy, they asked me to pass along their thoughts and see if we couldn't come to some sort of understanding."

"You mean Hart asked you to pass along his thoughts, don't you? I recollect that he does the talkin' and the rest of your crowd does all the listenin'."

The merchant reddened slightly, but kept his tone lowkey. "Seth's smarter'n you give him credit for, Dallas. While everybody else is runnin' around poppin' off at the mouth, he sits back and figures which way the frog is gonna jump."

"You're readin' the cards wrong, Doc. I'm not sayin' he isn't smart. I just don't want him meddling in my game. He's got his own ax to grind, and I'm not real sure I want any part of it. Not just yet, at any rate."

"For the life of me, I can't figure you out. Seth Hart is probably the most honorable man in this town, bar none. The only thing he wants is to get El Paso back in the hands of the people. Can't you see that, or is it that you just don't trust anybody?"

"Sure, I trust lots of folks. Just not all at once." The lawman left off paring his nails and pointed the blade in Cummings' direction. "You're the one that's got a lot to learn about who to trust. Nobody does nothin' out of Christian charity. Seth Hart included. Saintliness went out of style when they started feedin' people to the lions."

"Is that a fact?" The storekeeper's words came out a little

waspish in spite of himself. "Well suppose you just tell me what Seth's got up his sleeve."

"Can't say as I've given it much thought, what with one thing and another. But just for openers, let's suppose I've gotten rid of Banning, and the political goodies are up for grabs. Who do you think is gonna step in and fill his shoes?"

"Why Seth Hart, naturally. Every respectable person in El Paso looks to him for leadership. But that's no reason to suspect him. Good Lord, somebody has to run things. A town just doesn't run itself, you know."

"Nope, I guess not. Leastways there's generally plenty of people willing to take on the job." Stoudenmire regarded his nails critically for a moment, then snapped the knife shut. "Maybe Hart's everything you make him out to be. I'm not sayin' yay or nay. We'll more'n likely find out soon enough, and until then I'll just keep on playing 'em close to the vest."

Cummings bounded out of his chair and paced across the room, flailing the air with his arms. "Damnation! That beats anything I ever heard of. Do you want to know why Seth Hart called that meeting tonight?" Whirling, he advanced on the lawman. "Because he's worried about you, Mr. Doubting Thomas."

"Me?" Stoudenmire echoed skeptically.

"That's right, you. He believes you're in danger, and he means to do something about it."

Cummings' terse statement neatly skirted what had actually been said in the meeting. For over an hour Seth Hart had lectured his political cronies, building as always toward a predetermined and entirely logical conclusion. The Bannings were boxed in, damned if they did and damned if they didn't. Marshal Stoudenmire had become too popular with the townspeople for the city council to fire him, yet he was daily drawing closer to fitting the Bannings for a noose. They had no choice but to kill him. That or run. And the Bannings weren't the type to just fold camp and sneak off into the night. Still, one man wasn't a match for an entire gang. He could flush them, but when it came down to a shooting war, he

couldn't stand alone. The conclusion was obvious. Stoudenmire needed help.

"Dallas, we've discussed this matter thoroughly and the
solution is as plain as a bump on a log." Cummings met the
lawman's gaze squarely. "What El Paso needs is a vigilance committee."

"Not on your tintype!" Stoudenmire's hoarse growl buf-
feted the storekeeper back on his heels. "The first sonovabitch
that takes the law into his own hands is gonna get his ass
handed to him on a platter. And I don't draw the line at anybody, Doc. Not even you."

"Man, stop and think for a minute. You're bucking impossible odds. The Bannings have to be made aware that this
town won't abide further killing. Otherwise, you'll wind up
trying to kick the slats out of a pine box. What we need is a
group of armed citizens willing to back your play. That's
what'll turn the trick, and once the Bannings see the town's
behind you, we can end this dirty business."

"No dice. When a town resorts to vigilantes, they've the
same as admitted that the law won't work. I'm tellin' you
right now, Doc, that won't happen while I'm wearin' this
star."

"But, Jesus Christ, you haven't got the chance of a snow-
ball in Hades. Are you so pigheaded you can't see that? Or
are you just set on gettin' yourself killed?"

Stoudenmire ignored the merchant's nasty tone. "Doc, I
appreciate the gesture, but I'll have to finish this job my own
way. I was hired with no strings attached, and that's how
we're gonna play it out. Worryin' about a bunch of amateur
gunslingers would just slow me down, and right now I need
to keep movin'."

Cummings started to object, but the lawman stilled him
with an upraised hand. "Now let me tell you something for
your own good, Doc. What would happen if Hart formed the
vigilantes and I still ended up in a basket? Think about that,
real hard. You might be trading one political kingfish for another. Maybe I'm pigheaded, but I reckon I'll take my
chances without Hart standin' behind me with a gun."

When the storekeeper seemed inclined to argue, Stoudenmire decided it was time to make the evening rounds. But Cummings wasn't about to be put off by that old dodge. Like a feisty dog worrying a bone, he tagged along, talking a blue streak. Crossing the plaza, he extolled the many virtues of Seth Hart, lambasting Stoudenmire for being overly suspicious of the very people who could save his hide. When the marshal merely grunted and kept on walking, Cummings forgot about logic and launched into a harangue about the folly of pride and rockbound stubbornness. Turning off the plaza onto Oregon Street, the lawman headed for the southside, trying his best not to listen as Cummings haughtily pronounced him a brute for punishment.

Short of jailing his own brother-in-law, there seemed no way to end it, so Stoudenmire just plowed on, nodding every now and then to let the little storekeeper know he wasn't talking to himself. The southside dives seemed no more rowdy than usual, and the pair made quick time as they strolled through the quarter. Apparently the saloons and dancehalls had been able to handle their own troubles, and for once it appeared that Stoudenmire would get through a tour without making a single arrest. Still, the night was young and anything could happen. As a matter of fact, it usually did. On the southside every night was the same, some more so than others, and long before closing time the jail was generally packed to the gunnels with a motley assortment of belligerent drunks and weepy rumdums.

Nearing the end of Texas Street, the lawman was only vaguely aware that Cummings was still rambling on about the need for a vigilance committee. Leaving the boardwalk, he took to the street and headed for the far corner, figuring to shuck Doc for the night once they again reached the plaza. Suddenly there was a deafening explosion only yards behind them, and a load of buckshot kicked up dust at their feet. Cummings howled and grabbed at his leg, crow-hopping forward a few steps before he toppled over.

Staggering drunk, Bill Johnson wobbled from behind a stone pillar of an old mission and raised his scattergun for a better shot. But the lawman made a hellishly poor target. With the first report, he had hit the ground, rolled sideways, then reversed himself in the middle of a roll. Even as Johnson pressed the trigger, he swung around on his belly with his pistol out and cocked. The Colt roared a fraction ahead of the shotgun's hollow boom, and Johnson stumbled backwards into the crumbling pillar.

The buckshot tore a sign loose over a store on the other side of the street, and even as it fell, Stoudenmire dusted the former deputy with three quick shots. Johnson hung against the pillar, jerking with the impact of each slug, then pitched face down in the street.

Stoudenmire came to his feet just in time to glimpse a man dart from the shadows and take off running down Stanton Street. Hurriedly, he snapped off two shots as the dim figure disappeared around a corner, knowing even as he fired that he had missed. There was no sense in giving chase with an empty gun, and he turned back to see what could be done for Cummings. But the storekeeper was already up and hobbling toward the fallen bushwhacker, gripped by a curiosity that for the moment overshadowed the pain in his leg. Both men reached the body at the same time, and Stoudenmire toed it over with the point of his boot. In the faint starlight, the dead man's glassy eyes shone like cloudy agates.

"Well I'll be double-dipped," Cummings croaked. "It's old Bill Johnson. Who'd have thought that miserable bastard would've had the guts for it."

Stoudenmire started kicking out empties and reloading.

"They've all got the guts for it when they're shootin' at your back."

Holstering the Colt, he draped Cummings arm around his shoulders and took off at a slow walk. After a few steps he nodded down at the storekeeper's bloody leg. "That's the very reason I didn't want your vigilantes roaming the streets. Amateurs always end up gettin' shot."

CHAPTER EIGHT

—◅◦▻—

1

Early next morning Stoudenmire sent word to Seth Hart calling for a meeting. Things were coming apart at the seams, and unless they did something fast, the whole damn town was going to look like a shooting gallery.

Johnson's assassination attempt had fooled no one, least of all the respectable element. The Bannings were behind the bushwhacking just like they were behind every other dirty thing in El Paso, and trying to gun down a peace officer was the last straw. The town had split right down the middle, the southside scum against the decent folks, and battle lines were already being drawn. Word about the proposed vigilance committee had somehow leaked out, and knots of men were even then gathering on the plaza, bolstering one another's courage with loud talk and cheap whiskey. The general feeling seemed to be that Stoudenmire needed a hand in ridding the town of its undesirables, and for the first time, the people of El Paso were openly declaring their opposition to Boss Banning.

Stoudenmire wasn't too keen on meeting with the Hart

faction, but he saw no alternative. The townspeople had to be headed off before armed mobs took to the streets, and much as he hated to admit it, that was something he couldn't handle alone. Hart and his cronies had started this crazy business about vigilantes, and they were the only ones who could quell the hotheads gathering on the plaza. The important thing now was to get the leaders talking against mob action, and damned quickly. Otherwise, good men were going to die needlessly.

Although he would have been the last to admit it, the marshal could have used a little breather himself. Getting bushwhacked hadn't bothered him so much, but things were getting pretty fierce around the house. Kate had given him the roughest night yet, railing at him for getting Doc shot, then blistering him in the next breath for being so careless with his own life. Stoudenmire couldn't tell which had infuriated her more; she had skipped from one to the other for the better part of two hours. Finally he had stalked out of the house and returned to the office, leaving her to stew in her own juices. Women were damn strange creatures, temperamental as a mare in heat and about as predictable as a landslide.

Still, taking the shooting back to back with Kate's tantrum didn't gall him nearly as much as this meeting with Hart. The plain fact was that he would have to ask for their help, and it curried him the wrong way to be forced into that position. Seth Hart was a horsetrader from way back, and an exchange of some kind would have to be made before the lard-faced politician agreed to back off. But Stoudenmire didn't have a hell of a lot to bargain with. Except maybe to reveal the next step in his war on the Bannings. And that really grated on the bone! So far no one knew what he was going to do until he did it, and that was the biggest edge a lawman could ask for. Once somebody else was made privy to his plans, the cheese could get binding, real fast. Yet it was sort of like the fellow caught in a blizzard with only the shithouse in sight. He had damned little choice.

The morning passed uneventfully enough, but a hard core of troublemakers were still congregated on the plaza.

Stoudenmire resisted the temptation to send them packing; they would only gather somewhere else, and as long as they remained on the square, he at least had them in sight. The time to start worrying was when he couldn't see them. With the way things were breaking, that'd be the time some spell-binder would get them all fired up and start a march on the southside. Crossing the plaza on his way to the meeting, it occurred to the lawman that El Paso was a town that seemed damned set on getting itself leveled to the ground. Oddly enough, some folks had the quaint notion that the only way to bring about change was to burn everything down and start all over. And unless Seth Hart got off his ass, the hammer-heads in town might just get their way.

Upon arriving at Hart's home back of the mill, he found the clique assembled and waiting. Looking them over as Hart led him into the room, the lawman was struck by a certain sameness about their appearance. Then it came to him. They were seated in exactly the same chairs as on his first visit to this house. Each man probably had squatter's rights on his chair by now, and doubtless there was some hierarchy in-volved that made the whole thing seem vastly important to them. *Little men playing for big stakes.* That's what it all boiled down to, whichever way a man came at it.

Doc Cummings was the only one who greeted him by name. Horace Adair merely nodded, letting the lawman know that he hadn't forgotten their last encounter. John Simmons and Nate Hobart ran a dead heat to see who could cake the most ice around the word *marshal*, and curiously enough, they both won. So far as Stoudenmire was concerned, the whole damn room was swathed in frost, and he had the dis-tinct feeling it was going to be all uphill in the next few min-utes. Hart waved him to a chair, then took his own seat and sat back with his hands folded over his ample stomach. Watching him, Stoudenmire was reminded of an old bullfrog hunkered down on a lily pad flicking his tongue at passing flies. The trouble being that he seemed to be the only fly in sight.

Hart purposely let the silence build for a moment, then

looked over at the lawman with a gloating smile, "Marshal, I'll have to admit you've got us curious. Doc relayed your feelings about a vigilance committee, and I suspect he toned them down for our benefit. Be that as it may, you called this meeting, and we'll listen to whatever you've got on your mind."

Stoudenmire didn't even bother looking at the other men. They reflected Hart's mood like images on still water, and he addressed himself directly to the miller. "Mr. Hart, I'm gonna give you some cold facts. What you do with 'em is your own affair. But I'm warnin' you straight out, if you jump the wrong way, you'll wind up getting a lot of people killed."

"Like I said, Marshal, we'll listen." Hart's eyes roved around the table, and the other men nodded hastily. "I can't promise any more than that."

"Suit yourself. I'm just hired to keep the peace. Whichever way it goes, it won't be any skin off my nose." Horace Adair's jaw popped open, but Hart stilled him with a sharp glance. The lawman went on as if the Irishman didn't even exist. "Let's take first things first, just to clear the air. You're out to form a vigilance committee, and I mean to stop you. If I have to, I'll toss every man here into the hoosegow and forget where I hid the key."

"That's pretty strong talk for a hired hand." Adair broke in before Hart could silence him.

"Nothin' I can't back up, Mr. Adair. But unless I'm pushed, I'd prefer to handle it another way. Right now it's between the Bannings and me. That's the way I'd like to keep it. If you fellas organize the vigilantes, that means Banning will have to muster his own army on the south-side. Since he controls the vice district, it wouldn't be any sweat to raise more guns than you could count. Once your vigilantes cross the line, it'll mean open warfare in the streets, and nobody knows where that'll end. Not even Mr. Hart, here."

Seth Hart moved his hand in a dismissive gesture. "We're not the amateurs you think, Marshal. These same thoughts have occurred to us. But we figure to raise enough men to counter anything Banning could scrounge up."

"What kind of men? Clerks and bank tellers." Stoudenmire's lips curled back from his teeth in a grin that was more like a grimace. "Maybe you men can run a business, but when it comes to killin', you haven't got sense enough to wad a bird-gun load. Those hardcases on the southside would eat you alive and spit out the seeds. But that's not what troubles me."

"Well now, that's a damn curious thing for a lawman to say," Hart rumbled. "Just exactly what is it that troubles you, Mr. Stoudenmire?"

"Anybody that goes huntin' trouble deserves what he gets, no matter which side of town he's from. But if you turn the vigilantes loose, a lot of innocent people are gonna get killed in the bargain. I've seen mobs before, and once they get a taste for blood, there's no telling where it'll stop. You people have just missed a couple of showdowns with the Mexicans by the skin of your teeth. Seems to me it'd be damned foolish to start a war among yourselves that could be just as bad. Maybe worse."

Horace Adair snorted derisively and slapped the table with his open palm. "By God, Stoudenmire, for sheer gall you take the cake. You haven't got any evidence, your witnesses have all been murdered, and the Bannings are still running El Paso like they had a patent. But you have the audacity to come in here and ask us to hold back. Hell man, you haven't done the job you were hired to do. It's time somebody else took a crack at it."

Stoudenmire's flinty gaze swung around and settled over the Irishman like a cold mist. "Mister, I'm tryin' to overlook your bad manners, but it's gettin' to be a chore. Don't press your luck."

"All right, boys," Hart said, "let's not fly off the handle. Suppose everybody just calms down and tries using a little reason for a change."

"Seth, I'm all for reason, but it seems to me that Horace has a point." Nate Hobart rarely said anything, and his unexpected comment brought the other men's heads around. "Just think about it for a minute. The Bannings are so deeply entrenched in politics that we'll never get any evidence of corruption. All the witnesses that could link them to these killings are dead, so there's no way we can legally bring them to justice on that. Now the marshal tells us they're too well organized for vigilantes to be of any use. If that's the case, then just what is it he's suggesting?"

There was a moment of profound silence. The normally laconic hotel owner had deftly hit the nail right on the head. *Just what the hell did Stoudenmire have in mind?* Doc Cummings had held back up to this point, not wanting to put his own brother-in-law on the spot. But he could see Adair priming himself, and he decided to jump in before the meeting disintegrated into a real donny-brook.

"Dallas, don't get your hackles up. John's question seems like a fair one to me. If you want us to keep sittin' on our thumbs, then you've got to give us a reason. Have you got an ace in the hole, or are you just giving the Bannings more rope in the hopes they'll hang themselves?"

The lawman looked around the table, fixing each man in turn with a probing stare. Finally he spoke, not to anyone in particular but to the five men as a whole. "I'm not in the habit of tellin' people my plans. The fewer that know, the less chance of a leak. You figure you've got a right to hear it, so I'll tell you. But if it gets out, I'll know where to come lookin'."

Stoudenmire's cold eyes again traveled around the table, and the men felt their innards shrivel under his gaze. The threat was only thinly veiled, and not one among them doubted that he would kill the first man who opened his mouth in the wrong place. Like he said, they wanted to hear, and with it they accepted the responsibility of keeping their traps shut.

"The Bannings are vulnerable in three spots." The marshal selected three poker chips from a rack in the center of the table and stood them on edge, side-by-side as he spoke. "Their rustling operation, their corrupt deals with city officials, and the protection racket they run in the vice district. Starting tomorrow, I'll be probing for the weak links in each of these operations. What I'm after is hard evidence that'll stand up in court. It's a gamble, I grant you, but keep in mind that it

only takes one informer to topple the whole shootin' match."
Stoudenmire flicked one of the chips with his finger, and it
fell sideways, toppling the others in turn. "With a little luck
I might just have a songbird in the bag within a couple of
days. But even if that peters out, we'll still be giving Banning
the cold nose every time he squats."

Seth Hart nodded solemnly, studying the top of the table
for a moment. Then he looked up. "Marshal, we want shed
of the Bannings, but by the same token we don't want you
killed. Quite frankly, I'm not sure you can pull it off by yourself."

Stoudenmire's mouth quirked a little at the corners. "Well
if it doesn't pan out, you can always storm the Coliseum.
I might even go along with you."

Hart's belly rumbled, and his mouth parted in a wet
chuckle. The decision had been made. Stoudenmire would
have his chance, but the vigilantes would be held in reserve.
Just in case.

2

When the train pulled in next morning, a swarthy, dark-haired
man stepped off onto the platform and stretched his arms,
like a great black cat warming itself in the mellow sun. The
only baggage he carried was strapped to his hips, twin Colts
with darkened walnut grips and as deadly looking as the man
himself. There was nothing fancy about his hardware, just
tools of the trade, weathered, well oiled, and always close at
hand. But two guns singled a man out, even in a border town,
and it didn't take a swami to come up with his profession.

Still, guns and all, the thing that made people stare after
this man were his eyes. Sort of dark and impassive, like thin
ice on a winter pond. The kind of eyes a fellow didn't forget
and, more often than not, went out of his way to avoid meeting directly. They weren't cruel eyes, or even pitiless, they
were just black orbs that looked at nothing, yet saw everything, and registered absolutely no emotion whatsoever.

Somehow he put most folks in mind of a sleek carnivore

stalking its supper, moving sort of soft and lithe like he was walking on padded feet. And if he came scratching at the door some dark night, a smart man would have blown out the lamp and thrown the bolt.

After working the kinks out of his back, the man ambled off toward the vice district. There was a certain arrogance to his walk, like maybe he had just foreclosed on the sidewalk, and even burly, ham-fisted teamsters gave him a wide berth. Though his gaze touched on everything and everyone along the street, there was no sign on his face of either like, dislike, or even passing curiosity. Just a stoic disinterest that looked through and past whatever happened to cross his path. Which wasn't a hell of a lot. Most people just naturally got out of his way and left well enough alone.

Ten minutes later he walked into the Coliseum Saloon and planted his foot on the brass rail. When the bartender meandered over, the man nodded just once, as though he was conserving his strength. "Where can I find Ed Banning?"

The stranger's slow, guttural words put the barkeep in mind of a mission-schooled Kiowa he had once known. But something about the man warned him that this was one pilgrim who wouldn't take kindly to questions. Jerking his thumb toward the rear of the room, the barkeep said, "That's his office back there. Best knock before you go in."

The man didn't even acknowledge that he had heard. Moving away from the bar, he crossed the room, rapped once on the door, and entered. The bartender shook his head in a mild quandary and went back to polishing glasses. Some minutes later the door opened again, and the stranger came out, trailed closely by Ed and Sam Banning. The men bellied up at the end of the bar, with the soft-spoken jasper between the two brothers. Ed Banning signaled for drinks, and the barkeep hustled forward with a bottle, growing more puzzled by the moment. The boss looked fidgety as a whore in church, and that was one for the books. Up till now he had always thought the skinny bastard didn't have any more nerves than a gorged snake.

"Jack, let's have some of the good stuff," Banning ordered.

Looking about the saloon, he called out to a scattering of early morning patrons. "Boys, the drinks are on the house! Step up and name your pleasure."

The men sitting about the room exchanged startled glances, them made a rush for the bar. Ed Banning wasn't especially noted for his generosity, and everybody figured they had best get to drinking before he recovered his senses. The hubbub gradually died down after the men got their drinks, but Banning waited till everyone was swilling contentedly before he let them in on the reason for the celebration.

"Boys, in case you're wonderin' who this gent is, I'd like you to meet Choctaw Tyler." Banning placed his hand on the man's shoulder, then pulled it back like he had touched a hot stove. "From now on he's gonna be my right-hand man. Next to Sam here, of course."

There was a sudden stir of interest from the men crowding the bar. The name was known and feared, at least by anyone with sense enough to pour piss out of a boot. Choctaw Tyler, the scourge of Indian Territory, deadlier than smallpox and scarlet fever back to back.

Although facts were sketchy, he was reputed to have killed a dozen men in gunfights, maybe even twice that number. No one knew for sure. They only knew that, next to Doc Holliday and Wes Hardin, he was the most feared gun in the west. Perhaps the most deadly of all according to some folks, for it was a well known fact that gut-eaters placed no value whatever on human life, their own or anyone else's. And a man had only to look at him to know that Choctaw Tyler was a full blood, just a hop and a skip from carrying a scalping knife instead of a six-gun. Even the US marshals working out of Ft. Smith steered clear of him, and with good reason. Word out of the Nations had it that he was tougher'n boiled owl, and some even swore that wherever he spit, nothing ever again grew on that spot.

Now he was standing right before their eyes in the flesh, and he looked just about as mean as his reputation claimed. And the Bannings had imported him all the way from Indian Territory! By Christ, that would make folks sit up and talk, sure enough. But not a man at the bar needed to ask why Choctaw Tyler had been brought to El Paso. They knew. Just as sure as they knew their own names.

After a couple of drinks, the Bannings and their new hired gun returned to the office. The little charade at the bar had been nothing more than a means of letting everyone know that the Indian was in town. Word would spread through El Paso like a dose of clap in a whorehouse, and by noon folks wouldn't be talking about anything else. Maybe the uptown crowd wouldn't like it, but they'd wait around to see how it came out. Even Bible-thumpers had a certain morbid curiosity about such things.

Once they were seated in the office, Ed Banning briefly related the events leading to the present stalemate with Stoudenmire. Choctaw Tyler sat and listened, making no comment one way or the other about the killings, the political maneuverings, or the near misses. When the gang leader finally wound down, Tyler just looked at him, like he was watching a talking dog and waiting for the next trick.

"Right now we've got ourselves a Mexican standoff," Banning declared, slightly unsettled by the Indian's fishy stare. "But sooner or later, there'll be a showdown. Stoudenmire will either come lookin' for us, or else the vigilantes'll suck up their balls and start a free-for-all. Whichever way it falls, we want your gun backing our play."

"Money talks." Tyler's dark eyes hooded, revealing nothing. "Five hundred now. Another five when it's done. Sundays extra, and I buy my own shells."

Banning wasn't sure if the inscrutable sonovabitch was pulling his leg or not, but he let it pass. "Fair enough. We've got no gripes about payin' top dollar. This shitheel marshal has got the whole town walkin' on eggshells, and it'll be worth every penny of it to watch him eat dust."

Choctaw Tyler's mouth set in an ugly grin, like a skull-head covered with burnt rawhide. "Just pick a spot. I'll drop your hick lawdog like a load of bricks. They all go down when *Tai-me* rattles the bones."

Banning didn't have the least idea who *Tai-me* was, but

he had a notion that the fullblood seated across from him would tackle a turpentined catamount if the price was right. While he started counting out five hundred in greenbacks, Sam got busy pouring another round of drinks. Maybe their celebration was jumping the gun a little, but what the hell! Choctaw Tyler had just signed on for the duration.

3

Seth Hart was as good as his word. Along with Doc Cummings and his other cronies, the miller had circulated around the plaza talking his own brand of horse sense. The time wasn't right, he cautioned the men standing on street corners and crowding the boardwalks. The Bannings knew every move they were making, and the only way to invade the southside without needless killing was to take them by surprise. Wait, he told them, stand ready. Vigilantes may yet be needed, and when the right moment came, he would put out the call. Until then, everyone was to go about their business just as usual and avoid trouble with the Banning crowd.

When a handful of hotheads tried to argue the point, Hart gave it to them straight. Lay off or get your ears pinned back, he growled. Any man who started trouble today would find hard times camping on his doorstep. The warning had its effect. Once the Bannings were gone, Seth Hart would be the most influential man in El Paso, and everyone knew it. Crossing him now would only make for lean pickings farther down the road. The miller would eventually wield the power in the basin, and the man who got on his wrong side might just find himself starved out of town.

But Hart was too good a politician to send them away disgruntled. He had given his word to the marshal that the townspeople would hold off until the law had had its chance. That meant that the vigilantes would probably be needed after all, since Stoudenmire was fast working himself into a corner. Keep it confidential, he told them, but sleep light and have your guns handy. The call could come at any time.

Seth Hart had few illusions about his fellow townsmen.

They would keep it about as confidential as a medicine man
hawking elixir water. By nightfall what he had said would
be all over El Paso, in ten different versions. But it had gotten them off the streets, and as long as they had some burgeoning conspiracy to occupy their minds, they wouldn't be
out hunting trouble.

Stoudenmire and Gillette watched Hart's performance
from the door of the jail. While the fat man wasn't exactly
their cup of tea, they grudgingly admitted that he was a slick
operator. The crowd had been manipulated without even
knowing it, which was the mark of a true bunco artist. Maybe
Hart called himself a politician, but he was a kissing cousin
to a con man, and the two peace officers found the knowledge a little unsettling. Still, the mob had been dispersed, and
for the moment that was the only thing that counted.

The lawmen stepped back inside the jail and started tus-
sling with their own problems. Stoudenmire had purposely
held off discussing the next step in their campaign against
the Bannings until they could get more information on the
latest development. Namely, Choctaw Tyler.

Word of the redskin gunfighter had spread through town
at a dizzying pace, and rumors were flying thick and fast. The
Indian was here, that much they knew, and everyone suspected why he had been imported. After that it was pure
speculation as to how the Bannings intended to use him.

Stoudenmire had his own ideas on the subject, but right
now he was more concerned with other matters. Tilted back
in his chair, he spoke absently, as though trying to flush his
mind of distractions and focus only on the job ahead. "Jim,
we've been losin' ground fast in this deal, and it appears to
me we've got to play hurry up and catch up. Everybody in
this town seems bent on givin' us the fast shuffle, including
the ones that're supposed to be on our side."

"Ain't that the godawful truth," Gillette agreed sourly. "I
never seen people so damn set on gettin' their brains blowed
out. Seems like they're bound to get in a fight with somebody.
Now that you put a damper on the greasers, they're half froze

to start cuttin' on one another. Beatenest thing I ever run across."

"Well in a way it is, and in another way it's not." The marshal flipped his hat on the desk and locked his hands behind his head. "Most folks'll live and let live if they're left alone. Hell, wolves and cougars live right alongside one another, and they hardly ever tangle. People are the same way. They figure every man has a right to his own game, whether it's crooked or straight, so long as he don't step on their toes."

Gillette ran a hand through his unruly shock of hair, and his forehead wrinkled in a bemused way. "Pard, you just lost me on the turn. People ain't much different than the beasties, I grant you. But what the hell's that got to do with live and let live?"

"Why, I reckon I'm tryin' to say that, whether it's man or beast, they just naturally don't go huntin' trouble. Now you take wolves, for instance. Sometimes an old stud wolf'll get the hots for another outfit's territory. Before you know it, he'll start a battle royal and get his whole pack chewed to shreds just because he wants what the other fellow's got. Same thing happens with people. They let some sorry bastard get 'em all riled up, and before anybody takes the time to think it through, they're squared off lookin' for the other fellow's jugular."

"You're sayin' it's the leaders that cause the trouble. If the people was left to their own hook they'd figure out some way to get by without all this fightin'." The deputy scratched his head and mulled it over, unmindful of the shower of dandruff that flaked down over his vest. "Well, it's somethin' to think about. Don't know's I ever heard it put just that way."

"No other way to put it," Stoudenmire commented. "Just take a look around you. Ed Banning's got this town locked up tighter'n a drum, and Seth Hart figures he oughta be king of the hill. Between 'em they're liable to get half the people in El Paso laid out with their toes curled backwards. What folks oughta do is let those two fight it out man to man and then hang the winner. That'd solve most of the probems this town's got."

"Well you sorta set Hart back on his haunches for the time bein'. Leastways he called off the vigilantes."

"Not for long. He's only giving us enough time to make himself look good. If we don't come up with something fast, he's gonna have that mob back on the street yellin' for blood."

"You wanna know somethin,' Dallas? If I didn't know you better, I'd think you had rocks in your head. You got a hired *pistolero* sniffin' your trail, and you sit around worryin' about what's gonna happen to the little folks when the big dogs finally tangle. That's some kinda nervy, but I ain't sure it's too bright."

The lawman just chuckled, more amused than offended by Gillette's tone. This crotchety old fart was the only man on earth who could talk to him like that, and they both knew it. In some curious way, that made it all right. Perhaps everybody needed their own personal devil's advocate, someone who constantly looked on the dark side simply because they were too damned cantankerous to play it any other way. Oddly enough, it helped to keep things in perspective, and he always felt uneasy when Gillette wasn't around to nettle him with testy remarks.

"Jim, the way I see it, Choctaw Tyler's the least of our worries. The Bannings can't use him openly 'cause it would ruin 'em politically. Course, they could have him bushwhack me, but I sorta doubt that, too. I've got an idea they brought him in as a bodyguard more'n anything else. Like as not, the only time I'd trade lead with him is if I went lookin' for the Bannings."

"Jesus Pesus!" the deputy woofed. "You make it sound like a shootout with him wouldn't be no more'n a friendly game of mumblety-peg. You better check your paint pots again, *amigo*. I hear tell that gut-eater has already filled a couple of graveyards all by his lonesome."

Like most peace officers, Gillette and Stoudenmire kept themselves fairly well informed on the activities of the West's more publicized bad men. Even now they knew that Wyatt Earp and Doc Holliday were involved in a fracas out in Tombstone. Luke Short was still in Dodge, and Billy the Kid had recently gone under at old Ft. Sumner. Wes Hardin was serving twenty-five years at Huntsville, of course. And incredible as it seemed, Ben Thompson had been elected city marshal of Austin. There was just no explaining some people's taste in lawmen. Then there was Choctaw Tyler. Never been indicted, much less in jail, and reportedly as sudden as a snake with either hand.

Stoudenmire slowly unfolded from his chair, then crossed to the stove and poured himself a cup of coffee. Turning, he gave Gillette a searching look. "Jim, think back to all the gunslingers we've run across in our time. Every one of 'em had a reputation about a mile long and a yard wide. But when it got down to cases, their rep assayed out to one part fact and nine parts bullshit. Seems to me they trade on the fact that people are scared of 'em, sorta bluff their way through just because folks have heard they're sudden death. When it comes to shootin' at somebody that's gonna shoot back, they head for the hills. *Muy pronto.* I'm bettin' Choctaw Tyler's not any different. Just more so."

"I can't argue it. Likely as not you're right." Gillette returned his look levelly. "But I still say it's a piss-poor bet. What we oughta do is come up on either side of that knothead and throw his ass in the can."

Before Stoudenmire could reply Doc Cummings popped through the door. The little merchant's bearing was square-shouldered and somewhat martial, like he had just led the Light Brigade through the Valley of Death. Halting before the marshal's desk, he stuck his thumb in his vest pocket and puffed out his chest.

"Well gents, we've disbanded the troops and sent 'em home. But all you have to do is say the word, and we'll have 'em formed and ready to march before you can bat an eye."

Gillette and Stoudenmire exchanged sardonic looks. After a moment, the marshal returned to his chair and glanced up at Cummings, who seemed frozen in his pose. "Relax, Doc. Have a seat. I was just getting ready to fill Jim in on what we discussed at the meeting. Maybe you could give us some advice."

Stoudenmire saw Gillette cover his mouth to hide a grin,
but Cummings didn't tumble to the joke. The storekeeper
dragged up a chair and plopped down, immensely gratified
that his expertise in such matters had at last been recognized.
"Fire away, Dallas. I won't interrupt unless I see something
that's out of kilter."

"Thank you, Doc. I appreciate your help." The lawman
cocked an eye in Gillette's direction and stifled a smile. "Now
here's what I've got in mind. Jim, I want you to rent a packhorse, lay in some supplies, and go find yourself a spot where
you can spy on the Banning ranch. What I'm hopin' is that
they figure it's safe to start rustlin' again. If so, you trail 'em
and spot the outfit they hit. Assuming it works, we'll call in
the Rangers, get the Mexican rancher over here to identify
the cattle, and sack the Bannings with a federal warrant."

"Sounds fair enough to me," Gillette observed. "But what
if they've retired from the rustlin' business?"

"Good question," Doc interjected soberly. "That leaves us
out in the cold."

"Not exactly," Stoudenmire noted. "While Jim's gone, I'm
gonna visit every dive in town and put the pressure on 'em
for evidence of kickbacks to the Bannings. Along with that,
I'll also be nosin' around to see if we can turn up any political payoffs. Like that waterworks contract to Pud Brown's
brother. We'll be hittin' 'em from three sides at once, and all
we need is one good lick to bring them to their knees."

"Yeah, it might work," Gillette allowed. "But if it don't,
they'll suck their ass up so tight we'll never get a hold on 'em."

"We'll cross that bridge when we come to it." The marshal paused, watching the other two men intently for a moment. "If we come up between a rock and a hard place, I've
still got an ace in the hole. I had a meeting with the mayor
after I left Hart's this morning. The second meeting, as a matter of fact. He's scared shitless, and I've about got him sold
on testifying against the Bannings. The only thing holding
him back is that he wants another witness to back up his story.
He's afraid we won't get an indictment otherwise." Again
he hesitated, looking them both squarely in the eye. "I don't

have to tell you to keep this under your hats. And, Doc, that includes Seth Hart. If this ever got out, Isaac Porter is cold meat. Savvy?"

Both men nodded solemnly, and Cummings came up on the edge of his seat. "Dallas, I just volunteered to help you. By God, if anybody knows what's happening in this town, it's me, and I'll betcha I can turn up a wagonload of evidence on corruption and bribes."

"Doc, I appreciate the offer, but I'll have to turn you down. The stakes are just too damn high. Banning and his crowd play for keeps, and they'd kill you dead as hell if they caught you diggin' for skeletons. This is a rough game, and there's no room in it for eager beavers."

Cumming's face purpled with indignation, and they argued briefly, but Stoudenmire was adamant. Under no circumstances was the storekeeper to get involved, and that was final. If he did, he'd find himself locked in a cell under protective custody. With that, Cummings kicked back his chair and marched out with his nose in the air. As he went through the door, they heard him muttering to himself. "By Christ, it's a sorry goddamn mess when your own brother-in-law treats you like a snot-nosed kid. Believe you me, Kate's going to hear about this."

Stoudenmire just grinned and went back for a refill on coffee. Some folks just didn't know when they were well off. Especially storekeepers trying to convince themselves that they didn't belong among the fainthearted.

4

Overnight some disturbing rumors had drifted back to Ed Banning. Stoudenmire was making the rounds of various gaming dives and whorehouses on the southside. The message he carried was blunt and to the point. Cooperate in greasing the skids for the Bannings, or else. The latter part of his threat wasn't spelled out, but it was plain enough. Those who refused would be hauled down and trampled in the shitstorm that was sure to follow. Clearly the marshal had begun

a war of nerves with the madams and gamblers in the vice
district, and he damn sure wasn't pulling any punches about
what he had in mind.

That in itself didn't disturb Banning. The trick was as old
as the hills, and every highroller and whore on the southside
knew what would happen if they opened their mouths. What
really bothered him was the fact that only two dive owners
had reported the incident. That meant the sporting crowd was
spooked, uncertain who would win in the end; otherwise they
would have come running to him the moment they were con-
tacted. Sam's bullying tactics had kept them in line in the
past, true enough, but in a deal like this, nothing could be
taken for granted. Even the threat of Choctaw Tyler couldn't
be counted on now that Stoudenmire was out cracking knuckles. Some dunghead might get a case of the shakes and decide to hedge his bet. It only took one loose tongue to start
the ball rolling, and it might just turn into a goddamn ava-
lanche if something wasn't done fast.

Then, along about his third cup of coffee, Banning's morning turned even darker. One of the boys brought in word that
Deputy Gillette had ridden out of town shortly after dawn
leading a packhorse. The stablehand who had passed the information along didn't know Gillette's destination, but any
numbskull could figure that out. Even Sam had tumbled fast
enough. The old lawdog was headed for the ranch, only it was
a cinch he wouldn't be paying a social visit. Once he got into
the hills back of the spread, even a bloodhound couldn't track
him down, and with a spyglass he could count the whiskers
on everything that moved down below. The rustling operation would have to be shut down tight as a drum. Banning
sent a rider pounding out of town with a terse message. Until
he gave the word, nothing moved!

Ten minutes later Banning began wishing he had stayed
in bed. One of his men from city hall came tapping at the
back door and damn near wet down his leg while he was trying to spit out the story. These political hacks were all alike;
they never made a move without mulling it over for at least a
day, and even then you couldn't be sure they weren't playing

both ends against the middle. Still, this one had finally decided his bread was best smeared with Banning butter, and the story he had to tell was the worst news yet.

Yesterday Stoudenmire had paid a call on the mayor, and they had holed up in the politico's office for the better part of a half-hour. Although the man didn't know what they had talked about, Isaac Porter appeared visibly shaken when the marshal left, and it seemed pretty certain they hadn't been discussing official business. Banning gave the man a good tongue lashing for not reporting sooner, then booted his ass out the back door.

Turning back to Sam and Choctaw Tyler, he had the look of a man who had just been served fried dog turds for breakfast. "Well you have to hand it to that goddamn German. When he cuts the wolves loose, he goes all the way. The bastard's kickin' over rocks in every direction."

"Yeah, but what's it mean?" Sam frowned, now thoroughly baffled by the morning's rash of problems. "Is Porter talkin', or did Stoudenmire just brace him the way he did everybody down here?"

"I don't know," Banning pondered aloud. "After all we've done for him, I'd hate to think the mayor would double-cross us. On the other hand, I'm damned if I'd put it past him." Then he blinked, glancing around at his brother. "But I'll tell you one thing. Porter could be real trouble. He knows enough to put us all away, and if he ever got on a witness stand, we're lookin' at a jail cell. Maybe even a neck stretchin'."

Sam's bemused look suddenly turned to anger. "Goddamnit, it's just like I been sayin' from the start. We gotta get rid of that fuckin' marshal once and for all."

"Don't worry, little brother. We're gonna dig his hole real soon. But we have to pick the time and the place, and it's gotta look right. Otherwise, the reformers'll start beatin' drums all over town."

Choctaw Tyler grunted and smiled like a cat with a mouthful of feathers. "Anytime you say, suits me. Sooner I earn my money, the sooner I can hit the road."

Banning darted a glance at the Indian. "I'll tell you when.

And you can bet your boots it won't be long in comin'." He seemed on the verge of saying something else, then fell silent, and after a moment looked over at Sam. "What we need is to buy a little time, and it occurs to me there's a trick we haven't tried. Send the swamper over to Stoudenmire's office. Tell him I've got something to say that he'll be real interested in hearin'. But only over here. Nowhere else."

Sam's mouth popped open, but he never got a chance to speak. Banning shot him a withering look, and the burly ruffian obediently made tracks for the door. Choctaw Tyler just smiled and pulled out the makings. Watching him, Banning decided that the gut-eater would be hard to take as a steady diet. All he did was look at you with that shiteatin' smile and stink up the place with his goddamn Bull Durham.

Sam returned shortly, and they all sat around looking at one another in deadened silence. Twenty minutes later Stoudenmire walked through the door, and it escaped no one's attention that Tige padded along at his side. The brute looked meaner than ever if such a thing were possible, and it was clear that he hadn't forgotten his trip to this room. It was equally clear that the lawman had come loaded for bear. If the gang leader wanted trouble, he figured that between Tige and himself they could dish out enough to go around.

Stoudenmire ignored the Indian as though he didn't exist, leveling down instead on Banning. "Whatever you've got to say, get it said. I haven't got all day."

Banning smiled, but only with great effort. "I don't think your time will be wasted, Marshal. But first I'd like to ask you a question. Just what do you hope to gain by badgering my people down here? They're not gonna spill their guts to you in a month of Sundays."

"Banning, you'd be surprised what folks'll spill when they see the writing on the wall." The lawman saw the other man's eyes narrow, and he drove the needle a little deeper. "Your outfit's got more leaks'n a rusty sieve. Damned interestin' the way people'll talk when they know the string's about played out."

Ed Banning's thin blade of a face suddenly lost its smile. "You oughta've been a poker player instead of a lawman. With a bluff like that you could've made a fortune."

Stoudenmire's chuckle had a mocking ring to it. "The only way to find out is to call the bet. Course, when you take another peek at your hole card, you're gonna discover I've got you by the short hairs."

"One hand don't make a game. Not the way I play." Banning dismissed the subject with a wave of his hand, plastering another shallow smile across his face. "Look, I didn't call you over here to trade insults. I've got a proposition to make, and I'll give it to you straight out. You're not gonna turn up anything I can't handle, but you are sort of a nuisance. Not that it bothers me all that much, you understand. Just takes my mind off more important matters. Suppose I was to open the safe and count out . . . say three thousand dollars. Hell, I might even go as high as five thousand. Don't you reckon that'd get your mind back on your own business?"

Stoudenmire felt his pulse quicken. The bastard was running scared! One more push and he might just crack. "Banning, I've got a better idea. Why don't you stuff that money up your ass and set a match to it. That's about the only way you'll get me off your back."

Sam started out of his chair, but the gang leader stayed him with a short, chopping motion of his hand. Then Banning leaned forward and nodded toward the Indian. "Marshal, I don't think you've met Choctaw Tyler. He's been hearin' about the big *pistolero* we've got for a lawman, so we brought him down to have a look-see for himself."

Stoudenmire gave the gunslinger a slow, appraising look. For a moment Choctaw Tyler just puffed on his cigarette, seemingly absorbed in the aimless drift of the smoke. Finally he turned and met the marshal's stare with an insolent smirk. His mouth was like a hard slit that had been traced across his face with a razor, and when he spoke, his words came out a soft, guttural hiss.

"Mister, you'd best listen to reason. Else you're gonna end

up on the short end of the stick. Shit, he's offerin' you more
money to stay alive than he's givin' me to kill you. Take it,
'fore I decide to do the job for free."

The lawman's pale eyes riveted into the full blood, and his
voice was gritty as ground glass. "Tyler, I'm gonna give you
some advice, maybe the best you ever got. Start makin' tracks
out of here and don't look back. If you do, you're liable to
lose an eye."

Choctaw Tyler tensed, ready to come up out of his chair,
but Banning stopped him cold. "Choctaw, leave it be! He's
just tryin' to get you riled up, and we can't afford a shootout
in here."

When Tyler eased off, the gang leader looked back at
Stoudenmire. "Marshal, I reckon we know how everybody
stands, so let's just play the cards as they fall. Only don't
ever say I didn't warn you that you're playin' with a cold deck."

"That's real white of you, Banning. I'll remember it when
I put a noose around your neck."

Stoudenmire walked from the room with Tige bringing up
the rear. Sam jumped out of his chair and spat a wad of
phlegm at the door as it closed. Banning and Choctaw Tyler
exchanged disgusted looks and watched silently as the spit-
tle slowly wormed its way toward the floor. There wasn't
much left to say, and besides, it had been one turd-knocker
of a morning, start to finish.

5

That evening Banning sent for Isaac Porter. Things were at a
point that he couldn't afford another miscue, and one way or
the other he had to find out if the mayor was going soft in the
guts. Something was boogering the old scoundrel, that was
for damn sure. Over the past few weeks he had steadily grown
more jumpy, almost choleric in his drunken fits of gloom.
That was another thing, his drinking. Since becoming mayor,
he had religiously avoided the booze, finding solace instead
at the gaming tables around town. But lately he had been
soaking up whiskey like a sponge, and so far he hadn't shown

any signs of slackening off. Having a rummy as a frontman was a risky proposition, particularly in a business where corruption and graft were the order of the day. The cause of Porter's dismal moods was easily traced. In a word, Stoudenmire.

Until the German came to town, Isaac Porter had been a glad-handing, back-slapping, bon vivant. The rotund, rosy-cheeked, little charmer that everyone liked to think typified the warmth and casual hospitality that made El Paso what it was. This jocular, ever sprightly disposition was the big factor in getting Porter elected, and it had made him a perfect show-horse for Banning's political machine. But with Stoudenmire's arrival, a gradual transformation had taken place, almost as though Porter had been sapped of his vitality and amiable wit. Banning didn't give a tinker's damn for the dissolution of the man himself, but when it endangered the organization, that was a different ball of wax altogether. And if Porter had any notions of talking out of school, he would become expendable faster than a bat fart in a windstorm.

When the mayor arrived, he looked like a man with a mild touch of St. Vitus's dance. His face was pale and drawn, and he couldn't seem to sit still, squirming nervously in the chair like his chubby rump was stuck to a hot griddle. Around the Bannings he was normally as docile as a circus elephant, accepting their sarcasm and biting remarks with quiet good humor. But tonight he had a real case of the shakes, and Choctaw Tyler's flat stare did little to settle his nerves. Obviously he had spent the afternoon in company with John Barleycorn, for he reeked of stale whiskey, and his eyes were a watery shade of red. Yet even the whiskey had had no apparent effect on his frayed spirits. He was a bundle of raw, suppurating nerves, and whatever rode astraddle his shoulders had raked him bloody with fear and uncertainty. A man had only to look to see it gnawing on him, and none saw it more clearly than Ed Banning.

The gang leader worked up what passed for a smile. "Well, Isaac, what's new over at city hall? We haven't seen you much lately. Thought maybe you'd forgotten old friends."

"No, no. Nothing like that, Ed." Porter's eyes flicked around the room, like timorous sparrows unable to find a perch. "Just closing the books on the fiscal year and preparing the new city budget. Have to keep burning the midnight oil, you know."

"Sure," Banning agreed congenially. "Running this town is a big job. And we're damned lucky to have a man like you to shoulder the load. Being mayor's not all rose water and kissin' babies, is it?"

Porter dredged up a spastic smile, trying to ape the gang leader's easy manner. "That's right, Ed. It's more of a burden than folks suspect. Carries a great responsibility, and sometimes it gets to weighing on a man."

"Now it's funny you mention that, Isaac." Banning motioned over at Sam and Choctaw Tyler, who looked like a couple of men watching a snake mesmerize a plump field mouse. "I was just telling the boys today that we've been workin' you too hard. By God, overseeing this operation is no soft touch. Man needs a little time off every now and then. Fact is, I was thinkin' of treating you to a vacation. St. Louis maybe, or Kansas City. That wouldn't be too hard to take, would it?"

The mayor's rubbery features brightened with surprise. "Why no, that wouldn't be hard to take at all. Tell you the truth, I have been off my feed a bit here lately."

Banning lit a cigar and casually drifted into a long monologue on the merits of various eastern cities, making it clear that he considered Chicago the best watering hole east of the Big Muddy. Isaac Porter listened and nodded like an eager schoolboy as the gang leader spoke. Slowly he began to relax, inwardly deriding himself for the groundless fears he had conjured up about this meeting. Banning just wanted to chat, deliver one of those rambling, disconnected lectures he was so fond of on occasion. Porter slouched back in his chair with renewed confidence. Hell, he wasn't in any danger! Banning had himself a captive audience, and he was going to make the most of it. And if Mother Porter's youngest son played his cards right, he might just get a ticket east. A one way ticket! Where didn't matter, just so he never had to return to this murderous hell-hole.

Porter was jarred out of his reverie as Banning neatly switched directions. "Say, Isaac, before I forget it. Stoudenmire has been down here bracing my people with threats. The knothead actually thinks somebody's gonna rat on me. Heard anything about it uptown?"

The mayor felt cold beads of sweat pop out on his forehead. Should he jeopardize this trip back east by telling the truth, or would it be better to play dumb? It was a knotty question, but he hesitated only a moment. "No, not a thing. You mean to say he's actually making threats against the people down here?"

"Worse than that. He's telling 'em that the only way they'll save their own hides is to swap sides and testify against me. Matter of fact, a little bird told me he'd even paid you a call."

Porter was taken completely off guard, and he suddenly had the look of a trapped animal. He was sweating profusely now, fighting desperately to keep his hands from shaking. "You mean yesterday? Oh, yes, he dropped by for a few minutes. Completely slipped my mind till you mentioned it. Just wanted to tell me that he'd taken steps to put the quietus on this vigilante scare. Nothing really. Nothing at all."

The mayor's voice had cracked only once during his short recital, but he had lied poorly, unconvincingly, and even now his face had the look of a constipated warthog. Banning betrayed nothing of what he was thinking, nodding absently as if the subject had been only of passing interest. The gang leader easily returned to events of a lighter nature, smiling and poking fun in his usual caustic manner. Porter once again relaxed, congratulating himself for having brought it off so smoothly. *By damn, when it came to tricky dodges, it took more than these louts to outfox an old con-man like Isaac Porter.*

Shortly the gang leader's banter wound down, and he allowed as how it was time to get back to business. If the mayor wouldn't mind, he had some things to talk over with Sam and Tyler. They'd get together again soon, real soon, and work out

the details for his trip east. Porter's spunk and jaunty disposition were again restored, and he took his leave appearing
vastly relieved. Easing through the door, he cocked his hat
at a rakish angle and got busy planning a real rip-snorter to
celebrate his own devilish cleverness.

When the door swung shut behind the old politico, Ed
Banning put it to a vote. Not that his outfit was anything even
mildly related to a democracy, but he just wanted a sounding
board for his own opinion. Sam and Choctaw Tyler both
agreed. *Porter had been lying.*

Banning tilted back in his chair and considered the matter at some length. The minutes ticked by, and the other two
men began to wonder if he had gone to sleep. After a while
his eyes opened, and he came back to the present, outlining
in clipped, brutal words how it would be handled. They had
no recourse but to kill Porter before he spilled his guts to the
law. Tyler was to shadow him and wait until he headed home
for the night. When he caught the mayor alone on some dark
street, he was to finish him off. But it had to be done with a
knife. Make it look like the old prick had been robbed and
killed by some drunk greaser. That way the townspeople
would have something to piss and moan about besides the
Bannings.

Choctaw Tyler found the idea of using a knife vastly appealing. Somehow when a man felt it slip home, grating on
bone, rending flesh, there was a greater sense of accomplish-
ment; then, too, the smell of warm, fresh blood had always
aroused him in some strange way, and that made it all the
better. Happy to be functioning at last, he nodded to Banning
and slipped out the back door.

Some three hours later Isaac Porter was weaving along a side-
street when the Indian caught up with him. The mayor was
carrying a heavy load, but when he saw the knife, his deadened senses surged back with alacrity. Still, it was a short and
savagely unequal struggle. Porter managed only one bleating
cry before Choctaw Tyler sunk the knife up to the hilt beneath his breastbone. The politician shuddered like a bolt of

lightning had just fired up his rectum, then collapsed at the knees, and folded to the ground. Hunkering down beside the dead man, Tyler wiped his knife clean, then expertly went over the body for wallet, watch, and other valuables. Just as he finished, he heard the crunch of a footstep in loose soil.

Someone was standing directly behind him, and from the nearness of the sound, he wasn't more than ten feet away.

"Don't move!" the deadly click of a Colt hammer being earred back had a logic all its own. "Stand up slow and get your hands over your head. Then turn around."

The Indian obeyed, and when he came about, he found himself facing a Peacemaker in the hand of Dallas Stoudenmire. *Tai-me* was indeed a god of strange whims. Grinning, he jerked a thumb back at Porter's body. "Marshal, you're trickier than I thought. Looks like the fat man wasn't the only one being followed tonight."

Stoudenmire felt his guts constrict into a hard knot. The mayor hadn't been much, but he deserved better than this. "Tyler, I sure wish I had been on your tail. From the looks of things, I should've been. But just between you and me, I was makin' night rounds when I heard the ruckus. Course, it's not like I came up empty-handed, is it?"

Choctaw Tyler's guttural chuckle sounded softly in the narrow street. "Tell you what, Marshal. There's just you and me here. Why don't you poke that Colt back in the holster and give me an even break. If you don't, we never are gonna find out who's the fastest."

Stoudenmire just shook his head, his eyes cold and hard as hailstones. "No dice. I want you alive. The only choice you've got is between hangin' or doing some tall talkin' about who set this deal up. Course, if you're stupid you could go for your gun. But that'd just get you dead." The Colt moved slightly in a sideways motion. "Unbuckle your gunbelt and be real careful."

The Indian shrugged, a look of stoic resignation coming over his face. His left hand moved toward the belt buckle, but in the same instant his right hand snaked down and swept up with a six-gun. It was the old magician's trick with a deadly twist; distract the eye with one hand and work your magic with the other.

But as his pistol cleared leather, Stoudenmire Colt belched flame in a blinding roar. Three bright dots appeared on Choctaw Tyler's shirtpocket, and he stumbled backwards, tripping over the mayor's body. Dead even as he fell, he hit the ground with a dusty thud.

Stoudenmire walked forward and stood for a moment inspecting the Indian's spread-eagled form. Satisifed that the man was dead, he turned and headed toward the plaza, shucking empties and reloading as he walked.

Killing men was one thing, but he never could stand the stench when death released its grip on their bowels.

CHAPTER NINE

1

Jim Gillette awakened only moments after the dusky glow of false dawn erased the darkened sky. The stars that hung suspended in the heavens each night, all cold silver and iced blue, had disappeared, and he shivered in the chill morning air. The resinous, piney odor from the embers of his fire had a sharp bite, and through the cobwebs of his drowsiness came images of a cherry blaze and a coffee pot perking delicious aromas. His camp was high on a mesa overlooking the Banning ranch in the valley below. These huge orange and golden buttes jutted skyward from the flatlands, forming sheer palisades that dominated the countryside in every direction. Above the escarpment there was an expanse as level as a billiard table, as though the gods had cleaved the top away in a moment of petulance and outrage. Over this barren, windswept rock-pile nothing grew save a profusion of piñon trees, gnarled and deformed by time and altitude into a stunted mockery of green things. Yet even atop these grotesque battlements, a man always had the taste of grit in his mouth, as though powdery granules of some tasteless filth were forever lodged between his teeth.

The deputy curled up into a tight ball, drawing his blanket closer against the damp cold. Something had roused him, and he tried to push back the fuzziness that clouded his brain, but for a moment his wits slogged along like a crippled mule. Then it hit him. What he heard was the pounding of hooves, and it was coming from the valley below. Not just horses either but cattle, lots of cattle. *Great smokin' Jesus! The gang must have ridden out during the night without him hearing them. But how the hell could that be?*

Whipping the blanket off, Gillette scrambled to his feet and ran toward the forward edge of the mesa. Taking cover behind a huge rock, he eased down on his belly and peered over the cliff. Suddenly he went slack-jawed with astonishment, rocked back on his haunches as though someone had dashed him in the face with a pan of cold water.

The Mexicans were raiding the Banning ranch! Goddammit, it just couldn't be possible.

Unable to believe what he had seen, he rubbed his eyes and took another look. This time there was no mistaking what he saw. Maybe it wasn't possible, but it was sure as hell a fact. The greasers were rustling Banning's cattle herd, and from up there, it looked like they were flat going to clean him out.

Gillette was staggered, his mind reeling with this quirky turn of events. Christ almighty, what Stoudenmire wouldn't give to be here right now! Although it was the last thing they would have imagined when he set out to scout the Banning ranch, it was damn sure a fine joke on those meatheads down below. The best joke he had ever heard, in fact. The rustlers getting rustled! Jesus, that was rich.

Evidently, Don Miguel Salazar figured it was time the *gringos* had a taste of their own medicine. Banning's night riders had sure as shit driven off enough of his stock, and the turnabout was long overdue, no two ways about it. Hell, the Mexicans could raid Banning every night for the next year, and they would probably still come out with a hole in their pockets. Not to mention the number of men they had had killed trying to protect their own herds. *¡Bueno!* Now maybe the pack of scutters working for Banning would hit leather and keep on riding until they found a place where folks weren't so all-fired persnickity about a bunch of cows.

Though it tickled his funnybone to see the Mexicans raiding Banning, the old lawdog would have much preferred it the other way around. That way he could have stuck to the plan and maybe come up with some hard evidence that would carry a little clout in a court of law. But at least something was happening, even if it wasn't what the marshal had set his sights on.

Gillette had been perched atop this windswept mesa for two nights now, and he was growing dismally bored with the whole deal. The gang had done nothing but loaf around all day and drink whiskey far into the night ever since he arrived. They had no apparent concern for the operation of the ranch itself, and quite obviously weren't planning a raid any time soon. Things were so peaceful, downright stultifying as a matter of fact, that he had intended returning to El Paso that very morning. It was a waste of time watching rustlers who for all intents and purposes had retired from the rustling business. Broiling under a hot ball of fire during the day and freezing his ass off at night wasn't exactly calculated to improve a man's frame of mind. Especially when those sapsuckers down in the valley had all the whiskey.

But all that had suddenly changed. Maybe the Mexicans had thrown a monkey wrench into his plans, but they had sure as hell livened things up. Even now they were driving the Banning herd right past him as they pushed south toward the river. In the faint glow from the sky, Gillette could see the *vaqueros* using their *reatas* as whips, hazing the longhorns into a ground-eating lope that shook the earth with a dull rumble. They had a ways to go, near-about twenty miles before they hit the border, and it looked like the Mexicans figured to stampede the stolen cattle every foot of the way. Watching them, the deputy couldn't help but think that they were real greenhorns at this rustling game. They should have

hit just after midnight; that way they would have been across
the border long before first light. The way things were shaping up, they would be damned lucky to get that herd into
Mexico much before dinner time.

Out of the corner of his eye, he suddenly picked up movement around the ranch house. Changing positions for a
better view, he saw men running helter-skelter across the
compound, shouting and waving their arms toward the fast
disappearing herd. Then they turned and raced for the corral, grabbing any horse that came to hand in their haste to
get mounted. Within moments they were saddled and pounding out the gate, clearly intent on carrying the fight to the
Mexicans.

While the *vaqueros* could save themselves by making a
run for it, Gillette saw it as a profound injustice that they
should lose the cattle. That presented him with a thorny problem, one which he couldn't debate overly long, for the Banning
gang was riding fresh horses, and they would close the gap
in a matter of minutes.

*Should he side with the Mexicans or remain strictly an
observer?*

His instinctive reaction was to stick with his own countrymen even though they were outlaws, nothing more than
border scum when a man got down to cases. Simply by doing nothing he would be taking their side, and no matter how
it was sliced, it wasn't any of his business to start with. The
smart move was to just sit back and play like a spectator; let
them fight it out amongst themselves and devil take the hindmost. But then nobody had ever accused him of being smart,
or even bright for that matter. Besides, he felt a nagging sense
of loyalty to something greater than those two-bit despera-
dos, whether they were American or not. Like Stoudenmire
always said, personal feelings shouldn't get between a man
and what's right, especially if it's got to do with the law.

Just then a small band of *vaqueros* fell back to fight a rear-
guard action, and his debate came to a skidding halt.

Grabbing his rifle, Gillette jacked a shell into the cham-
ber and steadied himself against the boulder. Yet even with

the decision made, he couldn't bring himself to ambush the no-account bastards. Waiting until they passed beneath his hideout, the deputy drew a bead on the lead horse and squeezed off a shot. When the rider pitched headlong to the ground, the rest of the gang reined up short and milled around him in swirling confusion. Methodically, Gillette aimed and fired, dropping their horses from beneath them like cattle in a slaughterhouse chute. With each report another animal fell, thrashing and squealing in blind terror, and before he could empty the rifle, the gang had scattered over the countryside, running for their very lives.

The Mexicans were no less astounded than the Texans themselves, but only a fool would stop to question divine intervention such as this. Waving their rifles in salute, they wheeled their mounts and thundered off after the herd. Whoever the *hombre* was up on that cliff, he was a great artist with a rifle, and he wouldn't be forgotten in their prayers tonight.

Gillette wasted no time gloating over his handiwork. Striding back to his camp, he quickly packed his gear and saddled up. Ten minutes later he was riding down the narrow trail on the backside of the buttes and damned glad to be on his way. This deal had been a washout from the start, and it was high time to get his skinny rump on back to El Paso.

Suddenly he wondered what Stoudenmire would have to say about this little fracas. Probably wouldn't be too amused, but he'd be damn hard put to fault it. Compromise wasn't the marshal's way of doing things. He'd doubtless have shot the men instead of the horses. Still, all things considered, Gillette felt like it had been a pretty good morning.

2

Stoudenmire was discovering that there was more to catching fish than baiting the hook. The murder of Isaac Porter had silenced the sporting crowd as if a steel trap had clamped shut. Since he had caught Choctaw Tyler with knife in hand, there wasn't much doubt about who had ordered the killing. But

knowing it and proving it was sort of like spreading
horseshit on a soda cracker. Everybody admitted it looked
good, but nobody wanted to take the first bite. Rightly enough,
the marshal figured that the Bannings had somehow tumbled
to his deal with Porter, yet the knowledge did little except
add to his already sullen disposition.

Porter's death had soured his mood enough for one night,
but Kate had really finished the job off. After rousing the undertaker and getting the bodies attended to, he had gone
home prepared for another bitter argument. But Kate had
already heard the whole story from Doc, and she didn't care
to discuss the matter further. As it turned out, she didn't
care to discuss anything. She had decided that if yelling and
screaming couldn't sway him, then maybe the silent treatment would get better results. Not only was she silent, she
was downright aloof, even to the extent of turning her back on
him when they crawled into bed. While it was a childish
thing to do, and damned irritating coming on top of everything else, Stoudenmire found it to be a grimly humorous
joke on her. His tallywhacker wouldn't have stood on end
right then if a whole troop of vestal virgins had swarmed
over him buck-assed naked.

Somehow killing took its toll on a man in a way that he
had never fully understood. After the shooting was over and
the other man lay dead, it was like the hot juices inside him
had all been drained away. Often during the war he could
have laid down and slept for a whole week after an especially
busy day on the killing ground. It had always puzzled him,
even disturbed him in a way, for it was as though killing
sucked him dry of passion and left his twig as limber and lifeless as a doddering old man's. Over the years he had finally
come to accept it for what it was. Killing just plain wore him
out, and there wasn't anything to be done about it. But he often wondered if it had the same effect on other men. It wasn't
rightly something a man would talk about, and he had never
felt close enough to anyone to ask. Not even Jim Gillette.

Staring into the darkness last night, listening to Kate pre-
tend she was asleep, it came to him that the joke was really

on her. She thought she was punishing him by cutting him off, when all the time, he had about the same urges as a gelded hog. Still, wanting it or not, her peevish little contrivance had left him with a foul taste in his mouth.

The chilly atmosphere around the southside this morning hadn't done much to improve his mood either. The Bannings hadn't wasted any time circulating the word, and overnight it became known that the mayor had met the same fate that awaited any double-crosser. The warning didn't pass unheeded, and Stoudenmire had been rebuffed at every turn on an early morning jaunt through the vice district. Those who had considered talking yesterday now wouldn't even give him the correct time. Maybe he would end up putting them in jail, they conceded, that remained to be seen. But if they spoke out of turn, Ed Banning would put them in a box, and dead was a damnsight more permanent than a visit to the pokey.

Yet there was one aftereffect the Bannings hadn't counted on. Although Porter was generally regarded as a corrupt politician, the townspeople took a dim view of anyone murdering their mayor. Even if he was a crook. More than ever before, the people of El Paso closed ranks against the Bannings. There was even talk of forming a coalition ticket to defeat them in the forthcoming elections. Reflecting back over the vigilante scare, Stoudenmire was pleased to see that folks were thinking in terms of ballots rather than bullets. Once they were united against gang rule, they wouldn't have much trouble ridding city hall of its resident scoundrels.

But simply defeating the Bannings at the polls wasn't enough for the lawman. He wanted their hides nailed to the wall, and he had no intention of slackening the pressure. Gillette might return at any moment with evidence of rustling, and he had already made arrangements with the banks to inspect the records of various politicians. Still, he was going to need a witness, someone who knew all the details behind the Bannings' skulduggery. Gamblers, saloonkeepers, and madams had met his most recent overtures with stony silence, and obtaining proof of protection kickbacks now seemed highly unlikely. That left official corruption, and with nothing much to lose, Stoudenmire decided to brace the second most powerful cog in the Banning machine.

Judge Marcus Hamer was an imposing figure of a man. He was tall, stoutly built, with a mane of white, wavy hair, and he had the disconcerting habit of staring a man straight in the eye whenever he spoke. Moreover, he was a man of some refinement, cultured in his ways, highly educated, and obviously from a background of considerable breeding. Though it was common knowledge that his family had once ruled Atlanta society, not even his closest friends knew what quirk of fate had brought him west. Local gossip attributed it to a family scandal of some sort, but the only thing known for certain was that he had chosen El Paso for reasons of his own and, having done so, quickly aligned himself with the Bannings. He owed both his soul and his position as circuit judge to the machine, yet he gave every impression of being his own man. One who didn't flinch when the political waters got choppy.

Stoudenmire found him affable, somewhat amused by the Bannings' bumbling peccadillos, and quite willing to talk. But strictly off the record. After offering the lawman a chair, he lighted a thin cheroot much favored by southern gentlemen, then settled back with a patronizing smile.

"Well, Marshal, I presume you're here to offer me immunity from justice. Frankly, I'm just the least bit affronted that it took you so long to get around to me. I understand you have been all over town extending the same inducement to the more scurrilous element."

Stoudenmire missed some of the words, but not the tone. This man was an old campaigner, and he might just be the toughest nut to crack in the whole organization. "Judge, I won't waste your time beatin' around the bushes You know I'm after the Bannings, and I suspect you know I'll get 'em. What I'm offering you is a chance to come out on the winning side. It's as simple as that."

Hamer smiled wryly and exhaled a thick cloud of smoke

through his nostrils. "My boy, an Englishmen by the name of Spencer once said that the ultimate result of shielding men from the effects of folly is to fill the world with fools. Now by no means am I inferring that you're a fool. But I do believe that you are perpetuating a folly. If it won't offend you, I would be happy to explain why."

"Fire away." Stoudenmire returned the smile, finding himself liking the old reprobate even if he was a thief. "I've got a thick skin."

"So I've heard." The judge flicked ashes from his cheroot and glanced around slyly. "But it will take more than that to bring Ed Banning to earth. Quite candidly, Marshal, you put me in mind of a man trying to shovel quicksand. The faster you shovel the deeper you sink, and the only way it ends is when you have sunk into obscurity. Now, as a case in point. You've been flitting about town trying to drum up a chink in Banning's armor. But there's not a man in El Paso who would dare to speak openly. Isaac Porter's death was a deplorable thing, but most effective, you'll have to admit. The denizens of our vice district have had their lips sealed forever. Whoever talked would be killed even though the Bannings went to jail, and that rather salient fact hasn't gone unnoted. Your folly, my friend, is that whoever deals with you ends up dead. I might also add that it is a folly that has now been exposed fully in a most impressive manner."

"What you're trying to tell me is that I've played out my string. That there's no way to get the Bannings."

"Precisely. By election time this whole affair will have blown over. I regret to say that most people live out their lives in thimbles. The dolts that populate El Paso are no different. They will gladly take the path of least resistance and be quite content to return to their humdrum existence."

Hamer chuckled to himself, as if amused by the profundity of his own statement. "Ofttimes, to win us to our harm, the instruments of darkness tell us truths. You and I, Marshal, must suffer under the knowledge that nothing ever changes. Politicians and lawmen come and go, but corruption never falters. It feeds on itself as well as the people, and in our benevolent form of government, it is the only constancy that remains."

Stoudenmire's eyes narrowed, regarding the older man speculatively. "What about you, Judge? Haven't you ever had an urge to make it work better? Could be El Paso is the place to start."

Hamer blinked and gave him a wry look. "My boy, it occurs to me that you are considerably smarter than Ed Banning gives you credit for. But don't waste your energies trying to lure an old curmudgeon like myself into your schemes. I no longer feel a young man's compulsion to wager against time and life. Like the apathetic masses, I am content to exist."

Later, after having left the judge's office, Stoudenmire crossed the plaza under a cloud of foreboding. Maybe the high-toned old bastard was right. Everywhere he turned he found nothing but blank walls. And damned if each one didn't seem to be constructed of solid granite.

3

Kate had suddenly found her voice again. That evening when Stoudenmire came home for supper, she was primed and raring to go. The moment he walked in the door the lawman knew she was out for blood; even Tige crawled off in a corner and played possum. Her eyes crackled with a smoky brilliance that put him in mind of a treed wildcat, and he knew it was only a matter of time until her claws came unsheathed. Watching her bustle back and forth between the kitchen, clanging pots, slamming dishes down on the table, he thought again how complex and outright bewildering females became once they got married. Evidently a wedding band wrought some powerful change inside their skulls, and what it did to their tongues was an absolute marvel. Not the good kind, or even pleasant, just damned baffling and more than a man could handle on an empty stomach.

Maybe it had something to do with the moon. Hell, everybody knew what wild things went squirrely at certain times of the month, and the longer he was married the more certain he became that women weren't anywhere near as tame as folks made out. Leastways the one he slept with wasn't, and by Christ, now that he stopped to think about it, he had the scars to prove it.

After they were seated at the table, the silence lasted only as far as the mashed potatoes. Kate let him get a big glop piled up on his plate, but when he reached for the gravy, she came out swinging. "Dallas, there's something we have to discuss. Things have gone far enough, and I think it's about time we started being honest with each other."

"Goddamn, Kate, can't you pick some place besides the supper table to start these squabbles? Let me at least eat my meals in peace."

"Please don't blaspheme my house with your crude language." She got that prim look on her face, like she had just led a prayer meeting in scripture reading. "Just for your information, the only time I ever see you is when you get hungry. You're so busy being a rootin'-tootin' lawman that you've forgotten you're also a husband. You've even gotten to where you come home at night and flop down in bed like I was some kind of wooden Indian not worth talking to."

"Me!" Stoudenmire almost choked on a mouthful of corn bread. "Now, by God, that takes the cake. Last night you acted like somebody had hemstitched your mouth shut. You've sure got a lot of room to rake somebody over the coals for not talkin'."

"Well I had every right," Kate replied indignantly. "You can't come tromping in after killing another man and expect me to be a cuddly little furball."

"Why not, for Chrissakes?" the lawman grated out. "The sonovabitch was trying to kill me! What should I have done, took off runnin' and let him pump my ass full of lead?"

"Dallas, I'm going to leave the table if you can't talk civil."

Stoudenmire almost laughed in spite of himself. She was like a spoiled little girl trying to play the great lady. So proper and chock full of decorum. Except in bed. By Jesus, she

wasn't any lady then. After a moment he became aware that
she was waiting for him to say something. "Kate, I'm damned
if I can figure out what's got you riled up. Are you worried
about me getting killed? Or is it the fact that I have to use a
gun on other men every now and then?"

"Oh, what a horrible thing to say." Her face squinched up
tight, and she looked on the verge of tears. "Dallas Stoudenmire, you ought to be ashamed of yourself. Every time you
walk out that door, I die a little inside thinking you won't
come back." Yet that was only part of the truth, she thought
to herself. For she found it increasingly difficult to sleep with
a man who killed so callously, almost as if he considered it
his calling, maybe even enjoyed it. Still those were fears she
was barely able to admit to herself. Never to him. "Of course
it's you I worry about. With half the people in this town wanting to kill you, I'm almost out of my mind with fear."

"C'mon now. You're paintin' it darker than it is." He
smiled, letting a joshing tone creep into his voice. "Besides,
the other half's on my side. So that sorta evens things out."

"Very funny. But it's not a joking matter. You've risked
your life enough for this dirty town. After all, only so much
can be expected of one man, and it's time these people took
a hand in their own troubles."

"That's what they pay me for. If people were willing to
weed their own garden, then there wouldn't be any need for
men like me."

"But that's no reason for you to keep on doing it," Kate
insisted angrily. "They've stood by and watched it happen for
years, and whatever El Paso is, it's just what they deserve.
It's their fight, Dallas, not yours. If you can't see that, then
you're either bullheaded or blind as a bat."

"Maybe. But I'm a lawman, and you'd better get used to
the idea, missy. That's what I was when we got married, and
that's what I'm gonna stay. So you just might as well quit
flouncin' around with your tailgate up in the air and learn to
live with it."

Stoudenmire sighed wearily, noting the wounded look on
her face. "Let's talk about something else. I've got a meet-

ing, and I'd like to get through it without belchin' up this meal all night."

Later, walking toward Hart's mill, the marshal thought back to Kate's last stinging comment. *Bullheaded or blind as a bat.* Damned if he didn't know but what he agreed with her. The way things had worked out a man had to be one or the other just to keep on going.

After inspecting the bank records of various politicians that afternoon, he had reached the conculsion that crooks must bury their money in tin cans. Despite his time and effort, the idea was simply another in a long row of washouts. Then Gillette had ridden in shortly afterwards with an astonishing report. The rustlers not only weren't stirring from the ranch, they were now being raided by the Mexicans! Even if the Banning gang was caught crossing the river with a whole goddamn herd, it probably wouldn't stand up in court after this. What judge was going to sign extradition papers against men who were merely retaliating against Mexican *bandidos?*

Jesus, it was enough to give a man the blue swivets. And the hell of it was, he couldn't think of a damn thing to do to get things straightened out. It was like old Judge Hamer had said. He had shoveled himself ass-deep in quicksand, and nobody seemed to have a rope handy. Maybe somebody was getting their shits and giggles out of this sorry mess, but it sure hadn't given him any laughs lately.

Stoudenmire found Seth Hart and his cohorts in their usual chairs. As he took his seat, it passed through his mind that he was getting to be a regular member of this little conclave. But it was a damned disquieting thought. Still, these men had brought him to El Paso, and he owed them an explanation, if nothing else.

Looking around the table at their silent faces, he found that the words came hard. "Gents, I'll make it short and sweet. What I've got to say speaks for itself."

The grave tone hardly seemed necessary, for the businessmen could tell from the look on the marshal's face that the news wasn't good. Briefly, he outlined the latest setbacks in their war on the Bannings. The rustling operation had been brought to a standstill. There wasn't a solitary soul in the vice district who would consider turning on the gang. The political hacks absolutely refused to cooperate in exposing corruption, even if granted immunity. Ed Banning had everyone in town scared shitless, and without hard evidence, the law was running dead last. Shrugging his shoulders with a futile gesture, Stoudenmire observed that it was a Mexican standoff. Short of forcing the Bannings into a gunfight, he didn't know where to turn.

When he finished, the businessmen merely stared at him in stony silence. What they were thinking was best left unsaid, and much as they hated to admit it, none of them had any worthwhile ideas anyhow. Seth Hart finally broke the uncomfortable lull. "Well, it's not like we haven't gained something out of all this. The people are fed up with the Bannings and their methods, and by election time we might just put a reform ticket across. One thing's for sure, Ed Banning will never again exert the influence he has in the past."

"Horseshit!" Everyone turned to look at Horace Adair, startled that he would dispute the old miller so openly. "Elections are more than a year off, Seth, and you're just kidding yourself if you think Banning won't have the town weighed and sacked by then. Goddammit, what we need are the vigilantes! I've said it all along, and I still contend it's the only way we'll ever rid ourselves of those bastards."

"Horace, you might have a point there." Hart studied the Irishman for a moment, then turned to Stoudenmire. "I seem to recall that the marshal said if his way didn't work, he'd be glad to lead the first charge on the southside."

The lawman's face was wooden, clearly the look of a man absorbed in reflections all his own. "Mr. Hart, I reckon that's one charge you'll have to lead yourself. I don't believe in mob law, and I won't have any part of it. If that's what you decide, then I'll resign and leave you to do what seems best. Otherwise I'll keep right on till I find some way to put Banning under."

"That's all very commendable, Marshal," Hart said. "But

it appears to me you're fresh out of ideas. What's left to do that you haven't already done?"

Every man at the table regarded him with somber gravity, and a deep stillness settled over the room. The moments ticked by with excruciating slowness while the lawman considered. When he spoke, his words were as cryptic as his expression. "I don't know. Maybe nothing. Maybe more of the same. Whatever it is, it'll separate the men from the boys."

Seth Hart just nodded, then suggested they all think it over and meet again the next evening. There was a quick murmur of agreement, almost as though each of the men wanted to escape the tension that hung between them. Dispirited, they trooped from the mill and walked off into the darkening night. They had much to reflect on before the harsh light of day brought them face to face with themselves, and a man was best left to his own devices when he crawled away to lick his wounds.

4

Doc Cummings trailed along with Stoudenmire when they left the meeting. Not saying much, they crossed Santa Fe Street and headed uptown, each man lost in his own thoughts. The little storekeeper had remained silent during the brief exchange between Hart and the lawman. As far back as he could remember, it was the first time he had ever been at a loss for words. But how could a man speak up when he knew that every word out of his mouth would only add to a friend's already grinding misery? Stoudenmire had been brought to El Paso on his say-so, which sort of left him betwixt and between. Anything he said now would have the ring of sour grapes, and he wasn't about to badger the marshal like some old fishwife, particularly when recriminations would serve no useful purpose. Stoudenmire had failed and the less said the better. The whys and wherefores of that failure now seemed meaningless, something that required neither explanation nor discussion. They knew, and that was enough. Even Hart and the boys hadn't been too rough on the lawman, and Cummings was thankful for that. The man was being devoured whole by furies of his own, and he damn sure didn't need anyone to tell him that he'd fallen flat on his ass. He knew, and whatever he was saying to himself right at this moment was a damn sight worse than anything Seth Hart's crowd might be thinking.

Reflecting back over the past month or so, that first night flashed through Cumming's mind. The night Stoudenmire had come to El Paso to discuss cleaning up the town. He had seemed so sure of himself, cocky almost, and if ever a man looked the part of a town tamer it was Dallas Stoudenmire. *Town tamer.* That was the term John Simmons had used, and everyone readily agreed that such a man was exactly what they needed. Then, when Stoudenmire had walked into the room, they knew that this was the man for the job, sensed it somehow, like when a fellow gets a hunch at the faro table and goes whole hog. Whatever kind of inner steel that it took to belt other men in the head, intimidate them, shoot them if necessary, Stoudenmire had it. When he left that night to catch the train back east, they had laughed and carried on like kids. Slapping one another on the back, they had congratulated themselves on picking a real stem-winder, even drinking numerous ribald toasts to Ed Banning's early demise.

Now that night seemed long ago, as though each week had been a year in itself, and he felt like he had aged just about that much waiting for Banning to fall. Seth Hart always said that a man had to think big if he wanted to make his mark. What he forgot to add was that anyone who reached for the sun was just naturally bound to get blisters. *Blisters!* Hell, they had gotten enough to make them look like they had been scalded in boiling oil. Enough to make fools of them all.

Still, Stoudenmire's tenure as marshal hadn't been a complete loss. He had put the quietus on the Mexican trouble, and there was some solace in that. Not much, but you had to give the man credit. They had hired him to put the damper on the greasers as well as get rid of the Bannings, and he had done half the job anyway. But with the Mexicans peaceful again, everyone tended to ignore that and remember only that he hadn't axed Ed Banning's skinny neck. Christ, it was a grudging world. Full of fat old men who paid others to do their fighting and then bellyached like foundered mules when the hired gun didn't get himself killed just on cue.

Suddenly a very curious thought raced through Cumming's head. What if Dallas had been right all along? Maybe Seth Hart was another Ed Banning after all. Not so cold and deadly perhaps, but a man of ruthless ambition nonetheless, one who merely clothed it under the guise of civic benevolence. The more he thought about it, the better sense it made. Hart had never been overly concerned about the Mexicans, not even at the start. It was always the Bannings he harped on, and it stood to reason that he had engineered this whole deal just to rid himself of a troublesome obstacle. Namely, Ed Banning.

Even now the old devil was laying the groundwork to sack Stoudenmire as marshal. That benign little speech he made tonight was only so much crap. *Let's think it over and meet again tomorrow night.* Bullshit! He had seen Hart use that gambit a hundred times. Let the other man stew in his own juices for a day and then chop his head off with a few kindly, well chosen words. Stoudenmire wasn't going to get another shot at the Bannings. He was on his way out. Then, after things had returned to normal, Hart would recruit another fast gun and start the whole bloody business all over again.

Before Cummings could carry the thought further, he realized the lawman had said something. "Sorry, Dallas, I didn't hear you. My mind was a thousand miles off."

Stoudenmire jerked his head toward a sleezy cantina at the side of the street. "Just said I feel like a drink. Wanta join me?"

"Sure. I could stand a little fortifying myself, come to think of it." The storekeeper looked away, fearing his face would somehow betray the surprise he felt. Things must really be bad. Never had he known Stoudenmire to take a drink while on duty. The man was like a monk, spartan in his habits, limiting the pleasures other men took for granted to within the four walls of his own home.

Without another word Stoudenmire led the way into the cantina and took a seat at a table along the far wall. The men ranged around the room were mostly Mexican, and they studiously avoided any show of curiosity. *Gringos* seldom frequented this place, but if *el hombre* wanted to drink here, then who were they to object. Presently a barmaid materialized at their table, and the marshal ordered tequila.

When the girl returned with a bottle and two glasses, Stoudenmire calmly poured both brimful. Sprinkling salt over the web of flesh beside his thumb, he licked sparingly and tossed the drink off in one gulp. The tequila hit his gut like molten lead and bounced dangerously, but he held it down. Breathing deeply, he shuddered like a wet dog, then glanced over at the storekeeper.

"Doc, get that stupid look off your face. You've seen grown men drink before. What's so strange about that?"

Cummings still hadn't touched his glass. "Nothing, Dallas. Nothing at all. Except that you're going about it for the wrong reasons. Hell, tomorrow things won't look half so bad, and I'm layin' odds you'll figure a way out of this deal yet."

"Thanks for those kind words, brother-in-law." The lawman refilled his glass and stared at it listlessly. "But you and I both know that Big Daddy Hart is gonna give me the gate tomorrow night. So if I was you, I wouldn't be coverin' any bets."

The storekeeper started to say something, then tossed off his own drink and gasped when it hit bottom. After a moment he looked up. "Much as I hate to admit it, you've been right about a lot of things. Looks like old friend Seth is out to crown himself king, and near as I can figure, you're not arranging the coronation as fast as he'd like it."

Stoudenmire grinned wryly. "You figure pretty good, Doc. The old fart is gonna get rid of the Bannings even if he has to raise the vigilantes. That hogwash he was dishin' out tonight didn't mean a damn thing. Just as soon as he ties a can to my tail, there won't be anyone to stop him, and he'll put this whole goddamn town to the torch if that's what it takes."

"Yeah, but you're still US marshal. Don't forget that. You could stop him no matter what."

"Maybe. If I want to get myself killed facin' down a mob. I'm not real sure El Paso's worth it. The only other way is to send for the Rangers, and I doubt they could get here in time to head off what he's got in mind."

"Well hell, there's more'n one way to skin a cat." Cummings leaned over the table and tapped the lawman's arm. "Listen, there's plenty of good people in this town that won't hold still for that kind of crap. Why, I bet I could round up twenty, thirty men who'd stand with you when the time came."

Stoudenmire jiggled his glass, watching the tequila swirl around in tiny circles. "What good would it do gettin' them killed? It's like I told you before, Doc. When you've got two men who figure that there's room for only one kingfish, it's the folks in the middle who end up gettin' hurt. Maybe that's not how the Good Lord intended it, but that's damn sure how she works out."

Cummings nodded absently, staring into his empty glass. "Funny. When we were walkin' over here, I had it all figured out that Hart wanted to can you so he could hire another fast gun. Never occurred to me that the tricky bastard was just workin' up to an excuse for calling out the vigilantes." His voice faltered, as though the thought had touched a raw nerve. "Shitfire, let's have another drink. Maybe the sonsabitches'll kill each other off and we can start this town off right, the way it should've been."

Stoudenmire regarded the older man for a moment, then shook his head. "Guess I didn't want a drink as bad as I thought. Like the fella said, answers come sorta hard at the bottom of a bottle. Think I'll call it a night, Doc. Maybe tomorrow we'll wake up and find out we're both just a couple'a damn fools."

He tossed a coin on the table and headed for the door. They parted outside, and Cummings watched him walk off into the night, a deeply troubled man. Musing on it for a

moment, the little merchant hoped that Kate didn't give him
too hard a time tonight. Whatever else he was, Dallas Stoudenmire wasn't a quitter. But right now he was feeling mighty
close to being one. He would need all the understanding Kate
could give him, and then some.

Cummings wandered aimlessly for a while, then struck off
toward the plaza and his store. After entering through the
back door, he lit a lamp, broke open a fresh bottle, and sat
down to do some serious thinking of his own. If Stoudenmire
couldn't rid El Paso of the Bannings and hold Seth Hart in
check, then what the hell was left? The question disturbed
him, but the lack of an answer was downright chilling.

Puzzling over it, Cummings realized that the marshal was
essentially a man of action, one who always chose the most
direct solution to a problem. He wasn't a devious man, a
schemer, the kind who could employ subterfuge or guile to
put an opponent under. Moreover, he believed in the sanctity
of the law, respected it fiercely. He wouldn't bat an eye at facing another man's gun, but it would never occur to him to
acquire evidence in an illegal manner.

Like stealing the Bannings' records!

The thought came to him like a bolt from the blue, and
with it the gut reaction that it was the solution to their dilemma. The Bannings must keep records. They couldn't run
an organization without books of some sort. Whatever dirty
work had gone on in this town and whoever had gotten paid
off would be in those books. He knew it just as sure as he
knew his own name, instinctively and without a doubt in the
world. And the first place to look was the safe in Ed Banning's
office.

The storekeeper had another drink and mulled it over. He
wasn't a particularly brave man even by his own standards,
but by Christ, he wasn't a coward either. It would be risky,
and he'd have to be slicker than greased owlshit to pull it
off. But he owed it to the town to try. And to Stoudenmire.
Goddammit, that's what it all boiled down to! He owed it
to Stoudenmire more than any of those mealy-mouthed bas-

tards who sat around waiting for someone to save them from their own gutless palpitations.

By damn, he would drink to that. And to his first little sortie as a burglar. Down with Ed Banning and up Seth Hart's fat ass! Sonovabitch, that had a good ring to it, and if anybody could pull it off, it was that sneaky little shit by the name of Doc Cummings.

Late that night, after the southside dives had closed, Cummings gingerly stalked through the alley behind the Coliseum. He had downed the better part of a quart, just to steady his nerves, he told himself. Still, he wasn't feeling any pain, and his step was about as light as a bull elephant. After looking up and down the alley, he forced the lock on the rear door of Banning's office and scuttled inside. There he found himself confronted by what seemed the biggest goddamned safe in Christendom. It was an ugly, black brute that towered over him like a barge, but he had to snicker in spite of himself. In the dark its round, shiny dial looked like Cyclop's beady eye watching his every movement, and somehow that struck him as damned humorous, hilarious almost. Shushing himself he went to work.

Although he was a fledgling thief, he knew how to use a crowbar, and he tackled the job with all the finesse of an ore-crusher. Gouging and prying, he went to work on the safe's doors.

But as he heaved and sweated over the cold steel, he failed to see the door knob slowly turning. In his fuzzy euphoria, the storekeeper had forgotten one salient detail. Sam Banning didn't live at the Parker House with his brother. He kept a room upstairs.

The door suddenly flew open, and Sam leaped into the office, covering him with a cocked six-gun. Cummings didn't cower or beg for mercy. He was looking the grim reaper straight in the eye, and it wasn't exactly the moment to go fainthearted. Whirling, he threw the crowbar with all his strength and jumped for the back door. But he never made it.

The Colt roared twice, and the game little merchant crashed to the floor dead.

Lighting a lamp, Sam turned the body over and stared in slack-jawed bewilderment. *Doc Cummings!* He lumbered back a step, head spinning in a witless stupor, and for a moment he went cold with sweat. Then he slammed the lamp down on the desk and raced out the back door. Whatever had happened here was over his head, and right now the only thing he wanted was to get his big brother.

By Jesus, that was the ticket. Let Ed figure it out!

5

Early next morning Jim Gillette knocked on Stoudenmire's door. The deputy was filled with a sense of dread; unable to shake the feeling that he had unwittingly become a messenger of death. Last night he had restrained himself with no little effort from awakening the marshal, knowing full well what would happen if he did so. Instead, he had downed a pot of coffee and waited for the first, golden streamers of sunrise, telling himself that Stoudenmire would be more reasonable with Cumming's body already laid out in the undertaking parlor.

From years of watching men kick out their lives on saloon floors and dusty cowtown streets, he knew that time often worked a curious change on the dead man's friends and family. Those who were notified immediately experienced a mixture of shock, sorrowful bereavement for their loved one, and blind rage for the man who had killed him. But if they found out about it later, often even as little as a few hours, their pain and mindless fury was mitigated in a quirky sort of way. Somehow the hurt faded almost as fast as it began, and instead of mourning the dead man, they felt sorry for themselves. It was as if they regretted the poor fellow's death not nearly so much as they resented him leaving them in the lurch on such short notice.

Gillette had always thought it was damned odd, but then most folks were sort of queer in the head anyway if a fellow stood off and watched the numbskull things they did. Like trying to crack Banning's safe with a crowbar. Jesus!

Still that was over and done with, and there was no way to bring the dead back. Right now he had to face the living, and whatever gods were watching, he sure as hell hoped they would lend a hand in putting the damper on Stoudenmire's temper.

When the lawman opened the door, he knew immediately that something was bad wrong. "C'mon in, Jim. You look like a man carrying a heavy load."

Gillette stepped inside and pulled his hat off, twisting it nervously between his fingers. "Dallas, I wish to Christ I wasn't the one that had to tell you, but there ain't no other way. Doc Cummings is dead."

Stoudenmire just stared at him, showing nothing. "Who got him?"

"Sam Banning." The deputy knew what was coming and he added hurriedly, "But it ain't like it sounds."

Stoudenmire's face went ashen, and every muscle in his body seemed taut as strung catgut. "Tell me."

"Doc broke into Banning's office and tried to crack the safe. Hadn't no more'n got started when Sam caught him." Gillette's voice faltered then, and he looked down at the floor. "Doc heaved a crowbar and took off runnin'. Sam drilled him twice goin' away."

"What about witnesses?"

"Nary a one. Just the two of 'em involved. The sign's all there to read though. Sam went over and rousted Banning out of bed, and then they come and got me. I went over it real careful, and it's just like I said."

The marshal's color had returned, but his eyes were like death warmed over. "When did it happen?"

"Somewheres after two this mornin'." Gillette hawked and cleared his throat. "I had Doc taken over to Pritchard's funeral parlor."

Stoudenmire nodded vaguely, suddenly aware that Kate would have to be told. Then he glanced back at Gillette, and his gaze hardened. "What'd you do with Sam Banning?"

The deputy shifted his cud of tobacco and swallowed heavily. Now came the hairy part. "Nothin.' There ain't no way we can touch him legally. Doc was caught in the act, and every man's got the right to defend his own property. Even if his name's Banning."

Some moments passed as the lawman digested that. Then he grunted skeptically. "That sounds like something Ed Banning would say."

"Matter of fact, he did. Just used more words, that's all." Gillette took a hitch at his belt and met the younger man's look head-on. "Dallas, I got an idea what you're thinkin', but it won't wash. Whatever Doc was lookin' for in that safe, he was out of line. There ain't nothin' we can do to the Bannings, and you'd best set your mind to it."

"What's that about Doc and the Bannings?" Kate's voice came from the kitchen doorway. Turning, they found her staring at them with mild alarm. Gillette was reminded of a young doe, all wide-eyed and nervously alert at some strange sound, and he suddenly wanted very much to be somewhere else.

Stoudenmire spoke without looking around. "Jim, you'd better get on back to the office. I'll be down a little later."

The deputy shot a glance at Kate, seeing her tense, then ducked out the door. Stoudenmire was left with the dirtiest job of all, but he was damn glad the lawman had let him off the hook. Relieved was more like it, as though somebody had just pulled him clear of a load of granite. Telling people their kinfolks had gone under was a messy business, and no matter how many times a man did it, he always walked away feeling soiled and kind of rotten at the core.

When he went through the gate, it came just about like he expected it would. First the stifled cry, then a scream of shock and disbelief, and finally the wretched, sobbing moan that was enough to tear a man's heart out by its roots. The wail of Indian women was worse, but not a hell of a lot. Whatever kind of female it was, animal or human, the sound stuck with a man for days, and even worse sometimes in the night when he couldn't chase it away. Lengthening his stride, the old lawdog struck out for the plaza, not the least bit shamed that it was Stoudenmire back there instead of him.

When Gillette reached the office, men slowly began drifting in to discuss this latest calamity. They cursed and grumbled, drank coffee, swilled whiskey out of pint bottles, and talked incessantly of raising the vigilantes. Seth Hart waddled in before long with his somber-faced cronies, and the crowd swarmed around him demanding some action be taken against the Bannings. The miller talked a hell of a lot without saying anything one way or the other, and the morning ground on with deadly slowness. Listening to them jabber on and on, it passed through Gillette's mind that, if a man was to put their brains in a jaybird, the sonovabitch would probably fly backwards.

Then, shortly before noon, Stoudenmire walked through the door. Tige was at his side, and for a moment the two of them regarded the crowded room with a hollow stare. The lawman's face was grim as weathered tombstone, and it was obvious that he had just come from a house where death now resided.

Seth Hart stepped forward and extended his hand. "Marshal, we all want you to know how sorry we are, and we'd be beholden if you would pass along our condolences to Mrs. Stoudenmire. Doc was a fine man, a friend to every decent person in this town, and he'll be missed around here."

The lawman's face remained blank, and he dropped the politician's hand after a perfunctory shake. "Thanks. My wife'll be glad to know he had so many friends."

Hart glanced around uncomfortably, wondering if the others had caught the marshal's sardonic tone. But he came right back, blustering with authority and purpose. "I might add that his friends mean to do something about this cowardly act, Marshal. The boys have been talking it over, and we think it's high time to call out the vigilantes. The Bannings absolutely can't be allowed to go any further. Naturally, we'd prefer it if you'd deputize everyone and make it legal and above board."

"Naturally." Stoudenmire's reply was clipped, with just the

faintest trace of insolence. "Tell you what, Hart. It's gettin'
along toward dinner time so why don't you get these boys fed
and meet back here in a couple of hours. By then we oughta
know what's what."

Seth Hart got a funny expression on his face, like he had
heard it but he couldn't quite believe it. There was something
more to this than met the eye, and he had the distinct feeling
that the marshal had just snookered him into a corner. But
he couldn't very well refuse, and it would look fishy if he demanded they march now. Stoudenmire's suggestion seemed
very practical and everyone knew it. Hell, nobody wanted to
fight on an empty stomach.

The men filed out with Hart in the lead, and within moments Stoudenmire and Gillette had the place to themselves. Gillette was more than a little thunderstruck himself
by this sudden turn of events but he just waited for whatever
was coming next. The lawman had something up his sleeve,
and knowing him, it would probably be a real ball-buster.

After a moment the marshal sat down at his desk, took out
pen and paper, and began writing. Finished, he unpinned his
badge and tossed it on the desk. Then he handed Gillette the
note. "Jim, that's my resignation. As of right now, you're marshal of El Paso."

Gillette studied the paper for a moment, then looked up.
"I reckon you mean to call the Bannings out."

"That's about the size of it," Stoudenmire observed.

"And you just suckered Hart into gettin' the vigilantes out
of your hair so you could do it all by your lonesome."

"You're a foxy old buzzard." Stoudenmire gave him a wry
look. "Didn't figure I had you fooled."

Gillette dropped the note on the desk. "You didn't have
Hart fooled neither. But that's nothin' one way or the other.
What's important is that you're settin' out to do something
that goes against everything you ever stood for. Call the
Bannings out and you're gonna be spittin' in the teeth of the
law you've sworn to uphold. Now you tell me how that differs
from the vigilantes marchin' over there and lynching 'em?"

Stoudenmire's mouth set in a hard line. "Jim, I'm fresh out

of answers. Maybe there's times when the law's just not enough. The Bannings toe-dance around it and make it bend to suit themselves. I couldn't stop 'em, and Doc got himself killed trying to help me. I reckon if I had put 'em under when I should've that wouldn't have happened."

He paused, staring at his scrawled resignation for a moment. "I failed as marshal, but I'm not gonna fail Doc. Sometimes a man has to fight just because he couldn't live with himself if he walked away. Right or wrong, that's how my stick floats."

Their eyes met and Stoudenmire flashed his old grin. Then the moment passed, and he came up out of the chair, heading for the door. "Look after yourself, pardner."

Gillette moved to block his path. "Listen goddammit, there ain't no law that says you get to have all the fun. I'd sorta like a whack at them pricks myself, so just count me in."

"Thanks, Jim, but it's no go. This is personal. Besides, this town's got to have some law even if it's a crotchety old coot like you."

Smiling tightly, Stoudenmire brushed past him and walked out with Tige at his heels. Crossing the plaza, he felt a strange numbness settle over him. He had lived with danger all his life; sometimes it seemed as though he had no memory back beyond those first bloody days on the killing ground. But this was different. There was a cold, icy feeling in his spine, like death's ugly, fleshless hand was squeezing down on his backbone. Maybe it was a sign. Something warning him of what was to come. Then he chuckled. There weren't any signs. Just fast men and slow men. The quick and the dead.

Absently he noted the shops and people on the streets as he walked along. Curiously, it was as if he were seeing it all for the first time. Again he chuckled to himself. Or maybe for the last time. Then it came to him that first, last, or never, it really didn't make a damn. The only friends he had in this town was the one he had just left behind and the dog padding along at his side. Come to think of it, they were the only friends he had in the world. Whatever the reason, he just naturally couldn't take people except in small doses. But what the hell, a man in his game needed allies, not friends. After all, the friends you didn't have couldn't weasel out when the shooting started. That was the nice thing about Tige. The surly sonovabitch wouldn't back off from a bull alligator if he was hamstrung and blind in both eyes. Which was a hell of a lot more than you could say for most men. Even the best of them.

Without realizing it, he found himself standing in front of the Coliseum. The icy feeling was still with him, but he felt calm now, loose and easy inside where it counted. Then he knew that it was all right. Once the tightness drained away, everything else fell into place, and he didn't even have to think. Just react.

The moment he pushed through the bat-wing doors, he sensed that the Bannings had known he would come. Ed stood at the bar, while Sam casually studied a shot on the billiard table across from the door. They had him in a cross fire, no matter who drew first. But even so, he liked the odds. Somehow it made the game sweeter, more inviting, just the way he would have wanted it.

Glancing from one to the other, he decided to take Sam first. The overgrown crock of shit deserved it, and besides, Doc would have liked it that way. Watching Sam out of the corner of his eye, he laid it out for Banning.

"Banning, I've come to punch your ticket. Maybe you recollect I warned you once not to be around when your number was called."

Banning turned from the bar, brushing his coat back over the handle of his pistol. "Stoudenmire, you'd better turn around and walk out of here. Cummings got what was coming to him, and we've got the law on our side. Don't push it."

Stoudenmire's pale eyes went cold as chilled stone. "Shit, there's no law here. There's just you and me and your dumb-ass brother. Make your fight, mister. You're about to get killed."

Sam Banning's nerve suddenly broke, and he clawed at the pistol on his hip. Stoudenmire's arm moved in a blurred motion, and a Colt appeared in his fist. The gun bucked, and Sam was thrown across the billiard table, dusted front and back.

Crouching, Stoudenmire spun around, noting that Ed was no slouch with a gun. The gang leader had fired even as Sam died, but Tige was leaping for his throat, and the big dog took the ball straight through his spine. Banning thumbed off another shot as Tige dropped at his feet, and the slug caught Stoudenmire in the chest. Hurled backwards, he crashed into the wall and felt his knees start to buckle. Banning's mouth tightened in an evil grin, and he popped off a third shot. But he had rushed it, overanxious for the kill, and the window at Stoudenmire's side exploded in a shower of glass.

Steadying himself against the wall, Stoudenmire raised the Colt very deliberately, as if he had all the time in the world. When it jumped in his hand a small fountain of blood spurted out over Banning's shirtfront. Drunkenly, he staggered away from the bar and began to sag, groping blindly with his hands like a man trying to break a fall.

Extending his gun arm, Stoudenmire drew a fine bead and gut-shot Banning just as his rump hit the floor. The gang boss jerked upright, as if he were rowing a boat, his eyes bursting with pain and shock. Then the stench came as death loosed his bowels, and he settled to the floor. His leg jumped once, then stiffened, and he lay very still.

Stoudenmire's eyes glazed over, and he wiped his hand across his face. When his vision cleared, he looked down on the dead men for a moment, then shoved away from the wall. Willing himself to stand, to walk, to remain erect, he lurched across the room and pushed out through the doors. Gillette was there, and he rushed forward, eyes glistening wetly without shame.

Stoudenmire looked up through a bright haze of pain and grunted hoarsely. "Jim, you'd better call the undertaker. They killed Tige."

Then the Colt dropped from his hand, and he fell into Gillette's arms.

EPILOGUE

Stoudenmire stepped to the door, then paused to kiss Kate once more. Her arms encircled his neck, and she planted one square on his mouth, long and slow with a naughty little probing just for good measure. The kind of kiss nice girls weren't supposed to know about. The lawman squeezed her in a bearish grip, feeling the soft flesh yield and melt against him.

Christ! She was a shameless hussy about some things. Putting a kiss like that on him, right in the doorway where all the neighbors could get a real eyeful. But who the hell cared what other people thought? They didn't know about the wildcat that crawled into his bed every night, and by God, if she wanted a little kiss every now and then, he was damn sure going to oblige her.

Kate's soft lips curved in a teasing smile, and she stepped back, straightening his coat lapel. "There now. That ought to hold you till suppertime anyway. You just make sure you don't wear yourself out jayhawking around town."

"Lady, you oughta be arrested for carryin' dangerous weapons." He spun her about and swatted her on the bottom. "And don't be givin' people advice about getting their rest. It's not me that yells uncle in the clinches."

"Oh, what conceit!" Her mouth curled in a tiny pout. "Run along, Mr. Stoudenmire. Go on downtown and let everyone gawk at the big bad lawman. You'll get your comeuppance tonight."

Stoudenmire chuckled, then turned and hobbled off down the walk. "Is that a promise or a threat?"

"Both. But I'll let you take it out in trade." Kate giggled wickedly and slammed the door shut when he looked back.

The lawman went through the gate chortling to himself. Damned if things didn't have a way of doing a bellyflop just when a man least expected it.

The last couple of months had brought a warm glow of discovery in the Stoudenmire household. Doc Cummings' death and the subsequent shootout with the Bannings had wrought a startling transformation in Kate. Somehow she had sifted it out for herself and come to the conclusion that certain men just weren't meant to be gelded. Once that dawned on her, and she came to grips with it, her entire attitude had changed. Now she made jokes about other women and their henpecked husbands, laughingly dubbing them *mansos*, the tame bulls, a term she had picked up from her Mexican housekeeper. Though Kate never said anything openly, she had become fiercely proud of her man, and quietly confident that he could handle anything that came down the pike. When she looked at other women nowadays, she felt something akin to pity, or perhaps merely compassion, for they would have to live out their lives never knowing what it was to take a real man to bed. And under the Stoudenmire roof, there was no longer the slightest doubt who ruled the roost.

Kate had become a woman, and she reveled in the sheer joy of using feminine wiles to get her way. Dallas Stoudenmire was just a big, lumbering teddy-bear now that she had figured him out, and Mrs. Stoudenmire had his number anytime she wanted to punch it.

The lawman himself had spent considerable time reflecting on this volatile and highly mercurial creature who now shared his life. But he still wasn't sure that he understood her, or for that matter that he ever would. Maybe the fact that he had broken with his own code to avenge Doc had triggered the change in her. Though she had never said one way or the other, he sensed that a bond of some sort had taken root between them the day he killed the Bannings. Love. Venegeance. An eye for an eye. Simple gratitude for not letting her brother go to his grave with the debt unsettled. Damned if he knew what made her tick, and somehow it didn't seem so important anymore that he try and decipher it. She had turned out to be the kind of woman he had always wanted, the loving, gutsy, spitfire who was "root hog or die" all the way. And that was enough.

Still, he had to laugh sometimes when he saw that sparkle come into her eye, and she started wheedling and conniving. Women just weren't happy unless they had some little plot going; scheming and finagling new ways to twist a man's ying-yang so he'd sit up and bark like a lap dog. But what the hell! Long as a man didn't lose his balls in the bargain, it was a pretty comfortable arrangement.

Strolling along the street, he greeted merchants and townspeople with an easy smile as they inquired after his health. The briskness of winter had settled over the basin, and it was good to be walking again, even though he felt slightly ridiculous using a cane. The crisp air made him forget the dull throb in his chest, and the sight of snowcapped mountains in the distance brought new strength to the rubbery joints in his knees. His recuperation had been slow and painful, and damned uncertain at times. But he was back on the job, part way anyhow. And that was what counted most.

After circling the plaza, he entered the office to find Gillette catnapping. The old lawdog roused himself with a lazy stretch and started grumbling right off. "Dallas, we gotta do something to stir up a little excitement around here. This goddamn town's so peaceful it's downright mortifying."

Stoudenmire hobbled around the desk and eased down in his chair. "Pardner, you name it and we'll do it. What'd you have in mind? A little mumblety-peg. Rackin' up some horseshoes. Maybe a fast game of marbles?"

"Aw, quit your joshin'." Gillette opened the door on the

little pot-bellied stove and tossed in a load of wood. "You know what I'm talkin' about. Maybe we oughta pull up stakes and find us a town that ain't had a dose of law yet."

"Christ almighty," the lawman snorted. "We've just got started in El Paso. As long as there's whorehouses and gambling dives, some bonehead is gonna try to get his meathooks on the whole box of goodies. The game's the same, Jimbo. Only the faces change."

"Like Seth Hart, maybe?" The deputy cocked one eye with a sly smirk.

"Maybe, Maybe not. Looks like the old devil might just run for mayor." Stoudenmire explored the thought for a moment before resuming. "Which means he'd have to play it strictly on the up and up, leastways if he wants the reformers' vote. But that doesn't change nothin'. If it's not him, someone else'll come along. There's always somebody that wants to sandbag the bets and skim off the cream."

"Damn me, if you ain't right. Matter of fact, it looks like that particular ailment is goin' around like measles." Gillette pulled a newspaper off his cot and tossed it on the desk. "Accordin' to that, the Earp boys just had 'emselves a turkey shoot over in Tombstone. Caught a bunch of the opposition in some corral and just flat plowed 'em under. You reckon Wyatt's tryin' to do the same thing over there that Banning done here?"

Stoudenmire studied the newspaper article, nodding to himself. Some moments passed before he looked up. "From what I saw of Earp in Dodge, I wouldn't put it past him. Course, you never can tell. Some towns need more law than others. Hell'sfire, there's even times when the law itself has to have its neck jerked back in joint."

"Well, much as I hate to say it, I don't look for no more trouble in this burg." The deputy wagged his head ruefully and squirted the stove with tobacco juice. "Folks've just naturally got the idea you're half-bear and half-alligator, and they don't want no part of it."

The marshal let that pass. Everybody in town had been goggling over him like he was some circus freak, and it was growing a bit wearisome. "I'll tell you something, Jim. It's the elections that are gonna tell the tale in El Paso. People have got a right to choose whatever kind of leaders they want, and they generally get just what they deserve. But whichever way it works out, lawmen can't take sides. We're sorta like spectators at a cock fight. The best we can do is try to keep the lid on and make sure the good ones don't die for nothin'."

"Like Doc Cummings?" Gillette observed.

There was a momentary lull, and even the pot-bellied stove seemed to be thinking it over, holding its angry crackling to a simmering whisper.

Gilette quickly shifted the conversation around to routine matters of policing the town, and after a while Stoudenmire decided he would call it a day. Cane in hand, he hobbled out the door and headed back uptown. He still tired easily, and he had begun to look forward to his afternoon naps.

Moving slowly along the street, it occurred to him how much he missed Tige trotting along at his side. Maybe this afternoon he would take a stroll over to the big dog's grave. They had buried him back close to Commanche Peak where the wild things still ran free. Tige would have liked that, being out there among his own kind. *El lobo hambre*, the Mexican kids had called him that first day in town. Well, hell, he never was what a man would rightly call civilized. Never wanted to be either, just like his master.

Stoudenmire chuckled to himself. Damn, they'd made a pair, sure enough. Maybe they would cut trails again when it came his time to cross over. The thought brought a warm glow deep down in his belly, and just a touch of the old cockiness crept back into his stride.

Hefting the cane, he slung it into the middle of the road and struck off at a fast limp toward home.

971 701
6097